ROTTEN COMPANY

AN EPIC FANTASY TRILOGY IN ONE PART BY

DREW BRYENTON

Rotten Company
Drew Bryenton

ISBN 978-1-910779-86-6 (Paperback)

sci-fi-cafe.com

This one's for Seth (who gets killed every time) and his mum and dad
For two great mums of my own
And for Mark and Steph, the most gracious hosts ever

The Sugarloaf
Cloven Scarp
The Brute Pits
The Black Garrison
Lake Shite
The Malevolith
St. Guthran
fleamarket
Chantry Heath
Bishopsbath
Gallowgate
Jade Palace
Sunderside
Bentsteeple
Unspeakable College
Temple of Pleasures
High Wittering
The Stilts
GRAND SEPULCHRE
Harbour Watch
A

Sinner's Mitre
Old Sarunjek Ruins
Ironhead Dam
Smattering Hill
Halfway House
Rooktower
Ironbelly Gaol
Belfry Roost
Lord Governor's Tower
Hammer's End
Dolmen Grove
Brickdeep
Tarback Scrubs
Phoraxian Cathedral
Piazza Della von Tuesday
Harridan's Reef

PRECEDING PAGES...

THE PRINCESS OF CITIES, GRAND SEPULCHRE

As She stood in the 671st year after the Great Urzoman Conquest

Welcome, traveller! Well met, and pleasantly encountered! Come, sit awhile, and hear the tale of this vibrant (and totally not at all crooked, violent and depraved) cityport where you find yourself! Let us speak of Her delights, Her pleasure-souks and streets of noble merchantry, while avoiding looking behind you, where Frank and Garry are sneaking up to...

(Paragraph expunged, by order of the Grand Sepulchre Benevolent Merchant's Anti-Dodginess League, who proffer this alternative -)

Grand Sepulchre, City of Several Non-nasty Surprises!

Capital of the now-defunct and decadently dissolute Urzoman Empire, the city of Grand Sepulchre is the last and only foothold of this once archipelago-spanning hegemonic force, sadly diminished by time, politics, circumstance and lack of Imperial ambition. Grand Sepulchre would seem rich and ripe for the plucking by some foreign power, save for one fact; this sweltering merchant hub lies under the protection of an entity known only as He Himself, the Dark Emperor, a brooding skeletal wizard of prodigious power and capricious moods.

It is for His sake that the city, long since gone to debauchery, capitalism and hedonistic vice, maintains a flower-garlanded veneer of darkness and evil, masquerading as the dread stronghold of an infernal potentate who has long since ceased to care about conquest, bloodshed and wholesale slaughter.

Visitors should expect humid tropical climes, and should also acquaint themselves with the strange customs of the Princess of Cities, richest in all the Arch' – including their division of the day into eight Octals, each with their own distinct bells and rituals, heralding times of work, rest, sleep and depraved celebration.

The Octals of Grand Sepulchre

Dawn – rung out by the lizard bells of the slave traders' manse

The hours of toil – begun by the kraken bell, atop the statue of tyranny

High sun – rung out with the jaguar bells, within the temple of pleasures

Daysleep, the siesta hours – the mosquito bells of the assassin's jade palace

Second Labour – tolled by the cobra bells, high on Lord Governor's Tower

The Hour of revels – announced by Ole Roger, the wizard's bell

Midnight – knelled by the dead man's bells of the Ironbelly gaol

Last watch – struck with the tamarin bells, at the thieves' chapterhouse

DRAMATIS PERSONAE

Just Who Are The ROTTEN COMPANY?

Vanquishers of evil? Imbibers of refreshments, both fermented AND deliciously distilled? Innocent nincompoops, working beyond a law which scorned them as vagabonds and freaks? Perhaps all of the above! This rogue's gallery of ſuper-heroic medieval non-lepers now comes with 32% less bubonic plague, and MORE of the communicable diseases that fight even hard-to-reach crime!

The Pugilist – Elder statesman of the group, if only he knew what this meant. The pugilist was once a dirty, low-down fighter known to use every trick in the book, and he didn't even know how to read! Now he's... still a nasty, cheating, eye-gouging bastard, but with super strength and a toga. Hooray!

The Honey Badger – The only would-be assassin ever fired from the guild's training program for killing too many people! Now she possesses a weapon that simply can't be dropped, the ability to heal almost instantly, uncanny vitality, and if we don't say she's as beautiful as she is deadly, she might do that horrible thing down in the trouser department with the…aaaaargh, yes, *that* one!

The Naked Flame – The man without fear. The man without remorse. The man without clothes, as the fact that he's on fire kind of means it's hard to make wardrobe choices. Horribly, he's the company's doctor, but at least this means his tools are sterile.

The Unstoppable It – Huge, blue, super-strong and hardly even slightly a little bit based on that other guy. You wouldn't like him when he's sober.

The Double Vision – No, you're not seeing double... unless you're as much of a lush as he is, in which case, there are four of him. When old DV separates into twins, one of him is a ghost who can walk right through you, leaving behind the echo of every bad comedown and hangover you've ever experienced. No, wait... that HE'S ever experienced. Trust me, that's *much* worse.

Slag Iron – Once, she could slap a grown man clean through the side of a longship using only a medium-sized turbot. Now, this ferocious fishmonger is encased in sorcerous iron armour, and it chafes something awful. This has done absolutely *nothing* for her temper.

The Grimshadow – Millionaire. Playboy. Lackwit. Hypotenuse. These are all words which this brooding, dark hero is usually too high to comprehend. He has absolutely zero superhuman powers, but he is jolly wealthy, and all of his friends are real heroes, so... he's determined to have the best lines, and the best costume, even if he has to hire every bard and tailor in the city.

The Atomic Fop – The only man who can change faster than the trends in baroque men's fashion – the Atomic Fop lives a life of debauchery and designer lacework by day, and fights crime by night, using his uncanny ability to do *anything* remarkably quickly. Except choose an outfit with matching shoes. His wig holds more than just a whole ecosystem of parasitic lice.... it also holds *justice*. (But also the lice thing).

The Scarlet Spectre – A poor orphan boy who discovered amazing, impossible powers in a cliché so hackneyed that nobody cares! Now he must... you know, with the fighting, and the mystical quest, and a birthmark or something, so that, I don't know, let's say some princess doesn't need to get tonsil surgery. Some say the plague of heroism sweeping the city of Grand Sepulchre is his fault, but we say that nobody has swept this city in centuries, and the dead body piles now have their own historic monument plaques.

And who are their friends, foes, acquaintances and fellow citizens?

Rhaegulus Cratt – Master of the Harbour Watch, Commander of the Evil Empire's excise fleet and architect of all manner of anti-pirate activities. A short, angry little man who missed out on being a Dwarf by failing the intelligence test.

Chep Palaquat – Nephew of a very important man in the city of Grand Sepulchre, and hence, a spotty, chinless and self-important prat. Also, a prodigy in the arts of alchemy, more's the pity; fifteen years old and knows it all.

Multhazar Threck – Lord Alchemist, Jack Somewhat's employer (grudgingly) and a man who firmly believes that a spoonful of mercury a day keeps the barber-surgeon's hacksaw away.

Master Saulis Lurien – Chief poisoner of the Guild Lachrymose, a kindly man who has killed more people than most plagues manage, through his study of the demortifying arts and his teaching of the same to young aspirants.

Lord Archivole Foxmallet VII – An aristocratic lord of the admiralty who is far too mad to actually go to sea; he spends most of his time and a considerable fortune re-enacting great naval victories in his flooded basement, using models.

Lord Slave – The ex-barbarian warlord who now serves as Grand Vizier to the Throne of the Urzoman Empire. A gigantic, one-eyed, leather-masked and oily muscleman, clad in straps, chains, spikes, and underpants, thus leading to all kinds of suppositions about his private life.

Gathur Sagh – A highly respected tailor who specialises in 'protective wear' for the military gentlemen, the sporting gentleman, the fighting gentleman – in fact, everyone who wants to remain a complete gentleman in situation that involve knees, boots, daggers and claw-hammers on a low trajectory.

Morthrag – The genuine half-ogre gatekeeper of the fighting pits. He acts as a fairly good first test for aspiring knuckle-artists; if they are too scared to approach this hulking, flat-nosed apparition, they are not gladiator material.

Toothless Frank Hamsmiter, Golto the Demolisher, Mandak 'the menacing nickname' McGurk and **Grindolph 'three toes' Van Peltd** – Just a few of the merry crew of crooked gladiators who entertain the crowds daily in Grand Sepulchre's Brute Pits.

Clorance Gryssle – Detective Inquisitor of Throne's Shadow, the not-so-secret secret police force of the Evil Empire. From his regulation shorts to his push-broom moustache he is every inch a copper, and he's so bent he needs a corkscrew to take his socks off at night.

Himself, the Undying One, Dark Emperor of the Urzoman Realm – Nobody except Lord Slave has seen this reclusive, skeletal, undead wizard for some time now. It's rumoured that all he does is play chess against the rotting corpses of dead mages, brood gothically, and compose gloomy harpsichord solos. Still, you don't tell a fellow who can turn you to cosmic dust with a wiggle of one pinky finger to 'snap out of it' and 'cheer up'.

Ranulf Rothgarsonson – Master of the Guild Errant, the trainers of mighty heroes, of the old fashioned, axe-swinging, pithy-one-liner spitting, 'barbarian from the north with biceps like turtles in a rubber sack' school. He's the owner of a beard which almost deserves its own listing here.

Issimmus Kroome – Grand High Thaumatarch and Archmage of the Clenched Fist – a wizard of the thin and curly-bearded variety, well known for his aversion to actually teaching students, and his obsession with dissecting things.

Lady Belladonna Immacolata Lachrymosa, *Assassinatrix exemplary* – Mistress of the Guild Lachrymose, the hired killers who act as the 'scalpel of the aristocracy' in matters of honour, politics and, usually, lots of cash.

Invigilator Malmsley Vermish – A spy for the king of thieves, and commander of his 'nasty squad', who 'rehabilitate' non-guild criminals with the aid of a mince grinder.

Othis Greave, *Snagpurse, King of Thieves* – An immensely obese, warty, balding, and piggy-eyed hulk of a man, who has carefully cultivated this image to act as an effective master of all thieves, burglars, pickpockets, and general scumbags in Grand Sepulchre. As if this is not bad enough, he also invented insurance.

Gebhard the Obtuse, *A disgraced wizard* – Wizards are not defrocked when they cock up mightily, as nobody wants to see what's under those robes. Instead, this wretch was thrown out of the Unspeakable College until such time as he is able to pay his dues again. Massive, crippling gambling debts from the competitive pie-eating circuit prohibit this, for now.

Ranulf Rothgarsonson's Beard – It looks like it DID get its own listing here. It's quite a beard, this, and looks like a small bramble patch which has been rolled with the sweepings from a barbershop floor and then electrified.

Sethric 'Demonsbane' O'Crummage – A very highly strung trainee wizard, who does not have the obvious advantages of a mysterious scar, murdered parents or a natural aptitude for being The Chosen One. Instead, he has to actually study, and work part time at a greasy Zollish takeaway joint, just to scrape by. The middle name is made up, and he hopes he'll grow into it one day.

Ian, the Eternal Horror – The Unspeakable College quite sensibly hired an undead keeper for their monster pit. He tastes awful, can be stitched back together in a pinch, and he saves the faculty a fortune on uneaten dinners.

Dreevil Vulct, *Snagpurse the Next, King of Thieves* – Front-runner for the position of arch-larcenist, and not above hastening his career prospects, if he can find a roll of flab on his boss where a dagger might fit.

Doctor Vaspides, *Master of the Physicians* – A stylish, androgynous and mysterious figure, who is the last word in medicine. Unfortunately, seeing as medicine in Grand Sepulchre involves plenty of leeches, that last word is usually 'time of death, 6pm, time for a drink'.

Garith Smembly – High priest of the least popular religion in the whole of Grand Sepulchre, this jug-eared little berk nevertheless tries to take his necessary rota of blood-soaked sacrifices and ritual beheadings seriously. Of course, he has to make do with mouse blood and cockroach heads, but this might just be for the best.

Smeeves, *(real name unknown)* – First Gentleman of the Butlers and Footmen. No matter what you ask of him, from polishing a small ornamental statue of a corgi to garrotting a travelling salesman, his answer will always be a polite 'very good, sir'.

Quazirath, the Almighty Demon-God – Actually a fairly unimportant *genius loci*, the spirit of a harbourside hot-spring who has bartered his impressive powers of illusion (and creed of total debauchery) into a franchise religion. Famed for the enthusiasm of his raunchy acolytes and the lemon bars of his temple-roof-repair bake sales.

Dolores Blatterly – Grand Madame of the Wenches, Strumpets and Actual Prostitutes. A jolly old lady of the 'quick, hide the sherry' variety, Dolores conceals a sharp mind for business (and an even sharper cigar cutter) behind an expanse of powdered cleavage and petticoats which defies belief.

Slidney Chunt, *of the Merchants and Bankers Guild* – A round little twerp who got everything in life by the accident of being born to the right mumsy and dadsy; like all such human pimples, he never shuts up about his business acumen, self-made grit and sheer gumption. Would melt in the rain, but so long as the rules and some payable thugs are on his side, he's as vicious as a cut weasel.

Jimjo and Waldrick – A pair of downside, outcast bandits who steal from the rich and give to themselves, the poor. Thus making themselves rich, which is when the internecine fighting breaks out...

Elizabethany Rantoon, *of the Numinous Guild of Holy Priesthoods and Bishoprics United* – The top god-botherer in a city with nine official religions and two hundred and seven others. Rather than becoming spell-slinging Cleric or a cunning scholar of divinity, Pope Beth is the master of those things all organised faiths have in common – gossip, funeral catering, bake sales, bingo, and dressing up with a more impressive wax-fruit-covered hat than the other old ladies.

Darby Hardwicke, *the city of Grand Sepulchre's chief engineer* – A tall, thin man with a flat cap and a pair of callipers always about his person, he was invited to be a Dwarf despite his obvious 'deformities' (he's 6 foot 2!) after inventing a new kind of steam-powered mining shovel.

All these and more will appear in the following volume, being
An Accurate History of the Recent Strife in Jansamrana;
'As true as you are handsome, m'lord'

Chapters

A handy guide for those who, like your author, feel that using a press-dried rat as a bookmark is a waste of valuable protein

Prologue	18
CODEX ONE: ROTTEN CIRCUMSTANCES	23
1. The Imbecilic Juxtaposition	24
2. The Cognoscentical Proxy	36
3. The Belligerence Mandate	46
4. The Demortifying Conundrum	54
5. The Pugilistical Gambit	62
6. The Pugnaciousness Contradiction	75
7. The Reciprocatory Protocol	90
8. The Dauntlessness Quandary	105
9. The Subterranean Altercation	117
10. The Extrajudicial Indignation	132
11. The Thaumaturgical Ingression	151
12. The Leviathanic Outrage	168
13. The Irrefutable Contractualization	186
14. The Countermunicipal Destructification	197
15. The Climactic Paradox	214
CODEX TWO: ROTTEN DEVELOPMENTS	231
16. The Preventative Incarceration	232
17. The Malefictorial Manifestation	247
18. The Identificational Braggadocio	267
19. The Anxietal Exacerbation	285
20. Slag Iron and the Grimshadow in – House of 10,000 Thieves!	295
21. The Naked Flame and The Atomic Fop in – Temple of Terror!	305
22. The Jolly Tale of Mister Bun Bun	312
23. Th Doub e ision and T e Unstoppa le It face – The T w ring Innuendo!	320
24. The Pugilist and the Honey Badger in – Daggers and Duplicity!	324
25. Episode the Last – A Hero's De#!*	333

CODEX THREE:A ROTTEN END   345
  26.   The Arachno-Draconian Excession   346
  27.   The Truculent Ascendancy   359
  28.   The Regicidal Reflux   369
  29.   The Gemini Contingency   381
  30.   Chapter the Last – The Death of Heroism   392
  31.   Chapter the Actually Last – Rotten Expectations   400
  32.   Epilogue: Unhappy Landings   416
  33.   Appendix I: Becomme An Wyzarde! Todaye!   421
  34.   Appendix II: The Noble Sport of Urzoman Death Cricket 426

Prologue

The Fate of the Fatuous

SPACE GETS FRAYED around the edges.

Not many people know this, because the kind of people who manage to trek their way out to the Shallows (as the treacherously unreal margins of reality are called) are not the kind of people who usually want to come back and write scientific papers about it.

The Shallows attract wild-eyed voyagers who have seen the glorious breakdown of conventional physics, long before they reach the edge-places. Usually, thanks to the kind of naughty substances that come with either a stern health warning or a little paper umbrella in them.

The power of the gravitic torsion rams or toroidal mass-compressors needed to get there, in any case, means that the Shallows are only rarely visited by the more serious species of the Galactically Involved. The sheer waste of resources is akin to a rock star painting a brand-new Rolls-Royce paisley and jumping it into an Olympic-sized swimming pool full of Dom Perignon. So, it's people of a similar persuasion that come.

Long ago – so long ago, in fact, that terms like 'long' and 'ago' lose meaning behind the background static of sheer entropy – some whimsical race had come here to geoform a structure so interesting that, were its existence more widely known (beyond whispered rumours in the more salacious kinds of spaceyard taverns) it would be debated as to whether it was an act of art or science. It would have been a bastard to build anywhere else, where the rules of space and time were not so easily tricked - that was certain.

The legend goes that these alien jokers built two tiny suns; one red, one white. Then they encircled them with an ever-turning twist of salt sea, and studded this ring with asteroids, making a glittering chain of islands. It might have been designed as a beach resort. It might, as mentioned before, have been art. It may even have been a very obscure warning to other sentient races, not to trespass into the deeper reaches of consensual three-dimensional space; though whatever was being warned, it's best not to speculate. All that's rumoured is that the Archipelago exists. It's not valuable in and of itself, but working out how it was constructed could be worth more than a reasonably sized planet or two, to the right sentience. It's too bad that it shares the same kind of reputation as the Bermuda Triangle did, back on Old Earth. And that, or so the story goes, during the Diasporic Age, when wormhole gates were two a penny, it got infected with life.

In short, the Arch' was not something you aimed at.

But it was something that got hit.

Once, anyway.

The pod had been sent out from a dying world.

Not in the sense that all worlds are dying, by the slow and terrible grinding down of thermodynamics. *This* one was dying in a more kinetic and grandiose fashion, as a swarm of gigantic asteroids tumbled into its orbital track, promising a light show of the kind that ruined the holiday plans of several billion dinosaurs.

The people there were advanced enough to see it coming, but not quite advanced enough to do much about it, so there was nothing for them to attempt but the construction very deep bunkers and very powerful rockets. Or, (the more popular choice) to get so rat-arsed inebriated that the resulting planet-wide party would obliterate any thought of impending death - with the added bonus that this time, there really *wouldn't* be a hangover.

As is traditional in these circumstances, the great and the good fought tooth and nail to bribe, wheedle, extort and cheat their way to safety. But two of the rocket scientists (who had been working on reverse-engineering the drives from a recently crashed alien craft) had their own plan. It was, perhaps, very silly in one regard, but in another, it was a bona fide classic.

They jury-rigged a small but exceedingly powerful spacecraft with that alien tech. They programmed it to seek out the nearest habitable planet it would pass on its flight. Then they put their only child, a tiny baby, inside, and launched it, just as a rock the size of Australia came 'dozering in to blot out the sky, and suddenly, all the recreational narcotics in the world seemed insufficient.

Now, we're all clear on how this is supposed to go. The pod is supposed to skip across the surface of hyperspace like a smooth stone across a pond, and end up on a planet where, for no good reason, the people look exactly like the poor kid's parents. He's supposed to grow up to have some kind of strange powers, and save the world, which would have come in handy back where mum and dad were from.

But not this time. This time, the little pod strayed into the fray. This time, it skipped up into the Shallows, where willpower exerts pressure on reality like a fat lady perched on a beach ball.

And *this* happened instead.

The pod curved into a gentle arc around the two suns of the Arch', avoided by a whisker becoming part of their gravitonic cats-cradle, and was slung out towards the glittering ring of water which twisted around them. A force which we'll call luck, (but which might be considerably more sinister) saw to it that the little craft was aimed directly at one of the slowly tumbling islands which protruded from this moebius strip of ocean. A big one – both the top and the bottom poked out on different sides, with one in shadow and one in daylight at any given time. Right now, the lumpy, forested day-side was just turning toward night, and the pod streaked across its sky with a sonic whipcrack, piercing the tube of atmosphere which bound up the entire vast structure of the Arch'.

From this point on, it was all just physics - for a few minutes at least. The pod came down hard, skipping across a lake, then ploughing through a swathe of green, incinerating trees and shrubs and anything too slow to get out of its way. It was a dense and tropical forest, so it didn't take too long for snagging vines and clawing branches to bring it to a stop.

When it did, it lay in a trench of its own creation, plinking and hissing for a while.

Then someone poked it with a spear.

"Well, I don't know, Jimjo! I'm not really an expert on giant silver eggs falling from the sky!" Another prod, this time more forceful. A figure dressed in rags and mis-matched armour cringed back for an instant, but nothing happened. The figure's companion shouted something unhelpful.

"A dragon? Naw, they don't just lay eggs when they're in the air."

"Could be an incontinent one," suggested a second voice, pushing through the underbrush. It turned out to belong to a similarly ragged small man, armed with an axe. His face looked like the result of an argument between a cut-throat razor and a side of corned beef. The first figure rolled its eyes.

"Jimjo, I never cease to be amazed at your idiocy. If this was, in fact, the egg of a large incontinent dragon, it would be down here looking for it... right... now..."

The two men made a dive for the undergrowth. The pod, left alone, determined that it was now cool enough to open. A pair of curved doors popped and hissed, revealing its cargo to the humid air of Jansamrana, the great tropical island which stood at twelve noon in the god-sized clock of the Arch'. This was its less civilised side, and these two were, to put no finer point on it, bandits. They shuffled back in, warily, weapons at the ready.

"Well bless my bunions, Waldrick! It's a little baby! This must be the egg of an... well, I suppose, if a woman were real big, like, and made of metal..."

An image of the Statue of Tyranny, (which upheld the beacon of the Harbour Watch in a city they had both fled) came hastily to mind. But there were no twenty-foot-long sandal prints anywhere to be seen. Waldrick edged closer.

"A baby?" he sucked his teeth. "Best leave it alone, then. Trouble, that is. A baby discovered in mysterious circumstances by two honest peasants, out in the forest..."

Jimjo's brow furrowed.

"And what about if it's found by two nasty cut-throats like us, then?"

"I was speaking metaphorically, you nincompoop! What I mean is, it's probably a king or something. Gonna grow up as a swine-herd or a miller's lad or something, and then *wham*, he'll have a birthmark shaped like a crown on his bum and a sword he pulls out of a rock and it'll be trouble with the Emperor, mark my words. Mysterious heirs last about as long around here as merchant caravans with no guards on 'em."

Waldrick prodded with a dirty finger. The baby gurgled.

"No, Jimjo, I know when to leave well enough alone. Now, help me loot everything we can carry off of this big metal egg, right? Armourers guild will pay good money for nice shiny steel, and there's all kinds of other bits, too."

So it was that, an hour or so later, a baby was left in a clearing in the jungle, while a pair of honest peasants (who were actually bandits) made off with a single piece of advanced technology they had no idea what to do with. Shouting, swearing, kicking, thumping and the application of knives and axes had not so much as dented the metal of the egg, but a blow to one circular hatch had ejected... something.

The sum-total of their haul was the power source of the pod, a rod of matter so exotic it should have been served up with a slice of pineapple and a cherry on a stick. This, they felt, would be good for a couple of beers, at least, as it seemed to attract and then vaporise small insects.

The baby was found, eventually, by one of the great red apes which lived in the arboreal forests of Jansamrana, and raised by their troop to understand the secrets of nature, and the wisdom of the trees, and how to tell which vines to swing on and which ones were snakes. In time, he'd develop a six-pack you could crack coconuts on, arms like pythons which have just raided a ham factory, and a mental age of nine. This is not his story.

Instead, this is the story of how two idiots lost a priceless Yanavarian Perpetual Power Rod in a game of poker with some pirates, and how those pirates were surprised the next morning by a party of excise men from the navy, and how, to avoid a date with a short piece of rope and a long piece of thin air, the pirate captain traded his new glowing peg leg for free passage to somewhere as far away as possible. He hadn't even been able to give it a try-out.

The naval commander's brother was a wizard of the Order of Nine Reeds, and *he* (ignorant of what the glowing green rod was, but certain it was an artefact of power) ordered it sealed up in lead, smothered with runes, wrapped in waxed paper and posted to an old acquaintance of his, the Chairman of the Guild Morphologic, the Alchemists.

This, then, is the story of how the postal service, in those latter days of the Urzoman Empire, left a hell of a lot to be desired. That, and the fate of a third idiot, who, at the time of Waldrick and Jimjo waking to a hangover so vile it made their teeth itch, was just heading off to bed on the other side of the great rock of Jansamrána, rolling eternally with the twisted skein of Mother Ocean.

We shall give him at least one more night of dreams. And then – oh, yes! And then, the nightmares...

CODEX ONE:

ROTTEN CIRCUMSTANCES

1

The Imbecilic Juxtaposition

Dawn in Grand Sepulchre, Princess of Cities, and the Lizard Bells ring out in disharmony from the rickety cupola of the Slave Traders' Manse, heralding sunrise.

At the top of the Malevolith, that great spiked tower of black stone, flocks of predatory bats swirl like ink in water, finding roosts away from the light. Ah, yes! For before the Jaguar Bells of the second Octal ring atop the Temple of Pleasures, it will already be hot enough to fry an egg on the red marble walks of the Imperial Precinct, up there tight beneath the Malevolith's great gnomon. Smart citizens – or those not afflicted by hangovers, dreamsugar, or sundry other vices of the flesh – are already out in the cool of the morning, giving the metropolis, if seen from the air, the impression of a heaving, ant-infested smear of vomit.

Unpatriotic, perhaps, this comparison? Unfitting of the jewel of the Urzoman Empire, the residence of the Dark Lord himself, secure in his skull-carved fastness?

Don't worry. Your author is no government spy. Observe, where the shanties and barrios of the New Town cascade down the hill, dribbling toward the harbour. Past the butcher's shambles, and the fishmarkets, and the pleasure souks with their sweating eunuch guards. Past that sorecerous *alma mater*, the old Unaussprechlich Akademie (known in Urzoman as the Unspeakable College) where stout washerwomen pound the dust of centuries out of basketfuls of filigree'd robes.

Down, slipping in open sewerage, slopping and trickling further and further from the homes of the great and good atop the hill. Down Skizarian Street with its sailor's taverns, just as the wonky wagon comes creaking past, its hunch-backed driver picking up the dead and the dead-drunk from the gutters. A sharp turn into Peachcourt Alley, where the ancient voodoo priestess, Mama Lurga, is brushing her teeth at the fountain. Out onto the Stilts, where the buildings keep going despite the utter failure of the land.

Take one more left. Then a right. And straight ahead, past the reeking bait and tackle shop and the fortune teller's, you will find the Guild of Alchemists. It's built on bamboo, lashed up out of rice paper and straw and balsa wood. When your trade is in mutation, and your building often explodes, it's wise to take such precautions. The Guild therefore took the form of a Chungdojin castle, with sloping rooflines and narrow little windows paned with lacquered fish-bladders.

When the tides of Mother Ocean waxed fulsome, salt water lapped through the bamboo floors of the first storey, where the apprentices lived. When, as today, the tides drew slack, the whole edifice perched above a steaming, sucking mudflat on thousands of spindly spider legs. Cunning apprentices had already opened a welter of trapdoors beneath the guildhouse, lowering crab-pots filled with offal scraps down to the mud. Blue and purple bandit crabs, the size of fists, fought for the privilege of being tomorrow's dinner. Of course, the seventeen tenured Alchemical Masters and their Guildlord were still snoring. But there was one duty with which this ancient brotherhood was charged by Himself, the Dread Emperor. So at least one of their number was up and abroad as the twin suns broke the horizon, lighting up the great ring of Mother Ocean as she swept into the heavens.

The Alchemists were no fools. They delegated.

Thus, if you truly had followed that twist-scrabble path down through the city, right to the edge of the Stilts, you'd find a bent figure struggling along under the weight of a great bronze lantern. Inside burned the unquenchable fire of the alchemists, mixed up during the previous day's labours. Because it burned with the heat of Ijun, the white sun, the unfortunate figure carrying it was wrapped up in thick woollen robes, plated with ox leather. In the tropical heat of a Grand Sepulchre summer, this is rank insanity, and the figure's boots were already slopping half full with sweat by the time he reached the breakwater, and began his long trek out to the lighthouse of the Harbour Watch.

From the awful nature of this task, it was easy to understand exactly who the Guildlord had delegated it to. While he was still abed, perusing the daily news-sheets and sipping iced hibiscus tea, the least worthy of his apprentices was staggering along the breakwater, being slowly cooked alive.

Did the old man have any sympathy? Why, of course not! Guildlord Multhazar Florian Threck believed in three things: stern discipline, politics, and the demon-god Quazirath. The first made him a cruel taskmaster to his students. The third made him a devout parishioner of the Temple of Pleasures. And the second made him vehemently wish that he could simply expel his worst protégé, Jack Somewhat, from the entire institution of alchemy.

Unfortunately, the Urzoman Empire had a strict policy on unemployment. Foundlings, especially, were paid into guild tutelage by the government, so that they could enter the service of Himself when they were fully qualified. Jack, one such stray, had been bounced between the bakers, dyers, cutlers, fishermen, coopers, tanners, scribes and furriers during his formative years. Each guild had managed to make him quit, usually by assigning him to tasks of such stench, filth and unpleasantness that he voluntarily ran away.

So far, Multhazar Threck had been unsuccessful. But Jack, now seventeen and nearing his Maturity, could still carry the Day Watch Lantern, and so he was of some use to the citizens of Grand Sepulchre - even if he was held in the same general low esteem as the thousands of feral tamarins who infested its vine-choked alleys.

Long and sometimes bitter experience of the world and its wickedness convinced Jack that there was no use complaining. So he'd shouldered the ungainly wicker frame and harness which secured the Day Watch Lantern to his back, just before dawn licked the surface of Mother Ocean. He'd trudged along the breakwater, where it curved out into the city's great harbour. And, after what seemed like an eternity of sweat and back-ache, he'd reached the fortress of the Harbour Watch, where, exactly as on the preceding 422 mornings, the gate-guard was asleep.

Snores emanated from his little red-and-blue striped hut. Part of a belly and a pair of knobbly-kneed legs stuck out, gently cooking in the morning sun. They were clad in chain-mail undershorts and one yellow sock.

Jack knew that he'd get no acknowledgement for the fact that, in over a year, he hadn't whispered a word to the gate-guard's superiors about his skiving. If he turned rat, the harbour guardsmen would pull together in a jolly display of camaraderie to beat him to a boneless pulp. It was well known that their kind were recruited from the dregs of His prisons, and the soldiers of His armies who could not competently hold a sword and pick their noses at the same time, without a detailed series of scrolls.

It was not as if he could just shake the fat, scar-faced thug awake, either. So, he settled for the same farce he'd played out several hundred times, knocking on the door of the watch-keep until the man snorted his way into consciousness.

"Whaa? Mother? The cat's got no legs, I told ye, and bugger the donkey!"

The guardsman pushed his helmet back out of his eyes, and squinted at the figure before him, robed and hooded, framed by a blinding wash of white light. "Ahhh, it's you again, is it, maggot? Well, you can get that fecking furnace out of me sight, so you can. Look lively, you lazy offal-sack!"

Jack just tried to smile good-naturedly, as the guard fumbled among the keys at his belt and finally managed to open the door, puffing and heaving as he did so. Then he slipped inside, into the cool and shadowy watchkeep, with its familiar carvings of skulls and demons, and its globes of magical illumination hanging from brass chains. At least he wouldn't have to climb any stairs. The Day Watch Lantern was hooked onto a vast spiked chain of its own, deep in the salt-rot of the keep's basement, then hoisted up as the Night Watch Lantern came down, it's red fires guttering. Jack knew every hollowed-out stair and rusty gate on his route, which was marked by dour Harbour Watchmen getting about their morning business. Some of them nodded as he trudged past, and one or two deigned to mumble 'Maggot' at him as well.

It was not a name that Jack enjoyed, but it was better than some things he'd been called. In truth it was an ethnic slur, based on the fact that he was, like many citizens of the Urzoman Empire, a racial minority. In this case, an unnaturally pale skinned, blue eyed, straw-haired son of the Grailish Isles, some hundred degrees or more away around the arc of Mother Ocean. His people[1] had it better than others, in fact. Because, it was whispered, He Himself had been a Grailishman, until He'd passed through death and into his power. The majority of the citizens of Grand Sepulchre were the red-tan, black-haired Sarunjek, who had been native to this island before His armies ever arrived aboard their great death-hulks and battle-arks. Hence the background chatter in Low Sulj as Jack lumbered past, of which he caught only three or four words he could render into Common; these being the patois slang for 'imbecile' 'ugly' 'venereal disease' and 'your mother'.

---

1. If he'd had 'people', rather than an embarrassed diaspora, not one of whom claimed his parentage. It's hard to be part of a culture when they keep slamming the metaphorical door on your foot

Grinning as if he understood none of it, Jack made his way to the basement, where he stood ankle-deep in water and latched the lantern to its chain. He gave it the obligatory three tugs to prove it was secure. Hidden mechanisms, said to be powered by the tides, made the chain rattle and clank up into the darkness, lofting the alchemist's fire up a copper tube, toward the dawn.

All day it would blaze from the great glass globe atop the Statue of Tyranny's fist, where the Stingray Bells waited to ring out noontime. A much smaller, lighter lantern came jerking and swinging down into the dark after a while, the embers of a red fire sifting within. Jack unhooked it and lashed it to his back with leather straps. He paused for a moment, enjoying the sensation of cool water seeping into his sweat-soaked boots, then sighed and headed up the stairs.

On a usual morning, he'd trudge back across the breakwater under the hammer of the twin suns, then cadge what breakfast leavings he could from old Gilde Fane in the cookhouse. Then it was time for lessons; blowfly-blatter hours of hot boredom as Master Horgath and Master Sneel tried to inculcate his brain with the seeds of basic chemistry and Elder Chungdoji Arithmetic, respectively. This, however, proved to be an unusual morning.

Because, waiting at the top of the stairs, all unshaven and baggy-eyed, was the Commander of the Harbour Watch himself.

Rhaegulus Cratt was a bad-tempered, short, battle-scarred old bastard at the best of times[2], and this was clearly not one of them. He carried a dented enamel mug of strong coffee in one hand, and a waxed paper tube in the other, and he blocked the top of the stairs in a manner which made it clear that Jack was not getting past.

The apprentice alchemist gulped, his toes curling up in his soggy boots. In his experience, Jack had found that Authority only ever wanted to talk to him about a series of nasty punishments. Rhaegulus Cratt was known to upbraid his own men by whipping them bloody and throwing them into the harbour. Right now, he was frowning like a constipated thundercloud. Jack dithered.

"Hail His Wisdom?" he tried, giving a tenuous salute. Cratt grunted.

"Hail His glory," he replied, in the traditional fashion. His salute was a mere inclination of his coffee cup, which smelled absolutely delicious. The pay of an apprentice didn't allow Jack such luxuries.

---

2. To be fair, Master Cratt was short all of the time, which did nothing to improve his temper. He'd gone a long way in the military with careful application of the adage 'never underestimate a man who can uppercut you in the fruits'

"We've had a trireme in from the Underbelly last night. Brought a package for your lot. Something fell from the sky, they said." The Guard commander sighed. "So I've had to stay up all night to deliver it. Captain tried to tell me to bring it to old Multhazar by hand, but I'm no fecking errand boy, pardon my Sulj. I told 'em they sent a sniveller along each morning with the dawn lantern, and he could carry the bloody thing. By which I mean *you*, maggot."

With that, the black-armoured Cratt dumped that long, wax-papered package into Jack's hands. It weighed considerably more than it should have done for its size. In fact, it almost made his knuckles drag to the floor.

But over a year of carrying the Day Watch Lantern each morning had made Jack stronger than he thought he was. Truth be told, if he'd been pitted in a wrestling bout against the Guard Commander, (perhaps in the Brute Pits of Ramathagan Street, in the Old Quarter) the money could have gone either way. But Jack Somewhat was a young man unaware of his own size, which made him obsequious and clumsy instead of swagger-proud.

"Yes, sir. I mean *of course*, Commander. I shall see to it that the Guildlord receives it at once," he said, bearing up under the weight. His eyes darted to the open doorway, down the corridor. An arc of sunlight razored across the cobbles, already blowtorch bright. Rhaegulus Cratt caught the direction of his gaze, and smirked.

"I'll be off to a cool bath, me," he said, quite self-satisfied. "And if anyone asks, I delivered that bloody thing myself, you hear? That captain was a right pain in the arse, with all his paperwork and whining. Get on with you!"

So it was that Jack was swearing under his breath by the time he traversed the breakwater a second time, without even the opportunity to stop, as he usually did, for a cup of crushed and sugared ice. Ice was, happily, in plentiful supply in Grand Sepulchre, as it formed each night on the outer skin of the Malevolith, and was shucked off in glistening plates each morning by gangs of hook-men and barrow-pushers.

All Jack wanted when he arrived back at the guildhouse was to peel off his sweat-sticky robes and plunge his head under the pump. But his day was going from bad to worse. Chep Palaquat, the guild prefect, was waiting for him in the shadow of the house's bamboo portico, a horrible tight little smile on his face. Palaquat was an acne-raddled fifteen summers old, but he was a prodigy when it came to the alchemical arts. There was nothing he loved better than having power over the great, hulking Jack Somewhat. If girls could have been convinced to talk to him, perhaps with the application of a long-pointed stick, he would tell them all about his dire authority.

"You're late, you great Grailish oaf! *Late!* The Masters called a surprise assembly, and you were missing. *Again.* So now I'm wasting my time here waiting for you, to bring you before Lord Threck in chains!"

Indeed, the pinch-faced little prefect was carrying the ceremonial chains of disgrace, which he'd personally dug out of a mouldering old trunk in the attic, oiled, polished and restored for just such a happy occasion.

Jack may have been the worst apprentice ever, but he was no fool. The chances of Chep actually getting those manacles on him, without witnesses or assistance, were lower than zero.

"I got held up," he said, pushing past and into the shade. "The Harbour Watch gave me something for the Guildlord, so if you're going to be my escort, you can make yourself useful and carry it." He swung the package down from off his shoulder and offloaded it across Chep's stick-thin arms, causing him to collapse to his knees. Jangling chains bounced and rolled. Jack peeled back his hood, and shook out his straw-coloured mop of hair. Then he proceeded to dunk his head in the pump cistern, drowning out the prefect's howl of outrage. When he surfaced, the litany of rules and complaints was still forthcoming; he manhandled the great iron pump and dunked himself a second time.

"At least get it off of my fingers!"

Jack savoured the moment, just a little. He wasn't at heart, a bad person. But creatures like Chep Palaquat tend to bring out the worst in all of us. He stooped, dripping delightfully cool, and made a point of hefting the package with minimal fuss. Beneath it, the prefect's fingers looked like twin bunches of rotten plantains, all bruise-purple.

"What's in it, anyway?" sulked Chep, sucking a finger. "And why would they give anything of value to a maggot like you? We've all heard about *you people*, you know."

This, too, was nothing more than racial politics. The conservative Sarunjek party, God's Anvil, had determined with the aid of palmistry, phrenology and medical science that the Grailish were a race of hotheads, thieves and scoundrels, who should be eradicated from the city. In doing so, they not only charted a course perilously close to challenging Himself, but also made Jack's daily life that little bit less tolerable.

So it was understandable, if self-defeating in a larger political context, when Jack hauled off, dropped the package, and smacked Chep Palaquat square in the nose. There was a sickening crunch. There was a surprised honk, spluttering with snot and blood. Chep went down, hard, on his arse, and Jack recoiled.

Oh no! Not again. He really must remember how big he was! If that was broken...

"Du udder, udder pastard! Du proke by DOSE!" shrieked the prefect, staggering to his feet. "That's it! I'b delling old Bulthazar you did it! And that you stole that... that *whatever it is!*" He tried kicking the parcel, but only stubbed his toe, eliciting a further howl of agony. Seeing as the entire Guild of Alchemy was built from grass, bamboo, paper and lacquered fish guts, Jack was certain that everyone now knew something was going on. But his natural tendency to leg it was held in check as the paper split, and a long grey cylinder rolled free.

Chep was fascinated as well. There seemed to be no reason why, but the cylinder drew both their eyes with a magnetic attraction, similar to that of a large and untended hoard of gold. Or a doorway in the pleasure souks, without its usual eunuch attendant...

Two pairs of hands scrabbled for the cylinder. It was slippery and cold, fashioned from lead, and neither Jack, with his clumsy big mitts, or the twice-injured Palaquat could grasp a definitive hold. Instead they rolled on the floor like pariah dogs, demonstrating the kind of behaviour which traditional guild schooling is meant to stamp out. This failure of decorum continued, with many attempts at throttling, eye-gouging and knees to the fruits, until two things happened at once.

First, the clasp holding the cylinder shut gave way. A green, glowing rod some twelve fingers long clattered out, slithering across the bamboo. Secondly, Chep Palaquat, driven to an excess of rage by the siren-song of the strange artefact, actually managed to get both of his bruised and puffy thumbs into Jack's windpipe. He set about taking vigorous revenge for his broken nose, which still dripped blood and mucus with every honking breath. Jack, who had been holding back, following his previous excess, drew back his forehead and nutted him. There was a sound like a cabbage being pulverised with a war-hammer. Jack groaned, as sticky, snotty gore dripped down his face.

But he had three pressing problems. First, the lolling, unconscious body of his prefect, Chep. Second, getting out from under said body to scoop up the glowing rod. And third, with its numerical ranking rising by the instant, the sound of many, many feet descending the bamboo staircases within the Alchemist's Guildhouse.

Jack moved swiftly. He bundled up Palaquat and stuffed him into a convenient crab-pot, left here in the entrance hall near a set of large trapdoors in the floor. He shoved the snoring prefect inside, along with the lead tube and wax-paper parcel, then popped the hatch and let them swing out in the salt breeze, tethered by a length of rope. The footsteps and creaks were coming closer now, trailing muffled curses. Jack slammed shut the trap door and made a dive for the glowing rod, scooping it up in his fingers just in time to tuck it behind his back as the assembled Mastery of the Alchemical Guild came blustering into the room, dusty and black-robed, reeking of sulphur and vinegar and other vile concoctions.

It was a vulture chorus line. It was a brace of gargoyles sprung horribly to life. Multhazar Threck himself was front and centre, flanked by his Masters Alchemic as they staggered to a halt. Small apprentices poked out from behind the massed faculty like feral tamarins haunting a pack of street-dogs.

"What is the meaning of this unholy ruckus?" demanded Threck, his jowls quivering. "You! *Somewhat!* Explain yourself, or it'll be the latrine pits for you!"

Jack, who knew that he'd have to swab the dreaded latrine pits in any case, was less than terrified. But there were worse things than sluicing out crap, and he could just tell that old Muthazar's cronies were itching to suggest them. So he made a show of contrition, going so far as to fall to his knees. This also neatly covered the trapdoor beneath which poor, bloodied Chep Palaquat swung in salty space. Jack clasped the glowing rod behind him and gesticulated with his free hand.

"Fulminators, your eminence! Those mad puritans from the Creed of Stone. They tried to barge in, with their pamphlets and their sing-songs and that big hurdy-gurdy they carry around the streets. Called you a sinner, they did. So I sent them packing."

This was a stroke of genius. The Guildlord, a devout worshipper of Quazirath, was forever complaining about the abstinent, teetotal, utterly judgemental Creed, who just last Chainsday had tried to picket the Temple of Pleasures in a display of vigorous eschatological debate. Multhazar, who had been performing his religious duty by visiting the temple's prostitutes, had been struck in the face by a rotten melon. He narrowed his eyes.

"You, *all alone*, drove off a rabble of fulminators from the Creed?" He looked Jack up and down, noticing signs of obvious struggle. "Well, I suppose you are a hefty lad, and all..."

"I had the Dusk Lantern, your eminence," explained Jack, thinking fast. "Threatened them with unquenchable fire, I did. There was a little left. You know how they fear burning, what with their papers and ribbons and all."

The Guildlord nodded. Creedsmen did have a tendency to pierce, stitch and sew leaves of parchment to their naked flesh, clothing themselves in the words of their fool prophet.

"Where's Palaquat, then? I left him here to bring you to me. Seems there's something at the Harbour Watch I'm supposed to attend to. Mage nonsense, from those Nine Reeds charlatans."

Jack couldn't resist.

"He left with the Creedish, milord," he ventured, edging out onto the lie like a fat man onto Spring ice. It seemed to hold. "Said they made some very interesting points. Said he was going to pop along and read some pamphlets."

Multhazar's face was a study in acid and bile. His lips compressed to a thin and bloodless line for an instant, and a purple vein throbbed at his temple.

"Only one last question then, Somewhat, before you go back to the Watch for my delivery." His grin was one of cruel triumph. "*What have you got behind your back?*"

Jack reached around and scrabbled to change hands. His mouth formed a surprised 'O' of horror as he realised there was nothing in either of them. Had he dropped the glowing rod? Was it even now rolling across the floor, in plain view of seventeen assorted academic sadists? He held out his left hand. Multhazar sneered. He held out his right as well. The Guildlord's smile collapsed, like a tottering old ruin sinking into a swamp. There really was nothing there.

"N... nothing, your eminence. Nothing at all. I was... that is to say, I..."

"Oh, quit your blathering, your great Grailish turnip," sighed Threck. "Just go back to the Watch-keep, ask for that halfwit Cratt, and fetch whatever those imbecilic sorcerers can't seem to get their brains around, will you? You're excused lessons, on the theory that if you get any further behind, you'll be approaching enlightenment from the opposite direction. The rest of you – *back to work!*"

This last was delivered in a parade-ground bellow that rattled the bamboo and sent Alchemists scurrying in all directions. Jack took the opportunity to peer high and low, his eyes all but popping from their sockets as he tried to spy the rod. Threck turned back to him, finger extended.

"What are you waiting for! *Get!* And for the sake of the Demon, boy, wash those stinking hands of yours. My arse has to touch those latrine pit seats, you know!"

Jack didn't need telling twice. He was off and out the door, up Peachcourt Alley and onto Skizarian Street before he even thought to look at his hands, now allegedly filthy. When he did, he collapsed sideways into the doorway of the Black Hibiscus, a dive of such ill repute that it had become weirdly fashionable. The world spun. He smelled frangipani and fishguts, old sweat and razor oil.

Jack collapsed at a table, one hand clasped around the wrist of the other. He gurgled.

"Yeah, we get that a lot in here," said the bartender, a lady with a hook hand and a shock of blue-dyed hair. "Are you going to order up, or just make that noise all morning?"

Jack held out two fingers, largely on automatic. He couldn't take his eyes off of the palm of his left hand.

Where he'd held the glowing rod, there was a green after-image burned into his flesh. A stylised diamond, with a single rune branded athwart it. A shape like the curly-cursive-cut-out which graces a violin, crossed halfway up with a horizontal bar. He recognised it all too well. To a certain type of old-fashioned engraver, it was the first letter of his last name.

ſ for ſomewhat.

But that wasn't the problem. Not really. Jack, at the ripe old age of seventeen, had already woken up upside down in a haystack more than once, with a new tattoo, no memory of the night before, and a mouth like the nethers of a week-dead walrus.

What worried him was the *light*, pulsing green from under his skin. And the way it traced his veins, climbing up his arm with each thump of his heart. It was remorseless. Inches of his flesh fell to its advance as he gibbered, disbelieving.

This was definitely the time to have a wise, enlightened, good idea. They say that in times of incredible stress, the brain can think faster and come up with wild and untamed solutions, sparks of wisdom cast glowing from the forge of tribulation. Jack needed such an inspirational thought right now; indeed, he cried out for a good idea on so many subliminal wavelengths that he came within a split eyelash of formulating a working theory of time travel.

Then his glass arrived.

And thankfully, the rotgut brewed up in the basement of the Black Hibiscus was potent enough to let Jack consider a very, very bad one instead.

2

The Cognoscentical Proxy

THEY SAY THAT whenever you're in trouble, at least you have your mates to turn to.

Jack Somewhat, faced with a dilemma which had several equally horrible facets to it, certainly needed some friends, fast. It wouldn't be long before the Alchemists realised that he'd inadvertently consumed Multhazar Threck's important package. Then the Harbour Watch would know as well, and, like as not, the Order of Nine Reeds, those shifty elementalist wizards.

But, chin up, he thought to himself. He'd likely be dead by then, with this infection turning him to a glowing puddle of slop. He needed medical advice. Luckily, one of his old mates happened to be in the trade.

Well – adjacent to it. Parallel, if you will.

Jack pushed through the morning crowds in Sunderside, the louche artist's quarter of the New Town, trying to conceal his glowing hand inside his robes. Despite his best efforts, little pops and crackles of green dripped out from under his fingernails, slithering and hopping like fleas made of mercury.

Later, forensic mages would trace his route from Sunderside to Bentsteeple, and hence to the slums of Rown Cross, by the things that happened in his wake that morning. Sunderside, and especially Decameron Street, was home to Grand Sepulchre's fashionable cafes, sugar-houses and avant-garde theatres. A bubbling gumbo of social stratas moiled and squeezed through the alleys on each side of Decameron, where tamarins chattered amid the purple jacaranda blossoms, and cut-purses of the Guild Tenebral plied their trade.

Glowing green droplets went fizzing across tabletops, up trouser legs, and into plates of Grand Sepulchre's signature local dish, pan-fried scallops and moonfish, served in a spicy chilli and mango chutney[3]. Maybe a dozen people in all were so afflicted; strangers,

---

3. This was, in fact, a very different Sarunjek dish when the Urzoman conquest occurred – the story goes that one of His generals, seeing a Sulj laundry-man working to scour

each one, and as inconsequential as one could hope to be in a city of million souls. None of them realised the very specific doom which had befallen them.

Jack ploughed on through the crowds, staggering now, feeling feverish and cold at the same time. Part of this was the fact that he was still wearing the thick, protective robes used for the transportation of the Day Watch Lantern, and part of it was down to animal panic. He climbed the winding staircase past the Fountain of Sorrows, ignoring all the small, fussy little brick-fronted apothecaries there, and plunged into the stews on the other side of the ridge, down into Rown Cross proper. Down into the Fleamarket, where anything and everything was for sale.

How can we describe the Fleamarket? The smell of excrement, fried banana, wood smoke, sweat and flowers comes to mind. A great expanse of tents, bamboo stalls roofed with giant leaves, box-wood huts and blankets strewn with fruit and vegetables, guarded by vendors who sat slumped in the attitude of Underbelly's red apes.

Some of them wore the wide conical hats of the peasantry from out in the fields, and peered through basket-slats of flax. Others were got up in their own ethnic costumes, ranging from gaudy Uroshi pirates in their dyed silks and bells through to blue-skinned Thamars in loincloths and little else. They shouted, hooted, whistled and sang songs to advertise wares as varied as caged bats, fried stingray, wooden toys, bolts of cotton, treasure maps, love potions and trained, finger-length marmosets.

Jack was interested in none of them, even the Chalinese dancers who made the Thamar tribesmen look overdressed. He staggered through the Fleamarket, groaning, listing to the left, until he saw a familiar banner above a familiar wooden shack.

Soto Scalizari, master herbalist.

It's worth mentioning, as we sidle towards that slanty shanty of tar-paper and scavenged planks, that Jack's circle of friends weren't criminals, per se. It's just that, as noted, Himself had a definite policy

his bleach cauldrons, called on him to cook a traditional dinner, then and there. Knowing he would be short of one head should he refuse, but having the cooking skills of a dead rodent, the terrified laundry-washer made his best attempt at re-creating his grandmother's seafood curry, utilising mango relish instead of the usual Mace Pepper Death Sauce to account for the Urzomen's delicate palate. Of course the general loved this fraudulent bastard meal, and asked what it was called. The answer, Chulimajwek, actually means 'I can't believe they ate that', and has become known across the Arch' as the most authentic of Jansamrani dishes.

regarding unemployment, so it was very difficult indeed to be a free spirit in the realms of commerce. Nice, official, *taxable* guild jobs were His preferred form of mortal toil for the masses. It meant that His Vizier, Lord Slave, need only shake down the hundred or so heads of the Guildsbund each month to fill the treasure-vaults under the Malevolith.

Ostensibly, these monies were to be used to further the cause of evil, and the Urzoman Empire's conquest of the Arch' in its entirety. But the maintenance of Grand Sepulchre itself was an endless suck-sink for money, and the only way to keep generating more was to keep pouring gold into the jaws of its vibrant, sweltering economy.

Thus, it was hard work *not* to work. Some of Jack's friends chose not to have a job for political reasons, or because they were serious students of drinking, or because they were simply lazy ne'er-do-wells. This actually described the rainbow of excuses which covered just one of them, Jory Foxmallet. Soto Scalizari, on the other hand, had found a lucrative niche which was covered by no particular guild or order, and which only required him to work about an hour a day.

Luckily for Jack, he'd hit upon his master scam while trying not to do very much work as an apprentice doctor. Doing not very much was his professional speciality. This was why Jack was extremely surprised to come crashing in through the bead-hung curtain doorway of Soto's practice and find him actually ministering to a patient. Had he come in the back way, he would have found Jory, along with fellow scoundrel Billiam Knox, sharing a pipe of stumbleweed and talking politics; or rather, the politics of cricket[4], which divided Grand Sepulchre along sectarian lines deeper than any religion.

Luckily, Soto was very quick on his feet. He rallied magnificently, pushing the array of brass and bronze goggles he wore up onto his forehead, and gripping the lapels of his imitation doctor's smock in a statesmanly fashion.

"Aha! So, you Alchemists are after my secrets again, are you? What does that old miser Multhazar offer this time? His pocketwatch? His daughter's hand in marriage? A boatload of salted emu jerky? You can tell him, nothing doing!"

Soto's patient, an overweight woman of middle age, smiled approvingly, blinking a pair of eyes like runny eggs. Soto bullied up to Jack, who was twice his size, and stage-whispered behind one hand.

---

4. For the full rules of Urzoman Death Cricket, see appendix I

"Play along!"

Jack, who was mortally anxious, thoroughly stressed, and two cups deep on the old Black Hibiscus moonshine, made a noise like a kettle in intestinal distress.

"Yeessss. We, ummm... I mean to say, Master Threck... would really like to see you in person. *Now.* Yesterday, if possible."

Soto waved a finger theatrically, almost losing it in Jack's nostril.

"Never! My dear patients are more precious to me than all the gold that your guild can magick out of the empyrean! Begone, lickspittle... and as for you, Mrs Mulchaney -" he described a tight little turn, as though his feet were on oiled castors, leaning in to plant a kiss on her pudgy mitt. "Take three of these pills daily until you notice an improvement. Only by moonlight, of course, and followed by a half glass of best sherry. Herbalist's orders!"

He pressed a large brown glass jar into her hands and chivvied her off the couch and out through the curtain, his smile all but dripping sincerity - right up to the moment she handed him a fistful of notes. Then he turned, viper-quick, slammed shut the door, made the money disappear with a twanging of hidden elastic, and flopped down onto the room's only chair.

"Is she gone?" he asked.

Jack cracked open a gap between the split-bamboo blinds.

"She's tottering away. Seems happy enough. How do you do it, Soto?"

The thin little herbalist blew his wispy fringe out of his eyes. Like many of his countrymen from far Szerenica, he was fine-boned and slight, with a complexion tinted rose gold.

"How indeed, with you crashing in here like a hippopotamus in heat! It's all in their heads, Somewhat, and if you're about to show me some kind of rash or discolouration of the willy, I'll be forced to clobber *your* head with a length of bog-oak."

Jack slumped down onto the now-vacant couch and held out his hand. It was still faintly glowing green, though the eerie fire of it seemed to have dissipated. That diamond-and-rune marking stood raw and red from his palm, as if he'd tried to grab a torturer's iron. Soto peered, clicking several mis-matched lenses down over his eyes.

"Well," he said, with the kind of teeth-sucking inhalation that means 'this is going to be expensive'. "I don't have any pills for *that*, Jack. What exactly did you do?"

Jack waggled his hand experimentally. It didn't seem to want to drop off. In fact, the glow was fading, even as he watched. Still -

"What do you mean, you don't have a pill for it? You have a pill for *everything*. Even those horrible hangover cures made out of chillies and concentrated Zollish coffee!"

"Herbalism, Jack, is mostly mental. The pills are... the pills are like finding the key, when you've already broken into your own house."

"*Mostly mental*, Soto, describes my morning so far. I know you're a charlatan, and your pills are placebos, but..."

"But you're still asking for 'em. Alright. A lot of healing is done in the mind, Jack." Soto pushed his lenses away, and spun on his chair.

"A bit of a concoction of eucalyptus, cannabis, horseradish, turmeric and ginger sets those jangled nerves at ease, and frankly, quite a few of these patients of mine are just worried over nothing. Convinced they've got the zombie staggers or weepy liver or the shucks, when it's just a combination of stress, bad posture and a filthy diet[5]. Here. Have a bottle on the house. Just tell me what the hell actually happened to that hand of yours!"

At this point Foxmallet and Billiam came in, the pair of them grinning like lunatics thanks to the stumbleweed.

"Summink wrong with yer hand, Jacky? Too much jerkin' the merkin, is it?"

Jack rolled his eyes.

"If it was that, you'd have a pair of hooks, Foxmallet," he said. He necked a handful of Soto's pills, on the theory that they seemed to work for everyone else. At least these weren't the aforementioned hangover cures; Jack had tried those once, and had become so suddenly sober that he'd considered becoming a chartered accountant.

He slung a comradely arm around Billiam's shoulders, displaying his now-branded palm.

"It's actually a tragic and adventurous tale," he began, all

---

5. Soto Scalizari had come up with a new theory of medicine, which had nothing to do with his old guild, the Chirurgeons, as nobody got bits sawed off, and nothing to do with his current enemies, the Apothecaries, as his medicines were sold strictly as dietary supplements and herbal pick-me-ups. Soto had found that a certain class of Grand Sepulchites craved a cure for the general malaise, listlessness, fatigue and feelings of anxiety caused by modern life itself. Seeing as the only true cure was administered with a sword to the neck, a placebo was the perfect alternative. If the Apothecaries wanted to put him out of business, they'd have to admit that his fix-all pills worked, which they were too proud to do. And, as he held the patent for their concoction, they'd also have to buy him out for a staggering amount of money. Enough to fund his next scam, and a lot of drinks beside.

conspiratorial. "Have any of you got a beer or three?"

So it was that Jack Somewhat learned to stop worrying, and told the long and convoluted story of how he'd caught a band of smugglers trying to sneak past the Harbour Watch, who were all asleep. How he'd rescued Rhaegulus Cratt (who had screamed like a little girl when confronted with pirate steel), and sword-swashbuckled three sea-raiders, and swung on a dockside crane, and snaffled their treasure, a mystical glowing rod which probably had the power to turn water into whiskey, and men into marmosets.

There was a lot of embellishment, featuring swooning, big-bosomed wenches, unlikely sword-fighting moves re-enacted, and descriptions of heroes' deaths. More than one stout bottle of beer was passed about.

Until Jack got to the part about how he'd returned in victory to the Guildhouse of the Alchemists, out on the Stilts.

"And then, who had the temerity to try to stop me, but that stick-insect milksop, Chep Palaquat! I brandished my scimitar, but lately clawed from the dead hands of a seven-foot Chungdoji pirate, and still crimson with his crewmates' blood. I'll swear he crapped his under-draws at the very sight, but he's a crafty weasel, so..."

At this point, Jack's mind turned to what he'd *really* done with the loathsome Palaquat. How he'd stuffed him in a crab pot and dangled him beneath the Guildhouse. How the plan had been to spring him free as soon as the coast was clear.

And how now – as the Jaguar Bells down on the Temple chorused out Nine rising – the tide would be waxing full.

Sweet gods and demons, he was almost a murderer!

"So..." coaxed Billiam, the alleged apprentice wizard, making a grab for the bottle.

"So, I, ummm... had a couple of drinks and came up here and got Soto to have a look at the burn mark. See? Looks like a tattoo, doesn't it? The green was probably some kind of squid juice or jellyfish ink. They glow in the dark, you know! Now I've got to be getting back."

Jack's trio of mates looked crestfallen at this disappointing ending, to what had been a classic made-up load of hogwash.

"Shouldn't we come with you?" asked Foxmallet. "Just in case those pirates, or the Guildlord, or Cratt's thugs are after you?"

Jack thought fast. In his mind, water was already lapping through the bottom of Palaquat's cage. It would be good to have the lads around, even if only as a diversion when it came time to leg it.

"Right! Right! Just try to keep up! I've... erm... left something in the oven."

At this point, it's probably a good idea to fill in a bit of Jack Somewhat's history of running away. As a child, it had stood him in good stead, as he was a lanky and long-legged lad who was usually dressed in the one-size-fits-nobody oversmocks, robes and shapeless muu-muus of the guilds he'd been lumbered upon. This meant plenty of opportunity to put a fair length of hot cobbles between himself and anyone grasping at him, and a second-string plan for if all else failed – running off in his underpants while someone very angry beat up his clothes.

He'd never been too fast, really. But he'd been adept at switching direction unexpectedly, pumping his arms as his lower appendages flailed almost at random, and proceeding through the teeming crowds of Grand Sepulchre like a radioactive particle through a broth of quarks.

His three friends shot each other a look, grinned, and took off after him as he accelerated away through the Fleamarket, all but tumbling over a street puppeteer's tiny stage. Wooden mannikins of Sepulchrite folk-heroes like Mercy Jim and Baron Von Tuesday cursed and hooted at him as he threaded between the crowds. People were jostled. Things were spilled. Certain small objects, skewers of prawns, loose coins and sticks of incense may or may not have been scooped up by Knox, Scalizari and Foxmallet, following in Jack's wake.

And today, his feet surprised him.

Jack was well aware of his limitations, and he was exceeding them by the time he reached the Apothecary's walk. A six-foot Grailish teenage boy is not the Arch's most graceful beast, but today, his toes found grips between the cobbles through his ratty old boot-soles, and his eyes found gaps in the shifting crowds which he slid through, still accelerating.

Perhaps, he thought, *it was the fact he was racing to save a life. Would you call yourself a hero, Mister Somewhat? Well, only if heroes drink free, my dear...*

Then again, it was only the ragged little life of Chep Palaquat. That should hardly account for the way he came arrowing down the winding stair and up onto the rim around the Fountain of Sorrows, scattering parakeets and tuft-headed tamarins before him. He stepped lightly in a street-artist's palette, jumped over the head of a beggar, slid for a tottering second in raw sewage, then got his feet back under him and *really* got moving. Prajuragath Way blipped by as his legs pumped, operating on their own, it seemed. Spice-traders cursed as Jack's flapping robes stirred up miniature whirlwinds, flavoured with turmeric and cinnamon. He went over an ox-cart at full pelt, ripping his heavy attire away, and letting it fly back in his slipstream. There was the corner of Decameron now, marked by the wedding-cake ugliness of the Opera House, and he was running for the sheer joy of it, Palaquat all but forgotten.

Jack's mind traced a delicate trajectory as he approached the heaving intersection, where the Imperial Orchestra were out on the bricks, enjoying a spot of lunch. A drover had managed to intersperse an entire herd of steers with this black-suited mess, and from the other direction, a traditional Sarunjek funeral procession was approaching. Wailing professional mourners gave it their two copper bit's worth, got up in porcelain masks and yellow silks. A coffin, covered in gold leaf and paste gems, was carried on the shoulders of several family members, each ritually coated in ashes and clad in loose yellow robes. A high priest of the Ancestor-Gods dispensed firecrackers from a sedan chair made of bamboo and cedarwood.

Slide between the trombonist and that confused-looking bull. Twist around the high priest, avoiding the woodwind section. Straddle the coffin in a high-jump leap, then run across the backs of those cattle and off down Decameron, weaving between the street-side tables...

Jack wasn't amazed that he thought of it. But he *was* amazed to find himself actually doing it.

His mouth hung open, slack-jawed, as he spun upside down, the world in slow motion, firecrackers going off all around him and tiny hummingbirds exploding from the trees as his boots went spinning past. Then his feet were on the cobbles and he was off again, settling into the stride of the serious runner, arms pumping like the pistons on the Slave Traders' great water clock. He wasn't tiring, though. There was no debilitating stitch poking him in the ribs.

In fact, as Jack looked down, he saw that his legs were actually bigger and more powerful than he remembered. His guild under-robes were nothing but cotton, cut to mid-thigh for the sake of some modesty and ease of ablutions, and they showed off every corded slab of muscle. He stole a sideways look at one pistoning arm, and gurgled. That, too, had swollen up with biceps like ripe honeydew melons.

Now, to some people, this would be the stuff of dreams. But in reality, it was mildly horrifying. Imagine that unsettling feeling of putting on a pair of trousers that isn't your own, and the strange frisson of ennui it precipitates. Now multiply it by a billionfold, as your brain realises, belatedly, that it might just be the only part of your body that hasn't just received a colossal upgrade. An existential crisis? Assuredly! But... approximately the worst time to stop and contemplate the vistas of improbability is while you're pelting down a slippery, summer-sizzling cobbled street faster than a greased pig out of a slaughterman's embrace.

The signals from Jack's brain to his twitching new muscles suddenly tangled, and he found himself in a tumble, tripping over his own boots as he tried to corner from Decameron Street into the rickety-backed decent of Skizarian. The cobbles rushed up at his face as he winced, waiting for the pain to slap him sensible...

But it never came. His cheek bounced off the granite, deforming his lips into a fish-like expression. Then his shoulder barged into the side of a house, with the kind of impact that should have reduced him to wreckage.

Instead, the brick and stucco exploded.

Jack pinwheeled helplessly, a starfish of tender meat. But instead of the ripfires of agony he expected to feel behind his screwed-shut eyes, there was nothing. A pleasant tingle, perhaps. Jack felt a series of thumps as he slid on his back. Something warm and sticky glooped over his head. One more impact and he was, amazingly, back on his feet, which were still pumping of their own accord. Then he was off down Skizarian Street, bounding down past the crooked taverns and brothels, where they leaned one against the other in a drunken snaggle-tangle.

Foolishly, Jack dared to look back. And he saw, with the kind of awful clarity that usually only creeps into the frontal lobes at six a.m, a Jack-shaped hole in the side of a tenement block. A cloud of masonry dust and chicken feathers spreading into the sky. And a very old man, so ancient that he looked like a mummified knob of ginger root, waving his walking stick in impotent anger.

As Jack watched, two things happened. First, the facade of the building crumbled away, exposing a fat lady in a copper bath. And second, he ran smack-dab into something which finally stopped him, with a sound like a frying pan smashing a cabbage.

Whoooonnnnngggg!

It was the fountain which stood outside the Brujerierie of the redoubtable Mama Lurga; a depiction of a worried-looking merman spouting water from his pursed lips. It had been tucked away in the insalubrious neighbourhood of Peachcourt, hard up against the Stilts, because frankly, the sculptor hadn't been very good. The thing had a lazy eye that not only followed you around the square, but often seemed to be watching you hours later, as you took your ablutions in an entirely different part of the city.

Jack's impact hadn't improved things. Now the merman was bent at the waist, and sputtered water skyward with an expression of constipated outrage.

Voices blurred in Jack's head as the world trebled, then doubled, then settled back to a comfortable smudge. One of them turned out to be Lurga herself, shouting from a top storey window.

"If you've messed up my toothbrush, Jack Somewhat, I'll hex you with boils on the bottom 'til next Chainsday!"

The other voice, however, was smooth and calm, cool as chilled satin on a midsummer's night.

"You're doing fantastically. Go on. We'll worry about the costume later."

Jack got himself orientated, sprinted down Peachcourt Alley, and ran out onto the Stilts with enough force to rock the entire rickety, interlinked edifice. There was the Guildhouse, the water halfway up its oyster-crusted bamboo pilings. And there, half submerged in the tide, was a crab pot, in which a stick-thin and pitiful figure was stirring.

Costume? he had time to think, just as his pumping legs carried him off the edge of the Stilts and into what, despite its aroma, was thought of locally as fresh air.

A little later came the splash.

3
The Belligerence Mandate

JACK WOULD USUALLY have hesitated to jump right into the harbour. Not because of things like kraken, serpents, sharks and jellyfish, but because of the crust of excrement and rubbish which hugged the tide line like the pus around an ulcer. This time, however, his shiny new muscles propelled him into a perfect dive, sending him slicing through the film of unspeakables and into the shocking salt-cold below.

Was it fair to say that Chep Palaquat wasn't pleased to see him?

"You!" goggled the half-drowned wretch. "Get away from me! Murder! Rape! Thuggery!"

"Rape?" asked Jack, through gritted teeth. "Don't flatter yourself. I'm here to save you!"

"You're the one who *put me here*, you great Grailish turd! As soon as I get out of this thing I'll tell Multhazar..."

Chep realised, at that moment, that Jack could simply decide not to bother, and thus ensure that Multhazar Threck was blissfully ignorant of any such goings-on. The Bandit Crabs would pick the inside of his skull clean within mere hours. So he tried to grin instead. It was sickeningly ingratiating.

"My saviour! My pal! Please hurry!"

Jack sighed, and tore open the bars of the crab pot with one hand. He only noticed the grin sliding sideways off Chep's face a moment later, to be replaced with a mask of utter terror.

Jack looked down, between his paddling feet, and saw it too. Uprushing from the sea-bottom gloom, through jade green and shafts of sunlit gold. A shape all tentacles and spiny shell-spikes, the size of an ox-cart. A Hermit Octopus.

Now, this was not the great Pelagic Hermit Octopus, which has been known to take down whole ships in its wrath. This was merely a rock-hugging Lesser Barbed Hermit, the kind which scavenges the shells of dead giant whelks and goliath conches to protect its pulpy upper parts. Such things, on the scale of monsters from the belly of Mother Ocean, were hardly a blip on the page. But, if you see one rushing toward you, hooked tentacles grasping, it can be a sight you'll remember for the rest of your life.

All twelve seconds of it.

This Hermit was grumpy because a shark it had tried to munch for breakfast had managed to get away, taking one of its bone hooks with it. Its temper had not been improved by the mewlings and thrashings of Chep Palaquat, which were pitched at just such a tone to make the poor mollusc's spiked shell echo. So, when a second meat-creature had leapt into the water, redoubling the noise and fuss, it had naturally bullied its way to the surface to see what could be pulverised. Tentacles the girth of a fat man's thighs snaked out, hooks a-glisten...

Only to be caught in a vise-like grip, each one. The Hermit has tussled with giant crabs before, and even, on one ill-fated occasion, the secretive Colossal Shrimp, and the feeling of being pinched and pulled with implacable force was most unwelcome. Even less so was the sensation of being pulled up out of the water and swung around in a massive arc, up into the sunlight, then smashed back into the ocean. It snapped its beak, narrowed its quartet of eyes, and got angry.

Jack Somewhat, on the other end of those pale and sucker-studded tentacles, could not believe what he'd just done. But this was no time to marvel at the fact he wasn't yet being digested. The dire mollusc was after him with all six of its remaining free appendages, and he only had two arms and two legs to work with. Unfair! Perhaps, but such is the story of nature itself. And a recurring theme in Jack Somewhat's life.

"*Go!* Swim for it, you dunce!" he bellowed at Chep, as the sorry little Prefect floundered in the disintegrating ruins of a crab pot, robes leaking dye and ink. His cries, combined with a renewed assault by the octopus, did little but draw an audience to the edge of the Stilts. Fishmongers, anglers, sail-menders and drunks came sidling across to see what the fuss was about.

Thick tentacular ropes twisted around Jack, pulling him down into the greeny gloom, where spears of sunlight flickered. Once, twice, he lashed out and punched the great beast's bulk, making it squeal with eardrum-piercing force. Cracks skittered across its shell as Jack fought for air, making a fresh lunge for the surface. He dragged the Hermit with him, once again throwing it clear of the water to give himself time to suck in an aching breath.

"That's the way!" cackled an ancient fisherman. "Give it what for, lad!"

"Twenty silver on the octopus!" shouted a tattooed stevedore.

"I'll take ten on the hero!"

"Get your authentic octopus battle souvenirs here!"

"Where's that drunk bastard husband of mine? Haraaaaald!"

"Fresh clam fritters! They're loverleeee! On a sandwich! Only three coppers!"

Say this for Grand Sepulchre. Say that it didn't take long for a crowd to form wherever something interesting was happening. A gaggle of street-haunting locals were peering down into the water as Jack submerged for a third time, trying to pry a pair of twining tentacles from around his neck. A beak the size of a coal scuttle snapped, inches from his nose. And, finally, like a volcano awakening after centuries of peaceful slumber, to really give the villagers an appreciation of that old-time religion, Jack Somewhat got mad.

It wasn't his fault that all this was happening. He'd tried to do the right thing, hadn't he? Admittedly, as little of the right thing as possible, while doing none of the wrong thing, to be sure. Well, alright. A little of the wrong thing too, but only in terms of a bit of drinking with his mates. Was that so bad? Did he deserve the cruel fate which now saw him wrestling with an irate mollusc, in a bath of cold sewerage and salt water?

No.

It's fair to say that the Hermit Octopus didn't see the uppercut coming. Things with a black, chitinous beak made to snicker-snap through giant lobster shells don't usually take one on the chin. But this blow didn't just hurt. It propelled the entire octopus up out of the water so fast that the bubbles cavitating in its wake *boiled*. The poor thing went up so fast that it was just a blur of calamari, punching through three rickety floors of the Alchemist's guildhouse with a sound like a fist through paper.

"Ooooooh!" went the crowd, as it came out through the roof, spinning, yellow and blue bubbles smoking on its shell where it had smashed through several unrelated alchemical experiments.

"Ahhhh!" went the crowd, leaning forward as they watched the giant beast fall back toward the ocean, pulling in its tentacles to drop like a cannonball. Jack Somewhat was right in its shadow, treading water...

But in the last half-whisper of an instant, he reached out and gripped one of the great bamboo legs of the building itself. Mighty was the crunching and rending as he pulled it loose; a pillar as wide around as a bull's neck, crusted with barnacles and oysters. There was a curious heartbeat or two of utter silence as the crowd leaned forward, some with clam fritter sandwiches hanging out of their mouths, others frozen in the act of haggling with bookies and wager-makers. One (as is the rule of these things) was picking his nose.

The length of bamboo came whistling around in a blur which threw up a sheet of water, soaking the first three rows of gaggle-neckers. Then it struck the shell of the poor old Hermit Octopus with the force of a trebuchet's swinging arm, propelling it up and up into the twin-sunned sky, past the shreds of summer cloud, and away into unknown oblivion.

The cheer from the crowd was one that came partly from their innate appreciation for theatre, and partly from morphic echoes bouncing from one end of the universe to the other, carrying on their strange wavelengths the sound of jaunty pipe organ music and the smell of roasted peanuts.

"It's outtathapark!" yelled one drunken sailor, without knowing exactly what he meant. But just at that moment, as Jack Somewhat got Chep's sodden carcass draped over the floating bamboo spar, and all the fun seemed to be over, a dark shadow fell across the scene. A voice like half-chewed, yellow fingernails down a tectonic chalkboard sliced into the minds of all assembled, reminding them of past naughtiness.

"What exactly in the name of Quazirath's holy buttocks is GOING ON HERE?"

It was Multhazar Threck, resplendent in his robes of black, his gold-edged mortarboard, his ornamental filigree cuffs and collar, and a pair of belted-on opera glasses of an experimental nature. He stood in the hole where the skybound Hermit Octopus had ruined his building, trembling with rage. Veins stood out like purple hosepipes on the expanse of his brow as he scythed the crowd with his glare, his eyes, in their insectile brass magnification, searching, searching...

"JACK SOMEWHAT!"

The luckless apprentice looked up from where he floundered,

excess slabs of muscle now deflated away. Gone was the hero who had pulverised a sea-monster. The crowd winced.

"This is the last straw, Somewhat! I have been waiting for this moment oh, so very long. A moment to be savoured, indeed, yes, as I admonish you and declare that from this moment you are expelled from... urk!"

The crowd held their breath. Well, most of them.

"Where's Urk?" asked one medium-sized fishwife, squinting at the tattooed maps which covered the back of the sailor next to her.

"It's past the Grailish lands. Opposite side of Mograth, innit?"

But Master Threck was not lecturing on geography. Instead, one of the valves of his heart (weakened by years of alchemical fumes, vigorous worshipful intercourse at the behest of his religion, and the habit of taking a half-spoonful of mercury with his hibiscus tea to combat the effects of the syphilis which was eating his brain) had exploded. Sheer rage and fierce joy combined had done him in. The old master of alchemists went stiff as a board, and toppled from his perch, end over end, down into the drink. There he disappeared with a sad little 'gloop', sinking like a stone.

Jack, open-mouthed in astonishment, didn't know if this was a celestial reprieve or grounds for him to be hooked and quartered for murder. In either case, it looked like a good time to get scarce. He dived under, kicking away from the spar and arrowing into the gloom beneath the Stilts, under the maze of dripping, reeking wharves and pilings which formed the underbelly of coastal Grand Sepulchre. There were places in the oyster-crusted gloom where the dregs and the homeless went, and Jack knew enough of them to softly fade away.

Meanwhile, up top, things were going from bad to worse for the crowd. Because now, with the trained precision of utter bastardry, hard-faced men in black had appeared around what could only be called 'a perimeter'.

These were not regular Knock-men, of the type who cadged pastries and hot coffee and nobbled petty thieves with their truncheons. They weren't even the salty scum of the Harbour Watch, who were supposed to crack down on smugglers and pirates. No, these were the flinty-eyed, scar-faced veterans of the Other Squad. Throne's Shadow. When the dockside rabble who had watched Jack's fight turned to leave, they were subtly persuaded to remain right where they were, with nothing more than a look at certain sausage-fingered hands on the pommels of certain workaday swords.

Everyone in Grand Sepulchre knew who Throne's Shadow worked

for.

And now here he came. Why he was there was none of their business, but the fact that he was out of the Malevolith and roaming meant that someone was liable to end their days with a sad little squeak sometime soon. It was best not to be that person, or even next to him.

There are, of course, some Lords who like to make an entrance, with gold-armoured footmen, trumpeters, bards playing lyres, petal-strewing midgets in exotic furs and curly-toed slippers – you know the ones I mean. Lord Slave was not one of them. He created a chilly, empty space around himself wherever he went, just by being so big, and quiet, and looming. A mountain with scoliosis couldn't loom as convincingly as Lord Slave. People didn't see him coming and get out of his way; the sensation of skin-crawling wrongness which preceded him like a ten-day-old sewer funk simply hitched them up by the scruff of whatever parts were loose and made them *never have been in his way in the first place.* Part of this was because Lord Slave was seven feet tall, built like the spare parts bin at a heroic sculptor's bargain shop, and dressed almost entirely in black leather. Not much of it, either. He affected a massive, shaggy black wolfskin cape, spiked shoulder pauldrons, underpants designed for a barbarian three times smaller, and the usual silver-ringed, spiked harness such sword-swingers used to attach all their knives, loot pouches, axes, cleavers and claymores. In between, muscles fought with other muscles for the available sunlight, crushed in under such oiled tension that Lord Slave creaked like an overstuffed chaise lounge when he moved.

He also wore a tight leather mask, buckled on to cover his entire face, except for a mean little slot that showed his teeth. These had been filed to points. A single eye-hole, ringed in silver spikes, dominated the left side of this visage, while on the right was nothing but smooth black leather. Whatever was wrong with Lord Slave's right eye, nobody dared to guess. What was wrong with the left (as was clearly apparent to anyone who had the terrible misfortune to look into it) was that it has gazed upon Him, the Dark Eternal Emperor, one too many times.

This was because Lord Slave was His Grand Vizier, a title which already seemed to be rubbing its hands together and giggling about torture, *before* you bestowed it on what was clearly a body-building giant madman with fetishes unrecorded in the history of perversity.[6]

---

6. This last part was speculated about luridly, but the truth was, Lord Slave was not into any of the many strange kinks and interesting bedroom practices which his attire suggested. The fact was, he'd been going for the 'barbarian hero' look, and had been

He'd been, they said, the Dark Emperor's right-hand man, back when He was still alive, and Lord Slave's utter devotion (half the reason for his name) came from the fact that they had fought back-to-back as two out of five of what history called The Original Party.

That circle of cold and silence rippled out around him as he strode up to the edge of the dock, utterly ignoring the people who were now hemmed in between him and his guards. He looked down at Chep Palaquat, still spluttering and gasping in the water, and fixed him with the terrible pale orb of his one remaining eye.

"What exactly is going on here, boy?" he asked, in a voice which was part rasping whisper and part terrible, prickling ice-needles inside one's ear.

Chep Palaquat was born to snitch. Even if he hadn't been – even if he'd been a grizzled lifer from deep in Ironbelly Gaol - he would have talked at that moment.

"J... Jack Somewhat, Sir! He rescued me! From the octopus, Sir! And Multhazar's dead, Sir!"

Lord Slave inclined his head and sighed.

He hadn't come all this way to talk to gawking dockside dregs and a half-drowned apprentice. He'd been here to see Guildmaster Threck himself, regarding a package which the Order of Nine Reeds had sent him. A package which He Himself was keen to get his great, rusty-armoured claws on.

Still, it wouldn't do to appear weak. Not in front of these people, and not in these highly political times. Lord Slave gestured to one of the Throne's Shadow men, who snapped to attention.

"Gryssle, fish this creature from out of His harbour, and get it cleaned up." he peered down at Chep a second time. "What did you say that fellow's name was?"

"Jack, sir!" babbled the Prefect, scrabbling for the rope which Gryssle threw him. "Jack Somewhat. A fellow apprentice. But not a very good..."

"Shut up," suggested Lord Slave. He turned to face the crowd. Muscles creaked like timber under immense pressure.

"I hereby issue a warrant for the arrest, *alive*, of Jack Somewhat. The

forced to don the mask due to an unfortunate accident which left him horribly scarred. The realisation that he'd chosen a costume (and a title) which made certain suggestions with more than a nod and a wink had been so embarrassing that the only thing to do was to utterly ignore the issue. After all, people weren't about to bring it up, for fear that he might think they were interested in joining in...

charge is most dire."

The crowd leaned back as Slave's one-eyed stare flickered across them. There was always one... ahh, yes. The hunch-backed sailor with the wooden teeth.

"What charge, m'lord? For the reward, of course, to calculate, m'lord?"

Huh! And they thought Grand Viziers were wicked. Give any of these human rodents a big turban with a ruby on the front and they'd push their own granny in the viper pit for a basket of oranges...

"Why, one of the gravest of all," intoned Lord Slave, fixing the man with a glare that almost made his rotting dentures smoulder. He cracked his knuckles. It was like the sound of skulls under iron-rimmed siege engine wheels.

"Unlicensed heroism!"

4

The Demortifying Conundrum

BUT NOW, LET us consider another world, layered beneath the one we have just visited, in the way the celestial scribes of Utterith Zhang believe the realms holy and unholy interleave with the materia of the flesh. In the way that the philosopher Khysemius of Phloq described in his famous club sandwich paradox, wherein the realms of mortal man are likened unto that nice smoky cheese with the holes in it, and the virtues of morality permeate through like the piquant mustard which originates somewhere above the salad layer.

But enough of the Higher Mysteries! Enough, indeed, of thoughts pertaining to sandwiches, club or otherwise.

Turn your attention, instead, to the dank and steaming mazeways of sewers beneath Grand Sepulchre; those intestinal vaults of red marble, haunted by albino pythons, blind cave monkeys and the inevitable predatory bats. Whole under-clans and miniature empires are carved out in the teeming filth below, where organised crime holds sway, and life is cheaper than... well, suffice to say, cheaper than what is all too often underfoot.

It's *hot* down there. Secret springs well up under the city, bubbling from cracks in the marble and filling the sewers with shrouding mists. Deep down, they say, you'll find temples from the forbidden cults of the Sarunjek, the altars of the Harvester of Eyes and She Who Whispers. Deeper still, and madmen gibber about the things they have seen in the abyss, the ghosts of machines, the stalking minds without flesh, the...

But this is no horror-story. It is a factual account. And the fact we follow, insinuating herself through the phosphor-green glow of the mould-crusted tunnels, is in trouble.

Again.

If it was possible to see Amberelia Chance, there still wouldn't be much to see. Moving, she was a blur of those dark grey and drab green tones which hide a person so much better than ostentatious crowfeather black. Her clothes were rags for a reason – well, to be fair, they were rags because she was dirt poor, but also because the knotted strips and frayed hems broke up her shape as she ran.

Get her to stand still, and you'd be looking at a thin, tall, green eyed Sarunjek girl of about eighteen summers, her hair cut short and shaved close to her skull at the sides but for a top-knot of black, her long limbs bound up in wraps and tufts of cloth. Then again, you'd only see this apparition for a second or two, before it either disappeared or killed you, because Amberelia Chance was an assassin. A junior demortifex of the Guild Lachrymose, in fact, which explained the little tattoo of a teardrop on her right cheekbone.

And, of course, the fact that Danjo the Hook and his merry crew were right behind her, with murder on their minds.

"Come on! Come back! We only want to taaaaalk!" shouted one of the gang, in the playful tones always used by thugs in these circumstances. Any moment now they'd call her a 'pretty little thing', which always made Amber extremely angry. Compliments aside, this was *assassination*, not a fashion show!

Instead of meekly coming back to 'talk', the young demortifex used the sound of the man's voice to guess his position, and flung a poison-tipped needle off into the mist. A curse rang out, then unhinged laughter, fading to a thrashing in the water, and a final snap...

"See!" she hissed under her breath, to the tiny red mannikin perched on her shoulder. "Killed him! That's assassination!"

The little figure, who appeared to be made entirely of blood, and who held a crimson clipboard and pencil, tapped his teeth with the eraser end.

"No. That's just homicide. *Assassination* is when you get the one we were paid for. Remember our chess games, lass. The pawns are most assuredly not the king."

Amber adjusted her concentration as she came to a suspiciously straight, clear and well-lit section of corridor. She made a deep humming, clicking noise, and listened for the way it came back subtly changed. At just the right place she leapt into a dive-roll, then slid along the side of the tunnel, missing by a hair's whisper the series of cunningly placed tripwires which shimmered through the mist.

"Alright. Extra two points for using the hidden sight. But five off for not realising that there was a shorter way around... chess again, young lady. Diagonal moves often bamboozle the foolish player."

Amberelia skidded to a halt as she entered the chamber at the end of the tunnel, a huge octagonal sink-hole with hundreds of pipes emptying into it. The centre of the room funnelled down to a sluggish, bubbling whirlpool of ordure, shimmering with rainbow oils. High above, streetside gratings let in a few bars of light.

The smell... well, the smell was like half a horse left outdoors for half a moon.

But adjusting to the stench wasn't the problem. Danjo the Hook was the problem; he and twelve other men who, apparently, had a better map of the under-city than Amber did. Lurien would probably have another chess analogy; he insisted that they play five games a night.

"Proper exploration and reconnaissance, Amberelia," tutted the little blood-puppet on her shoulder. "Now, the right thing to do here, is just to escape as fast as..." it caught the look on her face. The furrowing of the brows. The tiny little grin. And it sighed. "Oh, not *again*, girl!"

But of course, he was too late. It had already started.

"Well, well, well. What have we here?" gloated Danjo, a lanky, scar-faced Mograthi man with skin tattooed black as charcoal and teeth inset with sapphires. One of his hands was indeed replaced with a trio of fishing gaffs.

"*Really?* 'Well well well'?" asked Amber, extending one hand out to her side and clicking her fingers. Something big and bulky moved inside her backpack, making a clattering, whistling noise. "Are you going to call me 'my pretty' next? Invested in the Big Book of Useless Clichés, have you?"

"I got up to page five. Uhhh.... my proud beauty!" put in a huge, doughy Grailishman carrying a hammer.

"Shut up!" hissed The Hook, sidling closer. "I don't care who sent you, or how much they're paying, girl. But I have to send a message to the Guild Lachrymose. Their territory stops just underneath the pavement, savvy? Down here, it's just me!"

"And that message would involve nailing me to the ceiling?"

Danjo tapped his glittering teeth with one hook. It looked remarkably sharp.

"Bloody good idea, that. Here, if it wasn't for the circumstances, I'd keep you on. *My pretty.*"

Amber felt countless little claws come spiralling down her left arm, even as she dropped a curved fighting dagger into her right palm. She felt the mantis shrimp lock its manipulators into the mechanism attached to her wrist, and smiled.

"Well, let's be fair, Danjo. It's just you, and Papa Griss, and the Black Crane Tong, and the Brothers Gryme, and the Hammerheads. Guess which ones called out this little visit?"

Danjo opened his mouth to answer, but that had already given the Other Girl behind Amber's eyes time to work things out.

Thirteen of them. Right.

First, the big one with the hammer gets it in the neck with the mantisbow. Then take his hammer, kneecap the ugly one with the nose ring, slide between his legs, (hold breath due to sewage) dagger in the fruits, pop up and take the sword from his sheath, left and right gets rid of stumpy and the one in the leather coat, by which point the shrimp's reloaded, and the tall Sarunjek with the axe can get one in the back of the head.

Throw the sword, pinning the archer with the weepy eye to the wall behind me. Duck under Danjo's hooks, trip him, use his own forearm as a shield when the thug with the mace makes his move, rip mace-boy's throat out with the dagger.

Throw Danjo across my back in a Chungdoji fighting roll, mantis-bolt to the face of the one charging with a spear, pick up the spear, swing low to break the legs of the little Thamar hatchet-man, then high to blind the Uroshi scimitar-swinger before she gets a chance to get close enough. Jump over the second spearman, the one with the pierced lip, and let him fall into the whirlpool.

Then it's just one more bowshot for the last swordswoman, the one with the red braids, and plenty of time to get a boot on Danjo's neck before he can get up from that throw... especially as that mace blow will have broken his arm in two places. Maybe three.

It all turned into a blur as Amber put her thoughts into action. The iridescent creature clamped to her forearm snapped its fighting claws forward, sending a barbed bolt flying at close to the speed of sound, and it went almost all the way through the Grailish hammerman's throat, sending him spinning backwards, his hammer left hanging in the air where he'd stood. Amber made a leap over the whirlpool and grabbed it, while in her head the wild music started, and the world became a haze of motion, crimson arterial spray and laughter.

Well. Laughter with an 's' on the front, anyway.

The little red mannikin on Amber's shoulder closed his eyes and put his hands over his head as it all unfolded, only opening them when the world stopped whirling sideways and splattering everything with blood. Amberelia had her boot on Danjo the Hook's chest, but he was on his back, aiming a nasty little pistol crossbow up at her. She had her mantis shrimp pointed right down at him as well; the definition of an Uroshi stand-off.

"Who... who sent you?" gasped the dreamsugar smuggler, his broken arm flopping uselessly at his side. "No. Scratch that. *What* are you?"

"I thought you said you didn't care," said Amber, cool as you like. Behind her, twelve broken bodies either groaned and sobbed with pain, or had passed beyond the need to do so forever.

"Well, I didn't care when it looked like you were going to be mobbed by my best henchmen!" raged Danjo. "You should be *dead!* Dead ten times over!"

Amber hunkered down, bringing her mantisbow with her.

"No. You see, *you're* the one they paid for. But I'll tell you a secret."

"Yes?" The smuggler's eyes were feverish. His pistol-bow dipped and did figure eights.

"The ones who sent me were..."

And she pulled the trigger, at exactly the same time as she cut the tendons of Danjo's wrist. His bolt, a wicked little poison-tipped thing, clattered against the far wall.

Hers, however, stood out from the middle of his forehead like an exclamation point.

"I guess you could say he fell for it, hook, line and sinker," said Amberelia, standing to brush herself off.

"Why do you *always* do that? The stupid little pun about their name? Or worse, some kind of dry one-liner before you kill them? It's just not *assassination* when you do all that stuff. It's... well, there's a word for it, but it's not very pleasant."

Amber made a series of whistling sounds, and fished a piece of dried squid from out of her pocket for the giant arthropod attached to her arm.

"Who's a good mantis shrimp?" she cooed, as the little rainbow-coloured horror snaffled up its treat. The thing scuttled back up over her shoulder, bubbling happily, and disappeared into her backpack, where there was a soggy ball of sea-sponges waiting for it to burrow through. Amber turned her attention to the mannikin. "He's dead, isn't he? *Assassination.* I expect that will finally be the end of all these tedious exams and practices, master Lurien? It's not as if I haven't killed... oh, I lose track. Enough to pay off my apprenticeship, anyway!"

The sorcerous image of demortifex tutor Saulis Lurien sighed. It was, of course, nothing more than a bubble of blood filled with the breath of sorcery; an artefact loaned from the Order of the White Ribbon. Far away, in the jade palace of the Guild Lachrymose, the real Master Lurien sat amid a pile of cushions, a pair of blood-red spectacles fitted neatly over his eyes.

"Yes, if all of them had been bought and paid for, girl! We demortalise the customer *only*, in case you hadn't noticed. We are *assassins*, not butchers!"

"There's precedent," said Amber primly, picking her way between the bodies to an iron ladder bolted to the wall. "Self-defence is perfectly acceptable. And you must admit, I followed all the fighting forms. The three stances, five variations, the use of available weapons, the mantisbow... you and I both know that was flawless work."

Lurien pinched the bridge of his nose, trying to suppress the headache which he knew was waiting for him.

"This is the ninth time, junior demortifex Chance, that you've been sent on your Master's Mission. Every single time, you've..."

Amber frowned, pausing halfway up the ladder.

"*Every single time* I've introduced the customer to his Gods, as you like to put it. Made him a metaphysical problem. Measured his shroud."

Lurien hazarded another sigh.

"And every time, you've sent at least another ten along with 'em. That matter with the mad duchess..."

"Who else but the mad would have that many guards in their bathroom?"

"And what about Lord Glaivebury?"

"How was *I* to know he was an orgiast?"

"What about that pirate captain, then?"

"Anyone could have had the bad luck to step on that parrot!"

"And the Witch of Bentsteeple?"

Amber paused.

"Allright. I'll give you that one. Her coven just pissed me off on a very personal level. Bloody moonlight and red satin and cheekbones like folded paper! But results, Master! *Results!* Tell me that I'll finally pass after this one! I don't think I can stand another week of novice's slops and those torture-slabs they call bunk beds..."

Lurien faffed about a bit with his hands. He often did this when he had bad news to impart, because, despite being one of the deadliest poisoners ever to blight the face of Jansamrana, he was just a little bit afraid of the chamber demortifexii, the actual cloak-and-dagger assassins of the Guild.

"Ummm... well, I'm glad you brought that up," he said, as Amber hung just beneath a streetside drain cover, working away at its clasp with the point of her knife. "You see, you *have* actually been granted a guild commission."

Amber smiled. It was an impossibly perky grin, when juxtaposed with her black eye makeup and tattooed tear.

"Well, that's good news, surely! When will I expect my ceremonial dagger from the Old Lady, then?"

Lurien inspected his fingernails with great intensity.

"Welll... ummmm... that's just the thing. You haven't gotten a commission from *us*. Not as such. More of a... an expulsion."

Amber's dagger scratched to a halt. She turned, very slowly, to fix the little blood-puppet on her shoulder with a single orange iris.

"WHAT?"

"But there's good news too! Great news! The best!" gushed the poisoner. "You've proven - and these are the exact words - *'thy prowess in the artes and sciences of combatte, pitted valiantly againste diverse oathbreakers, outlaws and affronters of ye Lord's Imperial Peace'*. The Old Lady showed the authorities some of the memory-shards of your... ahem... recent outings. They agreed. You're not an assassin. *You're a rogue*. And that means that there's a very noble, ancient and respectable guild that wants you instead."

He told her which one.

And while Amberelia Chance's mouth was open, screaming, a tiny glowing-green speck of something indescribably powerful fell through the drain cover from Decameron Street, and right down her throat.

Of course, she wasn't the only one.

Recall the wild flight of Jack Somewhat across the city, in search of his friends? Well, all along that route, people were infected by sizzling, popping fleas of green energy that day.

Here, a very well dressed young man scooped one up with his forkful of scallops and hot peppered rice. There, a man unloading a slab of beef into the jaws of a restaurant's ice-house felt something buzz into his ear, making him slap himself, to the head chef's amusement. Down an alleyway, two workmen clearing out the home of a deceased antiquities trader threw a crate of rusted armour off the back of their wagon to make room for better loot; inside the pile of metal, made for a battle nun of the warlike Phoraxian church, a bead of green power sizzled and melted into the steel. Even a bum, snoring drunk in the gutter with a dead rat for his pillow, inhaled a speck of the stuff which had so changed the destiny of poor young Jack.

In some, the power would sputter and die, causing nothing but constipation, indigestion, terrifying psychedelic dreams and a craving for fried chicken.

But in others, it would put down roots.

In Jack's head, alas, it had already grown a voice.

5
The Pugilistical Gambit

JORY, BILLIAM AND Soto had seen it all, of course.

Well, enough of it. Enough that they'd had to use their usual ruse to get away from the Other Squad; they simply pretended to be Foxmallet's entourage, what with him being an actual Lord and all.

Not that it meant much – Jory's running joke was that old money was like old everything else; it smelled terrible and there wasn't much of it. The fact that this was a terrible joke didn't matter, though, because the Foxmallets *were* old money, of the kind who would polish a title until it was see-through, and wear it like a tiara made of razorblades, all prickly and uncomfortable.

Back during the times when the Urzoman Empire had been a big deal in the Arch' – when His was a name to conjure dread on isles as far away as Chalinesia and Ysbogrod – the Foxmallet clan had controlled huge estates, owned armies of slaves, eaten off golden plates that they subsequently threw in the garbage, and generally lived in clover, both metaphorically, and (at least for Great Uncle Wexforth, who thought he was pig), literally.

Nowadays the Empire consisted of just the topside of Jansamrana, and the fiefdoms, duchies and counties of the Great Houses who served His Might were, to put it mildly, cut back a little. The Foxmallets were hereditary and absolute rulers, for example, of a very nice three storey townhouse in Chantry Heath, plus the row of shops next door and half of the apartment complex across the road.

The sundry treasures of an estate which used to cover most of the isle of Clourvonne were now packed into the twisting halls and dust-shrouded narrow chambers of the Red House, as it was called, with only a single elderly butler to take care of polishing the silverware.

Jory's bed was set up on top of a giant granite statue of the lizard God S'sthaa, inlaid with emeralds the size of pomegranates and leafed in platinum and gold. It was so big nobody knew how it had been manhandled into the Garden Wing of the house, and so generations of Foxmallets had simply worked around it, usually with the help of stepladders[7].

The upshot of all this was that Jory, despite looking like a stubbled and slightly hungover pirate, was in fact a Peer of the Dark Empire, entitled to wear the old skull-faced armour and ride out alongside Himself. Just not too close alongside, apparently. And, these days, not at all.

Being a Lord, however, was more than enough to allow Jory and his 'entourage' to bluff their way past Commander Clorance Gryssle, who was supposed to get everybody back to work, or at least rough them up a little. Instead, the trio were able to skulk through the salty, fish-odour-haunted back-scuttles of the Stilts, at last sidling furtively into Skizarian Street, and thence to the place they knew they'd find Jack Somewhat – the Black Hibiscus.

Inside that humid boozing den, where the walls leaned drunkenly on each other for support, a crowd of noon-day grog-artists were already deep in their cups as the Stingray Bells rung out from the Harbour Watch.

Some were determined lushes, staving off the dreaded shakes. Others were here for the atmosphere, for, as noted earlier, the Black Hibiscus was so louche, dangerous and excitingly deadly that getting your head bashed in with an ashtray there was seen as a mark of social favour.

The management, in keeping with this trend (and hoping it would continue) had installed deep, dark booths around the walls, furnishing them with tables made of stolen wagon wheels and chairs from a hundred mis-matched garbage collections.

Soto and the boys found Jack at the deepest and darkest, with a hood pulled up over his face. This had the effect of making him look unspeakably suspicious, even by Black Hibiscus standards. The group at the neighbouring booth, who had enough scars on their faces

---

7. The Red House was full of forbidden idols, unholy obelisks, weird, glowing orbs and levitating sarcophagi thanks to the Foxmallet clan's patronage, some three hundred years ago, of Throgg the Outlander, a barbarian hero of such unspeakably stereotypical proportions that it's said he *invented* bearskin underpants. Great-great-great-granddad Archivole Foxmallet simply had to keep sending him money for ale, busted-up taverns and sword polish, and he'd keep receiving the plundered thrones and other bits of furniture from a thousand lost, hidden and otherwise reclusive kingdoms. It was better than having Throgg actually turn up in person, what with the cost of replacing all the carpets and the contents of the wine cellar when he left again, 'in questly fearch of bolde newe adventuref!' The stuff was all still there because, to quote Jory's mum, 'the peerage don't have rummage sales.'

between them to constitute a full almanack of surgical anatomy, gave the crew a look which encouraged them to be amateurs elsewhere. "That was bloody *brilliant!*" enthused Billiam, before Soto cuffed him on the back of the head. "I mean... that was brilliant!" he hissed, slightly more quietly. "The thing with the octopus, and the huge piece of timber, then *whap*, and *pow!* It was terrific!"

Soto fixed Jack with a cool stare. He'd been practising. Then he reached out and pulled the hood of Jack's robe back, so he could actually see him staring coolly.

"You weren't kidding about that thing on your hand, were you?" he asked. "And I'm sorry. As a medical professional, I should have been more attentive."

Jack pulled the hood back down over his face. It squelched, and dripped something horrible and brown. He'd had to buy it off some homeless scavengers, under the Stilts.

"Go away." he said. "I'm thinking."

"It's pronounced *drinking*. With a D. R," said Foxmallet, signalling for a serving wench. The Black Hibiscus had the best in the business – cleavage you could lose a galleon in, and cunning, spring-loaded traps in their bustles so that if you hazarded a slap on the arse, you went home with less fingers than you arrived with.

"Don't mind if I join you in some pronounced drinking, Jory old son?" asked Billiam, grinning. "Come on, Jack. You've got all the reasons to celebrate. Old Multhazar's dead, and that means no more gainful employment for you!"

The erstwhile alchemist poked his nose out of the hood.

"And no more place to sleep. And no more pay. And... you heard the Vizier! I'm a wanted man!"

Foxmallet turned from ordering a round of drinks, his gaze lingering wistfully on the serving wench[8].

"I'd love to be a wanted man. Women want the wanted. It makes you cool. Interesting. *Dangerous!*"

"I don't want to be any of those things! I want to *not* be on Lord

---

8. Not a derogatory term in Grand Sepulchre; in fact, there was a Wenching Guild, who were very much separated from the Ancient and Noble guild of Prostitutes. A good wench knew how to keep a tray of crystal glasses upright during a class five tavern brawl, how to pass secret messages to adventurers, where to contact every kind of scoundrel, lock-picker, pox doctor, shady magical sword merchant and semi-retired consulting wizard in a ten-mile radius, and how to cripple a man in twenty ways if they 'took liberties'. They could also make a drinkable, palatable cocktail out of almost anything flammable, which was job number one in any establishment on Skizarian Street.

Slave's mind, that's for certain. Urrrgh! Can you imagine what goes on inside that mask?"

Soto sniffed.

"Can't be worse than what smells like it's gone on inside that cloak, Jacky-boy. But listen. Don't worry. I have a plan which will make all of this unpleasantness just faaaade away."

"He does, you know," said Billiam, unloading a quartet of large ceramic steins onto the table. He slipped an extra coin on top of the pile Foxmallet was paying with, earning a wink and a smile from the waitress.

"I've figured it out. We have to get you well away from the Stilts, and the Guildhouse, until this stink with the dead old vulture Threck blows over."

Jack nodded.

"We have to make sure you have some spending money while you lay low. So you need a way to make a few coins while incognito, like," continued Soto, as frosty as the Malevolith at sunrise.

Jack continued to nod.

"And we need to investigate the parameters of your specific physiological condition, vis-a-vis medical care and potential curatives. That's important."

Jack nodded to a halt, holding up one hand as he drained half his jug of beer.

"Alright. Sounds good. But what does it *mean*, Scalizari? It better not mean those hangover pills again, because I swear, I could taste blackboard dust for a week afterwards. I mean, do you *know* how awful it is for a person like me to think sensibly about my future prospects?"

Soto held his breath, looked left at Knox, then right at Jory. He held up one finger.

"It means we saw what you did to that bastard octopus, so we've enrolled you to fight in the Brute Pits. We can put on the most absolutely insane bets, and nobody will see you coming!"

Billiam managed to lean out of the way as a fountain of beer shot from Jack's mouth. The ex-alchemist choked in utter astonishment, slapping the table.

"You... I... I should have guessed you had a half-arsed plan, but I never thought it'd be this terrible! The *pits?* Are out of your tiny little mind, Scalizari? I wouldn't last ten seconds!"

Billiam leaned forward, his elbows in the puddle of spilled ale.

"Nonsense! You'd be *amazing!* We all saw the way you handled that mollusc. You looked bigger than old Slavey himself, what with the muscles and all."

Jory poked at him quizzically.

"What happened to those, anyway?"

Jack looked slightly embarrassed, and furrowed his brow with concentration. First his left, then his right bicep inflated, with twin popping sounds. His chest grew pecs like a pair of butcher's-blocks, and his neck swelled up into a tree-trunk of meat.

"Astounding!" said Soto. "I mean, from a purely medical point of view..."

"And from the point of view of gambling, and such, he'll look like a wimp until some sap gets a face-full of knuckles!" laughed Billiam. "How do you *do* that?"

Jack took another big slug of ale. It didn't appear to be doing anything.

"You want to know the truth? It happens when I think heroic thoughts. Which I have to keep suppressing, mind you. I mean, right now, I can't help wanting to swing on the candelabra, beat up all the obvious pirates, thieves, ruffians and no-gooders in this place, then give them a big lecture about justice. It's very distracting."

Foxmallet peered around the taproom. It was an ugly scene.

"If you're not counting us, and you'd better not be, that would be you against forty-three people, including most of the staff," he said. "*And* most of those thieves are licensed Guildsmen, too. Big trouble."

"I know!" wailed Jack, causing some pointy, serrated looks to be flung their way. "I know. But it only seemed to stop for a bit after I'd pulverised that octopus. Now it's back. It also says I need a costume."

The drink was definitely not working. Usually, by now, his mind would be floating along in a happy cloud of little bubbles, warm and numb. Instead, it was meticulously cold in there, and without constant care a little voice would pop into his thoughts like the mechanical cuckoo on an old Ysbogrod alpine clock.

"Come on. Just one bunch of cutpurses, and a small speech about the just and moral order. It'll be fun!"

Soto Scalizari steepled his fingers, and did his very best doctor's impression.

"So, you feel you need a costume. You say you want to engage in acts of violent heroism. And you recount that your symptoms recede when you give in to these impulses? Well, we have a good diagnosis, then. And I believe, my initial prescription still stands. *The Brute Pits*.

Heroically belt ten bells of shite out of some nasty old gladiators, and you might get it all out of your system. They want to fight you. You want to fight them. A costume is part of the deal. And, as a slight corollary, the matter of your emolument will be handily executed at the same time."

"The what of my who?"

"His money. The doctor's bill," said Jory. "By the way, are you feeling rascally drunk yet? We made sure your ale was a half-and-half with rotgut, so you'd come round to our way of thinking."

Jack drained the rest of the tankard, partly in hope, partly just out of habit. He slammed it down on the table, but the lovely warm bubbles were not forthcoming. Instead...

"Right. OK. *I'll do it*. Fine! Some of those gladiators could be considered heroes, with a tailwind and a squint. I mean, I used to have a poster of Forlaf the Crippler when I was a young 'un. That has to be worth some hero points."

Soto beamed.

"Excellent! You won't regret taking my very sage medical advice, Jack Somewhat! Now, about that costume..."

Jack reached out his suddenly very meaty arms and dragged his friends into a huddle.

"I have some ideas in that direction, as it turns out..."

Does it need to be mentioned that Grand Sepulchre, Princess of Cities, has not one but several all-night, all-day tailors to suit an adventurer's sartorial needs? From ballgowns and ornate regimental uniforms through to more esoteric work in leather and spikes, there were skilled hands at a customer's disposal to do it all.

For a little bit more, some of them wouldn't tell anyone what you were wearing underneath. The House of Sagh were reputedly the best in both categories.

Nevertheless, the little Sarunjek man in Krithnan Alley wrung his hands and dithered when presented with Jack Somewhat's bill of particulars.

"What do you mean, it has to be *stretchy?*" he asked. "You're only one size, boy! I mean, yes, it's a *big* size, but you're not likely to have a sudden growth spurt while you're in the ring. If anything, I've seen men come out shorter."

"No legs." whispered Billiam, behind his hand. Soto slapped him down.

"You're supposed to be the *best*, Gathur! And it's not as if we don't have the coin." He jangled a little bag of the stuff. Like any good Sarunjek merchant, Gathur Sagh followed it with his eyes like a cat following a speck of reflected light. It seemed to calm him down.

"Well, I do have some experimental fabrics from Urosh which might suffice. The thing is, attaching armour to them will be all but impossible! Have you tried to sew leather to anything stretchy? It's a nightmare, gentlemen!"

Soto grinned.

"Our boy doesn't need armour, master Sagh. He's a quick one."

Gathur Sagh gave Jack a quick up-and-down with his eyes, trying to ascertain if Soto was either mad or stupid.

"Well, it's your funeral," he sighed. "At least you'll be quite colourful. You know those Uroshi. Are you sure you wouldn't even like the usual codpiece? Helpful in the if-you-want-to-have-kids-later department, you know." He waggled his eyebrows in a way that he hoped made him look like a worldly man of the bedchamber.

Jack opened his mouth, but Soto stepped in front of him.

"No need, squire. Just the costume as detailed on this drawing here. That's all. And stretchy. Very stretchy. Except the cape."

Sagh squinted at the drawing proffered by Soto. It appeared to have been executed in crayons, on a napkin. There were sticky cup rings, and fingerprints, and Jolly Mister Sun.

"*Why* exactly is there a cape?" he asked. "Isn't that just something more for the enemy to grab, or strangle you with?"

Jack couldn't actually explain why there had to be cape. But he'd been pretty firm about its inclusion, and Soto wasn't about to back down.

"He's a cunning one," he confided, huddling in forehead-to-forehead with the specialist tailor. "Likely some kind of matador thing, like when the bloody Szerenicans do their bull-dance, you know? The hand is quicker than the eye, and all that?"

Gathur Sagh sighed. It wasn't worth it to argue with these four drunken fools, especially when they were dangling a small fortune in front of his nose. *So what if the big fat one got beaten up? At least he'd get beaten up looking absolutely fabulously stunning...*

"Alright. Give me three hours. And you're sure about this big insignia on the front? What is that, an 'f'? The bit cut out of a violin?"

"Secret identitititi...y," put in Foxmallet, who had managed to produce a pipe of stumbleweed from somewhere on his person. "So nobody knows who he is."

"There's already a mask," protested Sagh, weakly. Why did it fall to him to be the champion of common sense? "And nobody knows who he is anyhow. He's a rank amateur. A nobody. Pardoning your presence, sir."

Soto tapped his nose in a conspiratorial gesture.

"Ahh, see. But when everyone knows who he is, this way *they still won't know*. The S... it's an S, not an F, learn your cursive... is for Soto and Somewhat enterprises. Investors in gladiatorial futures."

"It is?" asked Jack.

"It is. But you never heard that, did you?"

This was aimed at Gathur Sagh, who simply nodded and smiled. Anything to get these madmen out of his workshop.

"Three hours, gentlemen. I'm sure you'll be very pleased with the results."

Which explained how, three hours later, Jack Somewhat was trying heroically to fish the very tight strapping of a very yellow codpiece out of his bum crack. Sagh, who was no sadist, had included what appeared to be a pair of undershorts over the long crimson tights which made up the majority of the costume, and they were lined with chain mail. Aside from that, the whole get-up was loud, bright red, and offered the same armoured profile as a rice-paper bathing screen.

Jack swivelled this way and that, trying to get comfortable. He was horribly aware that the material was not yet at full stretch, as he was trying very hard to suppress his impetuous muscles.

"Would you *quit* that?" asked Soto, in a terrible stage whisper. "They don't let madmen fight, you know. You look like you think you're growing a tail!"

Three hours had been more than enough for Jory and Billiam to get just nicely drunk, and for Jack to get a monumental case of cold feet.

"How *do* I look? Because, Soto, I feel idiotic. What if it doesn't work?"

The little herbalist reached up, gripped a hold of his ear where it poked out of the side of his stretchy red mask, and pulled him down to his level.

"If your condition subsides, as it were, of its own volition, then we can call that a win, can't we, Jack? And if the worst comes to the worst, I can call the fight off. I'm a doctor, after all. Sort of. Technically. So you might have to take one punch. How bad could that be?"

At just that moment the great iron portcullis of the Brute pits rattled open, hefted by the hand of a man who must have had at least a bit of ogre in his ancestry.[9] His knuckles looked like a row of individual butcher's slabs, and he was wearing a set of spiked brass rings which didn't just depict cat skulls – they had real ones nailed on.

"Larrrrst call fer volern...teeerrs," rumbled the man-mountain, reading this last word off of a tattoo on his forearm.

Jack pointed. His feet were already walking away.

"One punch from a thing like that? That's beyond all the doctoring you can do, matey! I reckon I'll..."

"Over here!" yelled Jory Foxmallet, cheerfully. The huge gladiator raised an eyebrow. "I say, my good fellow! We have one here! A strapping young thug in the prime of his... I don't know, pugilistic ascendancy. Yes! That's it!"

Jory pointed. Jack waved, defeatedly.

"He's got his own costume, and all," said Billiam, beaming proudly.

The gladiator shrugged the door across to his other shoulder and squinted.

"Nice. Nice. Though that's more the costume for the bar me brother bounces for. Well, I *say* bounces. Usually, they don't bounce much once the bone fragments go all floppy. The Purple Tiger. Lovely house band. And at the end of the night, the ladies who ain't ladies share the half-melons they used in the, y'know, chest area. Brilliant cabaret."

Soto puffed himself up like a pigeon full of helium and advanced on the man.

"I say, sir, my boy here is a fighter of rare repute! Would you believe he's never had an opponent leave the ring after facing him? That nobody has ever dared to go a second round against him?"

Both of these things were strictly speaking true, if only because Jack had never so much as fought a *first* round. Knox's mind was on something else, however.

"Melons?"

---

9. Ogres, despite the rumours to the contrary, are indeed real. Certain sages of the Order of the Secret Flame believe that Ogres are *made*, taken as children and subjected to the processes of certain Forbidden Conscious Artefacts from the Age of Hubris. Thus, true Ogres are rare indeed, and their strange, machine-worshipping cult is both the only way they can truly procreate, and the reason they are legendary for eating children. Very, very old scrolls say that the Ogre race was 'designed' to live in places where the very force which holds us to the ground would be enough to crush a normal man's bones, but of course, this is nonsense. Half and quarter Ogres, like the doorkeeper of the Brute Pits, are common enough through the 'Arch, though full-blooded Sons and Daughters of the Maw of Iron are secretive at best.

"Ohhh yerrr. Down the front of der dress, like, so them blokes like Dave the Ripper and Ice-pick Henry can pretend to be harem girls fer the night. Great song an dance. Worth the ticket price."

Soto wanted to tap on the thug's shoulder. He settled for a spot just above his horrible, crusted belly-button. A face like a hundred nightmares creaked around on an ox-like neck.

"He'll take *whatever* you want to put him up against."

Jack tried to look resolute. It wasn't happening. Now, as he looked into the dank, torch-lit tunnel that led into the undercroft of the Pits, this idea seemed less and less like a good one. But then the voice came whining its way into his mind again, like a mosquito trapped behind his eyeballs.

"OK. Loving the costume. *Loving* it. Cape and all. Is this where the criminals hang out? A den of iniquity? Let's give them a darn good thrashing, then a bit of a talking to about civic responsibility!"

"Just not *him* though," said Jack, clenching his teeth. "Wouldn't be fair."

Soto looked at the immense doorman. The doorman looked at Soto. They both looked at Jack. Then the giant burst out in peals of laughter, accompanied by a cloud of rotten breath like the exhalation of a dozen cesspits. Jory and Billiam got in on it too, until the massive thug wiped away a single tear with one arm-sized finger.

"Ohhhh, no no no. Fight *me*? What a larf! Not fair at all, not at all." He paused for a second, then unfolded one hairy great arm, ushering all four young men into the gloom. "I'm retired, I am. Too old for this mug's game anymore."

Wheezing laughter echoed after them as a midget with one arm and a clipboard showed them to the manager's office. There lurked a bald and swarthy man in a threadbare toga, with a wreath of poorly-made gold oak leaves perched on his head. When Jack and his friend arrived, he was giving a somewhat flabby fighter a neck massage and a little reassurance.

"It's only three man-eating lions, Swannock. Just think of 'em as little kitty-cats. Ones that think you're a mouse."

The man groaned, looking green around the gills.

"*Three* lions, though? I should have asked for a different judge, really. Should have had a better lawyer, too."

"Oh, hush," tutted the toga-clad Master of Gladiators. "My brother's a *perfectly* good attorney. At least you aren't just being hanged, or going for the old 'bit off the top'..." he mimed a whistling headsman's axe. "Nah, where's the spectacle in that? Tell you what, Swannock, you deal with these fleabags and there'll be something special in it for you!"

The man perked up a little, clenching his fists.

"You really think so?" He winced as the toga-clad man popped a muscle in his neck. Jack noticed that the Master was a lot stronger than he looked, and had a few too many scars to be in this game purely on an administrative level.

"Ohhhh yes. After all, when was the last time you had curried lion for dinner? Waste not want not, me mum always used to say! Now, you get out there and do it for that little crippled boy in the Sisters of Perpetual Complaint infirmary!"

Swannock looked a bit puzzled.

"You mean... the one that *I* crippled, Mister Creagle?"

The Master of Gladiators – for it was indeed the infamous, much-talked-about Zoltan Creagle – patted him on the cheek.

"You catch on quick, matey. After all, crippling a baker's boy is why you've been sentenced to see the inside of a lion, innit?" Swannock sagged. "Now now! No need to be so glum! At least Himself allows you to pick a nice shiny weapon! Go and see the man at the end of the hall, and he'll let you have a rummage in the spares barrel. Also, tell Gunnhilde to pour some gravy down your trousers. Gets 'em feeling peckish."

As Swannock wandered away dazed, Zoltan Creagle spun about as if on a turntable, and fixed them with a grin that was mostly carved ivory and the rest gold. He clapped his hands together, displaying sausage-sized fingers and more rings than you'd normally find in a thief's underpants drawer.

"Lads! Friends! Gentlemen! Fellow aficionados of the sweet science of punching people in the face! How can I help you on this fine, fine afternoon?"

Creagle did not look like the kind of man you should trust. In fact, he looked like the kind of person who would cheerfully sell you a second-hand horse, half of which was made of sack-cloth and sawdust. But he *was* master of the Brute Pits, by Imperial decree, and though his fighting days were well and truly done, he was still reputed to know more about inflicting pain with one's bare hands than any gaggle of torturers worth their floppy black hoods. Soto extended a hand warily, and had it mashed boneless in Creagle's enthusiastic grip.

"We... we have a volunteer for you," he wheezed, eyes popping.

Creagle laughed.

"Ahh, of course! A roaring lad keen for hot-blooded adventure, and of course... the ladies!" He wiggled his eyebrows so vigorously it looked as though they might escape. "And what is *your* speciality, son?" he asked, sizing up Jack with a flashing eye. "Charioteer? Sword-swinger? Chungdoji death-grappler? *Aha!* I know! You're one of those fellers with the net and the trident, aren't you! Old school! We had a brilliant one of those until that business last week with the rhinoceros and the two axemen..."

"What happened to him?" asked Foxmallet, swiping a flask out of Knox's hand.

Creagle clocked him with a condescending roll of his eyes.

"*He got very, very bad indigestion.* But come on! You've brought your friend here, a *strapping* young fighter. What does he want to try his hand at? Tell nice Mister Creagle, and we can have him on the way to *superstardom!*"

"You mean... you'll turn him to a huge ball of exploding gas?" asked Soto, who was wise in the ways of science.

Jack was just about to venture the proposition that it had all been a prank, and to apologise for wasting the man's time, but Soto finally managed to get his hand free, and popped up before he could open his mouth.

"He's a bare-knuckle boxer. Just done the circuit through the Grailish Isles. They call him... ummm..." he looked up and down the front of Jack's bright red costume, and fixed his eyes on that silly cursive 'S'. "The ſcarlet ſpectre!"

"Really?" asked Jack, under his breath.

"*Really?*" asked Creagle, trying to frame Jack's face between his outstretched fingers. "I can't see that on a poster. The ſcarlet ſpectre. Hard to pronounce with all yer teeth in."

"Really!" said Soto. "And what's more, he's ready to face anyone you care to mention!"

Creagle rubbed his chin, then leaned in, spitting in his palm.

"You'll get five percent of the house's twenty-five percent of all wagers on him, a hot meal each, second row seats, and if he wins... *if...* then we'll see about getting him a ranked match. First up, as a beginner, he'll face the other 'up and comers'. A nice easy one."

There was something nasty about the way he said that last bit. Jack remembered previous drunken visits to the Pits, and the curtain-raisers before the main show.

"You mean, the street-thugs and sailors who just fight for grog money and a dinner with identifiable meat in it? Some of them are meaner than the real boxers! But..."

Creagle raised an eyebrow.

"Chicken? I mean, not as an identifiable meat, like?"

"*But it won't do them a lick of good!*" put in Soto, a bit too quickly. "Is what the Spectre means to say. Because we'll – ummm - we'll take em all!"

Jack noted the collective 'we' clanging into place, even though it was him who was about to put his precious face in the path of several scarred-up knobbly fists. And boots, and other nasty hidden weapons, if memory served.

"Excellent!" beamed Zoltan Creagle, ushering them down the corridor where poor doomed Swannock had gone before. "Because tonight, we're starting things off with a grand melee *royale!* You'll be on in ten. Good luck!"

Jack gulped. Above their heads, the crowd cheered. He didn't like the sound of that *'royale'*...

Morthrag slammed the door shut behind him.

6
The Pugnaciousness Contradiction

So IT WAS that Jack stewed in the echoing, firelit gloom of the training dungeons, while Foxmallet, Billiam and Soto went and elbowed their way through the incoming crowds to their seats. The smells of rank sweat, fried mango, rotten fish and hot canvas assailed them, as tiny cotton-fluff tamarins scampered across the vines and awnings above, looking for a chance to swipe anything shiny or edible.

And there were crowds, all right. *Teeming* crowds, on their break during the Peacock Octal, the time of siestas, long afternoon teas and pleasing diversions before work began again at the cool of Mosquito Hour.

It was part of the genius of Himself (and of Lord Slave)[10] that the Pits served as rough-and-ready courtrooms, mass entertainment and a vast source of taxable income at the same time. If a citizen banged up by the Knock-men knew that a jury would find him guilty (so guilty that all the judge would have to do was pick out a nice rope), he could opt for trial by combat. In that case, the judge decided, based on the evidence, just *what* he should fight to prove his innocence.

Hence, peppered amongst the main events (usually fought by professionals who *wanted* to be there) there were bouts where murderers, rapists, tax evaders and other serious miscreants had to try to stop a rhino while armed with a teaspoon, for example, or were sentenced to face a champion or two picked by the victim's family. It turned out that this had been the speciality of Morthrag, the doorman, back in his heyday... dishing out bone-fracturing, face-ripping beatings to thugs who thought they'd get away with their

---

10. Some empires run on the principle that you can keep the people happy with bread and circuses. The Urzoman regime was always pleased to go one better, offering instead booze and bloodsports, which also neatly skirted around Lord Slave's irrational fear and loathing of circus clowns

crimes on account of being big and mean[11].

The pits were sunk into the red-rock flank of the great Sugarloaf, the massif which shouldered its way up out of the jungle at the landward side of the city, and which was girded with the traceries and jewelled necklaces of streets and avenues for the rascally rich. Where one knobbly protrusion hunched out over the fashionable district of Saint-Guthran-in-the-Outhouse, the old Sarunjek Rajahs had excavated an amphitheatre, where they had staged their elaborate operas.

Now, the many-levelled pits were for fighting, with the main arena reserved for the most egregious violence, and sundry other courts, cubes, fields and training oubliettes sunk in around it.

The second row was a wooden platform raised up above the terraced seating and shady awnings of the First, where Lords and Ladies preened, and high-ranking officers gave the 'old black and silver' an airing, carrying their tricorne hats under their arms and sipping wines from far-off Clourvonne and Zalois. Soto slithered through the crowd to the rail, while Foxmallet looked wistfully down through the gaps between the awnings to where his peers were eating grapes and melon slices from out of salvers of crushed ice. He snapped his fingers, summoning an urchin laden down with rental parasols, paid for one, and popped it open.

Billiam Knox, however, immediately began going about his business. This was the reason he never had to work a day in his life. Well, *this*, and the fact that he was apprenticed to a Wizard of severely advanced years. The Venerable Master was so ancient that he could barely remember what century it was (or if, in fact, he was a sock puppet called Geoffrey). In his day, he'd been a geomancer of horrendous power, able to raise whole castles from the bedrock by will alone. That day, however, was so long gone that it had passed from history into archaeology.

Knox had learned precisely nothing of magic, but he possessed the financial cunning of a feral accountant, and he'd been able to pay for a kindly Sarunjek nurse for Master Grimblewell by selling certain knick-knacks from around the old boy's apartment, then investing in his true vocation.

Gambling.

---

11. If that's your plan for life, remember that there is ALWAYS someone bigger and meaner, all the way down, until you reach your local version of Morthrag. Or even worse, one of those tiny little people who concentrate seven feet and 200 kilos of furious anger into a five-foot frame that's entirely made of sinews, knuckles and hatred.

Because Billiam Knox was the absolute, trophy-holding, big shiny belt wearing, heavyweight all-Jansamrana champion of looking like a rube. He could appear so naïve, so callow, and so dim that even the most ham-fisted, butter-fingered bookie would feel like a veritable mastermind in his presence. With his haystack haircut of fire-red, his adam's apple the size of an elbow, his watery blue eyes and his carefully cultivated peasant's accent, Billiam Knox couldn't just convince a man to take his money - he could convince him to loan him a large amount more, on huge odds, and almost (but not quite) feel sorry for him.

Then the numbers began to tumble, and the cards began to turn, and the horses came into the final stretch, and that gormless mug lit up with what sincerely appeared to be innocent, lucky joy.

This was the true genius of Billiam Knox. He could fleece an aspiring sharp down to the bloody stubble, and *come back again to do the same tomorrow*, to the same fellow, because he made it look like dumb, slap-faced luck.

Behind that slack-jawed visage, so carefully cultivated, lurked a mind like a well-oiled collection of sharp little gears and cranks – one which made numbers dance, and split and multiply like germs on a dockside tavern tabletop. Today, he had a perfect excuse. His old pal was fighting for the first time, and in the *grand melee royale*, no less! Why, he'd be a pretty poor friend if he didn't invest heavily in an untrained, untested, possibly unhinged pugilist who also happened to be his childhood buddy, wouldn't he?

While his friends were getting settled up top, Jack was feeling somewhat unsettled down below. An old lady wearing a chain-mail apron and big leather gloves (this had proven to be Gunnhilde) had shown him to a kind of wooden cell, told him to wait and read the paperwork, and then shut the door. There was a tiny bench to sit on, and a selection of dog-eared, blood-stained magazines, with names like *Mace and Crossbow*, *Soldier of Misfortune* and *Modern Face Puncher*. There were all kinds of forms and documents mixed in with them, but frankly, Jack was too nervous to read.

After a lot of sweating, a lot of uniform-adjustments, and a mounting cacophony of far-off cheers, the whole little room lurched suddenly, and began to rise. Jack realised it was actually a kind of elevator; or at least, a crude wooden box being winched up toward the light on chains.

Hidden machineries were making the same creakings and groanings as the Day Watch Lantern as it swung up into the air. Jack hung onto the splintery seat, aware that he was trapped in a levitating outhouse, as the roar of the crowd grew louder. Through the wooden slats of the walls he saw the mortared bricks of the undercroft turn to hewn red marble, then massive baulks of timber, and then...

The walls came away. He stood, shakily, under the double-blowtorch of the twin suns, in the middle of a vast circular pit, thronged on all sides with people. Hooting, gesticulating, boozing, half-naked, reeking humanity, all hollering and spitting, waving and cheering down at him in rank upon seething rank. The sound was like a physical force; Jack was drowning in it, his nerves buzzing as he squinted through the glare.

There were others out in the arena with him. Ten, twenty... more. Spaced around the edge of a great octagonal platform, and all looking equally dazed by the forge-hot heat rising up from the sand below, and radiating in waves from the crowd. The stench of old blood and fresh sweat fairly sizzled.

MAYHEM! MAYHEM! MAYHEM!

So chanted the crowd, and whether this was general advice, the title of the show, or the name of one of the fighters, Jack had no idea. He decided that he'd better get with the program, and raised his hands in the air, feeling his cape swirl out in a lethargic puff of breeze.

The other fighters were a mixed bag, to say the least. Jack had been right about the kind of people who took on a bare-knuckle battle-royale for grog money and a hot dinner, and they were every bit as desperate and mean as he'd imagined. There were sailors from a dozen of the ships in the harbour, wearing their tribal costumes, or in one case, nothing at all but a strategic sock. There were street monsters from all the worst parts of Grand Sepulchre, ex-convicts tattooed with the glyphs of the old Ironbelly, down-on-their-luck longshoremen, disgraced soldiers, and bar-room brawlers.

Not one of them was wearing a brightly coloured uniform with a cape. The rule seemed to be shorn-off hair, scalp-stubble fresh, tight leathers, burlap strips wrapped around the fists, and big, horrible boots.

"Ruffians? Criminals? Are they here to learn the error of their ways?" asked the voice in Jack's head. It was becoming increasingly worrying. He'd heard that hearing voices in your head was the first sign of going mad (even though this was the central precept of several important religions). Mad people, in Grand Sepulchre, were sent to the great rotting raft of broken-up ships they called the Sunken

Garden, where Wizards of the Order of the Three-Fingered Hand tried to cure[12] them. On weekends, tour parties came to poke them with sticks, listen to their rantings, eat roasted cashew nuts and pay a small sum for admittance.

"Am I going mad? Where does all this stuff about criminals come from anyway?"

So thought Jack, and he was not well pleased when the voice answered.

"Do you have *any* idea how long we were in space for? I scanned every single cultural broadcast about our situation, son. This is absolutely, *positively* what we're supposed to do!" The voice seemed to pause, looking over the shoulder it had borrowed from Jack. **"Look out, here comes that grinning thug in the toga again..."**

Indeed, a sputter of cut-rate fireworks and clouds of smoke were jetting up from a hole in the middle of the stage. Out of this display staggered Zoltan Creagle, coughing, fanning his face with one gold-crusted hand. He gathered his composure and beamed up at the crowd, raising his fists high.

"Grand Sepulchre!" he shouted, as if the people had forgotten which city they lived in. "Are you ready to be *entertained?*"

The replying wall of sound crashed like a breaker over Jack, but Creagle still cupped one hand to his ear, mugging like a pantomime duchess. "I can't heeeeear you!"

This time the roar stripped a layer of dust from the planks, and a thin film of dirt from several of the fighters, who seemed to be warming up to the idea of being here. Some were literally doing stretches and cracking their knuckles in anticipation.

"Then let's put the plug in this bloodbath!" Yelled Creagle. "This afternoon, sports fans, I present to you what was *going* to have been a thirty-way battle royale, between some of the most murderous bare-knuckle fighters ever to disgrace the ring! I'm talking the likes of Toothless Frank Hamsmiter!" He pointed to a man with a grin like a busted row of gravestones. "Golto the Demolisher!" This one literally had no nose. A huge hexagonal bolt was shoved in the hole. "Mandak 'the menacing nickname' McGurk!" A man-mountain all wobbling lard, and knuckles dragging the splintery boards. "And Grindolph 'three toes' Van Peltd, the pirate king in exile!" This one, at least, had

---

12. With all the zeal, vigour, interpersonal rivalry and accumulated classical ignorance of a gaggle of alchemists and barbers trying to cure a man of epilepsy, with the use of leeches, drills, various poisons and a big hammer

a costume, even if it was simply a rather threadbare and obviously fake Zollish pirate's coat, stripey pants and a bicorne hat. The three toes were on a necklace that he kissed and slipped into his top pocket. "Along with many other worthy fighters of impeccable repute! But..."

And here Creagle paused, one finger raised and quivering. The finger began to come down to the horizontal as the Master of Gladiators swivelled, aiming it like a small blackpowder cannon.

"But we have with us today a *new challenger*. Fresh from the Grailish Isles, that renowned land of salutary pugilism, by which I mean, they're so mean they beat themselves up to keep their bad tempers fresh! Ladies, gentlemen, and sentient beings who we let in purely to spend money, I present to you... the ſcarlet ſpectre!" Jack found himself staring down the barrel of that loaded finger, and an equally loaded grin.

"Oh, holy Quazirath, he actually bought it..." whispered the ex-alchemist under his breath. He tried a little wave. The crowd cheered. At this point, however, Jack was almost certain they would have cheered for a dead chicken, or a small bucket of yoghurt.

"Yes, a stout contender, in the full flush of battle-hungry youth, and equipped with a *most* amazing costume, you must admit! Doesn't the lack of any proper armour speak to his supreme, nay, *heroic* confidence?"

Creagle made huge, pantomime gestures toward his groin, indicating no visible codpiece. The yellow underpants seemed comically unsatisfactory. He mugged as if he'd been kicked in the fruits, wincing.

"Heroic! Yeah!" said the voice. At this point, Jack wasn't sure if he was sad to watch his sanity spiralling down the latrine hole, or happy to know that whatever supernatural bastard lived inside his skull was real.

Creagle's grin ratcheted up another notch, into areas where it was now obviously sinister. His tone became a metallic purr, quieter, but carrying to the backs of the stands on sheer menace alone.

"So there's a *new* prize, lads. First one that can rip off one of his ears, gets a fat purse full of gold, courtesy of the establishment."

"I thought you said something about a 'nice easy one'," hissed Jack, trying to retain his grin, while imagining Golto trying to figure out how to pull off his ears[13].

13. This was quite unfair. Despite looking like a brainless thug, Golto was smart enough to know his limitations, and had therefore hired a tutor to teach him the finer points of

"I never said easy for *you*," replied Zoltan, his mouth hardly moving as he waved to the crowd. "Anyhow, we have to test the merchandise. Worst case scenario, we'll find an ear in the bits bucket and sew it on for you afterwards. One in thirty chance it'll be yours."

"Really?"

"*Really.* And by the way. If you're one of them masochists, who comes down here to fleece poor old Zolt Creagle by having his mates bet heavily against him and then taking a dive, I've just sent your plans down the gurgler. Hope you weren't. We don't like those types round here. This is a place of *sportsmanship.* It was in the paperwork."

It'd be nice to say that Jack didn't have the heart to tell Zoltan he was doing just the opposite. But the truth is, he didn't have time.

The swarthy Master of Gladiators stepped backward into a new fizzle of sparks and smoke, winking, and disappeared. Then, up atop the stands, the great silver sheet of a sorcerous mirror rippled into life. It filled up with the image of a young lady wearing very little clothing, but carrying a gong and an hourglass.

"Fighters, prepare for MAYHEM!" she shouted.

MAYHEM! MAYHEM! MAYHEM! Roared the crowd. A desultory hail of fruit rinds, betting slips, spit, empty cups and other debris began to rain down around the periphery of the stage.

"Aaaaaaaaaaad.... **FIGHT!**"

Now, if Amberelia Chance, junior demortifex of the Guild Lachrymose, had stood in Jack's place, out under the double-hammer of the twin suns, her mind would have analysed every strike and counterblow which dictated the dance of combat. But she was currently stuffing her few belongings into a sack, and pretending not to cry.

So instead, Jack Somewhat simply stared at the approaching bulk of Mandak 'the menacing nickname' McGurk, heading toward him like a meat avalanche. And, in doing so, he missed the incoming fist of the man right next to him, who scored a jowl-slapping, tooth-rattling roundhouse on the so-called ſcarlet ſpectre before he even had a chance to conjure up some supernatural muscle.

"Ooh, that's *got* to hurt!" giggled the young lady on the screen, as purple explosions flared inside Jack's eyeballs. He felt his cheek grind across the timbers, his limbs flopping in a rag-doll tangle. Then green fire blazed up from his hand, where the scar pulsed angry and hot.

---

ear-removal years ago.

"Are you going to take that lying down?" asked the voice in his head. **"Come on. Open your mouth. Then get up!"**

Jack's jaw hung loose by default, but he was surprised as anyone to hear words come spilling out, in a deep and mahogany-rich baritone.

"Not today, evil-doer!"

He came up from the deck like vengeance in tights, watching his arm bulge and swell as it swung up and out. His fist connected with his assailant's chin with a sound like an axe splitting hardwood, and the man spun a full five times in the air before he hit the ground. Jack turned just in time to see the shadow of Mandak fall across him, and he grinned.

Mandak was none too bright, but his piggy little eyes narrowed as he saw his target go from prone, flabby and frightened to the kind of figure they usually cast in bronze.

Jack's fist might as well have been metal too, as it hammered right into the man-mountain's belly, sending undulating ripples of flab wobbling away from its impact point like waves on a pond. Jack swore he felt his knuckles kiss the huge man's spine, as twin rolls of meat lapped up to his shoulder. Then Mandak was thrown backwards as if from a catapult, spinning starfish-spread to *whump* into the arena wall.

The crowd were on their feet, mouths open, silent. Little dribbles of drool, liquor and other gustatorial juices dripped in slow motion as Jack spun on his heel, one foot flashing out in a red blur to connect with a third thug's head. The man's teeth came out like blunderbuss shot, and he spun like a drunken ballerina before collapsing to the ground.

Now they were cheering. *Now* they were shaking handfuls of betting slips and either cursing, crying or dancing a jig, depending on how the numbers fell.

Jack took stock of the remaining fighters, most of whom were faced off against each other, and zeroed in on the Zollish pirate, Van Peltd. He launched himself, leaping up and over two grappling slaughterhousemen in their bloody whites, and tackled the sea-raider to the deck with a mighty thump of timbers.

"Ahh! It was meant to be *staged!* I was meant to..." managed Van Peltd, as Jack's fist sent him lights-out. Then it was a quick left and right to send two more men sprawling, ribs cracking as they blew out twin fountains of bloody spit.

A ruffian behind him had pried up a plank, just to be extra villainous, but it broke across Jack's shoulders like a dried-out reed. He turned and landed an uppercut that literally popped the sorry cheater out of his boots, leaving his socks to curl up, smoking on his feet when he landed.

Jack looked up. The crowd were howling his name now, stomping in rhythm on the boards.

ʃcarlet ʃpectre! ʃcarlet ʃpectre! ʃcarlet ʃpectre!

He showboated a little, flexing his huge, improbable muscles. Across the arena, bolt-nosed old Golto put down the bloody wreck of the fellow he'd been headbutting, and narrowed his eyes.

"Lads, I reckon we have to take care o' this one together. He can't take us all at once!"

The hard-bitten fighters around the Demolisher agreed, forming up into a rough-and-ready mob. Fists were clenched. Illicit knuckle-dusters were adjusted. And Jack Somewhat smiled, the sunlight literally glinting off of his as-yet-unsmashed pearly whites.

"Come on then, if you think you're 'ard enough," he growled.

The voice in his head tutted.

"Not a very heroic war cry, is it? A bit coarse. Then again, we can work with it…"

The mob rumbled up to speed, charging with Golto at the tip of the wedge. Jack, who by this point felt all but invincible, waved to the crowd, tipped his non-existent hat at a swooning young noblewoman, and wound up one fist in a windmilling motion.

This time, the impact sent out a shockwave that blew the beer-glasses and paper packets of deep-fried crunchy bits out of people's hands, all the way back in the third row. Some of those who witnessed the fight swear that a glowing green bubble appeared right at the point of impact (Golto's stubbly chin), with the word KRUNT in it.

Bodies blew outwards like ninepins struck with a naval cannonball. Luckless bare-knuckle scrappers slid across the sand, planing off whole galaxies of rude tattoos. One or two landed in the stands; a broken-nosed brawler by the name of Octavius Grulk landed right in the lap of the huge, lace-wrapped Viscomptesse Scarberry, ruler of two small streets and an ornamental fountain. She ended up taking him home as a pet. A fair few others struck the walls, which were, mercifully, padded with leather and straw. Not one got back up again. Except…

Jack advanced on Golto, who had, amazingly, managed *not* to have been folded up like a cheap piece of lawn furniture by that colossal blow. The Demolisher cuffed blood away from his split lip, and put up his dukes.

"What are you *doing*, you bloody amateur? It's *rigged!* Didn't Creagle tell you? I take a dive to old Toothless Frank after all you little 'uns get biffed about a bit. It's supposed to be gravy for everyone!"

"But... the stuff about my ears!" countered Jack, leaning back as a huge haymaker whistled past his nose.

"Showmanship!" spat Golto, fishing a bloody-looking wax ear-lug from inside his pocket. At least Jack *hoped* it was wax. "It's all about the betting, see? You were supposed to be in on it!"

Jack's arm came up like a piston, cutting off any further elucidation by connecting with Golto's chin in a perfect uppercut. This time there was definitely a little green explosion, with the world PAF inside it. The bolt stuffed in the old boxer's nasal septum popped out like a champagne cork, ricocheting off of an ice bucket in the first row and then smashing Foxmallet's beer jug. Golto hit the boards, spark out.

Jack raised his fists high, but his grin wasn't quite as squeaky white this time. There *had* been an awful lot of paperwork he hadn't read. What if …

"Oh, no," he whispered to himself, as he saw horribly familiar black-clad figures pushing through the crowds. It was Throne's Shadow, armed with blackpowder pistols and short swords, and there, talking to a madly gesticulating Zoltan Creagle, was Lord Slave.

But Jack's problems had only just begun.

"Betting?" asked the voice in his head, with a definite tinge of incredulity. **"*Rigged?* Tell me, young man, are we fighting for *money*, here?"**

The smart thing, Jack knew, would have been flat-out denial. It had worked a charm for most of his young life, when confronted with angry figures of authority. But how could you disguise a horrible truth from a presence wrapped around your own brainstem? The reality of the situation leaked through, like a hot, embarrassing urine stain through the front of a pair of breeches.

"Well, that's not very heroic *at all!* I mean, *really,* young man! I go to all of the trouble of giving you amazing, superhuman powers to inspire and encourage your fellow citizens, and what do you do?"

Jack would have hung his head in shame, such was the tone of hurt dignity which blattered about inside his skull. But he'd seen something horrible happening across the great wooden octagon. It was Toothless Frank Hamsmiter, and he'd just finished crushing a man who looked like the poster-model for unsolved murder under his huge, callused foot. He smiled at Jack, levelling one hairy salami of a finger, and began to advance, his face twitching and gurning with a surfeit of unfocused rage.

"Well, that's *not* how it works. All the information I picked up was very clear. The cape, the costume, the justice... what would your poor blown-up parents think?"

Jack didn't quite have time to inform the voice that his parents hadn't so much blown up as never been around (they'd told him his mother ran away when the midwife showed her what he looked like). Because the muscles were collapsing under his stretchy suit like deflating pig's-bladders, and Toothless Frank was striding closer, his eyes as flat and cold as winter nail-heads on a gallows pole. Jack held up his hands in the universally accepted gesture for 'time out'. But his nemesis just smiled wider, displaying a rotten stump-scape of busted teeth.

"Ears off, lad!" he gurgled, miming a savage twist. "For real, this time!"

"I shan't help you out of this one," said the voice. **"You'll have to learn!"**

"Learn *what?*" wailed Jack, quite losing his composure. He scrabbled back across the boards as a fist came hammering down, almost losing his stretched-out trousers in the process. "How to die suddenly? Tell you what, can we just do the theory, and leave the practical for another four-score years or so?"

A second blow whooshed past like a runaway ox-cart as Jack staggered to his feet, ducking left. He turned to run, but one of Hamsmiter's huge fists closed around his absurd yellow cape, pinning him to the spot as his feet made a furious, slapping lack of progress.

Now the crowd were laughing. Now a fair few of them were baying for blood. Nothing makes a bunch of sports fans happier than an upset which has just been upset. The old home-town favourite looked like he was going to win again, by way of reeling Jack in and then making a pulverized waffle of his cranium.

That very-nearly-victim took a look over his shoulder, where Toothless Frank's face was rising like a scarred and horrible moon, chuckling to itself as it licked its lips.

"Alright!" he yelled. "*I surrender!* I've learned the error of my ways! Oh, that I could live long enough to hear a big boring sermon about right and wrong from a disembodied voice that won't shut up!"

If this blinding *non sequitur* put Hamsmiter off his stroke, he would never know. Because just as the huge man was cocking back a fist, a tingle sparked through Jack's limbs.

"Oh, all right then. You're young, and foolish, and it seems as though I missed most of your childhood. Lead does terrible things to my cognitive powers. It felt like we crashed one day, and I was integrating with a fully gown nervous system the next! Ahhh well. Let's try some of *this*…"

Some terrified, ratlike little remnant of Jack's hindbrain had been yammering about escape as loudly as possible for some time now. But when the world gave a lurch, and he found himself hanging in the air, ten feet above the arena, it wasn't as if the panic died down to a soothing background hum. For one thing, *hanging* was exactly the right word, because, as he started to make his wobbling ascent, Toothless Frank was still holding onto his cape.

"Ere! Mister Creagle dint say nuffing about wires and such! What are you playing at?"

Jack couldn't answer. He was struck dumb with confusion as he bobbed ever higher, level with the second row, and growing blue around the face as his cape starved him of oxygen. His fingers scrabbled at his collar, plucking at the stretchy, smooth material. Below him, Frank looked down between his swinging toes and gulped.

"Alright! You win, mister! I really, really hate heights!" A look of sincere pleading unrolled across his webwork of scars. "*Hang on*. Do you hear something teari…"

At that moment, Jack did. The ripping sound echoed like a great lusty fart, indicating that Sagh the tailor's handiwork had given out.

Poor old Toothless Frank was left holding a very large square of yellow fabric, thirty measures up in the air, looking down at a drop that would shorten his legs as surely and swiftly as a very sharp cleaver swung by a very mad dwarf.

"Mummy!" he squeaked in an unexpected falsetto. But Jack… Jack went *up*, much faster than his assailant went down.

He felt himself launched at jowl-flapping speed, like a rock from a catapult, or a bolt from one of those horrible living mantis-bows the assassins used. Air friction gave him a nasty burn, while at the same time ripping his trousers off, so that he ascended through wisps and veils of cloud half naked, utterly embarrassed and terrified out of his mind. The great twin-horned curve of the Arch' glittered in the purple sky, sweeping up and around past Urosh and Thamara in one direction, and showing the green speckles of Mirndeep and the King and Courtiers Isles in the other. Jack fancied he could even see tiny ships moving on the skein of waters as they rolled around to face the suns.

"*Concentrate*, won't you?" coaxed the voice, as Jack reached the very top of his parabola, following the exquisite simplicity of higher Chungdojin Mathematics to the letter. **"Just believe you can fly. It should be easy. You're already doing it!"**

Jack was ready with a sarcastic retort about how it was easy to remain calm when you were disembodied. But sitting there, weightless for a moment - pantsless too – and seeing all of Jansamrana spread out below him, Jack found it within himself to try, very, very hard.

He squeezed his eyes shut and tried to believe. He squeezed his brain to imagine the reality of the various Gods he'd been cajoled, cudgelled and bribed into worshipping, through his long, sad career as an orphan apprentice.

Unfortunately, he ran up against the same problem he'd had back then, sitting in all those incense-reeking temples and cathedrals, hands clasped in earnest prayer.

He was very self-conscious about expecting a miracle. Things that shouldn't happen – nice things, and unexpected ones – didn't happen to him. They were very much for other people.

And so, like Ridikulus in the Phoraxian legend, (who had tried to escape from the mad Hierophant's tower by fashioning wings out of lint, chewing gum, string and toothpicks, instead of being sensible like his father Antiseptikles and just bribing the notoriously bent guards), Jack fell.

It wasn't a smooth descent. Jack's mathematics tutor would have put his face in his hands and despaired at how the young lackwit could mess up such a simple parabola. Whatever power had launched him into the rarefied upper airs kept fizzing and sputtering as the wheels of his brain spun wild, like the gears inside one of those fancy clockwork gambling-engines you found in up-market taverns.

This led to a series of corkscrews, bumps, jerks, brief hops in elevation and skidding, sideways bursts of level flight, during which the voice shouted encouragement like a demented boxing trainer.

"Yes! Hold on to that... no! More with the legs and less with the arse! Just think light thoughts! You can do this... you can do this... oh, well, perhaps that's what the cape was for..."

The only way down, however, was *down*.

And while some of Jack's aerobatics slowed him considerably, he was still headed for a messy crater, and the kind of funeral where they scrape the bits off the shovel and hope that most of them landed in the hole. The green-and-red mosaic of Jansamrana rushed up to meet him, unfolding into a map of Grand Sepulchre with its soaring Malevolith, its tumbledown palaces and its sweltering arterial streets. Jack was reminded of the elegant theory devised by the great natural philosopher, Isambard Nugent.

One day, sitting under an apple tree, a falling fruit had conked the great thinker on the head, leading him to declaim: *"An inanimate objecte, when presented with the opportunity, will always seek to trippe over, inconvenience, injure or otherwise make a pratte of Man, for truly, the Universe is an righte bastarde."*

It was not often that an entire island got the chance to assault a person, unless they were fired from a catapult from the deck of a ship. Jack took one last look at where he was likely to land (inevitably, a jagged expanse of red rocks), and screwed his eyes tightly shut, waiting for the worst to be over so he could get on with more metaphysical problems, such as sneaking into a suitable afterlife.

However, even *that* went wrong.

That forlorn little spark of unfocused belief sent him skidding sideways at the last minute, limbs all a-tangle, to slam diagonally into one of Grand Sepulchre's greatest civic achievements at roughly half the speed of sound.

A tsunami of reeking filth slopped up from his impact point, immediately steaming hot, to sluther and slap up against the shanties and doss-houses of the city's poorest neighbourhood, Fevermarsh. Liquid excrement burbled in the gutters, doing admittedly very little to make the place smell worse, and in fact washing away a fair few animal corpses. Because Jack had managed to find a rare soft spot amid the iron-hard streets and paved plazas of his old hometown. He'd struck the municipal solid waste treatment ponds, otherwise known as Lake Shite.

In fact, he'd bounced off the bottom of one of those immense pans of ordure, skipped five times across a crust of algal slime, and ended up buried, to the waist, upside down in a mountain of horse manure, his naked legs still pedalling air.

When the basket-hatted, canvas-suited pole-men and muck-stirrers of the ponds thought it safe to come back out from their huts and workshops, Jack's bare, wind-chapped buttocks stood out like two pink marshmallows in a compost heap. They pulled him out, washed him down as best they could, and asked no questions; for these denizens of the lowest caste, misfortune was not something to be shared lest it be courted.

Commiserating indentured labourers brewed the young lad a cup of hot sweet tea, found him some pants, and sent him on his way. Needless to say, his mask and costume hadn't survived. The stinking figure in the too-big peasant slacks who staggered out of the gates of the sewage works hadn't spoken a word; he tottered through the streets with the blank gaze of a madman, his hair spiked up in a tangle with what can only be described as human shit.

Eventually he was discovered by a band of Creedishmen in Bentsteeple, who assumed he was a mentally deficient mute. They bundled him back to their temple, gave him several baths, wrapped him in a threadbare monk's robe, and rolled him into a cot, where he was snoring before his head hit the bale of straw they'd provided for a pillow.

7

The Reciprocatory Protocol

SO IT WAS a happy landing for Jack Somewhat, albeit a very smelly one. As the Dead Man's Bells tongued out their dolorous clangour from the tower of Ironbelly Gaol, the ex-apprentice was sound asleep in the depth of a Creedish Chapterhouse in Occipital Street, his snores rattling the hundreds of sheets of paper which were tacked and nailed to the walls there, covered in scriptures in a spidery hand.

But did the rest of Grand Sepulchre sleep?

Of course not!

The Princess of Cities heaved with humanity and its sordid traffickings, every octal of every day, and the bells which struck midnight from the great flea-infested prison on its eastern slopes heralded awakening for a whole army of night-people – night-soil men and whores, bartenders and dreamsugar merchants (both sanctioned and illicit) bakers, street cleaners and Knock-men, the Lord Mayor's Graddisher[14], of course, and members of those mighty twin Guilds, the Lachrymose and the Tenebral.

For Lord Slave, the day had not ended at all.

The alchemists had been singularly unhelpful when it came to the matter of the thing which poor dead Multhazar had been sent from Underbelly. Rhaegulus Cratt, master of the Harbour Watch, had sworn up and down on a stack of holy books that he'd delivered the package, and hadn't changed his tune even under threat of torture. This contradicted numerous reports of that short and horrible man

---

14. A ceremonial position which nobody knew the reason for anymore, but which was kept on for the sake of tradition. The Lord Mayor's Graddisher was paid to patrol the streets around the Civic House, under the shadow of the Malevolith, each night from Dead Man's Bells to dawn, wearing a costume which made him appear to have been attacked by carnivorous, swarming doilies, and brandishing an unlit lantern and a dead, plucked chicken. For this mighty service, he was afforded a yearly stipend of three (now defunct) Urzoman Groats, a bag of turnips, and all the coal he could shove into one stocking on the first day of winter.

singing in the bath until late into the morning.

Despite his investigative efforts, Lord Slave had been unable to get a coherent story out of the Alchemists themselves, as they were all officially in mourning – that is to say, they were engaged in machinations of a political nature which involved poisonings, knifings, garrottings and pushing people down the stairs in order to decide who would be the next master of the Guild. Lord Slave was smart enough to leave well enough alone, especially when it came to people who drank quicksilver and had fingers stained with antimony; he suggested to a handful of the front runners, (individually of course) the services of Old Lady Lachrymosa, and left it at that. Someone would rise to the top, and in the meantime, the factors of the government who produced blackpowder, naphtha and other ingredients of war could do without oversight, at least for a week or two.

Lord Slave had come to accept that the Thing, whatever it was, may well be at the bottom of the harbour, on the person of Multhazar Threck. He sent lackeys to hire pearl divers from the Quillish Isles and the Dry Scatters, and made a note to attend the fish markets come dawn. Threck may have ended up in the belly of something, neatly solving the problem of his whereabouts.

Of course, if Lord Slave couldn't sleep, neither could his much put-upon Majordomo, Gryssle. He'd been assigned to follow up a loose end, because, like policemen in every possible universe, he didn't believe in (or particularly like) coincidences.

Despite not being called one, and not really knowing what one was, Gryssle was every inch a copper. A nasty, bent one. From his black and silver helmet, which slid down over his eyes, to his push-broom moustache with the little turned-up corners, all the way down to his regulation black short pants and big horrible boots, Old Clorry (as his friends called him) radiated a certain smug self-satisfaction at being able to borrow the whole grim authority of the law, and use it like a crowbar chipped with tooth enamel.

Now he had in his custody a trio of known scapegraces, lurkers, loiterers and general scum, who had given him the slip earlier in the day. Known associates of a felon, in fact. Gryssle sipped his Zollish coffee and paced in front of the scarred-up blackwood table which the three lads were chained to, trying not to grin. His mug read – 'You don't have to rip people's thumbs off to work here, but it helps.' It had been a present from his mum.

In front of him sat a very dejected, slightly rumpled trio made up of

Soto Scalizari, Billiam Knox, and Jory Foxmallet.

They'd tried pretty much every last legal way of getting the lads to talk, including buckets of cold water, awful canteen-grade coffee, lack of sleep and incarceration in a tiny room that smelled of socks. The reason they hadn't gone further had a lot to do with the fact that one of them was a titled Lord, one was an apprentice Wizard (and, as such, had to be tried by a Thaumaturgical Court) and the other claimed to be the lawyer for the rest.

"Look," said Gryssle, tugging forlornly on his beard. "Just tell us how you made him fly, alright? Your mate Somewhat. That's all. We don't care about the gambling, or the money you..."

"Allegedly," put in Soto, very quickly.

"*Allegedly* won or lost," finished Gryssle, with a pointed look. "All that other nonsense is between you and Zoltan bloody Creagle, though if you want my advice, you'll look out for that baldy bastard for the next couple of weeks."

He scanned the three faces before him, and found nothing particularly cheerful among them. Soto had adopted the calculated blankness of a card sharp. Billiam Knox was picking his nose, which, on the surface of it, put him out of the running as a thaumaturgical mastermind. And the Foxmallet lad was very much the worse for drink. Worse still, his real lawyer would be here any minute, which meant politics, which Clorance Gryssle did *not* need. "Nothing? Not even you, mister wizard's apprentice? Didn't decide to liven up the fight by making your mate float off like a fairy?"

Knox offered up a cheerfully brainless smile, of the kind that had driven several bookies to strong drink.

"Sorry, officer. I'm not that good of a wizard, really. And the old master, well... he's Order of the Clenched Fist. Stone-magic. Not really the flying type, if you get the technical details. Rocks are *heavy*, like."

Gryssle scowled, but he knew the lad was right. Forensic mages working for Throne's Shadow had confirmed it – Billiam Q Knox hadn't nudged a thaumic particle in weeks, if ever. His hands were clean, according to the raven's skull in a rosewood box they used to sniff out such things. "Maybe it was something he ate?" burped Foxmallet.

"Oh, come on! People don't just bloody levitate! I don't care *what* they've eaten!"

Soto spread his hands open like a book.

"In fact, Majordomo, there are at least twenty-nine well substantiated cases of people levitating in the history of this city alone. Mercy Jim, for example…"

"Is the inspiration for a *puppet show for children!*" groaned Gryssle.

"Saint Guthran?"

"Quasi-religious legend who probably didn't exist!"

"The strange case of Lord Shrillbottle?"

"Aha! I know that one!" said Jory. "It was a very bad opera."

"No, he was the one who tried to make a flying sedan chair with three kegs of blackpowder and a very small parasol," said Gryssle.

At this point a menial popped his head in through the door and muttered something in the Majordomo's ear. He seemed to deflate, mopping his brow with a large monogrammed black handkerchief.

"Well, it seems that your actual lawyer is here. And that it's the formidable Mr Ludcastle, of Ludcastle, Sneers and Pinion. So, seeing as, against all bloody odds, it appears that none of you three have actually *done* anything… which is to say you have *bloody well done something*, but I am, as yet, still getting around to putting my finger on exactly what it is that you have *most definitely done*… I'm going to have to let you walk."

The trio stood up, and were caught short by the triple-chain of black iron which bolted their manacled wrists to the table. Gryssle used the jangle of cold metal as punctuation.

"*But!* I'm only doing this on one proviso. Which is this. You're to take a message to your very much wanted friend. His Lordship's already got Jack Somewhat's number for unlicensed heroism. Seeing as he's short a bloody guild, what with his Master conveniently keeling over and plopping into the briny, he's to show up bright and shiny to his new place of employment tomorrow… or else!"

"Or else *what?*" asked Soto, emboldened by the lackey who was even now turning the key in a ham-sized padlock to set him free. That, and the thought of the Foxmallet family's attorney, Grimshaw Ludcastle (who had once successfully defended an entire barbarian army accused with pillaging and burning the city of Travasq, on cultural grounds).

"*Or else,*" snarled Gryssle, prodding the little apothecary with one ragged-nailed finger "You're aiding, abetting, and providing succour to a known felon. Then, we can reconvene our little conversation someplace more… convivial."

Rarely, if ever, has a waggled set of eyebrows so vividly suggested the horrors of the rack, the bastinado and the thumbscrews. Soto gulped. Billiam opened his mouth to make a joke about the word 'succour', but thought better of it.

So it was that the finding of Jack Somewhat was left to agents of the Foxmallet clan's excellent legal firm, and particularly to Grimshaw Ludcastle himself, a painfully tall, thin man with hands of long-fingered delicacy, and (it was rumoured) a penchant for keeping great creaking, crackling scrapbooks full of fingernails from the defendants he'd sent to the gallows.

For his own part, the attorney couldn't give a vole's fart for Master Jory's entourage, but he *was* the sole male heir, and with Lord Foxmallet himself devoted utterly to his miniature dioramas of sea battles, and Her Ladyship now of the ripe old age of 73, it looked like he'd be the only one.

Urchins, mudlarks, scamps and other children of the moonlit gutters were retained by Ludcastle's agents, and it wasn't long before the Legend of the Shitman was retold in the neighbourhoods between Fevermarsh and the 'Cross, leading to a snoring figure in a cot of straw.

Meanwhile, not too far away, Zoltan Creagle sat perched on a very ornate, very high-backed briarwood chair, in a salon filled with tarnished mirrors and dust-sheets thick with the scurf of centuries. He was nervous, despite the fact that his giant doorman Morthrag had come along with him, and was perched on a chaise lounge, attempting to sip tea from a cup no bigger than his little fingernail.

Their host sat shrouded in gloom, on one of those thrones which, despite being indoors, has its own complicated arrangement of tent fabric, lace, gold thread and fiddly bits. This cast a deep, almost supernatural shadow over the face of the lady who lurked within, as the rest of the room was lit by nothing but a single hunch-backed candelabra in the middle of the long, long table between them. The remains of a great banquet sat mouldering on silver platters the length of this board, so far gone with age that they were more mummified than rotten.

Perhaps this was supposed to be a metaphor for something. Or perhaps it was just supposed to cast the face which eventually swum up out of the shadows in a better light.

"Surely you've lost money before, Mister Creagle?" sighed a voice just this side of the grave. "Some would say it's the nature of running a gambling establishment."

Old Lady Lachrymosa wore a wedding dress and pearls. Zoltan had never seen Himself, of course – very few had – but he imagined that this was what a lich must look like in the morning, although in this case, with the addition of so much pale lead makeup that it appeared to have been applied with a trowel.

"Ahhh... it's not the *money*, you see, your eminence. In fact, I've taken the liberty of bringing a small emolument with me for your delectation..." Here he gestured nervously to Morthrag, who shrugged a small, iron-banded chest around, popping it open. Gold glittered seductively in the candlelight, as gold is wont to do.

The Old Lady's mouth twitched up at one corner, then the other, cracking her perfect makeup and shedding one of several black velvet beauty spots which had been tacked on apparently at random. Her hands clutched into claws around the arms of her throne as she leaned forward, creaking like an armoire in a vice.

"I understand *entirely*, Sir. Pride is what they took from you. Gold is just a way of keeping score, for the rest of them, on the outside, isn't it? Pride is how we keep score in our own - dare I say it in such company - *hearts*." She spat the last word like a fleck of rotten gristle, dabbing her dried-up lips with a pearl-edged napkin.

"So... you'll do it?"

Old Lady Lachrymosa tilted her head to one side, her long, pointed nose giving her the shadow of a scavenging bird. It reared up against the dusty velvet curtains, monstrous and jagged-edged.

"But of *course*, Mister Creagle. We will do anyone the honour of a swift death... so long as we know the reasons why."

Zoltan (not used to being terrified) imagined, then, vast scriptoria packed floor-to-ceiling with tomes, and scribes scratching out with quills all of the hidden fears, grudges, secrets, feuds and insecurities of a city. It was said that there were many worse things the Old Lady could do than kill you, and he believed it, down to the very pit of his withered-up soul.

She snapped her fingers, and burly men who Zoltan could have sworn were not there just a second ago peeled away from the walls to relieve Morthrag of his treasure chest.

"Go and rest, you poor dear," hissed Lady Lachrymosa. "By this time tomorrow, your silly ſcarlet ſpectre will be in a nameless grave."

On the face of it, this should have sounded rather comforting to Zoltan Creagle. In fact, it was quite the opposite. He tongued those words in his mind as if they were an abscessed gap where a tooth had been, all the long carriage-ride home.

Across the city, the Tamarin bells in their spire atop the Guild Tenebral rang out the armpit of the night, that hot and muggy hour when vermin and pariah dogs ruled, and the Wonky Wagon was unleashed to scour the gutters for the drunk and the dead. But peaceful sleep eluded many, this night, as the moons rode high above Jansamrana amid fevered wisps of cloud.

In a shack on the waterfront, sleeping under a pile of nets, a redoubtable fishwife known only as Aunty Marjorie snored, rattling the cork floats which hung from the ceiling. In a crate at the foot of the bed, a set of discarded armour began to clink and stir. A single metal glove came scuttling over the dirt floor like a fat spider, slipping itself onto her hand, and changing her nocturnal visions to ones of violence and righteousness.

In a tall and fashionable town house, a young man in a gigantic white wig and candy-striped peacoat stared intently at a grandfather clock, its swinging pendulum cast in the shape of an idiotically grinning moon.

"Wuh... one," he counted, knocking back a cut-crystal glass of whisky as the pendulum reached the top of its arc. A blur and a snap of static electricity followed, then a small thunderclap. The young man's barstool spun around three times, and was about to topple over before he managed to be back in it, with another glass of whisky clenched in his hand. The pendulum finished its swing, slicing the second in half. At the other end of the room – and it was a long, lavishly panelled room indeed – a bottle rattled to a standstill atop an ornate black marble bar.

In the doorway of a pub in Rown Cross, a raggedy drunkard was hammering on the timbers, an all-but-empty clay jug of gin in one hand. A little slot snicked open, and a pair of beady eyes peered out, brows hunching in with disapproval.

"Go on with you! We're closed! Get yeself off to bed, you lousy sot!"

The face which pulled itself up to the grating was dominated by a red nose that had obviously been broken at least once, and a pair of pale blue eyes that seemed oddly out of place amid the scars and stubble.

"Please, good landlord... I mean publican... I mean... well, you know your business better'n I do, I'd wager. But... I can feel myself sobering up, y'ken, and that's not a situituituation that (burp) is conducive, right, to the public good right now. So if you'd take me silver for a bottle of something, I'd be most..."

The little hatch slammed shut. The poor drunkard held out a tarnished coin, all forlorn, then used it to tap on the door again. He didn't stop until the hatch snapped back a second time. This time, however, the nasty little end of a crossbow pistol pointed out.

"Right! I told you to leg it! If you don't bugger off, I'll..."

There was something in those eyes, though. Something in the pale blue depths, which seemed to explode and detonate, rushing up from within with all the urgency of a runaway stagecoach on fire. The publican burbled to a stop.

"You see," said Tarrence Bligh, as his shadow began to grow, looming up the front wall of the pub, "I *told* you I was getting sober. You wouldn't *like* me when I'm sober..."

In another establishment – the self same Black Hibiscus which we've visited before – a young lady was busy drinking. She sat and drank with the kind of cold, detached professionalism that an undead accountant would bring to a great big pile of ledgers. Because she was young, and pretty, in a sharp-edged, dangerous kind of way, she'd begun the evening in merry company. She was alone, now, with a group of unconscious, snoring, drooling and bloody men slumped on the table around her.

They'd been playing the knife game[15], for money, and so of course Amberelia Chance had plenty of change to pay with.

It's just that she wasn't getting drunk. Not even a little bit. She'd toyed with the idea that the barkeep was watering down her drinks, but after buying an unopened bottle of Szerenican Amnsinthe[16], and carefully watching the blue-haired woman blowtorch off the traditional lead seal, she was pretty sure something else was going on. That, and the fact that every other person who she'd shared a glass with was now off in that mysterious realm where hangovers are manufactured. Now she was onto the novelty spirits with dangerous animals pickled in them. These, in most bars of ill repute, sit on the second-to-top shelf, just below the almost-never-touched brightly coloured sticky drinks with sad raunchy names. When you get to this stage, the party is either raging or dying, or a curious undead amalgam of both.

Amberelia looked into the eight forlorn eyes of a bright blue

---

15. The regular knife game involves trying not to stab your own fingers while chanting a traditional song. The Urzoman version involved trying to stab everyone else's, while avoiding getting stabbed yourself.

16. Amnesia in a bottle, along with several healthsome herbs and tinctures. Otherwise known as the 'sledgehammer fairy'

tarantula in its bath of tequila, sighed, and put down her glass.

Not because she didn't want to drink it – that was a foregone conclusion, once you've gotten into the things with exclamation points in their names and embalmed arthropods at the bottom. But because a man was standing behind her.

She hadn't turned around, he hadn't made any noise, and trying to spot trouble in the crust-raddled mirrors of the Black Hibiscus would be like trying the scry the future in a privy pot. Amberelia knew because she was what she was – or at least, she was what the Old Lady had decided to label her.

She didn't even bother to turn. One hand came up from the table, and a hooked dagger blurred into view between her fingers.

"You see this?" asked Amber. "It's got two numbers for you. One's the amount of seconds you've got to explain yourself. The other is the address of a very good barber-surgeon, who can stitch your bollocks back on the right way round."

"Whoa! Hey now! I don't want no trouble!" said the man, who was robed in utterly impractical, very villainous-looking black crushed velvet. He held up his hands, and no less than three small knives clattered out of his sleeves.

"Funny, they all say that," said Amber. "Yet it's all the bastards ever bring me!" She pitched her voice into a mocking falsetto, "Oh, I don't want no trouble, now that I see that it's *me* who's in danger of being entroubulated. I just wanted you to very reasonably die, or something, without being any trouble, see?"

The man shook out his sleeves, checking for more instruments of death.

"Bugger it! Look, I borrowed the robes, OK? This is not what I usually do! I'm a poisoner, not a field agent!"

Something about that voice was familiar, even though Amberelia had never seen the man outside his guildhouse chambers. The thought of him in a bar like the Black Hibiscus was like thinking of the Dark Emperor performing a striptease.

"Lurien? What are *you* doing here? Fancy a drink?"

"Has it worked for you?" he asked, slumping down to the table.

"To be honest, no. But trying is half the fun, or so they say. So *you* say, in fact. Trying ten bloody times, then getting kicked out on your arse... *that's* where the fun stops."

She poured him a generous measure of tarantula grog. Lurien fidgeted with the tumbler in both hands, but didn't drink.

"That's kind of the thing, though. They sent me after you because, well... the Old Lady said she'd give you one more chance. It was pure luck. Some poor fellow who has to be... *demortalised*, I suppose, is going to be joining up at the same time as you. She got me out of bed, or rather, those two big lads in the black armour did. Brrr! Gave me the creeps, and I poison people for a living!"

Amber rolled her eyes, and made 'come on' gestures with her dagger-holding hand. The point dipped and weaved in the candlelight.

"Ahem... well, anyhow, she said that *this* time, if you could get it right, you'd be fully accredited. Master's dagger, black robes, the whole tea party. But..."

"But I still have to join *them*," said Amber with obvious distaste. It looked very much as if the tarantula (which she plopped out of the bottle and plucked up with chopsticks) was more palatable than the thought of joining that particular guild.

"I'd phtiiir hrvv thart on mr rechud..." she managed, tucking in the last few legs with ladylike aplomb. "I mean, it looks bad on one's curriculum vitae, doesn't it? Or curriculum mortis, in our business, I suppose." She looked pointedly at Lurien's full tumbler. "You gonna drink that?"

"I can't get drunk. Built up a tolerance to every single poison under the suns. Liver like cast iron, me."

Amber grimaced.

"It's not working for me, either. But we live in hope, right? Treat yourself."

He shrugged, and knocked it back.

"Seems a shame, really. According to the bottle, it's distilled from a kind of purple cactus that only grows in the Skeleton Shoals, and which defends itself with clouds of hallucinogenic spores. That spider you just ate nests inside the cactus as a symbiote, and kills off anything that gets too close. Makes you wonder how the natives harvest it at all."

"A very long stick with a saw on the end?" suggested Amber. "Trained monkeys in adorable little gas-masks?"

"See, *professionally*, I'm wondering about how the spores control the spider. Could we devise a poison that works on humans in the same way? Makes them unthinking, mindless guards, with no compulsion except to kill?"

"You're describing most of Throne's Shadow, Lurien," said Amber. "And speaking of those ghouls, I don't meddle in politics. What's this feller who needs 'special attention' done?"

The master poisoner winced.

"We don't ask what they've *done,* girl! We're assassins, not vigilantes! Asking what they've done leads to nothing but questions of justice, hence litigation, and our whole Guild exists to circumvent that particular stench-mire."

"Correction, Lurien. *You're* an assassin. I'm apparently a bloody r..."

"*Don't say it.* I never believed it for a second, and I won't have a trainee of mine being so self-derogatory. It's bad for morale! You take this job, and you'll be an assassin, with a capital A, and you'll never have to wonder about what the customers have or haven't done again. Promise. I might even let you win at chess, for once."

Amberelia wanted to weigh it up in her mind, give it some thought, and, essentially, make Lurien squirm. But the fact was, he was already squirming. Dangling on the Old Lady's hook, barbed with the assumption that he would be very, very persuasive...

A little silence was all it took, in fact, to knock an extra morsel of information loose.

"It's just a pay job. Someone ripped off the master of Gladiators. He seems to think they used magic, but the Orders would usually be down on that like a ton of dragon shit from a great height, and so far tonight, nothing in the city has exploded."

Amber looked wistfully at that long, horrible top shelf, filled with drinks in every shade of the vomitory rainbow. She'd have to report for duty in four hours, she knew. And there was no doubt that a horrible, servile, good-girl part of her mind wanted to say yes. Just as a vast, spiky, hissing-mad part wanted to tell the Old Lady to do what it suggested on the sparkly pink bottle third from the left.

"Fine," she said. "I'll do it. But you owe me one, Master Lurien. If I ever come calling for a very special poison or two, your door had better be open."

She punctuated her sentence by slamming her dagger down through the table, right up to the hilt. *Huh! Maybe it was true. Maybe she didn't know her own strength...*

The master poisoner rolled his eyes.

"Child, there's no need for the theatrics. You'll be needing that dagger, I'd wager. Now, take this woodcut of the customer, memorise it, and burn it. You'll need to make this one look like an accident..."

Amberelia pulled the knife out of the table with a grunt. She didn't notice, however, that it hadn't just been jammed through three inches of greystump wagon-wheel and a tatty chequered tablecloth. A goodly portion of the dagger had gone right through the table and into her leg. As she pulled it loose, blood welled up for an instant, but was replaced with a sizzle of green fire. The skin knit together perfectly; she never felt a thing.

"Right you are, Lurien," she said, unfolding the piece of parchment he slid across the table, navigating around puddles of drool, liquor and blood. "This Mr Jack Somewhat is going to find that his new job has all *kinds* of health and safety deficiencies. It's really too bad."

The dawnglow was shimmering up through the edges of Mother Ocean's vast ring by the time the Black Hibiscus shut its doors. But there was one little chore left for at least one denizen of the night, before some new apprentice (yes, it was that unlucky little cockroach, Chep Palaquat) had to heave the Day Watch Lantern out along the breakwater.

High in the Malevolith, in halls which had not known the tread of any other human feet for decades, Lord Slave approached the throne room of Himself, ready to deliver some bad news.

Many others would have preferred ritual suicide, using the little hooked blade which the Sarunjek cultists of She Who Whispers carried just for this purpose. But Lord Slave felt he owed it to his old friend to speak the truth, rather than simply make Him infer it from a disembowelled corpse kneeling on His doorstep. Whatever He had become, Lord Slave still remembered, vaguely, times when they had laughed together, and fought together, and even sung campfire songs in the long dark.

He passed between the tall and skeletal Gholem with their four arms and their massive *naginata* blades. He passed through the murder-hole tunnels, where acid and molten lead bubbled overhead. He sensed the swivel and blink of living eyes mortared into statues and gargoyles, watching him approach the final doors.

It was no surprise that they sighed open at Lord Slave's approach; he knew that massive water-cisterns and counterweights hefted the tall slabs of bronze and ironwood aside. The real sorcery in the room beyond was encased in the great rusted pile of armour which sat slumped on the throne.

"Ahhh, Slave. Welcome. I have, of course, expected you these many hours..."

The hook was implicit. Behind his mask, Lord Slave swallowed, his mouth gone dry.

"It's gone missing, Your Villainy. Lost to the sea, most likely. The master of alchemists..."

He cut off His Vizier with a gesture of one great claw, its metal the colour of dried blood. His armour was built on a scale which would have you think that He has been a giant of a man, but it was long gone to corrosion, and only moved with a creaking, groaning and torturous slowness. Motifs of bats, skulls and devils had been cunningly worked into every surface.

"We have heard of your difficulties. We find it impossible to care. What We want to know, is *what you are doing about them*, Slave. Things are out of balance in Our city, and We can feel it, like toothache." The thing on the throne chuckled, a sound like bubbles escaping from a metal pipe. "Yes, We remember having teeth, Slave. Just as you likely wake up some nights and try to scratch the nose that's missing from your face."

It was true. Not only was His guess about the itch precisely accurate, it was true that Lord Slave had no nose under his mask. His lack, in that department, was part of the reason for all the leather. Some said he was lucky, considering the terrible, freezing-cold stench inside the Malevolith, like some arctic offal-pit. None said it where Lord Slave could hear, of course, or else they might be given a personal lesson in the subjectiveness of luck, amputation, and the choices thereof. Very few now alive remembered the smell, in any case.

"*Pearl divers*, Your Sinfulness. They are scouring the harbour for the corpse of Multhazar Threck. Soon the item will be in your... hands."

Lord Slave stared into the iron-crowned, empty-faced helm of the suit of armour, watching a vile green light bubble and roil down inside it. Those hands sheared their finger-blades open and shut like scissors.

"This disturbance I speak of, Slave, has nothing to do with the dead alchemist. Though I would enjoy his company for one of my little games of chess..."

Here the armoured fingers gestured to a marble chess board, all set out in mid game. Across from Himself sat a skeleton in spider-webbed mage's robes, its mouth half open in what looked like a frozen grimace of discomfort.

The figure on the throne sighed, and a soft exhalation of decay threatened to make Lord Slave's single eye water.

"Even the best ones only last two or three games before they unravel. So yes, bring me his body. But this other business..."

Now the light was climbing up the gorget and throat of the armour. Now two incorporeal eyeballs, dripping clear ectoplasm, manifested behind the slot of the helm, cruel and ancient.

"No, I sense something magical, which is yet not magic. Something the rest of this Empire's washed-out old mages could scarcely comprehend. It tastes of hot ink, and cheap paper, and sugarcane, and sunshine, and... urgh... *hope*. Worse. The pathetic hope of small children. It is *horrible*, Slave, in the extreme. We have built our empire in the image of Evil, because Evil is what men understand. This disturbance must be crushed out. It would suggest that the strong can be good, and the good can be strong. *Blasphemy.* If that were true..."

For a second, the wistful tone in His voice set up strange harmonics inside Lord Slave's skull. He saw a dim and half-forgotten face, smiling down at him, and a hand reaching out, pulling him up to the surface and out of agony...

It snapped and writhed out of his mental grasp, slippery as a dream. The cold and the stench wrapped him up, slapping him back to the here and now. *Where he didn't have a friend. Where he had a Master.*

"Tell me who to kill, and their deaths will become legendary," he rasped, kneeling.

The thing on the throne chuckled again, rust cracking away from the slits that hid its mouth.

"*Of course* they will, my Slave. Has it ever been otherwise? But that would be too simple, I fear. Instead, I'll merely tell you what to watch for."

He leaned forward, steel creaking, spiderwebs pulling taut and snapping. A few big scuttling cobs flailed away, tiny sailors in the ratlines of a sinking ship. The terrible smell fanned out, like velvet curtains steeped in manure.

"Beware of those who feel they have the right to punish others, Lord Slave. Beware of *heroes*. Because the bigger the hero, the bigger the monster who will rise to face him..."

One particular monster was in both their thoughts. Things would have ended up much, much simpler, if these had actually turned out to be the same one.

"You think this... not-magic can help us with *that* little situation, Your Duplicity?" asked Slave, with a subtle inclination of his head.

The figure on the throne leaned forward, exhaling a cloud of rancid chill. Razor-sharp metal claws pared slivers of marble away as those terrible, disembodied eyes blinked, like a double eclipse inside His helm.

"I think that everything special and unique should be used up before it's destroyed, my Slave. Wrung out to the last drop. You know of my suspicions. You know what waits for me to... become unsubtle. Do what must be done. Then end this anomaly. Subtract it. Divide it. *Extinguish* it. Do what you do best."

There were three steaming imprints left in the frost when Lord slave left, swirling away into the darkness behind his huge fur cape. Places where he'd knelt, and pressed one fist against the cobbles. The knee-prints obscured the name on a tombstone that had been set into the floor; one that the man who would one day become Lord Slave had bought, while drunk, as a grim joke during their adventuring days.

So much had been forgotten. But other things just grew longer, more serrated shadows as the lamp of life grew dim with years...

Lord Slave, for his part, was thinking about Jack Somewhat. An idiot who'd been slotted into the only peg-hole that fit him, next to another square peg who'd been treading water for decades. Someone who was just about to become useful again, if His intimations were to be believed. Was it coincidence that the young fool was in the wrong place at the wrong time?

Perhaps.

But then again, being doomed was not a yes-or-no proposition. Doom had its own rainbow, every stripe of it black. The Somewhat boy had only just dipped his toe in the pot at the end of it, and suffice to say, it wasn't smelling very fragrant.

For just a heartbeat, Lord Slave felt some reservations about what he was about to do. Then the thought was blown away.

He couldn't remember the name of the man who he had once been. But he knew very, *very* well the name he went by now. Under the blank side of his mask, a phantom eyeball much like his master's twitched in its ruined socket. It was branded with the Urzoman symbol 'Zahash'. Literally – 'one who is bound in thrall until death'. There was no eyelid. He saw it sleeping and waking.

He found it was a wonderful aid to memory.

8

The Dauntlessness Quandary

THE LESS SAID about Jack Somewhat's hangover the better.

It was all the worse for not having been caused by drink, and it had the curious effect of making it feel as though his teeth had been welded in upside-down and coated with velvet. It was so bad that he'd even considered trying to rub the lint off one of Soto's infamous wake-up pills, found deep in his third best pair of trousers.

But that was nothing – *nothing* – compared to the prospect of starting out from the bottom of another bloody guild. The lads had been adamant that there was absolutely no choice. When, sometime around that soul-searching hour before dawn, a gaggle of what appeared to be street urchins, lawyers, Creedish deacons and his erstwhile mates had dragged him out of bed, he'd been bleary-eyed and slack-jawed, unable to hear their yammerings through the acres of cotton wool hammered deep into his ears by sheer fatigue.

Now, after being fed hot Zollish coffee through a funnel, shouted at, doused in cold water and dressed up in fresh, ill-fitting clothes (courtesy of the wardrobes of Foxmallet), Jack was bleary-eyed and slack-jawed still, but he'd been deposited outside the correct address, slapped on the back of the head, and left to fend for himself.

He looked at the piece of paper in his hand again, trying desperately to make his limbs and eyeballs move without causing the sensation of vertigo. Wax seals, loops and swirls of cursive calligraphy blurred in and out of focus. It was a *very* official document. It was stamped by the Vizier himself, then countersigned by a descending demonology of hierarchical lawyers, capped off with a blotted scrawl which Jack could remember signing for himself. It had taken three other people to guide his hand, but it was real. So, this must be the place.

If an award for the worst house on the best street in Grand Sepulchre was going to be dished out (perhaps by the Guild of Estate Agents), then this place would be in the running. Wheezing, clutching at its chest, smoking a sly roll-up, but in the running.

It was a low and sloping half-timbered anachronism round the back of a fashionable row of shops in Bishopsbath, inside the old city walls (and so close to the Malevolith you could keep your milk frosty by hanging it out the window at nights). The Guild would probably call it 'a handyman's dream', if only because handymen, like the rest of us, sometimes have dreams where they are being chased through an abandoned fun-fair by a living cheeseburger.

It was dank, and thatch-roofed, and sprouting mushrooms. Its chimney was curled around in a corkscrew twist, and over the door hung a warped and mouldy sign-board.

"A Place For Heroes"

For this was the Guild Errant, a group who Jack Somewhat had not heard of until very early this morning, and who he heartily wished would all die of the pox in the next ten minutes. He sidled up to the door of their noisome den, his sphincter puckering and his gorge rising, and, screwing up what remained of his courage, he pulled the bell-chain.

The ground collapsed out from under him.

Jack caught his chin on the edge of the Guild's doormat (*"If ye were a mighty barbarian, ye wouldst be home by nowe!"*), then swooped sickeningly around a slippery tangle of tubes, screaming. It didn't help that his head clanged against the chute with every corner, pummelling his tender brain. At last, he was spit out into absolute darkness, and flailed to a stop in a pile of what he desperately hoped was mildewed hay. Several soft and squeaking somethings scattered, on little scritter-scratch claws.

Jack spun about, clambering to his feet. It was so dark that he could see absolutely nothing at all.

Unfortunately, this heightened his sense of smell. Just yesterday, he'd ploughed into a lake of excrement so fast that it had begun to boil, but this was worse. This was a smell that had been a long time maturing, and which drilled into the brain like the whine of a mosquito on a sopping-humid summer night.

Suddenly, Jack felt a hand close around his arm in the dark. He stifled a yelp, and swung wild, clobbering his invisible assailant with his fist. There was a meaty **thwack**, and the hand disappeared.

"Good! Good! They *said* you were a feisty one! Now, where did I put those matches..?"

Jack, the one-time alchemist, wanted to issue a warning about smells this bad and naked flames, but he didn't have time. Fire bloomed and guttered, illuminating a big, broad, grinning face almost hidden behind the most unruly beard Jack had ever seen. It hadn't the topiary crispness of the razor-thin little beards in fashion at court. It wasn't even the snowy waterfall of an aged wizard, or the wild chin-mane of a warrior. It was a vast, tangled thicket of a thing, festooned with random dreadlocks, gold rings, bone beads and lashings of leather. It wasn't so much grown out of the face that smiled through it... it looked more as if the man behind the beard had been fired into it from a cannon, and stuck.

"Sorry about the trap door!" twinkled the Beard, shuffling off into the gloom to light more torches. "Part of the mysterious initiation rites. You know how it is."

Jack sighed. He knew *all* about mysterious rites. As a kid, he'd often been humiliated, dunked, pelted, soaked, ridiculed or down-trousered in the name of Ancient Ritual.

"Sorry for punching you in the face, I suppose," said Jack, who had definitely done so. The crinkly, wire-wool feeling of his knuckles sinking into that beard was indelible.

"Ahhh, it's good that you did! The first ritual of the initiation is to test your fighting spirit! It's called the Eye of Trismegiston!"

"You mean there's a *name* for the part where you drop someone down a trap door and expect them to assault you?"

"Oh yes!" enthused the Beard. "No use heroing if you can't come up swinging after falling down a simple level-one trapdoor. Now, onto the next test – The Scouring of Amoshemothep!"

Before he had a chance to move, the bearded man – who was actually quite large, even to Jack – closed the distance, did something clever with his footwork, and struck the young lad a massive slap across the cheek. Purple sparks popped inside Jack's head, but the voice, which had been silent all morning, had nothing to say about this. So he spun around, took aim, and landed another punch square in his tormentor's chops.

It was like punching a scratchy hessian bag full of bricks.

"Great! You passed that one too!" The mouth behind the beard was grinning, as if it hadn't just been clobbered with a horrible big Jack-sized fist. "And now, the third ritual, Crossing the Wasteland..."

Jack held up one finger.

"Hang about. How many of these ancient rituals of the initiation are there?"

The bearded man pursed his lips in thought.

"Twenty-three, all told. The All-Knowing Obelisk, the Riddle of the Old Ones, Braving the Tempest, the Leap of Fortitude..."

"Do they all involve seeing if, after some kind of minor annoyance, I'll punch you in the face again?"

"Well, broadly speaking, in a non-mystical context... yes."

"Can I ask why?"

A set of eyebrows, welded strategically to outlying regions of the Beard, waggled significantly.

"Oho! A thinker, eh? Well, yes, that's one way of completing the tests. Bodes well for heroes who want to solve mysteries, but you don't look the type. The *idea* is for you to have a good old go at me, and for me to demonstrate my masterful fighting abilities, thus establishing the dynamic of master and apprentice right away."

Jack thought back to how he'd launched the much bigger, much meaner Mandak McGurk halfway through a wall with a single punch, just yesterday. He smiled.

"I could give that a try," he said.

"Capital!" beamed the Beard. "Just so we're doing this right, I'm Ranulf the Butcher, by the way. Tenth generation barbarian, forty years in the fur undies and horned helmet, all that."

"What happens if I win?"

Ranulf shrugged.

"I guess *you* teach *me* how to be a questing hero, then. The old guild ain't what it was. You'd be in charge of the whole thing."

"The whole *thing?*" asked Jack, limbering up his punching arm. "That would be about how many of your so-called heroes?"

He pulled back his fist, trying to think grim, muscular thoughts. Ranulf just stood there with his arms outstretched, like he was going to give Jack a big uncomfortable hug. Power fizzed and popped as he let loose a wild right, his arm inflating like a sack of footballs...

And the old barbarian wasn't there. Instead, a knee came up into Jack's fruits with the force of an executioner's axe, and a pair of arms wrapped around his neck, throwing him up and over to hit the wall upside down. He squelched down the slimy stones to land on his head, dazed.

"Fancy another go? The answer would be, basically, you, me, and one other recruit who hasn't turned up yet, by the way. Come on! I thought you said you wanted a *fight!*"

This time the voice was awake as Jack charged into battle, swinging left and right as his muscles swelled up to heroic proportions.

"What exactly are we fighting now? I must have dozed off there... uuurgh, the amount of lead in this city's plumbing..."

"This woolly old bugger wants to be our mentor," said Jack, in the echo-chamber of his thoughts. "If we can beat him, we won't have to bother with Guild nonsense ever again!"

This looked like an outside chance, as Ranulf the Butcher was unspeakably quick for all his bulk. He ducked and sidestepped Jack's blows, keeping just out of reach.

"Is he actually a villain, though?" asked the voice. **"Kind of an important distinction..."**

"He wants to be punched in the face! He has all kinds of excuses!"

"Being mad isn't necessarily the same as being *evil*, though. Does he go around stealing things? Cackling about world domination? Hiring armies of identically-uniformed henchmen?"

Jack actually felt Ranulf's counterblows, even with liquid green lightning pumping in his veins. The man seemed to be carved from teak, and his grin never faltered, even when he was forced to roll backwards over a barrel to escape Jack's scything high-kick.

"Well... not as such..." admitted Jack to the voice in his head. "He claims to be a *hero*, actually!"

Jack caught a brief burst of second-hand clarity and understanding, as the voice made up its mind.

"Oh, then this is *easy*. Fighting him's not heroic at all! It's just a silly misunderstanding."

Comprehension dawned, just in time for Jack's final strike to land with all the power of a dropped dishrag. Ranulf looked down at Jack's fist (where it had demonstrably failed to punch clean through his chest) sighed, and did something fast, painful and physics-based which catapulted the ex-alchemist across the room, where he landed upside down in a pile of rotten hay.

"How... how did you *do* that?" he croaked, feeling the outlines of a massive bruise already forming across most of his back.

"Level 40 barbarian heroing, that's how. Well, we used to keep track of levels and things. Put it down to experience, lad. I've wrestled with monsters like trolls, and ogres, and dragons, so a bit of a punch-up..."

"But – those things are all *mythical!*"

Ranulf looked a little crestfallen at that, as though someone had reminded him that his dog had been run over by a night-soil cart.

"*Endangered*, is how they put it, toward the end. Seems like the less heroes there were, the less monsters we had to deal with, until one day, it was just me, all alone in this basement. But you're good hearty material, lad. Strong enough, for sure. 'Mighty of thew', as the old books would have it. Slower than a game of poker with a senile sloth, mind, but *strong*."

Just then, a sound like a fart through an alpenhorn belted out through the cellar. Ranulf skipped lightly over to a panel on the wall, and pulled a series of levers. Hoods dropped over the torches, plunging the place into darkness, while the Mentor of Heroes peered through a pipe that had dropped from the ceiling.

"Stay where you are, and stay quiet!" he hissed through his beard. "It's the other one! Ooooh, it's so good that Himself is finally getting the old Guild back up and running again!"

Jack had only just managed to get himself turned the right way up, and the rotten straw from out of his mouth, when he heard a now-familiar clunk, whoosh and scream. Someone else had just fallen through the trap door, which meant, any second now...

There was a series of sharp, muffled noises, and no less than three tinkling, metallic sounds off to Jack's left and right. Then a whistle, and a reverberation like a tuning fork struck just next to his ear.

"Exceptional! I see you've been practising on your own time!" said Ranulf, before a whoosh and a meaty thud indicated that he'd just thrown someone fresh across the room. "But knives aren't until textbook three. Now, those bloody matches have gone missing again..."

This time, the torchlight illuminated not just Ranulf's big beardy face, but also a four-inch dagger, still vibrating gently in a wooden joist an inch form Jack's ear. That, and a girl dressed in a ragged grey cloak and hood, pointing what appeared to be a lobster at their host.

"Say hello to my little friend," said the girl, as the brightly-coloured creature on her forearm clicked and bubbled. "His names Skrx, and he's a Rainbow Mantis Shrimp[17]. That means he'll put a poison dart

---

17. The Old Earth Mantis shrimp was able to punch its undersea prey with a pair of bony 'clubs' on its forearms, generating 1200 Newtons of impact trauma as they accelerated at over 10,000g, so fast that the water around them boiled. They had the most advanced visual system in the entire animal kingdom, able to see infra-red, ultraviolet, and apprehend colours with 16 kinds of visual receptors, compared to the human being's pitiful three. Such creatures must have been brought to the Arch' during the diasporic age, and bred or deliberately altered into the semi-amphibious, relatively intelligent crustaceans employed by the Guild Lachrymose, and, it's said, certain Wizards of the Order of the Secret Flame. The Mantisbow is a double-action weapon – first the shrimp punches to charge a clockwork mechanism, loading the bolt

through the first one of you that looks at me funny."

Jack raised a hand, very tentatively.

"Ummm, excuse me miss, but I'm a bit frightened *not* to look at you, in case you do something I have to get out of the way from. What's your definition of funny?"

Ranulf was, if anything, even happier to have a mantisbow pointed at him than he was to be punched in the face.

"That's an *assassin's* weapon! Where did 'y get it from?"

"If you have to know," said the girl, "I was kicked out of their apprenticeship program, and I stole it. *Him.* He's a very good little shrimp, and I couldn't just leave him to get all lonely, back there in his aquarium."

"I suppose the poison is viper's venom? Spinebark? Weeping deathcap?"

She nodded. "A bit of each. Who taught you your poisons?"

Ranulf chuckled.

"Go ahead and shoot then, lass. I wouldn't want to hurt your aquatic little friend there, but I learned those particular poisons by being bitten by vipers, stabbed by mad acolytes and tenderised by traps in ancient temples. The bolt would sting a bit, but by the time you could reload, we'd be in a situation where we were all sadder, wiser, and had sushi for lunch."

Amber – for such it definitely was – considered her mission here, her hopes of earning her diploma if she broke the very strict rules, and the fact that the bearded bastard was actually *smiling*. She gave a little whistle, and Skrx disengaged the bow mechanism, letting its internal clockwork wind down. He clattered away up her arm and disappeared into her backpack. This seemed to be all the invitation Ranulf needed to stomp over and wrap her in a huge, hairy embrace.

"Welcome! Thrice welcome, to the Guild Errant, and the training *bozo*[18] of Ranulf the Butcher! What a day for Heroism! Not only this

---

and tensioning a pair of springs. The second punch combines that mechanical force with the speed and accuracy of the shrimp itself, which can make tiny alterations to its master's aim in dynamic combat situations, even having the ability to 'fire at will' in conditions of darkness.

18. While more serious (and less deadly) masters of the martial arts train in a dojo, the adherents of the secret Chungdojin sect of the Wu Hu Comedy Monks practice their grim Pun-Fu, Slapstick Fighting and Stooge-Do in a many-chambered training hall known as the *bozo*, after the learned master who invented the razor-sharp custard throwing pie. The arts of the Wu Hu are so lethal that practitioners are only allowed to engage the most sage, skilled and knowledgeable opponents with honour. Hence the

big lad over in the corner, who I must introduce as Jack Somewhat..."
He bowed, causing Jack to consider that he hadn't received such
courtesy. "But now *you* as well. A genuine, actual Rogue!"

Amber winced.

"Amberelia Chance, at your service," she managed. "And I was
trying not to think about that word," she said, pushing gently clear of
the enthusiastic barbarian. "Heroing, I can stomach. But the R-word
means you're half thief, and I don't want anything to do with those
smelly bastards."

Ranulf tutted as he pottered about the cellar, re-lighting his torches.

"A common misconception, young lady. But suffice to say, the pair
of you could be quite complimentary. As in, he's strong as an ox, but
slow as a damp weekend, and you're accurate and slightly quicker, but
weaker than a spider's fart."

Both of them bristled as the lights came on.

"Hey now!"

"What gives you the..?"

Ranulf cut them off with a gesture.

"Just the truth, children. I've done a lot of this. Well, back in the
days, perhaps, *some*. And there's no use lying to each other about how
bloody mighty we are, when this is the beginning of a very, very long
training program."

Well, neither of them liked the sound of that much, but neither of
them were listening terribly hard, either.

Because Amber was taking a long, cool look at Jack, comparing him
to the crude woodcut she'd been slipped in the Black Hibiscus last
night. He didn't look like the kind of cove who'd come out on top of a
thirty-man bare-knuckle brawl. He didn't, in fact, look like the kind of
person who'd even volunteer to enter one. Sure, he was big, and young
– *very* young – but cheating, gambling and scrapping for money?
He looked more like a naughty schoolboy than a hardened criminal.
Especially with that stupid haircut, and those watery blue eyes...

Jack, on the other hand, hadn't moved by what seemed like a single
atom. Not since Amberelia Chance had dropped her ragged grey
hood, revealing a cascade of straight black hair, shimmering like the
reflection of the night sky in Mother Ocean. Her face blurred into
view in what seemed like a halo of smashed diamond reflections; a
wry little smile on her lips, that absurdly cute button of a nose, the way

---

Wu Hu ritual challenge: "So, you think you are a wise guy, do you?"

her eyes seemed to be staring right through his head, plastering the smoking remains of his brain to the wall behind him...

Jack tried to swallow, but his tongue seemed to have swollen up and dried out, like an entire mattress jammed in behind his teeth. This was probably a good thing, as the limit of his cerebral function, at that moment, was 'blurble'.

"Oh dear," said the voice, riding pillion inside his buzzing skull. "The data said this was likely to happen. How very complicating!"

Ranulf just kept on talking as though he'd seen none of it, which, in a very real way, he hadn't.

"Oh yes! We've got a lot of work to do before you two can claim to be heroes, let alone mighty ones. Somewhere around here I've got a stack of wooden dummies that need assembling, and a weight bench, and some throwing-axe targets. We're going to have so much fun! I mean, there'll still be the sausages to make, and all the steak and kidney pie fillings to get out by next Maidensday, but with you two helping..."

"Wait a second! What sausages?" asked Amber, slightly quicker on the uptake than Jack. "The Old La... I mean, the *brochure* didn't say anything about sausages. When I, you know, looked into this whole heroing business."

Ranulf looked pleased.

"You mean the brochure I've been hand-copying out for the last three years, and posting up in all the youth hostels and pubs? *'Be alle thou canst be! Pillage exotic landes, meete excyting people, then fmite them!'* Some of my best work, other than the number three pork, cracked pepper and applesauce."

The two uncomprehending stares levelled back at him made Ranulf switch gears amid the clockwork siege-engine workings in his head.

"It's not just a heroic name, you see. Ranulf the Butcher. I'm an *actual butcher.* The shop round the front is my... how d'y pronounce it... *boo-teek booshe-err-ree.* Por las provizzyon of victuals most, well, most expensive, really."

Ranulf's Clourvonnaise accent was stronger and less palatable than the cheeses of that self-same nation[19].

"An actual butcher? But I thought, with the heroing, and the pillaging, and all that..."

"Unfortunately, Jack me lad, one must pay one's bills, and all.

---

19. Such as the infamous ultraviolet-veined hextuple cream Chateau Cri-Degoute, which has a smell that assaults your nose several years before you actually even see the cheese itself, causing recurring nightmares until such time as you finally eat it.

Chopping up all kinds of exotic creatures gave me a certain lack of squeamishness, which is good for boiling the tripes, and a thorough knowledge of anatomy. So it'll be four hours on, down here, and four hours up top, making sure we have a Guildhouse over our heads. Of course, I might be able to farm some work out to Signore Zafarello and his sons, if this hero business really picks up again. Plundering the jewelled thrones of empires long forgotten is pretty profitable, once you pick the first throne clean. But a good chorizo is its own reward!"

"Would it matter if I told you I was a vegetarian?" croaked Amber, envisaging cauldrons of boiling tripe. Jack goggled.

"Wait... you were going to be a vegetarian *assassin?*"

She fixed Jack with a 'certain look', the likes of which he'd have paid more heed to, if he hadn't been raised almost exclusively by men wearing dresses who were saddled with vows of chastity.

"It's not like I was going to serve up my dear departed customers with horseradish and a nice pinot gris," she replied. "And anyway, they must have *done* something, if someone wanted them dead. A cow, what's *it* ever done?"

"Guilty of being delicious," said Ranulf, rubbing his hands together. "But don't fret! If you don't have the stomach for... well, the *stomachs*, and all, I do need someone to do the books. I know you trainee assassins can count, on account of the getting paid."

Amber rolled her eyes. *Making it look like an accident already looked like an accident waiting to happen. Butcher's shops had all kinds of sharp, nasty, spiky, bladed bits in them. If Jack Somewhat fell into a sausage grinder, it might actually improve his IQ. The output would have a lot of pork in it, after all, and pigs were supposed to be fairly smart.*

Ranulf was still bustling amid the further reaches of the cellar, obviously as happy as he'd been in years.

"It was *so* good of the government to let us start hiring again. You don't know how it's been. I mean, this heroing thing is the only game I know. Dad was a barbarian hero, granddad was a barbarian hero... even granny was a half-elf sorceress, and uncle Gurnwald was a pretty good cleric when it came to smiting things with a big gold hammer. I thought the day for that kind of action had passed, but you youngsters do my heart a world of good."

Jack and Amber shared a slightly apprehensive look. Some kind of wire-thin, wobbly little edge to the Butcher's voice made it apparent that his love of heroing was a bit too single minded.

"There's ummm... no *Mrs* the Butcher then, is there?" asked Amberelia, tentatively.

"Where does the time go?" replied the big-bearded brawler, popping up from behind a wall of packing crates with an armful of weapons and a rubber skeleton. "Oh, there were one or two temple maidens, and of course, Alectra the Archeress back in the days, but you know. Heroing's about all I really do. That, and a mean venison salami. You could say it's a bit of an obsession."

Jack had seen how Jory Foxmallet's dad (a man with so much money he barely even had to look at a single copper spothin[20]) felt about his model sea battles. A huge part of the Red House's basement had been flooded so that Lord Foxmallet could sit waist-deep in a tiny version of Mother Ocean, conducting engagements between quinqueremes and galleons he'd built out of matchwood. That was the look in Ranulf's eyes when he talked about his calling. It was slightly worrying, like a door-to-door salesman finishing his pitch by buying all his own merchandise, and telling you that you couldn't have any.

It could all have become quite awkward, then, except that something worse happened. For the second time that morning, Jack clapped his hands over his ears, as a sound like trumpeting flatulence filled the cellar.

"Lights out!" enthused Ranulf. "Three in one day! Cor, that's one for the books!"

Then came the sound of a body banging and clattering down through the trapdoor. Then came a muffled yelp in the dark, and a snap-flash of lightning, and no less than three whipcrack-fast slapping sounds.

"Aroint, sirrah!" said a nasal, aristocratic voice. It was a voice with not just a plum in it, but a selection of fruits pickled in cognac.

"Blimey!" said Ranulf. "I think one of my fillings has come loose!"

Light flared, orange and sooty, and both Amber and Jack beheld a young man in a huge, powdered wig which seemed to contain an entire gold carriage clock. His coat was crusted solid with lace and gold leaf, his buttons were jewels, and his shoes were platformed, candy-striped monstrosities with white spats and pearl-studded silk gaiters. He was holding a smoking glove in one hand, and a ribboned walking stick in the other.

---

20. It's true. The richer you are, the less you actually have to have to do with real money. Does the King or Queen of *your* country, for example, ever have to have a rummage under the sofa cushions before they go down to the corner shop to buy a sausage roll?

"Apologies, my good man, for the slappings," he said. "But in the dark and all, I fancied I was being molested! I trust this *is*, in fact, the Guild Errant, and not some den of knaves?"

Jack, who had often been accused of knavery, and who associated it with drinking, making dirty jokes, and singing bawdy songs about milkmaids, didn't really know how to proceed. But Ranulf the Butcher, (who now sported a red handprint across the part of his face not obscured by beard) seemed ecstatic.

"Now that was *speed!* Pure, gold-edged, 100-carat dexterity! Where did you learn to do that, son?"

The gent tucked his gloves away and feigned a little yawn.

"It's really most tedious. I've been getting faster and faster with the hour, it seems, after eating a very nice seafood kedgeree yesterday morning. My natural philosophical investigations having come to naught, I've given in to a whim I fancied, to do a spot of heroism." He extended a pale hand, with more rings on it that even Zoltan Creagle had managed. "Montmortimer Pettigrew, at your service. I believe I may be the world's fastest fop."

9
The Subterranean Altercation

So, while Jack Somewhat's friends got drunk and toasted his success as a barbarian hero-to-be, and while Lord Slave supervised a gang of pearl divers from atop a tar-caked black barge out past the Stilts, training happened.

There's little doubt that you've seen this kind of thing before, no matter where in the wide and watery Archipelago you hail from. War, that ever-hungry monster we glorify with saga and song, requires young men to march willingly into its crimson jaws. So, societies as diverse as the Thamari and the Zollish have established ways of tempering both the body and the mind for hackmeat-hero's work. Quite a bit of it involves peeling potatoes and polishing boots, though those two skills will not see you very far on the actual battlefield.

Ranulf the Butcher knew this well. His training regime (which he'd often considered writing up in a neat little guidebook and selling to impressionable youths) was heavy on the talk of honour and valour, short on the shoeshine, and big on muscle development and smashing things.

Amber, Jack and Montmortimer Pettigrew were put to the test against an array of straw men, wooden posts, expired melons, painted targets and heavy weights. Due to the peculiar nature of the Heroing they were meant to undertake, there was much talk about secret traps, blow-darts hidden in statues, bladed pendulums, scorpion pits and puzzles involving jumping between flagstones as well.

It was hot and thirsty work, down there in the huge cellars of the Guild Errant, which Jack soon comprehended as being ten times bigger than the butcher's shop above. In fact, so many of the rooms and chambers featured moss-crusted, dripping carvings and realistic replicas of ancient booby-traps that he was fairly certain that it had once *actually been* a subterranean temple. Part of the cellar was ice-cold, where it burrowed close to the roots of the Malevolith, and there,

Ranulf kept several large barrels of ale. This was dished out in plentiful supply when the trio took a break, but it absolutely failed to get Jack drunk. However, the tedium of sober, repetitive practice *did* give him a chance to interrogate the voice in his head.

He waited until he was alone, of course, because there *is* such a thing as not wanting to look like a raving lunatic.

"Right! Don't pretend you're not in there, because I know you are. I want some explanations."

As he spoke, Jack's fist slammed into one of the outstretched planks which jutted from an entire tree-trunk in what Ranulf called the Chamber of Wooden Soldiers. The great log spun, bringing another plank around to slap him in the kidneys. Meanwhile, hidden gears rotated a second log, lashing at his head with a padded ball on a chain.

"What's to explain?" said the voice. **"You're doing amazingly well. Did you see the smile on that man's... well, through his beard? Now that we're doing proper hero practice, I can predict a bright future for us both."**

"That's just it," puffed Jack, blocking the ball and snapping off a jab as the board. Gears clattered. Sundry other baulks of timber attempted to batter his teeth in. "Why is there such a thing as 'us both'? I was perfectly happy being alone in my head, thank you very much."

"No, you weren't," said the voice. **"I can read your memories, you know. You secretly wanted more out of life than carrying a big bloody lantern and scrubbing privy seats. Which is why I'm glad, if I couldn't serve the master I was supposed to, that I chose you."**

Jack blocked a wooden axe-head, ducked low under a whistling timber fist, and executed a high kick that bent an entire log backwards. Images assailed him of the voice sifting through his more sordid memories, like the pages of some sailor's crusted-up pornographic periodical.

"That's what I mean. Who *were* you meant to serve? Why do you want to be involved with hero nonsense? And what about the other two? Can they hear you as well?"

It should have been quite impossible for an invisible voice to look sheepish, but this one managed.

"I... umm... sort of lost my mission parameters, somewhere out there in space. I was a rod of programmable exotic matter, both the brain and the engine for a kind of... ship, you'd call it. A 'star ship'. And on board, see, was this little baby..."

Jack heard about the long, boring flight of several thousand years which had seen the pod crash land on the Arch'. He heard about the cosmic storm which had wiped the pod's memory, and how it had searched through all the weird signals and strange wavelengths of the universe to find out what it was supposed to do in its interesting and quite complicated situation.

"Turns out there's a bit of an archetype for this kind of thing. So *you* have to grow up big and strong, inherit all my powers, and fight crime. No two ways about it. The others – well, there might have been some overspill during the transfer process. These two, the girl and the fellow wearing a ton of horsehair on his head, they got a little bit of it too, but not enough to talk to me. You're really all I've got, kid."

He let that little bit of heart-string-plucking wistfulness go by.

"So, you're not a demon, I'm not mad, and I'm not possessed," said Jack, who didn't know if the voice's outlandish explanation had really been an explanation at all. "Still, I don't think this idea about fighting crime is going to work out. Ranulf here's getting us ready to fight *monsters*, which are pretty nasty, but not what you'd call criminal."

"Do you get a lot of them around here? Rampaging, crushing the city, kind of thing?"

"I've never really seen one," shrugged Jack, timing his shrug perfectly between twin blurs of tempered pine. He splintered two assailing planks, left and right, breathing in sawdust. "But crime, yes, alright... it's just that the thieves guild and the assassins guild won't like that."

"And they do *what*, exactly?"

"Well, steal things and murder people, of course. But it's part of the government. Sort of. There's taxes. It's complicated."

"Well, *that* doesn't sound too heroic! Why does the government put up with it?"

"Because the government is a huge skeletal wizard in a suit of armour, basically," replied Jack, coming to the end of the ranks of wooden soldiers. With a last wobble and click, the final timber assailant swatted feebly at him with a club. Jack snapped it off clean. "Look, about the other day... I'm sorry I tricked you, right? The lads put me up to it. But you have to tone down this crime-fighting thing, or we'll *both* be in trouble. Just promise that if we *do* end up fighting a monster, you won't have a hissy fit and turn off my powers. I don't fancy being something's lunch..."

"A *hissy fit*? Young man, I..."

"You know what I mean. And, if we're going to have a reasonable dialogue, I have to be able to call you something. If you're living in my head, getting mud on the carpets and all, I'd like to know your name."

The voice seemed to sulk for a moment – or maybe it was simply thinking.

"Alright. You've still got plenty to learn that this Ranulf fellow can't teach you, though. So you can call me Rodney, seeing as I was stuck in the form of a power rod for the past few millennia. And we'll talk about your other powers when you've done training with him."

That sounded ominous. That sounded, in fact, like more attempts to fly, which Jack would rather leave for another eight decades or so, at least until senile dementia made sure he didn't know he was doing it. But there was no time to mull over what the voice had said, because here came Ranulf, grinning for ear to ear (or at least, those locations in his facial thicket where ears were supposed to be), and carrying a huge mug of beer.

"You three are *astounding!* I mean, if I could package all of your abilities in one person, then we'd have a ready-made hero right there. But whatever your mums have been feeding you, it's done the trick. The young lady with the pet lobster made such a mess of the straw dummies that there's not enough left to feed a guinea pig, and the fella with the make-up on has already passed through the hall of the whirling knives, the corridor of the three nasty surprises *and* the fireball gallery without so much as breaking a sweat! I reckon, after we finish up upstairs, we should go on Patrol. Unless you think that's too..."

Jack, by this point, would have eaten his own toes to see the outside of Ranulf's dungeon.

"No! Nonono! I'm keen as mustard to get out there and... ummm... spread the butter of justice on the toast we call this fair city!"

Ranulf looked at him with a squint.

"That's funny. Both of the others said something absurdly similar, with the same weird poetic turn of phrase. The one with the wig said something about Grand Sepulchre being like a woman! Tell you what lad, if you ever meet a woman who smells like this town, run the other way, fast!" Then he slapped his meaty hands together, and rubbed them as if he was trying to start a fire. "Patrol! Ahh, just the word brings back great memories! Splattered kobolds! The smell of orc guts in the morning! Lovely days!"

Which really raised more questions about the nature of Patrol than it answered. But Jack had other things to contend with before then...

Like a crash-course in bacon slicing, while Montmortimer served at the front counter, Ranulf hacked several frozen carcasses apart with a giant cleaver, and Amber tackled the butcher-shop's ledgers, a vast and musty column of books wrapped in cobwebs and greased paper.

Ranulf really did run a very up-market little gourmet establishment, and it really was full of sharp, spiky and dangerous bits. The under-butlers, cook's assistants, pantry lads, and even one or two persons of nobility who came through the door exchanged a few quiet words with the old barbarian, and left carrying paper parcels which would, in the fullness of time, become gourmet dinners.

Once, while Jack was paring prosciutto with the spinning razor of the meat slicer, Amber gave him a desultory nudge, just to see what happened. He put his hand out to keep from falling into the machine, his fingers gripping the sharp edge of the wheel with a whine of sparks... but there was no blood. *He didn't even notice.*

In the spirit of assassination, she tried a similar experiment while he was manufacturing a series of frankly rude-looking deformed sausages (that only a tabloid's joke page could love). But the big, spiked tenderiser that fell from its hook above him failed to bash his skull in like an eggshell, and *also* failed to send him face-first into the funnel of the sausage grinder.

"Oops! Can't be Mr Clumsy with things like that lying around!" he'd said, favouring her with a wobbly grin. "Better get a new hook for it, before someone gets hurt."

Amber had bit her finger with quiet outrage and decided to bide her time. There was something funny about this one. *Perhaps the Old Lady had set her up.* Perhaps there was more to Ranulf's silly training regime (that had seen her lifting boulders and chasing chickens all morning) than 'twould appear to the untrained eye.

Perhaps she was just going mad from the mangled mathematics of Ranulf's book-keeping. If she were him, she'd be more worried about Lord Slave's tax department than supernatural horrors!

A bit of time-biding and whole lot of creative arithmetic later, the Peacock Bells went chiming out over the city, from their tall slim tower atop the palace of the Guild Lachrymose. Amber felt a pang of homesickness, hearing them echo from so far away. Ranulf gathered his three students together, after closing the butcher's-shop door, and disabused them of the notion that they'd be getting a siesta this afternoon.

"This first patrol is crucial," he said, pulling down a chart from a hidden alcove in the ceiling and whacking it with a pointer. The chart proved to be the many delicious joints and cuts available from the common pig. He rolled it up again and pulled down the right one – a map of the underside of Grand Sepulchre.

"Monsters, the undead, various skulking, stabby varieties of nasty eldritch folk – they all like to live underground. Like the humble ant, they are compelled to burrow and hoard, so there's plenty of mysterious chests, bags, barrels and loot crates in any given dungeon labyrinth, even for a party as woefully level-one as you three. We could encounter anything from skeletons to orcs, so keep close behind me, keep your eyes open, and hold onto your weapons."

Amber, who'd heard this kind of speech before, just smirked. But Ranulf had something tucked away under the counter for Monty and Jack.

"For you, Montmortimer, a set of steels which will play to your strength, which is *not*, by the way, strength. Zalois fencing swords, long and short, the most dexterous way to poke holes in your foe, fast. And for Jack..." Ranulf heaved with all his might, eliciting a rasping sound from under the bench. He emerged holding a double-edged sword the size of an ironing board, its immense flats etched with skulls and lightning bolts. "One from back in the old days. Proper troll-cleaver, that. I reckon you've got the strength to wield it, at least two-handed for a start. We'll get you onto a shield as well, as the training progresses. Miss Amberelia, you already have just what you need. So, all that remains is for me to find my axe, and we're off on Patrol!"

Monty gave his pair of swords a practice swish through the air.

"Can we have a little time to make our weapons look fabulous? Some emeralds on these hilts, a bit of gold on the basketwork, perhaps some ribbons for the scabbards..."

Amber held up one hand.

"We're going to patrol the under-tunnels? The old sewers, and all that? I can tell you from experience, there's no monsters there. I've checked."

Ranulf leaned forward, pointing to his face.

"You see this scar? Well? OK, it's a bit covered in beard, but it's a bloody good one. Got that the very last time I went down there, from an ogre berserker with a nail-studded club. Nearly caught me death of tetanus. So don't you be telling me what is and isn't under this city, young lady!"

What he *didn't* say – and a worry that was gnawing at his secret heart – was that that last time had been twenty years ago. Before the Emperor, (He Himself) had retreated into the Malevolith, and wound up the Guild Errant in all but name. But second thoughts were not really the thing for barbarian heroes. First ones rarely even came into it. Considering *why* you were leaping onto the back of a dragon while wearing nothing but a codpiece and some strategic sword-straps was a huge impediment to actually getting the job done, not least because stopping to think gave the monsters pause to snack.

"Just meet me in the basement in ten and be prepared. Old Ranulf the Butcher knows what he's doing!"

Twenty minutes later, they were quite lost.

It seemed that a period of two decades had been enough for a combination of municipal works, gangland skirmishes, re-drawn underworld borders and seismic occurrences to re-write the map of Grand Sepulchre's intestines. Ranulf tried to bluff through it with a grin and a wave of one gauntlet-clad hand, but pretty soon they'd passed the same suggestive-looking stalagmite three times, and not even the whiff of a monster had been detected.

"I say," ventured Monty. "Doesn't that rock formation look a bit like someone's…"

"Cock and bull story if ever I heard one…" muttered Amber, "*Oooh, we're not lost!* Then why is this the third time I've seen that massive stone…"

"Boner! That's what the shop could use!" mused Jack, far away in a reverie that didn't involve smacking his head into the roof of the tunnel every five steps. "A device for taking all the ribs out of roasts, and such. *Hang on.* Haven't we already seen that sticky-up bit that resembles someone's…"

"Privates! Fall in and listen to your commanding officer!"

Ranulf mopped his forehead with a chain-mail handkerchief, and sat down on one of the humorously round boulders which sat at the base of the stalagmite. "It's come to my attention that I may have taken a wrong turn somewhere back there. Hence the lack of monsters, and all. Do any of you have any notion of where we are?"

Jack, Monty and Amber peered into the humid mists on all sides, down the radial spokes of several identical red-marble corridors intersecting this cave. Hot vapour swirled and eddied, concealing everything in a cloak of grey. Ranulf frowned.

"The thing that gets me, right, is that even the *sewers* used to be crawling with beasts of one kind or another. Noble families would get a baby chimera or predivore for Baron's Tuesday or Carnival Muerto, then flush it down the privy when it got too big for its litter box. Let me tell you, fighting a thing with three heads and a snake for a tail that's been surviving on sewer alligators – that's no sport for the faint hearted!"

Amber reached up past his face and brushed some dust away from the big stone phallus. There was something carved there, and it didn't look like a predictable dirty joke.

"*Real estate*," she said, stepping up on tiptoes to read the inscription. "These tunnels vent out into the harbour all over, and there's smugglers who would kill for a way to bring untaxed rum, tobacco and dreamsugar into Grand Sepulchre. Quite often they do, in fact. Look here. Shark jaws, with the number 22. Your magical monsters have been driven down deep, Ranulf, and replaced by human ones."

"Excuse me for being a stickler," said Monty, "But as a natural philosopher, I have discovered that the common shark can only survive in salt water. Indeed, it has to keep swimming forward in order to..."

Jack, who was just a sliver more streetwise, cut him off.

"*The Hammerheads*. Dreamsugar mob. They own most of the Old Town and the docks. I'd heard they'd got rich enough to call out a contract on Danjo the Hook and his boys, but nothing ever came of it."

Amber blushed scarlet in the dark, suddenly very glad for the hood which came with her Rogue's costume. Which somewhat put her off-guard when a sardonic, slow round of applause came echoing out of one of the tunnel mouths.

"Very good, youngsters. Very good indeed. You've solved the mystery of who cleared out these very lovely tunnels and put them to good use. Thing is, there's a bigger mystery afoot, as the Knock-men would put it." A definite snicker and leer entered the phantom voice, alongside the sound of an oiled blade slipping from its scabbard. "*What ever happened to your dead bodies?*"

Now the part of Amber that was still 100 percent assassin heard all kinds of sharp, sparkly little noises from all around them – the sound of people trying to remain quiet while limbering up an array of razored steel.

Horribly, embarrassingly, Ranulf strode up to the figure who swum out of the mist, smiling. He produced as he went a huge, ribboned, wax-crusted document from somewhere under his ancient armour.

"Come on now! There's no need for a fuss. We're not interested in your business, we're just getting in a bit of training. Guild errant, heroes for hire. You know - 'evil vanquished for reasonable rates...' and all that. Look, I have a pass to be down here, and all. *Exterminator Royal of Abominations*. It's got a stamp on it."

The figure cut a fine figure indeed. He was tall and heavily muscled, wearing a shark-skin suit with double rows of buttons, and with his hair pomaded up into the shape of a fin.[21] His associates – who now crowded in from all around – were similarly dressed, though with subtly less finery to the cut and quality of their attire.

"Well, that's alright then! No problem! You just go on with your 'scouting for boys' nonsense, and we'll trust you not to tell anyone about the vast, illicit smuggling empire we've got going down this part of the underside. Wink wink, nudge nudge, eh?" The man held up two fingers in a kind of miniature salute. He smiled, with a mouthful of sharpened ivory teeth.

Ranulf, whose grip on sarcasm was never the best, grinned even wider. Jack, who was halfway between mortified and fascinated, wondered if the Hammerhead knew exactly what he was tangling with. After all, the Butcher had put Jack on his arse, and that was with a spoonful of supernatural strength behind him.

"Good idea, sir! Nice to see that there's still a wide streak of pragmatism among the criminal classes. We'll just be heading on down deeper, where there's something worth fighting."

Now, even Montmortimer knew there was *everything* wrong with that sentence. First off, there was the distinct insinuation that the Hammerheads – twenty of them, now, and all armed with curved Chungdoji-style swords – weren't worth a scrap. Then there was the unfortunate use of the word 'criminal', which made the voice lately known as Rodney perk up inside Jack's head. He could feel it regarding the Hammerhead underboss through his eyeballs; an itchy, sizzling

---

21. The Hammerheads were part of an international criminal organisation often called the 'Chalinese Mafia', but referred to in the tongue of their native land as the *Jaccuzza*, after the practice of their most powerful bosses conducting all their business in a hot tub, with lots of plum brandy and 'ladies of negotiable affection'. The Jaccuzza boss of Grand Sepulchre, for example, had a three-room spa built around a mineral hot spring deep under the neighbourhood of Bentsteeple, where his many henchmen called him 'Bert the Walrus' behind his back, and he complained about the difficulty of getting a decent Chalinese *smushi* selection delivered to his secret address.

sensation.

"Now you listen here, you old bum! We're legitimate businessmen, see? And that's why we're... ummm... going to have to murder the lot of you. On account of not being criminal scum!" He looked angrily left and right at his companions, who appeared dumbstruck. "Don't expect it to make sense! Just expect it to be nasty and painful!"

"Criminals!" sighed Rod, with the mental impression of a Labrador locking eyes on a fresh new tennis ball. **"At last!"**

Ranulf actually laughed.

"*You* shower of pillocks? Level-one human bandits? I wouldn't get me axe dirty. But the kids need some exercise, and there's not a goblin to be seen down here today..."

For an instant, the Hammerhead underboss looked into the black, glittering eyes of Ranulf the Butcher, and saw hellfire capering merrily within. He wasn't, at heart, a stupid man, which is how he'd clawed his way halfway up the underworld chain of command. He certainly knew that look – the one you got when you'd just pushed a huge chunk of chips and coins across the table, and the other guy was about to lay down four aces. But just then, one of his newest henchmen made the decision for him.

"'Ere! *I know you!* You're that assassin girly what carved up Danjo the Hook!"

It was a familiar face to Amber, all right. The spearman with the ludicrous lip-ring, who she'd recently pushed down a whirlpool of sewage. Seemed he'd been quick to find new employment.

"We *have* to stop meeting like this, you know," she said. "And you really need more than just one bath, after what I did to you last time. I can smell you from over here. Unless... yes, folks, he's wetting his pants right now."

The underboss scowled.

"Assassins, is it? You Guild Lachrymose bastards won't take me alive!"

"Logic's not his strong suit, is it?" asked Rod, as twenty swordsmen settled into fighting stances all around them. Jack felt his muscles creak and expand, and he reached for his own huge blade.

"You really want to do this?" asked Ranulf, one eyebrow raised.

"You haven't left me much choice, you beardy idiot!" hissed the Hammerhead.

"Well, a word of advice, friend. Once my little lads and ladies here mangle the first couple, you'd best start running. I'll be over here enjoying a cigar."

"Wait, *what?* There's *twenty* of us, old man! Armed with traditional ancient *No-Touchi* blades, from the Fractiously Violent Monks of the Temple of Oi Yu![22]"

"Yes. And there's *three* of them, armed with the traditional 'what happens when the heroes get set upon by numerically superior enemies who don't all have first names'," said Ranulf the Butcher, leaning nonchalantly up against the wall. "Monty, Jack, Amber – points off if I have to get me axe out. You know what to do."

The voice in Jack's head was laughing with innocent glee as he leapt forward, swinging his immense battle-blade in a silver blur. But the voice in Amber's head – the one that had nothing to do with heroism – had already planned it all out for her.

A punch dagger in the chest for the underboss, pinning him to that dodgy-looking stalagmite. Then up and over, a mantisbow bolt through the back of that one's head, slice the tendons on the next one's arm, use him as a human shield to block a sword-blow from the right, then spin him around, plunging a blade clean through his chest and into the next assailant...

It was perfect. It was beautiful.

A ballet of demise, traced out in arcs of arterial spray.

But Amberelia hadn't taken into account Monty Pettigrew, who was considerably faster than she was. Her punch dagger missed the Underboss by inches as he was flattened by a blur of wig-powder and cologne, the Fop's uppercut lifting him clean out of his shark-skin loafers. Amber's dagger bent against a crust of crystallised limestone, making her whole arm jangle with shock. Then the next man she'd marked was slapped aside by the flat of Jack's sword, sending him spinning, arms and legs flopping, off into the mist.

"Come *on*, young lady!" encouraged Ranulf from the sidelines. "Get your head in the game!"

She improvised, letting Skrx pick a target with his excellent infra-red vision. A bolt pinned one of the gangsters to the wall by his collar

---

22. These single-edged, curved longswords of beautiful hand-forged steel are the traditional weapons of the Chalinese warrior caste, who are said to prize them as much as their immortal souls. Regardless, enough have been bought and smuggled out of that island kingdom over the years that they are also now vital accessories for gangsters of the Jaccuzza crime families. When asked about this, the great Chalinese swordmaster Zato Ichikawa replied – "When even a man of great martial honour is hungry enough, he'll admit you can't eat your immortal soul".

as Amber slid under a wild sword-stroke, swept the Hammerhead thug's feet out from under him, and whipped his cranium neatly off his shoulders with a piece of garrotting wire.

"How's *that* for 'head in the game', old timer?" she shouted, as blood painted the ceiling… and before Jack's elbow caught her square in the stomach. He'd tripped over the severed head, sending it skidding off across the smooth floor on the stump of its neck. It was all Amber could do to turn her bent-double gasp into an attack, planting a dagger in another Hammerhead to steady herself. He looked down at the blade, held up one finger to protest, gurgled up a mouthful of blood, and died.

"Watch it!" she snarled. "I could have missed the artery there, you big oaf!"

"*You* watch it! That head almost snapped my ankle!"

"Auuugh!" shouted Monty, off behind them both. "*It just bit mine!*"

The fop's scream was loud enough to make Jack miss his stroke, allowing a rat-faced thug to duck under his sword's swing. The blow buried the oversized claymore deep in the shaft of that suggestive rock formation. Now a pair of beady little eyes were sizing up his neck…

But Monty was there, blurring into focus just long enough to deliver a solid knee to the man's fruits. His eyes crossed, and he let out a horrible little whimper before he toppled over, conveniently falling on his own *No-Touchi*.

Then Jack was beset again, this time by two sword-swinging crooks who came at him together, their blades spinning and whirling. He shrugged, hoped that whatever sorcery Rod provided was up to it, and grabbed both weapons, bending them backwards with a creak and groan of tortured steel. Then he pulled both men in at once, and delivered a devastating headbutt that shattered both their noses, knocking them out cold.

Right behind Amber.

She was backing away from a huge Hammerhead, blocking a storm of savage cuts, when she tripped over the two prone bodies and fell. The gangster didn't waste his opportunity. His sword lashed out, and sliced clean through the young assassin's arm, severing it neatly just below the elbow.

It was one of those moments when time seems to break, like brittle glass. *Jack shouted something incomprehensible, his eyes wide, his own heroic bulk getting in his way as he tried to turn…*

Green fire flashed; a bracelet clamped around the wound. The fingers of Amber's chopped-off hand opened, and her dagger flew wide, clattering to the floor as she rolled, her cloak concealing her for an instant. But the Hammerhead kept his eyes on his goal. He stepped over his two fallen comrades as Jack launched himself into a flying tackle... too slow.

Monty was fencing with three men at once, all the way over the other side of the chamber, his mouth an open 'O' of horror.

There was no stopping it.

The thug's sword came up, strings of crimson whipping away from its edge, and his teeth showed white in a savage grin as he chopped down, finishing the job.

Sparks flashed. Metal ground on metal. The sword broke, snapped in half. And a pair of long pale claws swiped up the front of the Hammerhead's suit, unzipping sharkskin and flesh alike. He screamed as his intestines spilled out in a steaming coil, falling to his knees and trying to cram them back in with both hands. Unfortunately, he made this attempt just as Jack collided with him, and they tumbled away together in a bloody, offal-tangled mess.

Jack fought the urge to vomit as he wobbled to his feet. There were still more of the Hammerheads left, so he staggered toward them, growling, a coil of lower intestine wrapped around one leg, a large flap of liver in his hair. They took one look at the gore-soaked, muscular abomination lurching in their direction, dropped their swords, and ran. But there was time for one more casualty; Montmortimer himself, who was arrested in his pursuit of the fleeing thugs by that trailing intestinal loop. He caught his foot in it and slammed headlong to the floor, with a puff of cosmetic powder and a shrapnel of velvet beauty spots.

The last, sad little sound of battle was his swords clattering and rolling to a standstill, like the last, miraculously intact plate which rolls out of the kitchen following an epic food-fight.

That, and the sound of Ranulf the Butcher applauding. He was still leaned up against the wall, and when he inhaled, the cherry-red tip of his cigar lit up his face like a cheap horror mask.

"Bravo! Well done! I mean, you were awful by proper heroing standards, but you were proper heroes, by today's awful standards. Or is that... reverse it? No? You know what I mean." He leaved himself up to his feet, exhaling a perfect set of smoke rings.

"Montmortimer was quick enough, but he only had the confidence to take on the very little ones. Amber tried to play it like an assassin, all cold and cool. You have to *feel* the fight, instead of planning it out like a charity barn-dance, girl! Jack... was just Jack. That which he managed to hit, stayed down. Now, it's not like I'm criticising you personally see, but that was *rubbish*. Fine slapstick, but no cohesion. There's no 'I' in 'Party', you know, and if you want to be heroes, you'll need to learn to work together."

Jack helped Monty to his feet, getting nameless and sticky red juices all over his coat sleeve.

"Easy for you to say! You're all talk about monster slaying, but *that*, if you don't mind me saying so, was no monster. That was a *gang war*. Monsters don't find out who you are, come round to your house later, and set it on fire!"

Ranulf regarded the ex-alchemist coolly.

"Fair point, justly made," he said, tapping the ash off the tip of his cigar. "I'll be the first to admit, you'll never learn without getting in some real monster practice. I mean, do you feel more experienced and skilful after besting those ruffians?" He shook his head. "And not even any decent loot."

"I think one of them dropped a candy bar," said Monty.

"And the severed head has gold earrings," added Amberelia. "I almost got the garrotte caught on them."

"Be that as it may," said Ranulf, "Those items don't account for a whole lot of prime schnitzel, at today's prices. No, what we want is a nice big target that will help you co-ordinate your strengths. A *real* monster, from the old *Beastiarium Bellicosa*, the kind that you could really get your teeth into. Before it got its teeth into you!"

Amber gave Skrx a little scratch behind the antennae and sent him scuttling back into his backpack home.

"But you said it yourself. Most of them are either dead, endangered or a long way off, aren't they?"

Ranulf's smile was just a bit crazy around the edges – a bit too wide, and a bit too wobbly for Amber's liking. She reminded herself that there was no better way to do away with Jack Somewhat than to keep on getting into deadly situations.

After all, she *was trained to get out of them alive! He, on the other hand, was just an untrained mess of what appeared to be tempered, rippling, battle-sculpted muscle and...*

She shut that thought off very, very quickly. That way, madness lurked in a dark alley, teaming up with hormones to bash her over the head and relieve her of her common sense. *You had to admit, though, he didn't look half bad, in this light...*

No! Amber's second thoughts waved the equivalent of a very big stick, getting her mind back to business. Back to the sobering vision of Ranulf the Butcher's big beardy grin, in fact.

"I know where they've got one," he said, leaning forward all conspiracy-quiet and twitchy. "I was saving it for my birthday, but what the heck! You only live twelve times, with an optional thirteenth for good behaviour![23]"

Monty finished tucking his swords back into their scabbards and wiped his brow with a silk handkerchief. It smeared the blood about like abstract art.

"May I ask, from the point of view of a man of science, what manner of beast you think we should contend against?"

"Oh, indeed you may!" nodded Ranulf. "Indeed, you may... indeed! I'm only talking about one of the most hideous mistakes of occult biology ever to be spawned in the charnel-shops of mad wizards! A thing they keep around the Unspeakable College to eat all of the failed experiments, kitchen scraps and dead students!"

"Oh no..." said Jack, who could see where this was going.

"Oh, *yes!*" said Ranulf, rubbing his hands together gleefully. "Let's get back, have a big manly dinner, and get ready. Because tonight... we're going to slay the Mantigore!"

It was only when they were halfway home that Jack remembered what had happened to Amber's hand. But by then she'd remembered too, and she kept it tucked right up inside her cloak until she was able to get some time with it alone...

---

23. Ranulf, like many barbarian heroes, was a believer in the old sea-reaver's religion, from whence Urzoman society had taken the days of the week. He was a devout adherent to the creed of the Axefather, Gordin, who revealed in his excruciatingly long poetic gospels that each warrior had twelve chances to prove himself worthy of fighting in the ranks of the Thunder Gods during the battle that would end the universe, with a possible thirteenth attempt granted for warriors who died in unsportsmanlike circumstances. This dispensation was granted by Snalric, referee of the Gods, whose black and white striped raiment represents, so it's told, the dark and light side of fate and human nature. There were twelve whole saga cycles explaining the correct conduct of a warrior in battle, including an offside rule so difficult to comprehend that it was inscribed in runes of fire on a series of forty-foot menhirs beneath the ice mountains of Nastiskaarsfjord, and still caught people out.

10
The Extrajudicial Indignation

WILD STORIES STALKED the streets of Grand Sepulchre next morning. Not just tales of the Shitman, the manure heap that walked – no, there were others, too. Rumours of war in the docklands, where a gaggle of pirates reported being attacked by a dwarf made of iron with glowing green eyes. Their reports were garbled thanks to the fact that this apparition had forced them to eat their hats, lest they be rolled up into a tube and stuffed somewhere thoroughly uncomfortable. There was also disruption and doom on the Stilts, as the struggle for control of the alchemist's guild reached a pitch of actual warfare, and their building burned to the waterline for the fifty-fifth time. Chep Palaquat was missing, presumed evaporated.

Then came dire rumours that an alehouse on the corner of Ricketback and Decameron had been torn apart by a 'thirsty blue giant' – a fact which had yet to reach the ears of the city's bonded monster hunter, Ranulf the Butcher. But Soto Scalizari had heard, and so had Jory Foxmallet and Billiam Knox. They'd joined in at the back of the crowd to look at the four walls of the place all peeled outward like a masonry banana, and they'd been more than happy to see Clorance Gryssle and his men hard at work, all otherwise occupied. The trio skulked off to Soto's shack amid the noise and stench of the Fleamarket, there to lay low and ponder their worries.

Worries? Yes indeed. There was ample reason for the trio to be worried, even though they'd kept their end of the bargain, and delivered Jack Somewhat into the slavering jaws of gainful employment. Those worries called for a council of war, or at least a council of heavy drinking, and Soto was known to have a big stone crock of Quillish firewater hidden under his floorboards.

It came down to voices, and compulsions, and the question of whether Jack Somewhat was contagious.

"You know, I saw a pickpocket out there before," said Soto, peering out between the bamboo blinds. He knocked back a gulp of firewater and winced. "Great technique. Sliced the fella's trouser seams neat as you like, and off she went."

"So what?" asked Foxmallet. "There's a hundred more out there right now. So long as they're licensed by the Guild, no one will be getting their thumbs chopped off."

There was a certain twinge in his voice, though. Soto pounced on it like a terrier on a fat dockside rat.

"So, it doesn't bother you to know that there are *burglars* out there too? Safe-crackers? Pirates? Extortionists and blackmailers?"

Foxmallet tried to copy Billiam Knox's famous poker face, but only managed to look blackjacked.

"Not in the slightest. Some of my best friends are ex... extortionists and blackmailers. Not to mention f...f...fraudsters. People have to eat, after all. It's just that I'd rather you didn't mention..."

"Cutpurses? Swindlers? *Assassins*, even?"

Three distinct twitches hinked up the side of Jory's face, as if Soto was pulling a needle and thread through his friend's skin.

"Those kind of ... professions. Yeah. And in fact, it would be nice to have another drink about now." He rattled his cup, ice cubes clinking. "While we deftly change the subject."

"So *you* feel it too," mused Soto, grabbing the stoneware bottle before Jory could. "A kind of weird compulsion to... *do something* about it. Like the little voice that tells you that you need to pee."

Knox, who had hitherto remained silent, slapped his knee with one hand.

"That's exactly it!"

Soto spun on his chair, bringing with him one of his surgical lamps, a gas flame in a jar backed by a big bowl-shaped mirror.

"Aha! It all makes sense now! It's some kind of pox. Perhaps magical! It's gotten into all of our heads, and fostered a terrible, probably dangerous, likely *suicidal* urge to..."

"No, I mean I need to use the outhouse," said Billiam. "I've put away a fair few of those cocktails you were slinging earlier. What did you call them?"

"Quillish Forget-Me-Lots," said Soto, peering around the lamp. "Well, go on then! The street, nay, the *world* is your chamber pot, Mister Knox. Just don't try to deny that you feel all funny when I say the word *bundlescullion!*"

"Ummm... I don't know what that is!" wailed Billiam, holding the doorknob in one hand and his privates in the other.

"Someone who seduces kitchen maids in order to steal the silverware," put in Foxmallet, finally snagging the bottle. "How about now?"

Billiam twitched as though a horsefly had stung him somewhere horribly intimate.

"For some reason, I'd like very much to punch one. But first..."

He slipped outside, leaving the illicit apothecary and the feckless peer alone in the hot gloom.

"So you think we've caught something off Somewhat, do you?" asked Jory, after taking an adam's apple shuddering gulp of firewater. "Perhaps you even think that we've gotten a little sprinkling of whatever weird occult power is messing with him? *You*, especially."

"Why do you say that?" asked Soto, squinting suspiciously.

"Because, old son, your head has been on fire for the last five minutes, and you haven't seemed to notice."

Soto jumped into the air, dropping his lamp and flailing at his hair with both hands. This simply caused the little tiny purple flame which had hovered over his skull to spread, rippling around his fingers in a violet nimbus.

"Waaaah! *It burns!*" he shouted. Then he stopped. "Actually, no it doesn't. Hold on a minute..."

He reached out for the jug of booze with one finger. As soon as the flames surrounding it came close to the fumes from the potent liquor it belched a plume of fire, hissing like an angry tomcat.

"Hey! I was drinking that!" yelped Foxmallet, shying away from the heat.

"Interesting. So, I'm on fire, but it doesn't hurt me. While at the same time, I feel a distinct predilection for... I suppose you'd call it *justice*. Or being an interfering busybody. It's just that..."

"It's spreading," warned Jory, trying to retreat back over his chair. "Old chap, this is perhaps an (hic) experi...meriment not to be undertaken indoors, right?"

Soto looked down, and found this to be true. The flames were boiling all across his skin, now, sizzling from the tips of every strand of hair without so much as a tickle. But...

"Ahhh! Pants, man!" shouted Billiam, holding his hand up over his eyes as he came back through the door. Soto looked down, and realised that his clothes were not as immune to the supernatural fire as his skin was.

"EEEEEK!" he exclaimed, strategically covering his groin with both hands. "I think I have some chain mail around here somewhere..."

"Won't that just get red hot?" asked Foxmallet. "You *do* realise you're on fire?" asked Billiam, who had obviously paused to smoke a pipe of stumbleweed while taking his ablutions.

"He thinks he caught it off Jack," put in Foxmallet, rummaging for another drink. He found a bottle of surgical spirits with an eyeball floating in it, shrugged, and took a swig.

"Well, that makes sense. Fire's contagious. My gran's house was right next to the old bordello on Grindmarsh Street when it went up, and..."

"No, he means that whatever occult nonsense has gotten into Jack, has gotten into *us!*"

"Ahhhhh," mused Knox, with the philosophical, skew-eyed look of the pleasantly stoned. "I get it. The weird compulsion to meddle in people's business. The strange urges to fight crime, even though I'm not being paid by the Knock-men. And, this, of course..."

The apprentice wizard shut his eyes tight and clenched his fists, looking for all the world like a constipated bear. He trembled for a second, then something popped, and another Billiam Knox appeared, right next to the other one. It was identical in every way, except that it had the rainbow sheen of a soap bubble if you really squinted hard at it. "Knox!" yelled Soto, who was now holding a metal plate over his nethers with one hand and a tea tray over his bum. *"How did you do that?* I thought you were rubbish at magic!"

The phantom Knox slapped palms with the real one, and they performed a few interlocking steps of a Grailish jig together.

"Well... you know how when you get rascally drunk, you can sometimes see two of things? He's the other one."

"That... that makes no sense at all..." bubbled Foxmallet, who had slumped down behind the chaise lounge.

"He turned up yesterday, when we had a little drink or three to celebrate getting away from old Gryssle and the lock-up. If I try really hard, I can get him to move very small things. But he's not magic. He's just... well, he comes along with this kind of urge to get out there and..."

"Fight crime," said the other two. Knox's doppelganger faded away as the trio looked at each other.

"Do you think we could charge money for it?"

"I reckon if you saved the right people, they could be usefully grateful, kind of thing..."

"Nonononono. More important. What does Foxmallet do? I'm... quite clearly I catch on fire, and old Bill goes double, so what's gotten into Jory?"

The young Lord stared down at his hands.

"Well, I get the twitches, and I feel a lot like bashing criminals, but dash it all, lads, I don't seem to have any kind of special magic..."

"It's not magic," put in Knox. "Doesn't feel like magic. When the old Master does magic, and it's usually by accident these days, the air feels like it does before a thunderstorm, and you taste metal on your tongue. This is... something else."

"Well, I haven't got it," huffed Foxmallet. "Most unfair!"

"There, there," said Soto, patting him on the shoulder. "You already have a power. You have tons of money. That's never a bad thing, surely?"

Jory grinned from ear to ear.

"So I do, by Josephat! And this crime fighting lark sounds like a good laugh. I mean, it's *exciting*, you two will give us a heck of an unfair advantage, ladies will think we're heroes, and we can all get spiffing costumes like the one Jack wore in the Brute Pits!"

"We'll only punch some *little* criminals, though, right?" asked Billiam. "No real assassins, or paid-up guildsmen? I mean, those guys are pretty heavy..."

Soto furrowed his brow, concentrated hard, and extinguished his full-body flame with an audible pop. He was left standing there covering his willy with a badly burned plate, his hair still gently smoking.

"We're not *idiots*, Knox. Just little ones. Just to... umm... explore the economic possibilities. What do you reckon, Foxmallet?"

He shrugged.

"Well, old sausage, I reckon that with silly powers come bugger all responsibilities. If Jack's been packed off to hero school and we don't want to join him, we'll have to be careful."

"Circumspection-asity will be our (hic) watchword!" said Knox, waving a freshly found bottle in the air. Soto whipped it out of his hand at the last possible moment.

"Not *those*, you noddy! Those are the hangover pills! The last thing we need now is a super-sober Billiam Knox weeping about his poor life choices, and swearing to devote himself to chastity, financial security and – urgh – *sobriety!*"

Which is how the trio managed to be lurking behind boxes in an alleyway, as the Cobra Bells rang out the descending veils of night. All three were dressed in uniforms designed by the genius of Mr Sagh.

Their enthusiasm had grown with every drink, and they had drunk to curb their nerves, which fairly jangled with enthusiasm. As Jack Somewhat girded his loins[24] to go and face the Mantigore, his erstwhile mates were peeking from behind a stack of rotten old crates, watching a robbery unfold.

It was a classic ruse. Two thugs had managed to pilfer a sedan chair from somewhere, give it a lick of paint and a spruce-up, and had gone out on the streets posing as members of the Guild Transportational. As soon as a tipsy Lord had stumbled into their trap, they'd locked the door from the outside and trotted off to a nice secluded spot to conclude their business.

"Right, Dennis, get him out of there! He looks a ripe 'un! Did you see the size of his coin purse?"

"Bit of a personal question, Ralf! I mean, modern fashions with the tights and all leave little to the imagination, but..."

"I meant *literally*, you fool! Come on! Get that door open!"

A pair of rough, tattooed hands threw the bolt, and hoisted a lace-trimmed figure out of its seat, none too gently.

"I *say!* This isn't the opera house! What are you two playing at? I'll have you know that..."

"And we'll have *you* know that this is a robbery, mister! Now, put your hands up nice and slow, and we can just relieve you of your gold without any violence."

The rather drunken lord tried to draw his rapier, discovered it was already gone, and bristled with fury.

"And what if I *want* violence? You... you're no match for a gentle... entleman! Where's my pistol? Would one of you be so good as to load it for me?"

Ralf gave the man a kind of desultory conk on the head with a short truncheon.

---

24. Nobody knows how to actually do this, though it's suggested in all manner of ancient religious texts as something which people do before battle. The modern interpretation is 'hiked up their courage', that emotion being oft-connected with the danglier parts of the male anatomy. However, it could just be practical advice; if those old vases are to be believed, blokes used to rush about with their willies out 24-7, so girding the area with a bit of something solid before facing up to another fella with a mace and a bad attitude seems only prudent.

"Shut up. Coins. Now. We've not got all night."

His victim gave a yelp.

"Hey now! Come on, boys! I'm fully paid up with guild insurance. There's no need for any of this. Look, here's my policy card. You can burgle my house for any furniture I'm sick of, and artworks the missus picked out, thrice yearly. No muggings, though. I paid extra."

Dennis grinned horribly, waving a notched old hunting knife.

"Here's the thing though, granddad. We're not really what you'd call guildsmen..."

That was what Soto had been waiting for. All through the long conversation that had just passed, he'd been holding in the urge to dispense justice, like a bladderfull of finest rotgut. Now he leapt over the crates, casting aside the cloak he'd been wearing, and bursting head to toe into flame. No less than two Billiam Knoxes, dressed in blue tights and silver knuckle-duster gloves, followed.

"Ummmm! Dennissssss!" wailed the more perceptive of the two thieves, as improbably-clad peril rushed up on him. "It's a couple of angry male prostitutes and a man on fire!"

That was all he got to say, because Soto was already on him, flailing away with a flurry of punches. Now, the apothecary was not a big man, so each of his blows was far from devastating. The thing was, though, that he was both consumed in a halo of super-hot flame, and completely, utterly naked. This was a combination of pain and embarrassment which any fighter worth their salt would be keen to get away from. So, Ralf turned and ran – right over the stuck-out leg of Billiam Knox. Another Knox was there to meet his chin as he fell, with a rising uppercut.

Ralf hadn't become a seasoned scum-of-the-streets by dropping at the first punch, however. He massaged his jaw as he came up growling, swinging a wild blow at the wobbly, blurred outline of his assailant.

His fist went right through. And as it did so, a hideous sensation twisted its way up his arm and into his head. It was the concentrated power of a hundred groaning, sweating hangovers at once, and it exploded behind his eyes with sickening intensity. The real Billiam Knox twisted Ralf's arm up behind his back, just in time for Soto to tag in and smash him with a plank of wood, putting him out cold.

"The Naked Flame strikes again!" crowed the blazing, bollock-nude figure with the halo of sizzling hair writhing on its head.

"And so does the devastating...ummm... Double Vision!"

"I just want it made very clear that I never hired these pillocks," pointed out the drunken Lord, tapping on Dennis' chest with one finger.

"Not to worry, Guv. They're just leaving," snarled the bigger of the two thieves, fishing an even bigger hunting knife out of his waistband to match the first. "Your regular mugging will resume after these horrible screams and slicing noises..."

It was at that moment that something very stylish and black descended from above on a zipline, a dark cape fanning out around it like nightmarish wings. Leathery billows flared, enveloping Dennis in darkness, and something evil glinted within as he was caught up, crunched down, rolled under and bundled away to smash through a pile of steaming garbage.

There was a short, truncated scream, then a gurgle, then silence.

A figure stood up, caped and cowled, utterly black, like a template punched through into the void between worlds. Well, except for where it was now covered with used tissues, banana skins and greasy stains.

"Awww, come on!" it wailed. "You know how hard it is to get that kind of mess out of suede? And as for the *velvet!*" It aimed a kick at the thoroughly trussed-up, garbage-slathered form of Dennis, ex-freelance mugger of the parish. "That's from my butler, and the washerwomen who will be up *all night* trying to make this very expensive costume look cool again!"

The figure strode forward into the light fuming, and unclasped one of the small metal pods from its belt. This turned out to be a tiny, shot-glass sized dram of liquor, which the figure knocked back, licking its lips.

"What was I calling myself again, lads?" asked Jory Foxmallet, dressed from head to toe in the kind of black which even assassins would have found too ostentatious. His cowl sported a pair of dragon's-skull fins, and his cape was fashioned like a set of the legendary reptiles' wings. "Oh, that's right!" He turned back to his hogtied victim, who appeared to have been lassoed with wire. "Fear the judgement of the night's dark messenger, the mighty Grimshadow!"

"Worth every penny you paid that street poet, I reckon," said Billiam, scratching his arse. "What do we do now?"

Soto emerged from behind their original hiding place, shrugging a cloak around his (now extinguished) shoulders.

"Now we gauge the generous gratitude of our gentleman in distress, you nincompoops. After all, those two seemed pretty bloody murderous..."

He turned to bestow a wide and ingratiating smile on the drunken aristocrat in question, only to find the end of a rapier up his nose.

"I don't have the foggiest notion where you shower of prats came from," snarled the man, who turned out to be not only sober, but also angry and thoroughly ungentlemanly. "But King Snagpurse is gonna be livid! Two weeks we've been after this pair of noddies, so's we can give their employer a bit of the old hot-pliers persuasion! Two weeks down the crapper, and all thanks to a flying umbrella, a flaming fairy, and a pair of twins too stupid to have separate bodies!"

He pulled off his wig and threw it to the ground, as shadows clad in amazingly good camouflage peeled away from the walls of the alleyway, appeared out of crates and, in one case, rose up out of a horrible filth-choked drain, wearing its mesh grille as a hat. Two sidled away and knelt by the bodies of Dennis and Ralf, both of whom were snoring obliviously.

"Follow 'em back to their masters, said the chief! It'll be *easy*, said the chief! I've even paid the bloody knockers to leave well enough alone..." He sighed, shaking his head. "Well, I won't go in empty handed! You three prize berks are prisoners of the Guild Tenebral, and I'd suggest you help us with our enquiries. For all I know, you're part of this rebel faction of freelancers who've been giving us a bad name!"

Billiam, now condensed back into one body, raised a tentative finger.

"How can you give a guild of thieves and burglars a bad name?" he asked.

"I'm *so* glad you enquired," beamed the fraudulent Lord, as huge hands reached out for all three of Jack Somewhat's friends. "You see, you could make people fink we *weren't good at it*, right? And that would make ol' Snagpurse... what's the word?"

"Emotional?" ventured Soto, who discovered that he was all out of fire.

"Upset?" tried Foxmallet, backing away from one hulking Guild Enforcer and into the grip of another.

"Morose?"

The false aristocrat rubbed his chin, with a sound like sandpaper. "Naw. I fink what I was going for was *homicidally, face-rippingly angry*," he said. "Boys, put em in the sedan chair. None too gentle-like. Make sure the one in black don't have any more nasty toys on 'im. And then take the bunch of them to the Halfway House. Snaggy will want words with 'em, and if he leaves any bits worth a ransom, I bet the Knock-men would love to hear about people out there doing their job for them."

Jory tried his ace in hole, as two men the size of brick outhouses attempted to fold and compress him into a space made for half a midget.

"I'm a lord, you know! I can pay you!"

The false gentleman patted his cheek as the door was sandwiched shut.

"Always nice to know, guv. I was one too, a few minutes back. Don't fancy all the lace, though. Plays merry hell with the boils on me neck..."

It was not a fun sedan-chair ride. It was an even less happy arrival, as burly thieves with crowbars levered the three ſuper-heroes out of confinement, and dragged them through the dripping, creaking corridors of the Halfway House, that perpetually-unfinished monument to thievery (which had been stolen during its construction by the first ever Snagpurse, King of Larceny).

They say the theft involved a complex scam involving squatter's rights, union intrigue, bribed stonemasons, crooked civic planners, and a duck. The original Snagpurse was also pretty handy with a meat cleaver, which helped immensely.

There are two ways you can go, if you are successor to a man like that.

One is to become nasty, sarcastic, unshaven, rail thin... and as twisted as a machine for making corkscrews. The other is to be all of the above, but so fat that your tailor has to have a nice sideline in circus tents.

The current Snagpurse, King of Thieves, was known as Othis Greave, and he was of the immensely fat variety. He was also incredibly proud of his collection of warts, and the idea of adopting false teeth made of ebony, for that authentic 'rotten black grin'.

Like his many predecessors (elevation to the post of Snagpurse was by dead man's boots, usually while they were still warm with toejam), Snagpurse Othis ruled his motley horde from a super-sized throne in a crumbling, half-finished hall.

But where once the Kings of Larceny had lorded over reeking great gambling-rooms or feasts of beggars, he looked out over a room full of busy scribes, each with his own desk, lamp and filing cabinet. Here, the raw stuff of thievery – fear for one's greedily guarded property – was turned into gold by the alchemy known as incrementally assessed insurance.

The Guild Tenebral still thieved, and picked pockets, and burgled houses, of course. It's just that, if you were wealthy enough, you could take out insurance to make them pay you back. They came down hard on non-guild crime of a larcenous nature, too.

How hard? Well, suffice to say that Dennis and his chum Ralf would have been taking up a bright, fresh new career as shark bait in the harbour if Foxmallet and company hadn't intervened. Unlicensed muggers were treated in a way that Snagpurse called 'firm but fair'; after all, people who have had their fingers chopped off and their tongues tied in a bow through their eye sockets rarely become second offenders. Othis looked every bit the stygian judge as he leaned forward on his throne, making its thigh-thick timbers creak alarmingly. From the dirty ruff around his neck, dripping congealed bacon grease, to his motheaten velvet coat and its straining brass buttons, all the way to the top of his reeking powdered wig, complete with live rats, the King radiated two things – stench and authority. He leaned on the handle of his great cleaver of office, *Spinesplitter*, and scowled his most jowly, warty scowl as the three strangely costumed prisoners were paraded before him.

"What in the name of all fresh and rancid hells are *these*, Invigilator Vermish? I told you to apprehend some o' them freelancers who're working for Uncle Thumbscrews, not raid a novelty brothel!"

The fake lord who had nobbled Jack's friends bowed, his wig scraping the slimy tiles.

"These three stupid prats biffed up the ones we'd been following, y'vileness. Ruined the whole operation. Seems they 'ave a bit of a hard-on for... *fighting crime*."

Othis looked shocked, his jowls wobbling.

"But my dear colleague! *We* perpetuate crime! Lots of it! We, dare I say it, *personify* crime! Did they think they were going to come here next, and scare us to death with their carnival costumes? The temerity!"

"Precisely my thoughts, y'decadence. Seemed a terrible waste to let 'em keep knocking about in public, as it were, perhaps convincing other citizens that they could ..." (he chuckled) "Fight back!"

Snagpurse cupped his collection of chins and fingered the bandage-wrapped handle of *Spinesplitter* reflectively.

"Alright. One chance. What were you shower of fops really up to?"

The triple intake of breath made all of the scribes' candles gutter out in long, pale filaments. Then Jory, Billiam and Soto were all gabbling at once.

"We were rascally drunk, see, with that firewater *Thought we'd only take out the ones that weren't with your noble guild and then* **Perhaps it could be impressive to the ladies** Mention we were pretty gosh-darned steaming *Little voice yammering about justice* **Probably count as being possessed, which under thaumaturgical law means** And then we had some more drinks, *and thought 'beat up a few little ones, and save you the trouble'...*"

They trailed off, as Othis stood, heaving himself up to his full height. For all the blubber, he was a big man, and he was more than able to lift *Spinesplitter*, bringing it down with an echoing great chop on a butcher's block put there just for this purpose.

"Oh, I honestly can't be bothered with all of this. Just kill them, and make sure you mince up the bodies properly, this time. The shark fishermen have been complaining."

Six suddenly very sober eyes bulged and goggled.

"No!"

"You can't!"

"I've got bloody insurance with you lot!"

A very muscular, very menacing group of guildsmen came looming out of the shadows as Othis slumped back into his throne, making the dust rain down from the sagging ceiling. One of them was pushing a very large mince grinder on a little cart.

"Wait!" shouted the King of Thieves.

"Yes!"

Hope spun in the wind like chaff...

"Is any of you called Jack Somewhat? Apparently he fits your description. Stupid, silly costume, meddling in things he shouldn't, young, drunk... you get the portrait."

The possibility of lying was shopped about with a series of panicked glances.

"No, sir. Not any of us, sir."

"That's a shame. Me old mate Zoltan wants him alive. Something about fighting for reparations, or some such. Never mind, then. On with the killing, and the mincing, and such. Which reminds me! Someone bring me a stolen pie!"

Wretched guild beggars scurried to find one, but it was to be the last meal Othis Greave ever ordered. Just as all hope seemed to have gurgled down the cosmic u-bend for Jack's friends, one wall of the Halfway House exploded, sending clerks, desks, papers and filing cabinets flying in a horizontal rain.

Through the breach charged an immense blue monster, all wild-eyed, and muscled like a whole gym full of wrestlers. It was wearing torn-off pants and nothing else, and its hands were the size of siege shields, each finger as thick around as King Snagpurse's flabby arm.

A couple of the largest of the Guild Tenebral's enforcers made an attempt to poke the creature with spears, but it simply growled, and swept them aside with one rib-cracking backhand. The rest cowered away, trying to look both dutiful, fierce and very, very small at the same time.

Behind this apparition came a short, fat figure which looked for all the world like a pot-belly stove come to life. It was, by the shape of it, undeniably female, as considerable ironmongery had gone into crafting for it a bodice like two cauldrons riveted to a fire surround. Below the waist it wore a dress of thick chainmail over full plate trousers, and the joins of its armour glowed green, as if it was filled with stolen auroras.

It also moved much faster than its gigantic compatriot, powering across the room, leaping from a tumbled desk to hurdle Snagpurse's row of guards and pin him to his throne. One of his piggy hands went thrashing in the direction of *Spinesplitter*, but he couldn't quite reach.

"Don't any of you *****ing mother******s move, or I'll ****** your ****** so far up your ******* that ********* ******** mongoose ***** tube socks **** ***** ******** next week!" bellowed the iron dwarf, using language so utterly foul that it literally sizzled in the air. A few thieves and beggars winced, and put their hands over their ears.

"Drink!" roared the giant, pounding a filing cabinet so flat it could have been used as wallpaper. His beady little eyes, burning blowtorch-blue, searched the room for bottles, casks, kegs or barrels.

"No drink! Not yet! We're here to shut down this den of thieves, and... oh! Who are *you* bastards?"

This was aimed at Jory, Billiam and Soto, as the eyes in the iron-clad woman's helm narrowed to slits.

"No drink! Then SMASH!"

"************!" she exclaimed, causing Snagpurse's ebony teeth to smoulder. "Look, if you're costumed heroes here to scour this pit of iniquity with righteous fury, we're sorry, but it was our idea first. I'm Slag Iron, and this is the Unstoppable It. Care to join us?"

Indeed, gnarly snaps and crackles of green energy were hissing through the air now, as like called to like. The strange infection which had hold of Jack Somewhat had these two in its grip as well, and their power was boiling over, screwing itself into the heads of the Double Vision, the Naked Flame and the Grimshadow with a fizz like cheap champagne.

Soto Scalizari burst alight, throwing aside his cloak. Billiam Knox blurred around the edges, then popped into two. Jory Foxmallet, powerless, nevertheless swirled his cape menacingly, as extending batons snicked open in both of his hands.

"Don't mind if we do," drawled the Grimshadow, in a voice that seriously needed a packet of cough lozenges.

"What's with the voice, Foxmallet?" asked one of the Knoxes.

"It's menacing, and dark, and edgy, and it helps disguise my identity," rasped his friend.

"So, they won't know you're the same guy, even though most of your face is still showing, and you sound like you've been smoking cheap cigars?"

Soto cracked his knuckles.

"They won't remember much about us anyway, once they've all got a nice case of concussion. You know there are three hundred pressure points on the human body that the apothecaries know of each of which can paralyse or incapacitate?"

Billiam shrugged.

"The wizards know about the one where you clonk someone right on the head. Seems to work."

Up on the dais, Snagpurse managed to loosen Slag Iron's grip around his neck, just enough to croak an order of his own.

"Don't just stand there!" He wheezed. "Seize them!" His fumbling hand managed to push a hidden button, making klaxons blare throughout the Halfway House.

"Awww, ******** this load of *******!" snarled the woman in armour. "Flatten 'em, It! There's a bucket of best brandy in it for you if none of 'em get out the door."

The so-called Unstoppable one didn't have to be told twice. With a bellow that splattered ropy drool halfway across the hall, the blue-skinned giant leapt among Snagpurse's lackeys, huge fists swinging. Broken, unconscious and otherwise mangled bodies scattered like chaff, some ploughing clear through the half-made walls of the Halfway House, others crumpled into their armour.

A doughty few fought back with axe and club and pointy stick, but the creature's skin was like leather, and its retribution fierce. Others tried to swat at the monster with fire, hefting torches from the walls.

Sadly for the Guild Tenebral, this also seemed to make the Unstoppable It even angrier. It pulped an axeman between two upturned desks, clapping them together like blackboard erasers, then advanced on the throne, where the erstwhile King of Thieves tried to cower. If it was possible to hide behind your own rolls of fat, Snagpurse would have managed.

"Guards! Lackeys! Chambermaids! *Anyone!*"

But there was nothing Othis could do as the great monster-man lifted his entire throne from the floor, with him as a passenger. The It glared at the Tenebral King, then unleashed a roar laced with apocalyptic halitosis.

"Driiiiink!"

Down on the floor, the Naked Flame, Double Vision, Grimshadow and Slag Iron had it all their own way. Thieves and other scoundrels came boiling in through the doors at the klaxon's call, but these weren't warriors. Some hadn't even had time to get their trousers on. Flying fists meted out swift justice (or at least nasty concussions) and soon the yawning doorways were choked with the unconscious. Slag Iron turned to her big blue friend, who looked like he was just about to swallow the King of Thieves.

"Come on, you massive waste of space! Finish him off, and we can... oh, *******"

It looked like there was a good reason for the sailor talk. Because, for the first time today, Othis Snagpurse had done something intelligent.

As the Unstoppable It hoisted him, all jowl-shuddering and lard-wobbling up in the air, Othis popped open one of the arms of his throne, revealing a selection of nicely stolen cut-crystal decanters, containing the finest Zollish rum, Clourvonnaise special reserve and even a cheekily nicked measure of Chungdoji Dragon Water, a spirit so potent that it evaporated in the air between the bottle and your tongue[25]. As the yellow-toothed maw of the It cranked open wide, Snagpurse tamed his flapping jowls, grabbed every last bottle, and

---

25. For the Sages of the Temple of the Forgotten Weekend, this had been an easy one. Just take every hangover cure known to science, find its thaumic opposite, brew it up in a big barrel, then freeze it not just in temperature but in time, waiting to see which bits didn't go solid. By their reasoning, this liquid would contain the essence of the lost time experienced by the serious reveller; the very spirit of intoxication. The side effect of Dragon Water, and what makes it so prized, is that due to magical entanglement, *someone else gets the hangover*. This also neatly explains those mornings when you feel like you've been dragged through a mile of brambles by your tongue, backwards, despite only enjoying a single white wine spritzer.

threw them in.

There was a sudden gulp. There was a hiss, as of an industrial boiler just about to blow its bolts and level the town.

Then the fire raging in the It's eyes flared and receded, sucking back down into his soul like bathwater down a plughole. At the same time the huge creature began to shrink and grow pale, withering away until it was revealed to be a middle-aged Grailish man with messy red hair, and a pair of pants far too large for his frame.

In the silence which gripped the hall, he burped. The pants fell down, revealing a tattoo of an anchor on his bum.

"Beg yer pardon, squires. What's going on here, then?"

"Oh, God's ******!' exclaimed Slag Iron, as physics reinstated the rule that a tiny little human can't lift a mountain of lard on a three-ton throne. Snagpurse took a tumble as the hitherto-Unstoppable It fell off the dais, arms windmilling.

"Guards! Lackeys! Menials! *Butcher them!*" roared the fallen King of Thieves, who knew a turning point when he saw one. Even more nasty guildsmen crowded in, for there was no shortage in a place like Grand Sepulchre when it came to beggars and burglars. There were even a few pirates thrown in, as part of a trans-guild criminal exchange program.

Worse – there was a wizard.

Gebhard the Obtuse, to be precise. The famous Curmudgeonly Conjurer, one-time all-Jansamrana champion pie-eater, and now in hock to the Tenebrals for gambling debts which could cripple a small country.

"Hold yer horses, hold yer horses," mumbled the old, ragged-bearded man in robes, who was literally wheeled into the accounting hall like an artillery piece. "This better be worth getting outta bed for, you slimy bastards! If it's just cockroaches in the jam again, I'll turn your eyelids inside out!"

Two hefty minders pushed the mage into position, then levered him out of what appeared to be a brass-and-wicker bath chair, full of blankets and empty bottles. He wobbled a bit, fished for a half full vessel, took a pull, then peered down at Snagpurse, who was unable to get up under his own power.

"I suppose you'll be wanting those ones vaporized, or something?" he said, gesturing at the embattled little knot of ſuper-heroes in the middle of the ruined hall. "One of them's already on fire, you know. He might not combust properly."

Down amid a closing ring of angry thieves, Billiam Knox gulped. Both of him did.

"Don't want to alarm you chaps," he said, "but that's a proper wizard up there. I can feel the thaumic charge, right in my back teeth."

"And I can see the big red robe with the arcane symbols on it, and yes, now here comes the pointy hat," said the Grimshadow. "What do we do?"

"Run away?" suggested the former It, holding his pants up in a desperate last stab at modesty.

"Well, we don't know if he's actually any goo..."

Slag Iron didn't get to finish, however, as the Guild Tenebral's pet conjurer flourished his floppy sleeves, causing every last crook and criminal to take a step backward. Then he spoke a Word, and a disc of white-hot fire appeared above his palm. Its edges appeared to be made of jagged teeth, dripping and sizzling with lightning.

"Run away!" conceded the ſupers, as the disc began to spin.

"As yer can see, there's nothing up my sleeves..." intoned the Wizard, in the traditional pre-spellcasting fashion. Then he threw the disc, sending it scudding across the hall at knee-height, ripping through overturned desks and chairs and filing cabinets with a sound like a silk being slit with a razor.

ſuper-heroes scattered and dived, narrowly missing those sizzling teeth as the disc spun up toward the ceiling and punched out through the roof, evaporating in a cloud of purple sparks.

"Ooooh!' gasped the members of the Guild Tenebral still on their feet, and with both eyes open.

"Aaargh!' gurgled Billiam Knox, who had stubbed his toe while looking at the fireworks instead of where he was going. And...

"You *missed*, you sozzled old charlatan!" roared Snagpurse. "What part of *incinerate them* didn't penetrate that rotted pumpkin you call a cranium?"

"Insults? Insults is it, you rancid walrus-skin sack of decaying offal? I'm a level twenty-three mage, me, not some grubby urchin you can talk to like *that!*"

"I paid good money for a murderous battle wizard! I got a drunken, arse-faced lunatic!"

"And your mother got paid good money to couple with a red ape, and what came out was a slack jawed, overstuffed buffoon with the intellect of a piece of occasional furniture!"

"Arrrgh! They're going to *escape*, you daft conjurer! Blast them!"

"Blast them, you say! Right! I'll show you, tubby! Get ready for a blast no one will soon forget!"

So -

"This way! Come on!" shouted Slag Iron, hustling Soto, Jory, Knox and the now-quite-stoppable It around a corner, down a flight of greasy stairs, and into an open manhole cover. The sound of scurrying and pounding feet echoed after them as she scraped the heavy iron lid back in place and followed them all down a ladder into the undercity. The last thing the ſupers heard was a bellicose bellow from the King of Thieves, who could shout loud enough to put the average sergeant of Marines to shame.

"*I'll find you, you meddling bastards!* By the sacred blade of *Spinesplitter*, and the honour of all Thieves past and future, I'll flay your bones red raw!"

"As you can see, sleeves, and all that," muttered the Guild's High Wizard, conjuring up a petulant fury of lightning...

And that was the unfortunate end of Othis Greave, twenty-third Snagpurse of the Guild Tenebral. Because with its intended target now six levels underground and running as fast as a man holding his pants up can waddle, the magical tangle of lighting simply zipped straight *upwards*, into the clouds above Grand Sepulchre.

And as is the way of lightning, it cleared a path for an even bigger bolt, that speared down through the hole in the Halfway House's roof, narrowly avoiding the rickety cupola with its big bronze bells. Instead, it earthed a titanic whack of electrical discharge down the brandished blade of *Spinesplitter*, and into the three hundred kilograms of flab and muscle holding it.

There was a very messy explosion. There was a stench of burning bacon grease. For an instant, the blackened skeleton of a very fat man stood there, holding the smoking remains of a giant cleaver, then it all fell to bits, clattering to the cobbles and smouldering.

The wizard looked very hard at his finger, then folded it carefully away.

"Ummm..." he said, testing the waters of deep, deep trouble with one toe. "That was *them*, wasn't it? Those mad, insane assailants in the funny costumes? We didn't see anything, did we? After all... 'honour among thieves', and all that?"

The assembled wretches of the Guild Tenebral looked sideways at each other, left and right. Honour was one thing, but a finger that could do that was not to be argued with. At least, not until the matter of the succession had been sorted out...

"We didn't see nuffing!" came back the chorused response, as somewhere halfway across the city, in the black rock of the Malevolith, a shrunken head in an ornate gold filigree cage began to scream the signal for magical murder. Below the swinging cage, tucked up in a set of fluffy pyjamas over his leather and spikes, lord Slave's single eye snapped open.

Someone was *definitely* going to pay for this!

Lord Slave sat up, clutching tight a pink stuffed rabbit which was also clad in a black leather zippered mask.

"Yes, I *know*, Mister Bun Bun! They *never* let us get any sleep! No rest for the wicked, after all! What's that?" He held the stuffed toy up to one ear-hole. "Whoever woke you up should be slowly grated into a pool of acid and undead crocodiles? A capital idea! Capital!"

By the time he was enjoying his cheese on toast (with a smaller pink plate for Mister Bun Bun), two nasty suspicious thoughts were already swirling in Lord Slave's mind.

The first concerned a missing magical artefact of allegedly terrible power.

And the second was Jack Somewhat, who couldn't possibly be as dense as he seemed...

11
The Thaumaturgical Ingression

Jack Somewhat had often had cause to wonder if he was mad, even though his life (thus far) had been comparatively short and uneventful.

There had been times when the question of sanity had been advanced by way of drink, or by drugs legal and illegal. There were times when he had been, (as many lads will be) smitten by the charms of women inaccessible, hostile or just plain uninterested. And of course, there were those nights spent in serious contemplation, as his huge feet hung out the end of yet another guildhouse's set of cheap bunk beds, when Jack wondered if the whole world was crazy, and following the path inscribed by tradition and law was the maddest endeavour of them all.

Usually, Jack had been able to take comfort from that old adage, that the truly insane don't know that they *are* insane, and thus to question one's sanity is a very sane thing to do.[26]

Right now, however, he felt that there was no accurate barometer to measure whether his brain was going the way of custard. After all, who could he consult with? The voice in his head, which was whistling a happy alien tune, content that he was becoming a heroic, muscular freak? The living lace-shop mannequin of a man to his left, who fussed over the cuffs and brocade of his costume, even as they trudged through a sewer? Perhaps the mysteriously clumsy yet attractive girl to his right, who had 'accidentally' stabbed, bludgeoned and (in one case) garrotted him since they'd met, all with absolutely zero effect. Well, apart from making him blush, and feel as if his clothes were too tight and full of steam. Certainly – and here Jack was quite sure of himself – certainly not Ranulf the Butcher, who was definitely a candidate for the extra-long-sleeved jacket and extremely comfy little cell.

---

26. So called 'Catch 23'

Here they were, following him down into the stygian, dripping depths, while he muttered under this breath about levels and treasure ratios and lugged a huge sack containing (according to the manifest he'd neatly written out on graph paper) A Wand of Scouring Flame, A Portable Hole, a Potion of Celerity, some mummy dust, three months' worth of elvish bread[27] and a very nice beechwood smoked pancetta.

Ranulf the Butcher clearly didn't think that going to fight the most fearsome magical monster in all Jansamrana was mad. So, by the logic of the sages, he was either absolutely correct, or so far round the twist he'd need a piece of curly string to find his way home. Then again, that endless mumbling about dexterity points and armour values could be the Guildmaster's way of questioning the function of the grey pudding between his ears - making him just as sane as Jack.

Who was *following* him.

By court order, no less.

The erstwhile ſcarlet ſpectre gnawed nervously on one finger as their little party slopped on through the murk and steam of the undercity, working their way toward the district of Bulbous Corners, the wizard's acreage. Where stood the Unspeakable College. And where dwelled (or lurked, depending on its mercurial mood), the Mantigore.

The Mantigore!

So many tales have been spun about this foul beast, the shameful 'secret' of the Wizards, that to recount them all here would be a sinful waste of vellum. They have to skin goats to get these pages, and that should make all writers feel terrible! Unless, like your current scribe, you are a clinical psychopath, and thus not obliged to contemplate the suffering of others, except as an abstract exercise.

Oh, soon they'll see! Soon those so-called doctors with all the silly letters after their names will see! When the machine is finished, and the moon is right... then we will separate the sinew and the sanity, the meat and the madness!

---

27. They say an army can march for a week on one piece of elvish bread, largely because it's so horribly good for you. That's not to say that the army would actually EAT the bread, which is absolutely stunning and perfect-looking from every angle. No, they'd rather scour the mud for worms or eat a bowl of thatched cottage roof, because elvish bread tastes so damn smarmy. One bite, and for the next three weeks, all mere human food tastes like duck vomit and wallpaper paste. Giving in to eating the elvish bread (which has no flavour to humans, who don't have the right number of taste buds to appreciate it) is like becoming addicted to licking drywall, while being compelled to tell all your friends how it's helping you lose weight. You'd rather eat the dwarf bread, trust me.

(Note – eighteen pages of absurd sacrilege and heresy, revenge fantasies aimed at doctors, wizards and officials of the Urzoman Empire, and crudely drawn plans for "The Blood-Curdling Reciprocating Mechanical Soul Flayer' have been excised here by the order of the Chamber Fendant of the Morality Department, University of Jansamrana, for the purpose of preserving the sanity of the populous. Signed, Bligo Slappense, Lord Redactor Superior)

… but of course, we were discoursing on the Mantigore.

For those from foreign parts of the Arch', some small illustration of the nature and temperament of this beast should be offered, if only to quantify the extent of Ranulf the Butcher's folly.

The Mantigore was *created*, not born. It was conjured into existence by the so-called Maniacal Mage, Enkalderon the Younger, some four hundred years ago, when the Urzoman Empire was in the full, fetid flower of its dominance.

Enkalderon, for his sins (and largely because of them) was the High Thaumatarch of the Unspeakable College, and he had made it his career's work to weaponise the essential nature of life. He had devised torturous and cunning methods to combine the essence of beasts together, spawning abominations such as the Vampire Pelagic Moose and the Fire-breathing Imperator Penguin. These (and a menagerie of other nightmares) were intended to fight alongside the Urzoman legions in a war of Arch'-wide conquest, but unfortunately, there was always something wrong with them.

Some were craven and paranoid, some suicidally depressed, some melted in sunlight, and some exploded when exposed to water. The Horned Titanic Musk Weasel, for example, may have been twenty feet tall and armed with acid-spitting fangs, but it was deathly allergic to the colour purple, which caused it to spontaneously combust. This made it singularly hopeless for armed conflict, where it's very difficult to tell your enemy which colours of banners he's allowed.

Despondent, gloomy, driven to drink and dreamsugar, Enkalderon retreated to his sky-piercing spire atop the Unspeakable College's gothic jumble of masonry. He sent out servants far and wide to bring him strange herbs, magical tinctures, vials of blood, slivers of horn and bone, an endless supply of jam sandwiches, and a selection of books so forbidden that they were stamped onto plates of lead and transported frozen in blocks of ice. The grim black chimneys of his manufactory spewed coloured smoke, tongues of strange fire and clouds of hissing sparks for weeks.

Until at last, he emerged; a skeletal, fevered shadow of his former self, but smiling.

He held an egg.

This, incubated in a furnace amid dragon dung and crushed sulphur, would eventually hatch into his finest creation. But Enkalderon would never see it take its first tottering steps, as he died soon after the egg was finished. It seemed that the Maniacal Mage had lived up to his name, and during the creation of the Mantigore he'd swallowed enough liquid mercury to cure a small army of syphilis.

When his successor, Rogath the Tartan, Archmage of the Third Sun, performed the traditional autopsy, there was enough exotic metal inside Enkalderon to justify melting him down for scrap.

As it's told, the baby Mantigore hatched just as they were dedicating a small statue to Enkalderon, in a suitably out-of-the-way place where students wouldn't be inspired to follow in his footsteps. Without an ambitious battlemage at the helm, the Unspeakable College was able to get back to doing what it did best; byzantine power struggles between the seven orders, rampant alcoholism, and teaching novices, in roughly that order of importance.

What came out of the egg was said to be like a small serpent with spider legs, but it soon grew fur, then dragonfly wings, then went and built a nest in the grand chandelier of the College's dining hall.

A hapless novice, sent to gather notes from Enkalderon's dark and smelly den, came back with papers written in the Maniacal Mage's hand, which concluded that he'd solved all his previous problems. He claimed to have discovered a new essence in all living things, which allowed them to change and adapt through inter-generational mutation, better fitting their environment. To make the Mantigore, the ultimate beast of war, he'd isolated this principle in several nasty species, turned it up to eleven, and baked the whole mess into an egg.

This explained why it didn't stay as a flying stoat for long, swooping down from the rafters to steal the wizards' cheese on toast. It 'evolved' (to use Enkalderon's heretical term) into something immune to fly swatters and rolled-up newspapers, and the more the Wizards tried to capture or kill it, the bigger and meaner it got.

Finally, it attained a form which even the Wizards were afraid of, and they did the unthinkable. All seven orders worked together to trap the Mantigore, now a beast with the body of a rhino, the head of a great white shark, a huge scorpion tail, dragon wings and the spikes of a hedgehog. It also had the temperament of a drunken sailor and the intellect of a deck chair, and had been lurking in the undercroft, feasting on the College's population of mastiff-sized rats.

Noting that attempts to kill the thing only led to further, more dangerous mutations, they sealed it up in a deep, craterous pen, covering the top with a spiderweb of iron bars. Then they put it to work eating all of the magical waste the College produced, in vast quantities, every week. As a creature born of sorcery, it could digest even the most eldritch of garbage, and poop out muck that made the geraniums come up something lovely.

On high days and holidays, the Wizards allowed citizens to pay a penny to look down into the Mantigore's cage and thrilled the crowds by levitating goat carcasses down through the bars for it to savage. After several hundred years of indolent captivity, it was looking a bit fat, motheaten and lazy, but it was still by far and away the most dangerous monster in Grand Sepulchre – or at least the most dangerous one known to Ranulf the Butcher. He was yet to hear, of course, of an entire tavern which had been demolished overnight by what witnesses claimed was 'a thirsty blue giant', clad only in a pair of ripped-up trousers, let alone what was going on just across town, right at this moment, vis-a-vis King Snagpurse of the Guild Tenebral.

For once, he was single-mindedly focused on his map and compass. He strode ahead of his apprentices with a grin on his chops and a pair of boarding axes in his belt, whistling a barbarian steppe-shanty off-key.

Behind him came Montmortimer Pettigrew, an embroidered silk bag of rose petals pressed up to his nose. His shoes were, of course, ruined, but it seemed this was the price of adventure. Amberelia Chance followed, cooing over her mantis shrimp while she fed it little scraps of dried octopus. She didn't look at all worried about facing a proper monster; in fact, she was even starting to think that this rogue business could be more fun than assassination. If it wasn't for the embarrassing problem she was still hiding from the rest of them...

Then came Jack, his mind pondering madness while his eyeballs, as is the default setting for young males, watching the motion of Amber's posterior in those tight leather trousers. He was all too aware of his lack of finesse in what Soto called 'the subtle arts of romance', his experience having been covered quite exhaustively by the catch-all phrase 'Gee, I'm pretty drunk and you're all right, fancy a shag?"

Amberelia could have worked out the ratio of slapped faces, kneed fruits and derisive laughs to actual intimacy this method (wholly endorsed by Knox and Foxmallet) rendered. Then again, Jack was certain if he tried it on her, he'd end up leaking in all kinds of nasty places.

Truth be told, he didn't know how he felt about his new companions in heroism. Ranulf was, as noted, completely off his wobbly little trolley. Monty was so upper class he'd probably cut the crusts off a teacup, so he counted as simply 'eccentric'. But Amber was both the most annoying person he'd ever met and a source of awed respect at the same time, after watching her fight. None of which explained why he kept trying to think of things to say to her that wouldn't come out as verbal mush.

"Right!" said Ranulf, derailing the little mine-carts of Jack's train of thought. "We ought to be in the right place, here. Everyone, look around for a secret door."

"How do you look for a secret door?" asked Monty. "By its nature, shouldn't it be... well... *secret?*" "Ahhhh," began Ranulf, rubbing his hands together as he saw the chance to dispense adventuring wisdom. "The thing is, see, the average secret door comes with a few, like, easily noticeable signs. Things like candlesticks that are obviously a handle, or wobbly bricks, or bookcases with a volume called 'the keys to enlightenment' or some such, with all greasy fingerprints on 'em."

"How about a big, obvious door that's not secret at all?" asked Amber.

"Well, that would be a whole different thing. Usually, one of those would be made of oak, about eight feet tall, have a gargoyle for a knocker and all those big iron studs all over it."

"No," said Jack. "I think she means, there's one of those right over here."

And indeed, there was.

The door was every bit as tall and oaken as Ranulf had said, and it really did have a gurning gargoyle face for a knocker.

"Awwwgh, it's bloody hideous, isn't it? Looks like the poster child for facial warts." Monty leaned over to inspect the gargoyle, with the practised eye of someone who only ever buys antiques. "I'm sure the sculptor had nightmares about this one. Probably ate some pretty nasty cheese before trying to get to sleep that night..."

The gargoyle opened one eye, then spit the large brass ring in its mouth at the World's Fastest Fop. Luckily, he was quick enough to duck out of the way.

"And yer a bloody oil paintin', are yer?" hissed the ugly little face. It was made of metal, but it moved just like living flesh, complete with some kind of nasty skin disease. "Who the hells are you lot, skulking around down here, anyway? I've got half a mind to sound the alarm!"

Amberelia was there in a second, making frantic shushing gestures.

"Shhhh! You want them to find out before the surprise is finished? Pardon Montmortimer there, he sometimes lets his sense of aesthetics get in the way of his manners. But surely you've heard of him?"

The gargoyle looked puzzled for a second.

"*Why* would I have heard of him?"

"You don't get the latest magazines and periodicals down here, do you? Read the news-sheets? That's Monty Pettigrew, the famous interior decorator."

Amber's eyebrows were working overtime as her face tried to convince the rest of the heroes to get in on the lie. The Butcher tapped his nose in way which left subtlety in the bushes, trying to get its pants back on.

"Ahhh... yes. *Quite* famous, in fact. And we're his, umm, crew. Ranulf the, mmm, pictographer, and Jack the vox-recordist. We're here to, errr..."

"Give this place a full-on, no expenses spared *makeover!*" enthused Monty, who looked like he actually believed it. "This dungeon look is *so* third century! We need to give the wizards a secret back passage that they can be proud of! I'm thinking shrubberies, some nice Grailish tapestry work, a Chungdoji koi pond, perhaps even a coat of paint for this noble and - now I look more closely - *ruggedly handsome* door."

"So, you don't want to get in, then?" asked the gargoyle, looking slightly puzzled by this turn of events. "No desire to open the dread portal and enter the haunted undercroft of the world-renowned Unspeakable College? Not even a bit?"

"Oh, not at all," gushed Monty, who had managed to find a tape measure somewhere among his many lacy pockets. "Do you think gold brocade and candy stripes for these pillars, or inset rubies and lots of cherubs?"

"Oi! It took *centuries* to get the slime on those pillars just right! And those spiders are an endangered species! Are you lot *sure* you don't just want a wee shufti inside the forbidden dungeons of the eldritch archmages? There's a really good riddle you have to answer, see, and..."

"We could put ornamental lighting all along this bit and tear down the rotting skeletons," said Amber, just as Ranulf grabbed Jack by one ear and pulled his head in close.

"*Right. When that 'orrible little door ornament is good and confused, you clobber it with this,*" whispered the barbarian butcher, slipping Jack a lump hammer. He squinted at the worried-looking gargoyle, which was still talking.

"It's just that it's my *job* to do the riddle, see, and then, right, you could come back and do your interior decorating later. I mean, it's all right for *you*, innit? *You* can't be demoted to being a toilet brush holder, can you?"

Jack, who had by now sidled up by the door, hammer clasped behind his back, felt a bit sorry for the hideous thing. After all, he had spent a lifetime doing all the horrible jobs for a variety of organisations. He knew what it was like to be a mere lackey with one pointless task, in a world that tried to complicate everything. Visions of a thousand well-scrubbed latrine pits danced in his head.

"All right," he asked, "What's the riddle, then?"

The gargoyle beamed, with a mouthful of mismatched gold teeth.

"Thought you'd never ask, guv'nor. Right... ahem... here we goes then... *What has no arms, no legs, and writhes around on the floor in a pool of blood trying to scream for mercy with a mouthful of broken teeth?*"

Ranulf scratched his head. Amber looked up at the ceiling. Monty kept taking notes on colours and textures.

"I give up," said Jack. "What does...."

The gargoyle cut him off with a cackle that should by all rights be called unhinged, except for the fact that it was uttered by an actual door.

"What has no arms, no legs, and writhes around on the floor in a pool of blood trying to scream for mercy with a mouthful of broken teeth? *A bunch of lying sods pretending to be interior decorators, after my mate Barry's seen to them!* BARRY!"

At once, a pair of huge bronze fists punched out through the wall behind the heroes, one grabbing Jack and the other Ranulf. A monster stepped through the rubble and dust, hoisting the pair of them off the ground.

It was huge, and hideous, with stubby bat wings, massive, apelike arms, hunched shoulders, and cloven hooves. The whole thing was cast in metal, and it gleamed sullen and red in the torchlight, just the same as the gargoyle which had summoned it.

"Hah! The old 'surprise home and garden makeover' routine! Oldest trick in the book![28] Now, prepare to quite ironically become a set of

---

28. The *actual* oldest trick in the book comes from the mud-brick civilisation of the city of Urp, famous for its utterly square beards and excellent kebabs. It was here that the first liar, Abshuhemmoroid, developed the trick known as 'Look behind you, yeah, over there, isn't that the ten-armed, aardvark-headed earthy manifestation of Dur, God of embroidered cushions and the lower delta of the river Urtestes?' - followed up by a slap on the back of the head. It says a lot for the civilisation of Urp that this remained funny for three whole dynasties.

new ornamental skeletons!"

The only thing slightly off about Barry, thought Jack, as he scrabbled at the relentless brass fingers about his throat, was his head. Where your usual giant animated death golem probably (Jack assumed, from a lifetime of reading cheap comic books) had a skull face, or the demented visage of some elder god, Barry had a football crudely tied on to the end of his neck, and a smiley face drawn on the front of that, in the style of a two-year-old's first finger painting. The drippy yellow and black visage with its wobbly grin was somehow more horrifying than any squid-and-skull combo from the nightmares of a frenzied cultist.

Especially when the thing's fingers were slowly crushing the life out of you.

"Yipe!" screamed the voice in Jack's head. **"Even the old super-strength won't help you much right now, I suppose. And getting this thing off the ground looks like a no-starter. Tell you what, I was going to wait a while to show you this one, but... try to focus on a point right through its face."**

"You mean its *football?*" croaked Jack, slowly turning purple.

"Exactly! And think heroic thoughts, of course..."

Montmortimer Pettigrew was definitely doing so, because he blurred forward and hammered his rapier right into the metal golem's chest, screeching like a scalded poodle. The thin metal blade bent for a second, humming at a tooth-shattering pitch. Then crumpled into the shape of a lightning bolt and clattered to the floor. The Fop's fingers were bent at horrible angles as he reeled away, cursing.

Amberelia was far more cunning, as befitted her assassin's training. She came in low as the monstrosity lumbered to the centre of the room, one choking would-be-hero in each fist. Something skirled and sparked down around the thing's ankles, and the young demortifex somersaulted away, hissing. Even Barry's achilles tendons were solid metal.

All of this gave Jack time to conjure a very hopeful image in his mind of himself, standing triumphantly on the prone body of the broken golem. Amber, of course, was swooning in his arms. Jack's rather imprecise first-hand knowledge of swooning meant that this hallucination involved a lot of cleavage.

"Come on! Focus, but kind of... don't." enthused Rodney, with fizzing disembodied abandon.

Jack crossed his eyes, furrowed his brow, and floated off into that half-conscious fuzzy place which is the second-to-last resort of the very drunk and the mildly asphyxiated.

All of a sudden, the world turned red.

Jack had a terrible sensation of staring into the noonday sun, accompanied by a kind of crawling, sizzling feeling inside his eyeballs. The fingers hinged shut around his throat snapped open as a truly abysmal smell filled Jack's nostrils, turning his first heaving breath into a coughing fit.

Good gods and demons! Was someone grilling a rotten donkey nearby?

Inside the ruby-tinted blaze, something went **pop**, then bounced around the chamber, hissing like a ferret. Something large – it must have been Ranulf, because neither Amber or Monty were that wide around – slammed into the wall, crumbling a row of canopic jars. A tirade of upside-down Nastiskaarsfjordian swearing assaulted Jack's ears – literally, as Ranulf's people had developed the weaponised umlaut centuries ago.

"That's the business!" shouted Rodney, looming large in Jack's mind until his muscles threatened to burst out of his tunic. **"The old heat-ray vision! I never thought you'd pull it off!"**

"Well, it was either that, or Barry would have pulled my head off," said Jack, ducking under the golem's windmilling arms. As the red cleared from his sight, he was able to make out what had happened. The crudely painted football atop Barry's neck had been roasted, and was even now being prodded to death with Montmortimer's rapier. It resembled a small, overcooked octopus. Now the decapitated monster was swinging wild, staggering like a drunkard. Jack did the old double take.

"Wait? What exactly did you *think* was going to happen?"

"Well, that laser blast was definitely in the multigigawatt range. Technically, if you weren't super enough, it could have welded your corneas to the wall opposite. Then again, no harm, no foul.[29]"

"Left! No, your other left!' screeched the gargoyle, as Amber sidestepped Barry's flying fists. "Go on! Get the big stupid one with the axe!"

Ranulf was indeed back up and about, with his best monster-slaying face on. He spun with terrifying grace for one so big and hairy, putting

---

29. This sporting reference translated extremely poorly into the Commonspeak of the Urzoman Empire, where most sports were of the type promoted enthusiastically by Zoltan Creagle. It came out as 'Nar zorlag fnarg, craddash ktim lorgai', which translates to 'So long as all your arms and legs are still on, you can compete in the next round.'

himself between Barry and the door which was acting as his eyes and ears.

"Come on then, if you think you were forged hard enough!" growled the barbarian hero, taking a firm grip on his axe handle. Barry flexed his giant metal fingers and charged. Ranulf sidestepped like a bullfighter, his axe coming down in a blur of silver...

And someone opened the door from the other side.

This wouldn't have been much of a problem, had it not been for the fact that on the other side of the door was a tiny little crumbling shelf of stone, and a rickety old rope bridge over a genuine chasm of lava.

It wasn't the brim-full, fat-bubbled stream of red-hot death it had once been, because magic was becoming old and comfortable in this Third Age of the Arch'. But it was still a long and spiky drop down to liquid fatality, and it was guarded, from the inside, by a proper wizard.

Well. Sort of.

The Orders had read the fine print some centuries ago, and decided that an apprentice was good enough. Jack would not have at all been surprised.

Hence, the lad on the spot was a thin and knobbly-necked young spectacle-wearer named Sethric 'Demonsbane' O'Crummage. He'd added the middle name in the hope of becoming a master Hexorcist of the Order of the White Ribbon one day, but, even when he bought several pewter skull rings and a robe with pentacles on, people still called him Seth. He'd been trying to work out a very confusing part of the textbook he'd been assigned[30], when something had started making a terrible ruckus behind the door.

Technically it was called the Dread Portal of the Ebon Vortex, but they all knew what it really was: the Unspeakable College's safety valve. Young students could nip out for a pint and certain other pleasures, and of course, no group of cosmic horror-botherers worth their star-spangled pointy hats would build a fortress without a secret escape route. Mobs with torches and pitchforks could be so unreasonable, even in the face of massed combat thaumaturgy.

So hence, the door, and the tunnel, and the attempt, by some self-important old Wizards, years ago, to make it seem appropriately grim. And hence, when Seth opened the door from the inside, and leaned through to hiss - "Could you bastards keep it down? Some of us are trying to *study* here..."

30. Professor 'loony pants' Fischer and G.W. St. Willoughby Price's *My First Nightmare Grimoire of Slobbering Monsters from the Dimensions of Pain*

A giant, headless metal statue stumbled into his arms like an overweight tango partner, sending him staggering backwards onto the bridge.

The designers of this edifice had really been far too keen on the look of the thing, rather than structural rigidity. The ropes and chains which held it up were at least a few centuries old, and they parted with a sound like harp strings being cut with nail clippers as soon as the combined weight of Seth and Barry got on board.

There was a horrible second while physics, not really a welcome visitor in the Unspeakable College, rushed to keep up. And then the pair of them disappeared, down into the red-lit depths, a diminishing shriek of -

"I regret everything!"

...the only echo that remained.

"Barry!" howled the gargoyle doorknocker, until Jack brought his lump hammer down and knocked it out cold, leaving a dent.

The heroes crowded in through the door, taking in the sad little workstation on the other side, cluttered in between the doorway and the bridge. Lava popped and boiled deep below.

"Oooh, I don't feel so good about that," said Rod, who gave the impression of trying to hide behind Jack's frontal lobes. **"He was probably not a bad guy, really. Even if he did have a lot of cheap skull jewellery on."**

Amberelia was similarly upset.

"Guthran's sake, he had pictures of his *mum* and a *puppy* over here. And look at that sad little bed. Scratchy grey blankets and all. Plus, it's about a foot too short."

This made both she and Jack consider, with a mixture of wistfulness and discomfort, the horrible sleeping arrangements of the respective guilds they'd both been shuffled around over the years. They shared a look that could have become meaningful, if Monty hadn't pushed through between them, brandishing his bent rapier.

"I don't suppose you could give me hand, big fellow?" he asked. "Just grab the end and pull when I say when..."

There was a brief blur. There was a hiss and a sizzle. Then the World's Fastest Fop was back in front of Jack, smoking slightly around his lacy edges, and holding a white-hot sword. Jack sighed and thought heroic thoughts as he pinched the glowing tip between his fingers. With a snap, Monty drew it out straight again.

"Much obliged. But what now? Which way to the mantigore

thingy?"

"I'm still worried about this Seth fellow," said Amber, picking up a poorly painted watercolour of what appeared to be a girl wearing massive, ale-bottle spectacles. "Villains don't have a pencil case with their name on it in wobbly handwriting. He even had a girlfr..."

"No! Nononono!" bustled Ranulf, plucking the picture from Amber's hands and throwing it into the lava trench. "Think of it as an industrial accident. And don't say the name. Henchmen don't get back stories. Makes the whole thing messy. One day, eventually, you find yourself standing in front of a yurt with your battle helm in your hands, trying to explain to *Mrs* Guldruk the Conqueror why her husband isn't going to be home for the big yak-herding festival..."

The way he trailed off made Jack suspect that this was not just a random example.

"It just didn't seem that heroic, is all I'm saying," said Jack, who was basically echoing the sentiments of the voice in his head. He scuffed one shoe in the black sand which lay thick on the flagstones.

Ranulf sighed.

"What you know about heroing, lad, would be able to be written on the back of a mouse's handkerchief. Let's just get to the monster, OK? Very clear-cut rules with a monster. No moral compass malarkey. It's heroism, or be eaten. Right?"

The saddest part was, there was no real need for the bridge. Not when Ranulf knocked the hinge-pins out of the Dread Portal, and threw it down over the gap, which Jack fancied he could have jumped over anyway. They tromped across, ignoring the little voice that came from underneath the door.

"Oi! Look, sorry about the Barry thing, but you're not going to leave me here, are you? That lava's pretty bloody hot, and I'm getting a bit of a sweat on! Guys! Guys! C'mon!"

At first, Jack was worried that vengeful mages would be down upon them like a shower of hot bricks, but he hadn't accounted for the sheer amount of undercroft with which the Unspeakable College was equipped. Indeed, the massive, seven-towered pile of spires and domes which tottered over Bulbous Corners was positively iceberg-like in its architecture. This was because real estate in the Dark Empire was severely limited, seeing as it was, to put a fine point on it, only one city wide.

When the fad for a certain type of magic swept through the Orders, the current Thuamatarch and his Council of Wisdomen could only really expand in one direction – well, two, if you could play fast and loose with gravity.

Downwards, though, they were helped by the fact that Grand Sepulchre was built almost entirely on top of Grand Sepulchre, and before that the ancient Sarunjek city of Krymm, and before that... well, all that talk of Disembodied Sentiences, and Iron that Walks, and the dreaded Artificed Vivisectors had to come from somewhere. Wizards had carved out everything from bingo halls to vaults of necromancy to volcanic forges under their rickety demesne, and when the trend for, say, reanimating the dead on an industrial scale had gone the way of wide lapels, they'd simply filled the resulting dungeons with junk.

Jack, Ranulf, Amber and Monty clambered through spiderwoven piles of garbage, slid down scree-slopes of mouldering papers, and navigated weevil-haunted, dust-choked squeezes between alps of worm-wracked furniture. Things unseen scuttled, clicked and hissed as they traversed dripping tunnels where pipes lined the walls, some freezing to the touch, some mummified in cloth and steaming. There was one vast room where Ranulf stopped, holding back the little party with one hand, until a pendulum the size of a house came whooshing down out of the darkness on a chain forged with links like cartwheels, then swung up again into the murk.

Through all of this tunnel-delving, Jack had begun to have time to think. And, thinking not being his strong suit, he'd done so very hard, and quite deliberately. The second thoughts he's come up with, then, were not fancy around the edges, but they were very, very solid.

"Ummmm..." he ventured. "Rodney? You there?"

The voice in his head turned its attention onto him, a feeling quite like opening the curtains while suffering a monumental hangover.

"Of course, Scarlet Spectre! What kind of sage, heroic advice would you like this time?"

"Well.... it's about that, see. I don't know if this whole concept is very practical. I mean, perhaps there's a reason why Ranulf's kind of heroes aren't around anymore. Let alone... whatever you've done to me."

"*Done to you?* Listen, matey, you're *super strong!* You can *fly!* You can shoot laser beams out of your eyes, which is not easy considering the relative squishiness of the human retina, let me tell you! That's the kind of thing little boys dream about!"

Jack, whose dreams as a small child had more often been about getting a bowl of gruel with identifiable meat floating in it, remained unconvinced.

"But what about what *grown-ups* dream about? Wouldn't it be more heroic to use these kind of powers for that kind of thing? I mean, a person with super strength could build an aqueduct in an hour, or reap a field in a minute. Someone who can fly could save people from drowning if they fell off a ship, or make sure medicine got to far-off villages. As for the eyeball thing, I suppose it might be good for welding? But..."

"But it's for *defeating evil!*" wailed Rod, metaphorically tearing his hair out. **"It's for vanquishing do-badders, individually, with a lovely big fight scene and all the sound effects! Isn't that enough?"**

"About that too," ventured Jack, who really didn't want to hurt Rod's feelings, presuming he had any. "If we go around, see, and just beat up all the criminals without asking *why* they're criminals, we're just being big bullies, right? I mean, what if someone's only stealing because they're very very poor, right? Isn't the greater evil poverty itself? Someone with ſuper powers... or a whole ſuper team... could help create prosperity, maybe even help peacefully change the concept of feudal government through public awareness..."

Rod gave the kind of groan usually associated with dire intestinal distress.

"No no no! Oh, I *knew* it would all go wrong! *Public awareness?* Listen, lad, there's a particular idiom here that must be followed. You become a big enough hero, you'll be *immortal!*"

Jack thought about Himself, then, alone in his dark Malevolith aerie, an undead monster who'd lived for hundreds of years. It was for His sake that the architecture of Grand Sepulchre was heavy on the skulls and spikes, though the people themselves weren't evil. People just... got on with being people, and the Dark Empire trappings looked more like pantomime every year[31]. Deep in his heart of hearts, Jack felt a bit sorry for Himself, alone with his dried-up dead things and his memories.

"Don't want to live forever, really. Just want to live a bit better now," he managed, his thoughts wobbling toward Amberelia Chance,

---

31. Not to mention that fact that, with overcrowding as it was, even the most evil bits of a Dark Capital will tend to get gentrified eventually. Bung some picket fences, hanging baskets and a coat of whitewash on your average Pain Pits, Dungeons of Eternal Torment or Dread Armouries of Darkness, subdivide them into apartments, and you can make a tidy profit. Dollars to donuts, a couple of decades after the big eye went out, orc real estate speculators were flogging sections in subdivisions with names like 'Nazgul Creek Estates' and 'The Grove at Mordor Heights'

unbidden.

"But that's not very heroic! Don't you want... ummm... sagas and songs and rune stones all about you everywhere?"

Jack knew that tone of desperation. He'd heard it before, when some of his guild tutors came slamming up against his general ignorance like a ripe cantaloupe hitting a castle wall. He softened a little, trying to put a bit of a smile into his thoughts.

"That's more of Ranulf's thing, I reckon. But, tell you what. We'll try it his way. This old mouldy monster can't be much of a big deal. After that, we'll talk. But I have a few ideas of how we could use these powers for *real* good!"

For an instant, green sparks crackled and seethed inside his skull.

"Maybe I just haven't given you the correct motivation," muttered Rod, in a very disturbing tone. There were harmonics in there that sounded like glass being sharpened on stone. **"But, oh well. They never said this was going to be a picnic..."**

Jack wanted very much to ask what the 'correct motivation' might be, but just then, he ran into the back of Montmortimer Pettigrew, who ran into the back of Amber, who cursed, and toppled into the back of Ranulf. Who had stopped. In front of a huge, scarred, skull-festooned portal, a door of the kind that doesn't need a sign on it saying 'beware of the dogge'.

It was made of iron, black as the bits of the night sky with no stars in them, and from behind it came the dreadful sound of...

"*Snoring?* Really?" asked Amber. "Hardly spine-chilling, is it?"

Ranulf had a look on his face like a kid on Baron Von Tuesday's Morning, all sly and gleeful amid a wire-brush explosion of beard.

"That door's two feet thick, lass! If you can hear the beastie snoring through *that*, it's a mighty foe! Now, come on, Jack! Grab one of those rings there, and let's be getting down to business!"

Deep behind his frontal lobes, Rodney slapped a pair of incorporeal hands together and grinned.

"This is gonna be fun! You'll see!"

Jack rolled the kinks out of his neck, felt a tingle and zap of green fire sizzle through his muscles and tendons, and clasped his fingers tight around the great iron door-pull.

"In for a penny, in for a groat," he muttered. After all, this was pretty much on government orders. Sort of.

And then, as is absolutely mandatory at a times like this, everything went suddenly and horribly wrong.

12

The Leviathanic Outrage

LORD SLAVE STRODE into the Halfway House trailing a nimbus of Throne's Shadow thugs, his black cape billowing like a thunderhead over the summer plains. It took a lot of technology and not a small amount of magic to get that billow just right – suffice to say that a whole new kind of spider was required to spin such black and light-devouring silk, and if you saw one in your outhouse, it would do the job of several bowls of sultanas, bran and concrete mix for a week.

Nobody strode quite like Lord Slave. It was a cultivated kind of walk, which suggested that he would keep on going no matter what stood in his way, and that if you were foolish enough to be that 'what', you'd soon feel the underside of a heavily hobnailed sandal. Thieves pressed back into the mouldering walls, in some cases leaving an imprint.

This time, as he was on official business, he carried his mace of office, a level-sixty cursed weapon which was said to sing when it reaped a harvest of blood and souls. It hadn't had to do so for a very long while, and Lord Slave didn't have the heart to tell his minions that it was the singing that constituted the curse.[32]

There were times when it was a good thing to have had one's ears burned off in battle.

Nevertheless, the Grand Vizier heard all, despite his lack of face-furniture. Right now, the lumpy bits that had floated to the top of the Guild Tenebral were helping him with his inquiries, and they all seemed terribly keen to unload their stricken consciences.

Maybe part of this was the way that Throne's Shadow thugs had tied them all to a row of mismatched chairs, doused them in lamp oil, and lit Lord Slave a cigar. Certainly, part of it was the very precise and careful way he'd placed Mister Bun Bun on the table in front of them, and then fitted him out with a tiny judge's gavel and wig.

---

32. Through some strange cross-dimensional interference, what the mace sung was in fact 'I want to break free' by Queen, though not in the original tones of Mr F. Mercury, but instead a rendition by a drunken long-distance truck driver in a karaoke bar in downtown Seoul, South Korea

"So it's all official," he'd chuckled, with a knowing wink and a tap of where his nose presumably wasn't.

It didn't take long for the assembled scum of the guild to tell their sorry tale. A tale of costumed freaks, rampaging monster-men, flaming nudes and gutter-mouthed metal dwarves, to be sure, but a tale which it seemed they all agreed on. In Lord Slave's experience, a gaggle of witnesses often found it hard to agree on the colour of the sky without the persuasion of thumbscrews. Hence, a whole table full of high-ranking (and highly rank) thieves, beggars and street monsters singing from the same hymnal was horribly compelling.

"So, a strike force of completely mad nutters decided to take on one of the most heavily armed, legendarily sneaky, underhanded and generally poisonous..."

"Not to mention totally officially sanctioned..." pointed out a Guild lawyer in judicial rags, before shying away from the cherry-red end of Lord Slave's cigar.

"....and of course *officially sanctioned* packs of bastards this fair city has ever known, and in the fracas..." (the lawyer winced) "... King Snagpurse was totally incinerated."

Lord Slave gestured to the giant, greasy stain which surrounded the late thief-king's boots. A wisp of smoke curled up from one of them, as happens in these circumstances. "Exactly!" piped up Gebhard the Obtuse, who, thanks to the use of a dramatic finger and some serious eyebrow waggling, had been kept well out of the story. The thieves knew which side their bread was buttered on, and would sooner that it didn't suddenly become toast. "Mad sorcery without a permit. What's the world coming to, eh? Why, in my day, the College would have been down on those miscreants like a very... ummm... skip bin full of... errrr..?"

The reason for his embarrassing failure to complete a sentence was a terrifying and far-off bellow, which literally shook the Halfway House to its rotting foundations.

"What in Von Tuesday's name was *that*?" asked a grubby little thief, pushing his hood back from a face with more scars than features.

The sound came again, a roar of mixed confusion and agony, of the kind you wish you could make when you stub your toe in the dark on the way to the lavatory. It jangled up and down the spines of all assembled, playing all 33 vertebrae like xylophone keys.

Lord Slave was in front of Gebhard in two strides, his cape swirling magnificently.

"These intruders," he spat. "Did they look like they were *questing?* Did they mention they were here to stop you from... committing acts of evil?"

The obtuse one gestured around himself at the lamp-oil sodden crew who helmed the Guild Tenebral. A more wicked looking bunch of gutter-scum could not have been imagined, even by the most lurid writer of penny dreadfuls.

"Oh, aye. One of 'em said something about righteousness, and villainy, and such. But that was sort of lost behind all the punching and fireballs and nonsense, you understand. It's one of the first things they teach you at the old UC. When your enemy's giving a big long-winded speech, that's the best time to start powering up a good hot lightning bolt."

The sound came again, this time accompanied by a counterpoint of far-off screams.

"Of course!" said Slave. "The Unspeakable College! That's the sound of a Mantigore in distress!"

Gebhard chuckled, producing a soggy roll-up from somewhere about his person.

"That seems a bit unlikely, squire. I've seen the beast, and it's usually the one on the delivering end of any distress that's lying about, if you catch my meaning."

He suddenly found a leather-clad finger right up under his nose.

"Don't even *think* about moving, spellcaster! We'll be back, and I will personally get to the bottom of this! Right now, however... it appears I have to go and save a monster from some bloody heroes."

Gebhard's eyes crossed. It occurred to him that while Lord Slave's finger was thoroughly unmagical, it did have one advantage over his own. It could likely poke right up his nose and into his brain with just a twitch of the huge Grand Vizier's muscles.

"B...b...best of luck?" he croaked, fumbling for his cigarette.

Lord Slave stepped back and gestured to Throne's Shadow. Twenty black-clad guards snapped to attention.

"Just don't try to light that thing, you dunce," sighed the Right Hand of Himself, as his troops marched out of the Halfway House. Gebhard the Obtuse looked down at the cigarette in his hand, then at the pools of lamp oil everywhere, then at the thieves and cutpurses on either side of him, eyes bulging in terror.

He popped the unlit roll-up into his mouth, closed his eyes, and swallowed.

Across town, and some few fathoms below it, Jack Somewhat was doing the same. He wasn't swallowing a damp twist of sailor's tobacco, however, but his terror. It may have tasted slightly better (being all but metaphorical) but it still stuck in his throat in exactly the same way.

Things really had started to go horribly wrong the second Jack pried open the huge doors to the Mantigore's pit. The initial wrongness was this: there'd been a dead man leaning back on a kitchen chair inside of them, enjoying a cup of hot cocoa.

"Wha! Alarm! Intruders! Spilled beverages! Disaster!" yelled the revenant as it toppled over backwards, its hugely spiked armour clattering. It came to a stop like a pile of discarded saucepans, peering up at Jack through milky white eyes. "'Ere! Are you lot supposed to be pokin' about down this part of the dungeons? Only there's lots of signs, see, about how you're not supposed to. Gotta Mantigore in there, and it's more than my job's worth if it goes missing."

The undead creature rose creakingly to its feet, all seven-foot tall and sinewy, its skin a patchwork of stitches and staples.

"We're students," said Amber quickly. "They... ummm... sent us to collect some things from the cellars." she flapped her hands around in circles at the wrists, in the internationally approved signal for 'help me out with this colossal lie, please'. Jack, veteran of far too many apprenticeships, knew just what to do.

"There's a list, and all. Left-handed screwdriver. A long weight. Double-positive battery. A sudden wrench. A pair of irreversible nuts. Aaaand…" (he peered intently at what was, in fact, a receipt for some of Ranulf's fine sausages) "an extra-long loose screw, whatever that is. The master thought it was quite risible, that one, though I suspect it's to fix the potions shelf."

The revenant grimaced.

"They're havin' you on, my son. Bloody wizards. Don't get me started. Three hundred years I've been down here, and not so much as a 'thank you'. Take my advice, lad, if a man in a pointy hat and a dress asks you if you want the secret to immortality, don't drink it!"

He stumped over to the door and leaned against it, moving the massive slab not one iota.

"Anyhow, if you lot wouldn't mind. There's a very endangered species down 'ere, and like I said..."

Montmortimer shrugged. Jack dithered. Amber simply couldn't believe it had worked. But Ranulf the Butcher was grinning from ear to ear, rummaging in his massive knapsack.

"It's been bloody ages since I've even *seen* an undead! Ages! I've always wanted to try that scroll of holy banishment I nicked from the Temple of the Inner Dawn..."

Amber noticed that her erstwhile tutor's mind was doing that thing again, where it clicked merrily along on little rails of insanity. She quickly stepped between the elderly dead man and Ranulf.

"An endangered species, you say? But there's only ever been one Mantigore. That's hardly a spec..."

The thing waggled what remained of its eyebrows. One appeared to have been replaced with a dried caterpillar.

"Not *it*, you pillock. US. If the beast wakes up, we're all for the chomp. Well, it'll spit me out, right, hence the undead thing, obviously. But it plays merry hell with the armour, and it's a lot of work with a tinker's hammer to get the tooth marks out."

Which was a very, very bad time for Monty to pipe up.

"Errr... gentlemen. And lady, in fact. The, umm. The snoring's stopped."

Everyone except Ranulf found their eyes drawn to the gap between the huge doors, their heads moving as if tugged by invisible strings. Something behind the gates snorted, sending a huff of dusty air rolling across the little collection of would-be heroes (and one mummified custodian).

"Ooooh, he can be a sneaky bugger, for all how big he is." moaned the undead, rolling back his milky white eyes as a shadow fell upon him...

There was a sudden lunge. There was a blast of reeking, summer-midden-pit breath. The doors slammed back on their wrist-thick hinges, and a great battering-ram triangular head bulled forth, beady little eyes burning with hatred. A mouth crammed full of arrowhead-shaped teeth chomped closed on the unfortunate custodian, then the darkness swirled, stirring up a menagerie stench, and the beast was gone.

It had been a lot bigger than Jack assumed it would be.

Too big to actually fit through the door, despite the door being immense.

And a lot more... *toothy*. In fact, Jack's overwhelming impression was one of a great enamel bear-trap, hinged and dripping like a dentist's nightmare.

There was a second or two of what sounded like an old copper bathtub being stomped on in hobnailed boots. Then something came sailing out between the gap in the doors, to slide and scrape along the flagstones trailing a comet-tail of mucous. It was half the custodian, from the waist up, and he groaned, slopping drool from out of his eye sockets.

"Oooooh, bloody hell! If he's swallowed my legs again, we'll need the extra-strength monster laxatives. And that always ends in tears, let me tell you!'

Monty pointed one trembling finger inside the doors.

"So, the big plan here is that *we* are supposed to fight *that*?"

Ranulf had found the right scroll, but seemed more than a bit peeved that his undead foe had been (as he'd likely put it) 'cloven in twain'.

"Not just fight. *Vanquish.* Heroically. Come on! If it was the size of a bichon frise it'd hardly be the work for heroes, would it?" He looked around at the frankly unimpressed faces of his students. "Would you like me to go first?"

As if to punctuate his sentence, a huge scorpion tail came whipping out between the gates, all segmented and scaly. The wicked barb on the end would have skewered Montmortimer, had he not been so supernaturally fast.

"Truth be told, I'd rather we all just went home," confessed the fop. "The wizards might not take kindly to us... vanquishing... their beast. It's the mascot for their cricket team."

Jack nodded in agreement.

"As I was just mentioning to someone recently, it'd be far more heroic to actually do some good, rather than just punch wildlife while breaking and entering."

Amber shrugged.

"The big thick one's got a point. And Monty, too. We've already killed one wizard..."

"Henchman," interjected Ranulf.

"By accident," said Jack.

"... and ruined an antique door. If we slip away quiet-like, we could all be home in time for breakfast."

The Butcher wrung his meaty hands.

"I can't help but think that you're not grasping the theory, here. Punching wildlife while breaking and entering? That's the very definition of barbarian heroing! Did Krot the Decimator worry about *trespassing* when he fought the evil spider priests and wrested the amulet of Zothnar from the mad god Xargenox? Did Blood-drinking Bardan the Bruiser care that the two-headed dragon

Grimnognir was a protected species when it ravaged the townspeople of Sportingroingaard? Do you think Throgg the Outlander, gods bless his furry underpants, filled out health and safety forms in triplicate before he wrested the black sceptre of the Necrodemon from the cultists of Sha-Behab and their four-armed, fire-breathing lord?"

He looked around, eyebrows raised.

"*Like bloody fun they did!* It's simple arithmetic. We're heroes. That's a monster. Jurisdiction sorted."

The scorpion tail tried again, and this time something huge slammed up against the door frame, fixing all assembled with a glare from one black and glistening eye.

"All the same, professor, but I'd like to be excused to go to the bathroom," said Monty. Ranulf sighed.

"Fine," he said. "Watch and learn!"

He unrolled the scroll, causing half a very sticky undead to cover his eyes with both hands, and then, after a second, turned it up the right way. He sucked his teeth noisily.

"Now, your average magic scroll is a one-shot. Point it at your monster, see, get a good deep breath, and read the word on the parchment. It's probably going to be in some heathen lingo, but the main thing is to bellow it good and loud, thusly..."[33]

Ranulf drew in a huge breath, filtered by his beard. Then he exclaimed a word which seemed to take on physical form as it burst from his mouth, filling the space not just with sound, but with a sickle-blade swirl of glassy shadows, all spiked and skittering. Jack tasted vinegar and dust as the Magic Word sizzled in through one ear, tracked its muddy claws across his brain, then popped out the other. Then it gathered itself up, aimed at the Mantigore, and buzzed at it like a swarm of hornets.

The scroll Ranulf had found was supposed to crumble the undead to dust, so the custodian of the beast-pits (who we never introduced properly, but who was called, in life, Ian) was glad it missed him. The priests of the Temple of the Inner Dawn were very cross about

---

33. Magic books, tomes and scrolls abounded across the Archipelago, ranging in power from fortune cookie inserts inscribed with a cure for verrucas, through to the most forbidden volume ever set to parchment, Jean-Pierre De Robichaux's magnum opus of insane pastry cookery, *Une histoire complète des gâteaux érotiques*, which contained images of cakes considered erotic by the Elder Gods, the Things Outside of Space, The Fairly Average Old Ones and the Loiterers in Darkness – pretty much all of those beings which look like an explosion in a mollusc factory.

undeath in all its forms and were subsequently banned from Grand Sepulchre as a discriminatory hate group. But their sorcery was most potent. It struck the Mantigore right in the eye, rippling through it in a burst, like gamma radiation through a ham sandwich.

Unfortunately, the spell was confused.

The Mantigore wasn't alive in the traditional sense, having been made by a mad wizard. But it wasn't really undead, either. Not in the 'grab your spade, Igor, we're having a recruitment drive' manner. So, the spell (a complex one, with just enough of a mind of its own to be nasty) decided to split the difference. Rather than crumbling the huge monster to dust, it simply made it feel as though it had been beaten up with cricket bats, then gave it a headache of the kind that would make you bypass the aspirin and go straight for a hacksaw.

Hence that first bellow of rage – the one that caught Lord Slave's attention, halfway across the slumbering city.

And hence something else.

Because Enkalderon the Younger, (origami expert, libertine, level thirty-seven mage and creator of abominations) had designed his masterpiece to *evolve*, if it was ever in trouble. Now, with pain twisting through its every nerve, the Mantigore threw off five centuries of indolence and gluttony, its flesh writhing and its joints popping as more muscle and sinew were added to its wings.

Those huge, draconic pinions slapped open, nearly spanning wall-to-wall in the creature's pit. And with a single great downstroke, which blew dust, guano and gnawed bones out in a radial blast, the Mantigore launched itself upward.

CLANG!

Several raging tons of beast smashed into the domed cage atop the pit. The bars bent under the terrible impact, but they held.

Now came the second great bellow from the Mantigore, the one which had convinced Lord Slave of just what was afoot this night. The creature slammed back to earth, shook itself like a wet labrador, then snarled, a sound which grated several square yards of tooth enamel up against even more of the same.

"What have you *done*, you silly arsehole?" wailed the custodian, propping himself up on the stump of his waist. "If that thing gets out, it'll eat half the city."

"There, there. Calm yourself," replied Ranulf, with a thoroughly mad grin on his face. It was the kind Jack had seen on the mugs of several alchemists, when the fumes got to them and they began to think they were a pretty yellow lemon tree named Arthur. "We're *heroes*. This is the kind of thing we sort out."

Montmortimer had drawn his swords, but was looking at the pair of them as if they were toothpicks.

"Sort *that* out? With *these*? Are you, as the servant classes would put it, 'avin a larf?"

The Butcher brandished one finger.

"Only the rousing, merry battle-laugh of the true barbarian hero. *Yo ho!* Go on, try it."

"Yo... ho?"

"Whooo," went Jack, unconvincingly. Amber just rolled her eyes.

"Look, it's all about teamwork, see. Monty there, can distract the beast without being so much as scratched. Jack's got the power behind his punch to stun it. I can tactically expose its weak points. Then Amber here can use her incredible accuracy and skill to strike the killing blow. We just have to work together as a team!"

The student heroes looked at him as if he'd just explained the unified field theory of space and time in fluent Chungdoji. Ranulf gestured with his axe.

"And if we *don't*, it'll definitely do the thing that the skeleton man said. Eat everyone. Wreck the city. All that. Come on! What are you made of?"

"Meat, unfortunately," said Jack, risking a glance at Amber to see what she thought of all this. The young rogue nodded once and slapped him on the shoulder.

"Just do the thing with the muscles, and everything will be okay," she said. "The voice in my head has a plan."

"Wait, what? You have one of those too? What am I supposed to do with the muscles once I... erm..."

Amber gave him a cool, appraising look as he dithered, all red and awkward.

"We're all a bit crazy, Jack Somewhat. But here's a tip. Try to let the muscles do the thinking. They're definitely better at it than your brain. And..."

Now came a second great hammer-and-anvil crash, as the Mantigore once again battered against the bars of its prison.

"And what?" wailed Jack, drawing his huge and ludicrous sword against his better judgement.

Amber smiled, a small and lopsided smile that kicked Jack's heart sideways in his chest.

"And at least I'll have something nice to look at while we get ourselves killed," she said, extending one arm to let Skrx flow down to settle on her wrist. Then she turned, sword held out to one side, and started walking toward the door. Inside, something huge and scaly slammed up against the wall, hard enough to crack the massive brickwork on this side.

"Well, go on," hissed Ranulf, leaning in so that Jack could smell his beard oil. "You can't let the lady do this all alone, can you? She'll be pulverised. Masticated. Discom... thingy... It'll be messy."

Not content to be left out of the bullying chorus, Rodney piped up as well.

"She's the closest thing to a princess we've got, so you'd better save her. It's the heroic thing to do."

Jack couldn't see that he had much choice, but he truly hated to have to agree with these two.

"First of all, I'm not at all sure about this hero business, and second, she's not my princess. Not in that kind of sense. It's...complicated, but..."

"Shush," said Rodney. **"Forget the princess bit, then. Just think of this as the motivation I was talking about earlier."**

The horrible truth was, he *did* want to rescue Amber. Even if she wasn't the type who usually looked like she needed rescuing. Images flickered across his mind of all the ways he could do it, and they were rendered in crisp black lines and bright colours. *Amber swept up in his arms as he swung away on a rope. Amber leaning against his manly chest as he stood on top of the Mantigore's vanquished corpse.* Newsprint images, flipped on pages in his brain...

"Fear not! The ſcarlet ſpectre is here!" he said, his voice coming out all booming and scratchy, like a bad connection between wizard's skrying mirrors. Jack felt his muscles twist and expand, his clothes ripping as his red, stretchy undergarments took up the strain. The big cursive character on his chest visibly glowed as a cape he didn't remember putting on flapped out behind him, all yellow-gold and tactically stupid. "Evildoers, prepare to feel the... ummm... *rich, meaty flavour of justice!"*

"Really?" asked Montmortimer, with a little shrug. "Oh well. If we're doing this, we'd better do it with style, eh?"

Ranulf whooped and brandished his axe. Ian the Custodian did not look well pleased.

"You idiots! It's got you outnumbered one to four!"

But the combined might of the Guild Errant wasn't listening. They were piling in behind Amber to face a monster.

The first impression Jack had of the Mantigore's pit was one of utter, nose-clobbering stench. As a lad used to cleaning privies for a guild who drank mercury for fun, Jack knew bad smells. This was something else. This was a stench that was almost visible, and which screwed itself into the sinuses like an auger covered in hot sauce.

The second impression was of a gigantic creature rushing straight for him, its shark-mouth gaping and drooling. Snicker-gnash teeth ground and dripped as four huge rhinoceros feet came pistoning closer, driven by cubic tons of muscle.

Amberelia was right between them.

Raw heroism fizzed wild inside Jack's skull, overriding the switchboards of terror and trepidation. Jack pulled back a fist. Muscles bulged. He closed his eyes, gritted his teeth, and waited for the impact as he swung...

PAF!

Amber actually saw the little green explosion as she made a desperate dive. She saw the nonsense word traced out in sparks within it. Jack's uppercut stopped the Mantigore like a fortress wall stopping a runaway manure wagon, piling up its bulk in scaly folds as its shark-nose bent double. A selection of tooth enamel flew wide, whipped on ropes of drool and blood.

But the Mantigore was a cunning foe. Its scorpion tail lashed up and over, the stinger on its end humming like a plucked rapier.

Which is exactly what parried it. Monty may not have had the strength of Jack, but he was supernaturally quick, appearing with a small lacy thunderclap to divert the sting away. It punched into the wall of the pit, leaving the beast stuck, its tail writhing.

"I say! Get at it, old sport!"

Ranulf didn't hesitate. He was in there with the axe before the Mantigore could rally, chopping at its neck scales and shearing off a glittering spray. Each one was the size of a saucer and hard as steel. But beneath...

Slide in, under that flapping wing, then spring off its knee as it collapses, driving a dagger deep into the exposed white flesh...

That's what the calm, cool voice inside Amber's mind suggested, even as her training took over. Time seemed to slow down as she pelted across a carpet of cracked and marrow-dry bones, sliding in a pall of dust, dagger spinning between her fingers...

This time, the bellow which came from the creature's throat was one of confusion and agony. A geyser of blood blew Amber backwards, drenching her to the toes of her boots as she tucked and rolled. One final thing. Skrx snapped forward with his powerful little fighting arms as Amber flew, spitting a quarrel directly at one of the creature's beady black eyes.

Amber hit the ground and rolled, the breath punched out of her lungs. Jack leapt backward, avoiding a massive tonnage of collapsing Mantigore. Ranulf swung his axe, severing the sting on the creature's tail. And Monty reappeared from a brocaded blur, leaning nonchalantly on his sword. There was a horrible little squelching noise and a pop, like someone stepping on a grape. The Mantigore's bellow clawed its way up through several octaves, then sputtered out, like a steam whistle running out of pressure.

"There," said Ranulf, neatly catching the football-sized stinger as it landed. "Teamwork. The bigger they are, the harder they... vanquisise, I guess. So, how do we reckon we could have improved on that little performance?"

"I'd vote for more style, and an audience," said the world's fastest fop. "I can't shake the idea that people are supposed to be watching us do this hero stuff."

Ranulf tossed the stinger in his palm a couple of times, as if to heft its weight.

"No lad. She's a terrible solitary game, the heroing. One minute you have a band of merry adventurers around you, next thing you know there's wall-to-wall orcs, and you're vowing vengeance for people whose names you didn't quite bother to remember." He frowned, memories bubbling like gumbo behind his eyes. "Now, as far as style goes..."

"We should have properly killed it," said Jack, taking a cautious step away from the carcass. There was a creaking noise from what remained of the Mantigore, a sound like corsetry under extreme duress. "I don't think we actually did. That was too easy."

Amber narrowed her eyes.

"Got it right in the peeper with some very nasty black stenchwort extract. Enough to demortify a small elephant."

"It's making *noises*, though. There! It twitched!"

Ranulf grimaced.

"Probably just gases escaping the carcass. They can often sound a lot like growls or moans. Where do you find a *small* elephant, anyhow? And why would you want to assassinate one?"

This time Jack was certain he wasn't hallucinating. Hallucinating, in his experience, was a hard-earned condition which didn't just trundle along to dish out handy excuses at times like these. It was usually pursued behind crumbling damp taverns, from the pockets of men with names like 'weasel-faced Percy', for large amounts of coin.

The Mantigore trembled. It made a sound like a bagpipe being slowly forced under the surface of a vat of treacle.

"There!"

"See?" Gases of decomposition and suchlike. Making sounds like those..."

"Oi! You down there! What have you done with our bloody mascot?"

"Sounds *very much* like those of an irate wizard?" asked Monty.

Ranulf grinned.

"Yes, exactly! They can often sound exactly like a very ticked-off wizard shouting at you. But there's no reason to..."

"If it's dirty unhygienic adventurers again, you'll feel the bloody edge of my staff, so you will! If I had a hot dinner for every time some sword-swinging, sandal-wearing pillock with more pectoral muscles than neurons tried to torment the poor old Manty, I'd... well, I be about as fat as I actually am! Ian?"

"That's a surprising amount of co-incidental gases," said Amber. "Incidentally, that man in the dress up there is about the size of a small elephant. Skrx?"

Ian, the undead custodian, came stumping into the pit on his hands, dragging his truncated spine in the dirt.

"Down here, master! It's heroes, apparently! And the Mantigore's got me bloody legs again, pardon my Zalois!"

By now it was apparent that there really was a wizard up at the top of the pit, leaning over the cage of bent and buckled bars. He was quite a sight, too – an Archmage Pursuivant of the Order of the Third Sun, in pyromancer's robes of red and orange silk. Wizards can go one of two ways with tenure and seniority; rail thin, pointy-bearded and vicious, or round, scholarly, bushy-bearded and equally vicious.

The technical term for a group of wizards is a 'thaumaturgical holocaust', and they only worked together as a college thanks to the metaphorical big iron hammer of Himself hanging over them[34]. Some distracted themselves from their natural tendency to murder or enslave their peers by turning to study; others became drunks, debauched libertines or, in this case, *gourmands*. One or two became so loopy they even tried to teach students.

"Don't just stump there, Ian, get them out of the way! The bleedin' thing hasn't gone through a moult for at least forty years, and it's going to be messy."

"Moult?" asked Monty, just as a loud cracking noise rang out from the carcass of the Mantigore, followed by a huge and lusty fart.

"Now *that* was definitely gas escaping the body," said Ranulf. But then he yelped, throwing away the bulbous stinger in his hands. For it, too, had begun to swell up and crack. When it struck the ground, it split right open like a ripe puffball, and something with an odd number of legs, eyes and mouths lurched skittering from its remains, scuttling over to the main mass of the Mantigore and wriggling inside.

"I told you!" shouted Jack, as the outer skin of the creature swelled up tight and glossy, losing its colour. Cracks ramified across this new, waxy outer skin.

"Don't let them escape!" hollered the wizard, hiking up his robes. *"I'll go and get the preceptor of the Three Fingered Hand. Put it to sleep so we can mend the cage."* He took a moment to waggle his staff menacingly at the heroes. *"You lot are in a whole shit-cauldron of trouble!"*

"No, we're not!" replied Ranulf cheerfully.

"Yes, you are!" said the pyromancer, disappearing from above.

"Don't let them escape? Sure, I'll just kick them all unconscious, of *course* master, three bags bloody full, master," grumbled Ian. He tried to make a rude gesture with one skeletal hand and toppled over sideways.

---

34. And of course, the real one. In the two hundred and ninth year of the Urzoman Dominion, He had adjudicated a magical duel between two Thaumatarch-Aspirants known as Gartho the Puce and Kelroth Skysplitter, both of whom were quite evenly matched. When the collateral damage threatened to turn a large part of Bulbous Corners into sapient breadfruit pudding, He took it upon Himself to show a certain amount of kingly wisdom. Smashing the pair of them to nasty pulp with his huge battle-hammer, the Dark Lord commanded that half of the unidentifiable mush should be shovelled into a barrel, and that this barrel should serve as High Thaumatarch until such time as the wizards got their collective heads out of their arses and just had a vote or something. *Side note – the barrel governed over a period of peace, expansion and fraternal wizardry which lasted ninety years, until it was thrown out by an overenthusiastic young janitor. The next high Thaumatarchy was decided by an egg and spoon race.*

"No, we're not..." repeated Ranulf, though this time less convincingly. He was watching the carcass of the Mantigore, which now seemed more befitting of the term 'cocoon'. It wobbled. Smoke puffed out.

"Unfortunately, yes we are," confirmed Amberelia, as the whole thing split down the middle, releasing a stench like a thousand hot latrines on a summer night. Skrx chittered and clattered his mandibles, strobing different colours.

The thing which emerged from the skin of the old Mantigore was still, definitely, a Mantigore. Because the whole complicated skein of the evolutionary heresy had been wrapped up inside its pith and marrow, the beast had simply changed to better face Jack and his friends. Its tail split into three with a sucking, sticky snap, scorpion stings becoming eyeless, fanged cobra heads. Its scales were replaced with the spiked carapace of a lobster, dull grey like beaten metal.

Extra legs thrust out from its sides, ripping through the scutes of its belly, each one a many-jointed insect monstrosity tipped with mantis barbs. Except for the front pair, which were equipped with lobster claws. Its sharklike mouth unzipped even wider, and a tentacle thrust out with *another mouth* on its end, this one ringed by spikes. A profusion of eyes popped up like mushrooms after rain, covering the front of the creature, which was now armoured and horned like some titanic jungle beetle, chitin curving up and down to from a beak and battering ram at once.

"Well, that's not so bad," said Ranulf. "Actually, I'd expected much wor..."

Then the Mantigore roared, spreading its new wings wide. There were four of them, and they were vast enough to scrape the dripping walls of the pit. They appeared along with a bellow that shook the whole Unspeakable College to its foundations, and a belch of flame, greenish-blue and hissing with sparks.

"Quick question, Mr the Butcher," asked Monty. "If I pee these pants, am I allowed to go back home and change into something different? Asking for a friend..."

Jack was also having considerable third, fourth and ninth thoughts about this hero business. Rodney, of course, was cackling like a madman in his head, and his pulse came pounding like war-drums, the air around him slippery with unmagic. Every movement seemed to be accompanied by the rustle of turning pages, and his arm, when he looked down at it, was made up of thousands of tiny, coloured dots. The urge to tackle the beast head-on fought tooth and nail with the part of him which was still, underneath it all, a scared and bewildered primate. He almost leapt out of his skin when something cold and clawed gripped him by the ankle.

"Little help?" asked Ian. "If you can get me upright, see, we might get out of here alive."

"How?" wailed the erstwhile alchemist.

"Well, it's *specialised*, right. To gain one thing, it has to give up something else. That's how the big hats described it to me. So, it's night time, in a pit, and it wants to avoid getting poked in the eyes. I'd wager it's gotten very, very bad eyesight right now."

Jack did a quick double take.

"How many times has this happened, then? Do you have some kind of plan written down?"

Ian shrugged, which tipped him over again.

"More than you'd expect. That's one of the most legendary monsters in the whole 'Arch, there. What with the rumours that its heart is a giant ruby the size of yer head, and that its blood is the elixir of eternal youth, we get people in here all the time having a crack. 'Course, it were the wizards what started them rumours, right? A steady supply of adventurers means that they bring in all kinds of enchanted codpieces and magical scimitars and such. They kind of do the questing for us."

Jack gripped the skeletal custodian by his shoulders and dragged him up until they were face to face.

"The *plan*, you mouldering waste of calcium! *The plan!*"

"Now, now. Hold yer' orses. The tubby bloke from before's gone to get the chief of the mindbenders – the Order of the Three Fingered Hand. A gaggle of those lads will put our mate there right to sleep. In the meantime, we have a specialist on staff who can distract the beastie, and you bunch can cower in a corner or something."

"A... specialist?"

"Yeah," nodded Ian, with a sound like a bag of maracas falling down some stairs. "Big bloke made entirely of metal. We'll pop his head off the door where he works, screw it on his body, and let him get chased around for a bit while the wizards get their night-night spell ready. Works every time."

Jack's heart sank to about the vicinity of his knees.

"Tall feller, is he? Bit of the gargoyle about him? Keeps a brass ring in his mouth?"

"You know Barry, then?" grinned Ian, who had, let's face it, very little choice.

There came a snort from behind them, pitched low down on the brainstem, down in the mess of wires and cables where the reptilian hindbrain hangs out, leaning on a lamp post and flipping a coin.

Jack and Ian slowly turned their heads until they were almost cheek to cheek. The Mantigore loomed over them, its face a prow of spiked chitin studded with eyes.

"It's just possible", hissed the skeleton, "that its sense of vision is based on movement. If we stay very, *very* still..."

A bellow blasted his helmet clear off and made Jack's hair stand out sideways. Gobbets of truly horrible drool pelted them like a horizontal rain.

For a second, it looked as though the story of Jack Somewhat, rather pathetic hero, would end with a gristly crunch.

Then Ranulf was there, leaping up on top of the beast's triangular skull with his axe reversed. Opposite the blade was a kind of mining pick, of the type used for winkling knights out of their armour. He smashed it down into the glistening carapace behind the Mantigore's horn and whooped like a madman.

"Come on, boys! Up and at 'em! Let's hit this big bastard with everything we've got!"

It was at that moment, as the beast reared up on its stubby legs, all four wings thrashing, that Jack realised something.

Ranulf the Butcher was completely insane.

Not the same kind of insane as Multhazar Threck, whose mind had been made up of the mildewed remnants of normality, shattered by years of chemical abuse and lashed together with the thin twine of tradition and ceremony.

Oh no. Ranulf the Butcher wasn't *out* of his mind. He'd managed to stuff himself quite completely *inside it*, and he wanted to drag the rest of the world in there along with him. For a brief instant Jack could comprehend some of the things this explosion of muscles and beard-hair had seen and done, the amount of death he'd ploughed through the world behind him, and just how that would engender a steely, fire-hardened resolve to never look back, to never question...

Heroes are Just. Heroes dispense Justice. And Justice is Just... Justification.

A part of his mind – one that didn't have Rod in it at all - gently took the controls.

You beat the villain, and they were the villain because you beat them. You slew the monster, and it was a terrible evil monster because you were left alive to tell the people how wicked it was.

The voice in that other part of his head was yammering and raving, trying to drown out these thoughts. But they were the clearest, most utterly perfect thoughts Jack Somewhat had ever had, even with the aid of Soto Scalizari's very best stumbleweed. When he turned his head, he heard the sound of crinkling paper, and smelled powdered sugar and freshly mown grass.

Jack looked down at the huge, improbable fist of the ſcarlet ſpectre. He willed it to open up into five fingers. And as the Mantigore came crashing down, its massive snout just inches away, he reached out and gave it a friendly pat.

"You're not so bad, are you boy?" he said, in a voice that sounded like two voices at once. "Just bored, and hungry, and sick of all the little creatures poking you with metal. Am I right?"

The Mantigore, in its tiny little brain, wanted to bite him in half. It settled for trying a bellow, and maybe a belch of flame again. But the little human reached out a finger and shushed it.

"How would this go, if this was your story? *Giant lonely beast tormented by idiots who were afraid of it?* Huh." Jack Somewhat, deep in his heart of hearts, was well aware of what that felt like. He leaned up against the Mantigore's spiked cliff of a face. He slung a companionable arm around its horn. "I bet you'd rather just have a... a nice big decomposing walrus for dinner, and a pair of slippers, the size of a cottage to chew on." he sighed. Was there a second there when the magical aura around the Mantigore wobbled? When the strange harmonics spliced into its sinews by Enkalderon the Younger thrummed to subtle wavelengths, reversing hundreds of years of toothscrabble survival? Amber was watching, and she was sure that for an instant, the beast shimmered and *shrunk...*

But just for an instant. Because just then, the combined coven of Wizards who had assembled above gave the signal, drawing down arcanum from those dimensions which lie at odd angles to our own. They let the power of creation seep in through cracks with too many sides, and from points which defined constellations that hurt your teeth to think about.

Fingers wove sigils dark and wild. Words were spoken that came out sharp and crooked.

And a blast of power that could have lit up all Jansamrana for a month blazed black and jagged from their hands, spearing down to strike the Mantigore right between several of its eyes.

13
The Irrefutable Contractualisation

Magic.

The greasy stuff, the lightning of the mind, the secret lore of the learned and sage - otherwise known as witches' fire, the Hidden Word, the Art Arcanum or, to all non-mages, as a bloody nuisance.

There have been many attempts to codify just how it works, throughout the aeons of the 'Arch. Ever since the earliest days of that vast and watery realm floating, (as we've noted), in a disreputable part of space-time.

The truth is, the Words of Command, the Meditations of Control, the Sigils of Balance and the Secrets of the Art are all different for each of the seven orders of wizards, just as they are different again for the Chalinese Sorcerers, Zalois Warlocks and the Red Sages of Khantif. But they're all doing the same thing.

Here's the trick. You can't - even with all the gothic jewellery, incense, mind-bending mushrooms and snazzy black robes in the world - whip the universe to your will. It's bigger, and older, and meaner than you, in a way which makes thermodynamics itself look merciful.

No, the secret is all in *moving yourself* to a universe in which, by a perfectly natural chain of causality, the desired effect has *already happened*. All magic, therefore, is a very complicated form of teleportation.

Imagine the now-classic (and probably a bit retro-chic) trousers of time. Make a choice – any choice, from what t-shirt to wear this morning to pushing the big red nuclear button while giggling maniacally – and you create two distinct pants-legs of reality. Now imagine that time and space are less a pair of slacks and more the kind of shapeless garment knitted by the granny of an Elder God, from one of those slimy cold dimensions of horror. Imagine that, in some places in the universe, the material which those tentacle-legs are knitted from is all stretchy and pliable, churning in the fabric softener of improbability.

Magic is all about very, very precisely explaining the series of causes and effects which would lead to your chosen outcome, from the subtle re-arrangement of neurons we call 'mind control' to the sudden occurrence of a massive localised earthquake, or the appearance of a custard square eight feet to a side. In an infinite universe, all of these things have already come to pass infinite times. Magic is simply all about going to the place where they have just happened, and taking credit for them in a loud and obnoxious fashion.

The best guess about the pyrotechnics, though, is that they're there *because we think they should be.*

The fireworks this time – when twenty self-important mages let fly with everything up their embroidered sleeves – were simply stunning.

A blast of jagged black lightning belted into the Mantigore's face with the heft of a sub-orbital hippo, making probability-disruption sensors all over the city howl, scream, chime (and in one case croak) their alarm. The skull in a gilded cage carried by one of Lord Slave's men shrieked, rattling against the bars as the poor fellow tried to keep up. In towers and aeries, dungeons and bordellos, the power-brokers of Jansamrana were woken from their slumber or pried from their distracting delights, all the better to batten down the metaphorical hatches.

And the real ones, of course. When wild magic started getting flung about, things tended to get crazy, and the great and good of the Urzoman Empire would prefer to keep their precious stuff unbroken.

In the steamy humidity of Ramathagan Street, Zoltan Creagle attended to the whispers of a raggedy little thief, then came rising from his bath of crushed ice and fragrant herbs like a drowned colossus.

"So *that's* his game, is it? Trying to take over the Guild Tenebral, is he? Well, Jack Somewhat, you may be smarter than you look, but you've forgotten one thing!"

The dripping wet, toga-clad Brutemaster screwed on his golden wreath and shuffled through the papers on his desk. "You signed a contract, lad! Eighty percent of what's yours is mine! Glurko, get the 'eavy mob. If he wins, we've got a guild to run. If he loses, we can nobble the bugger while he's down."

Down below the streets, in the intestinal maze of the sewers, the people who had *really* busted up King Snagpurse's party heard the echo of rusting horns in the deeps, and the bellow of a pissed-off Mantigore from above.

Something tugged inside the lot of them, like a fishhook in the soul. Billiam and Jory, who were carrying the cheerfully drunken Unstoppable It between them (and who had found out that It's name was actually Tarrence Bligh), came to a sudden halt. Soto Scalizari promptly ran into the back of them, causing the lot to go down in a heap. Slag Iron – still encased in her suit of battle nun's armour – turned a glowing green stare on the bunch.

"You felt it, didn't you?" she said. "****ing justice! ****ing monster up there, probably wants to eat some virgins or some such, and can I just walk away? Like ****** I can! Ever since I put this **** ****** ***** monkey ***** tuba **** three-olive martini ****** armour on, I've had the most horrible urge to save the world."

"Is that why you attacked the whole entire thieves' guild?" asked Soto, who was also a bit twitchy around the eyes. Visions of nebulous glory danced across his frontal lobes. "It's... well, it is kind of why *we* were there."

"It seemed like the thing to do," chipped in Bligh, who was at that pleasant stage of intoxication when the whole world seems to be wrapped in rainbow candy-floss. "...and of course, we figured, I mean, between the pair of us..."

"It might be a curse of some kind. It might just need that itch scratching, once, and then I can take this bloody **** ******ing cast-iron ball gown *off!*" Slag Iron looked at them all with her hands on her hips. "Ohhh, right, like you think this thing is *comfortable*, do you? And what about the necessaries, in the bathroom department? I don't dare stop for a curry, if you catch my drift. Don't get me started on chafing..."

"So, you reckon if we sort of sidle up there and, you know, we're at least present when that creature gets the old night-night..."

Slag Iron nodded.

"*Bingo*, as they say down at the temple of Quazirath on Chainsday evenings. Curse lifted. Then I can get down to the real business of the day."

"And that is?"

The slap and grind of metal fingers together gave a horrible intimation of what was going to happen to somebody's tender anatomy.

"I'm gonna find out which ****ing ******* cursed me with a sense of civic responsibility, of course. And introduce them to my haddock tenderiser, face first."

Billiam shuddered. He knew all too well the wrath (and sheer arm strength) of Grand Sepulchre's fisherwomen; he'd briefly dated a girl from the docklands who could open oysters with her bare hands. Suffice to say that after one indiscretion too many, he'd been forced to walk bow-legged for a week.

"Just to be clear, we're not actually going to try and *fight* that thing, are we? I mean, you heard that bellow. It doesn't sound like a feral tamarin, does it?"

"I think it might work if we're just in the general vicinity. To be sort of… *assembled*." said Soto, with the half-dreamy look on his face that all those present now associated with the green fizz of static.

"In that case, perhaps we had better start heading topside," growled the Grimshadow, pulling his very stylish black mask back across his face. "It sounds like there's plenty of assembling going on without us already!"

He was right, of course. Lord Slave himself arrived at the moat of the Unspeakable College just in time to watch a coven of mages scurrying across the high battlements above, their robes and vestments flapping in the updraft from that chasm of fire.

Admittedly, the moat was less impressive than it had been in earlier aeons, when the very rocks at the lip of the flame-moat had run like wax to make dribble-candle shapes, horribly suggestive of screaming faces. Now noxious gases rumbled and burped deep below, sending billows of flame up to lick the foundations of the College, and putting visitors who crossed the great iron drawbridge off their breakfasts.

"None shall pass?" quavered one of the wizards on guard duty, seeing the full bulk of Lord Slave bearing down on him like bad news personified. Muscles creaked and strained against oiled leather as he fronted up to the gates. The guard-wizard's outstretched finger fizzed and drooped.

"*Right,*" said Slave. "You see this mace? Very enchanted. Sings, and all. By its authority, I demand access, under the auspices of the civic power, may I not have to get Him to come down here and knock the plum pudding out from between your ears, alright?"

Which was not the correct speech, but Lord Slave could hear the sound of something massive slamming itself against iron and stone. He could feel, in his gnarly old twist of a soul, the warping and mangling of reality as sorcery made merry with the underpinnings of the world.

"Hang on, hang on," stammered the mage on the left, a tall, thin Geomancer wearing a neat little goatee and a robe patterned like molten lava. "Isn't it supposed to go 'Oh ye guardians of the dread portal of knowledge, we beseech thee... dumpty dumpty dum... something about secular majesty... diddly doo... and a thousand years of darkness, amen?"

Of course, *he* wasn't the one staring down the length of Lord Slave's mace of office, or indeed, noting how the huge man held it in *one hand*. The enchantments wrapped around the horrible weapon fairly boiled the air around it.

The second wizard – a fat little level-twelve necromancer – felt rather like a customs inspector who has just realised that the boat he's come aboard, *alone*, is crewed by gentlemen with hook hands, peg legs, eyepatches and very big swords. His skull-face mask slipped right down off his nose.

"Right y'are guv, lovely day for it, mind the step, Thaumatarch's office is third on the left, up the Winding Stair of Gnostic Wisdom, just past the cafeteria. *Shut up Eric!*"

This last to the geomancer, who had raised a single finger and opened his mouth, in the universally accepted sign for 'I've got a big rant about tradition to share with everyone'.

Lord Slave ignored Eric and leaned down until he was face-to-zippered-face with the little necromancer.

"I think, perhaps, this time, I should just take my lads right to your Mantigore problem, hmm?" he asked, all honeyed razors. The small round wizard goggled, suddenly wishing he'd paid more attention during vanishing lessons. He recalled that he was, in fact, supposed to keep everybody out, and thus protect the hallowed, cobwebbed sanctity of the halls of higher learning.

"Ohhh.... nah, mate, you've got it all wrong, see? We haven't got a Mantigore problem. It's probably the plumbing." Behind him, the College rocked from its roots to its many spires, as something huge belched flame and screamed, battering against the bars that held it down. "Ooooh. Blurble blurble clonk!" shouted the necromancer, while Eric put his face in his hands. "Quesadilla night, you understand. Very volatile for the bowels..."

Lord Slave's hand wrapped right around the top of his head, like a dragon's claws around a pumpkin. He leaned even closer, until his one twinkling eye was only an inch away. What the small mage saw there put the howling vistas of the realm of death in the shade.

"Good thing I've brought my big plunger, then," grated the Grand Vizier of the Urzoman Empire, just as his huffing, sweating retinue of Throne's Shadow soldiers caught up. "I think we can find our way to the... *blockage*."

The black-clad Throne's Shadow trooped in through the front doors, and Eric looked up beyond them, to the soaring battlements and spires of the College. Some of those towers were suspended by a single arching buttress and had pointy bits top and bottom. Some floated free of the main structure entirely and had upside-down ramparts and fiddly crenelations.

All of them were aswarm with wizards, some in their finery of robes and high turned-up collars, capes and pointy hats, others in their nightshirts and knitted beard-cosys, and at least one archmage in red long johns with hearts on them. The College was lit up like a Mercy Jim's Day Gateau with the multicoloured flames of staves, wands, amulets, magic rings and various numinous weapons, lofted in elderly fists. It's at times like these that the wise and erudite have the perfect *bon mot* to sum up the situation.

"Sod this!" said Eric, turning to his fat little associate. "You reckon any of the pubs are still open? We could pretend we weren't never here..."

But then...

...went a gigantic blast of black lightning, stuttering from the top of one of the towers.

It painted the whole world monochrome as it came. Power poured from the fingertips of twenty mind-bending wizards of the Order of the Three-Fingered Hand. Forty curly-toed boots and slippers levitated inches from the College battlements, as beards bristled, and feral tamarins burst screeching from the trees for miles around. The weave of magic focused in through a circle of glowing runes and belted down to smack the Mantigore right in the chops.

Eric and his mate, who were just on the periphery of the spell, both slumped down and started snoring immediately. Wild ricochets sizzled and bounced through the night-time air of Grand Sepulchre, inducing sudden narcolepsy wheresoever they landed. People face-planted into their dinners on Decameron Street, crashed their wagons on Skizarian's hump-backed cobbles, and even passed out cold in the middle of haggling in the Fleamarket. Crackles of green fire burst from the fingertips and ears of Jack Somewhat and his friends as the Mantigore copped the full force of the spell. All four tasted oily tin and smelled burning hair, as magic and ſuper-powers clashed, sparking wild.

But whatever was in Jack's blood was not so easily overcome. So it was that he, Amber, Monty, and Ranulf witnessed exactly what happened when twenty of the world's most powerful wizards gave the beast their all.

Absolutely nothing.

Well, that wasn't quite true.

Deep inside the new, nastily evolved Mantigore, that little knot of awful that had once been its stinger absorbed the magic and turned it into the equivalent of a bucketful of raw testosterone.

As we've noted, all magic is effectively a very cunning form of translocation. What the Mantigore had evolved, after several occasions of being blasted insensible by sorcery, was very much like the mysterious magnetic sense which pigeons and albatrosses use to navigate their way across the Arch', without maps or compasses. A thaumic lodestone-organ had burrowed into the creature's brain like a tick, telling it *exactly* where it was in the multiverse at all times[35], with such tungsten-hard certainty that no magic could move it, nor anything near it, to a more convivial set of eleven-dimensional co-ordinates.

Power was power, though. And the Mantigore wasn't about to waste the magical equivalent of several megawatts. Oh no.

Muscles bulged. Wings stretched. Spikes erupted. Eyes proliferated. Teeth lengthened and sharpened. And the damned thing GREW, bulking out until the four heroes who shared its pit were pushed up against one mouldering wall.

"Run away!" shouted Montmortimer, his wig trembling.

"Where to?" asked Jack, as the beast reared up on its hind legs, snouting out the source of its tormentors. "The door's behind it, and I don't think it's going to move out of the way anytime soon..."

---

35. Due to the now famous uncertainty principle, this means that the Mantigore was utterly unable to tell exactly how fast it was going, a point its lawyers would be able to use to great advantage if the huge, drooling horror ever received a speeding ticket.

He was wrong, however.

The panicked wizards up above them had seen their major incantation fail and had taken to pelting the Mantigore with a hodge-podge of whatever spells they had up their sleeves. Fireworks, shrieks, bolts of lightning and a rain of small, disgruntled chickens showered down from above as the creature braced its legs against the walls of the pit - and began to climb.

"Well, it's the College's problem now," said Amber, dislodging a chicken from her hair. "I suppose all we need to worry about is getting away before they can point their fingers and draw up a wanted poster."

Up above, the spells sputtered out, replaced by screams. Jaws like a meatwork's nightmare clamped around he bars of the cage and began to exert their terrible pressure, snapping spans of metal like harp strings. Rivets spanged off the stonework, making the College's sentient gargoyles cover their faces with their claws.

"Bugger this!" said Ranulf, who was pulling his beard with nervous tension. "If that thing gets out, it's going to eat half the city. We can't be heroes if we let that happen!"

Jack rounded on him, suddenly red with anger. It was all the frustration of the last few confusing, horrible days at once, and it had one of his improbably big hands wrapped around the Butcher's chain-mail collar before he could stop it.

"Get it through your head, old man! We're *not* heroes! Not your kind, with your levels and your monster manuals and your silly ideas about honour and valour. We're not the other kind either, with the capes, and the sad speeches about justice, and the one-liners that aren't actually very funny!" He sagged a little, realising that there were actual tears at the corners of his eyes, and that he had his erstwhile teacher halfway up the wall, pinned with one hand.

"We're screw-ups! We're *mistakes*! And if that bloody thing does eat half the city, it's your damned fault for bringing us here! We need *help*, not encouragement! This heroism's a disease, not a blessing!"

Up above, the Mantigore roared in triumph. The cage atop its pit was torn apart, the metal latticework savaged between its jaws and then thrown out into the harbour, where it sunk a small fishing scow.

Wizards legged it, faster than a bunch of elderly academics had any right to be able to. But down here, everyone was fixated on Jack's other fist. The huge, double-wide bunch of knuckles at the end of his very muscular arm. It was cocked back over his shoulder, ready to pound Ranulf the Butcher's head through the granite. And his eyes were glowing red, as well...

Jack realised what he was doing at the same time as Monty grabbed his wrist, and Amber slid in close, bringing her hand up to his neck. There was a curiously metallic sound, and Jack clearly felt several of the little hairs there cut through and float away. He looked.

"Erm..." he said, not daring to move his head. "Do you have big bone claws coming out of the back of your hand, miss? Because if that's not you, then someone else is perilously close to cutting my windpipe."

"I'd hardly want it to be anyone else, Jack. Now, put the mad old tutor down, nice and slow. I'll agree with you wholeheartedly about not being heroes. But we're not just murderers, either."

Jack shook his head, then let Ranulf slide down the scarred stone of the wall. The old warrior was looking past him, though, to the very empty space where the Mantigore had been.

"Gone," he croaked. "You're letting it get away. If you want to be right about not being murderers, lass, then you'd best be getting up and after it..." he chuckled, pushing himself to his feet. "As for you, Somewhat..."

A deep, oiled-mahogany voice cut him off.

"As for *all of you*, actually. My, my, my. I'd like to say I was disappointed, but I'd have to be surprised first. *And* have expectations above the ordinary, for the lot of you."

Lord Slave dropped into the pit as if he was stepping over a dry-stone wall in the countryside, landing with his mace slung over one shoulder. Behind him, crunches, screams and shouts rang out. Something exploded, sending purple flames billowing up in a spiral.

"Oh, bugger," said Monty, hanging by both arms from Jack Somewhat. "The jig's up, lads."

Lord Slave smiled.

"The jig, the polka, several line dances and a waltz, Mr Pettigrew. Jack, of course, we know from his aquatic escapades, and his much-discussed turn in the fighting pits. And Miss Chance. For all your talk of not being a murderer, it seems that your peers at the Guild Lachrymose found you a bit of a handful, hmm? Why don't you tell them which one you were sent to... what's the charming term you use... *demortify?*"

Amber blushed scarlet and jerked her claws away from Jack's neck. He noted that they sprouted from between the bones on the back of her hands, delicate pearly razors the length of her forearms.

"And *the Butcher*," continued Slave. "You know, I sent you Mr

Somewhat here because I wanted to see what he was made of. Your dungeon full of foolish training dummies and machines is outmoded, but quite rigorous. He could have been Throne's Shadow material. The fact these other two decided to join up should have been inconsequential. But you had to go above and beyond, didn't you?"

"It's what heroes do, m'lord," managed Ranulf, looking thoroughly embarrassed. Despite the leather, it was painfully obvious that Lord Slave had raised one eyebrow, with malice aforethought.

"Oh, indeed? And just after Jack here was explaining how you *weren't heroes at all.* But allow me to clarify. If you aren't heroes, then you are simply very stupid burglars, who have damaged a priceless antique building, released a horrible monster, and will, even if it takes Himself to banish the thing, face trial for all the damage it causes. There are places deep under the Malevolith that will hold you, no matter how strong, or fast, or cunning. Places *I* built to hold *me*, in fact, should I ever... but I digress."

The Grand Vizier had them all backed up against the wall now, his horrible, overwhelming bubble of personal space pressing like a heavy hand on their necks. "No. You get to have your wish. You get to be *heroes*, just one more time. Because, in the erudite words of one of our foremost archmages 'that bloody thing eats magic now, so sod this game of soldiers, it's all yours, guvnor!'

He turned, gesturing with his hideous, skull-faced mace of office. "Oh, for the erudition of academia, eh? That means we do this the old-fashioned way. By which I mean, we do it *Ranulf's* way, more's the pity. I need a party of adventurers. You're it."

Amber, quicker on the uptake than the boys, raised on hand. The bone claws protruding from her wrists slid back between her knuckles with a slick, organic sound.

"Mister Slave, Sir... umm... what happens if we win?"

The Grand Vizier made a strange sound, then, like sandpaper being flushed down a long-dry lavatory. It took Jack a while to realise it was laughter.

"Well then, Amberelia Chance, then you'll just have to explain to the Old Lady why you reneged on your mission and 'went native', as they say down on the Underbelly. I understand she's very... *understanding.* But as for the governing power, personified as it is, right now, by a horrible bastard – ME – well, we'll throw you a big parade. And then you and your friends will declare mightily that you're off to adventure somewhere else. You'll get on a ship, and wave to the adoring crowds, and never – this is the important part – *never* set foot in the Urzoman Empire, ever again."

"No more Guild?" croaked Ranulf.

"No. No more number twelve beef and bacon breakfast sausages, either, more's the pity. But those are your choices. Rot in prison, or perhaps – just perhaps – find a new life in exile. I might have one last job for Jack, though."

The big lad shrugged his shoulders.

"Why not? How could it be any worse?"

"Well, if you can hold your breath long enough, we still need to find a little something your old boss Multhazar Threck had on him when he died. Himself is getting a bit tired of waiting, and it's probably at the bottom of the lagoon."

The look in Lord Slave's one eye was flat, calm and frozen, like a sacrificial well in winter. Reading anything in it was like trying to read a spell book through lead covers.

Jack, never Jansamrana's best poker player, went through about five permutations of trying to keep a straight face, then played it off as an attempt at deep deliberation. He smacked one meaty fist into his palm.

"Right. We'll tackle this monster, then. Just you, me, Amber, Ranulf and Monty. That should be... umm..."

Lord Slave grinned behind his leather mask.

"Oh, it's not just us! There'll be one more member of our party who brings a certain, shall we say, legendary quality, all of his own."

For an instant Jack perked up. The Grand Vizier couldn't possibly mean it! He Himself, the Lich Emperor, was going to descend from his throne of ice and blades to help them? *Him?* A figure of such enormous power that he had confined himself to his tower for decades, lest his raw magic break the world?

"You don't mean...?" breathed Monty, obviously thinking the same thing.

"That's right!" enthused Lord Slave, pulling something furry and pink from out of the recesses of his cape.

He squeezed it. It squeaked.

"Mister Bun Bun is coming too!"

14

The Countermunicipal Destructification

THE FERAL TAMARINS of Grand Sepulchre were famous throughout the Arch', chiefly for their sheer numbers, noise, smell, and legendary sense of mischief. What the zoologists and natural philosophers of that watery realm didn't know, was that some of them were smarter than the people who studied them.

Certain troupes and tribes of the tiny creatures had infested the upper rooftops of the Unspeakable College for centuries, living among the forgotten coppices of chimneys, glass-domed orangeries, broken-down observatories and lead-banded cisterns which festooned the giant edifice. Magical leachate, stray spells, and no small amount of residue from Enkalderon the Younger's weird experiments had done things to the tiny primates, making them both more and less than they had been.

To put no fine point on it, they'd caught a bad case of civilisation. So it was, that as the Mantigore lumbered into the air on its four ungainly great wings, its passing caused a stir among tamarin scouts dressed in tiny suits of armour hammered out of plates and cans. Dire portents were read in marbles, pools of ink and cockroach entrails by tamarin sages, robed in used washcloths and UC cricket socks. The King of the Northern Transept, old and ailing, feared an attack by the combined forces of his treacherous nephew, the Baron of the Breakfast Kitchens, in alliance with the Witch-Queen of the Clockwise Expanse. The humans, running about in what, to the tamarins, was viewed as a kind of subterranean hades full of giants, barely factored into these intrigues.

But it was with a chittering wail of dismay that the massed forces of both the Transeptine Alliance and the Kitchen-Clockwise Axis witnessed something else huge and bloated floating above them, blotting out the moon and stars. All thoughts of conflict fled as the great bulbous shape of Lord Slave's air-cruiser, the *Truculent*

Righteousness, rose over the spires and chimneypots, dropping ladders from its gondola in a rope-tangle cascade.

Down deep into the Mantigore pit. The vast black dirigible was here to take on a cargo of heroes, the better to pursue that absent beast and bring it down. A crew of Mageineers and Techolytes fussed and sweated over the thaumo-clockwork motors which thrashed the air with their imitation dragonfly wings and maintained a wall of hissing brass valves and dials, feeding vile gases into the thing's air-bladders.

Every possible attempt had been, well... attempted... to make the *Truculent Righteousness* look less like a huge flying willy, but the state of the art had only come so far. The omen of a giant, disembodied phallus was exactly what the Tamarin sages saw.[36]

Amberelia Chance could have found some choice words to say about this, as she climbed up the swaying rope ladder and hauled herself into the ship's gondola. Words about insecurity, and patriarchy, and irony. But, from the view up here, it would seem that everything going willy-shaped tonight was the general rule, rather than the exception.

The Mantigore, first of all, wasn't really made for flying. Its wings had thrashed through the air for a while, hauling aloft a body which had no business being subject to the laws of aerodynamics. But as soon as gravity got a word in edgewise the great beast had fallen.

It had crashed down amid the tottering shingle-roofed rookeries of Rown Cross, sprawling uphill past the Fleamarket. Ten whole buildings had been knocked from the row that fronted Baskeline Street, punched out from the snaggle-toothed skyline like rotten teeth. In their place, fires burned, and Amber could see that they were spreading.

As she watched, clawing the hair out of her eyes and gripping the rail, she saw something burst from under the rubble, head whipping back and forth beneath a crown of horns. Flaming baulks of timber rained down across the hillside, and cedar shingles sizzled though the air, starting more tiny fires among the thatch-roofed slums that huddled in Chokeneck Gully.

---

36. Dress that up in theology any way you like, but it's still a tough prophecy to sell. The tamarin seers, perhaps much smarter than their human counterparts, declared that this was proof that the old Transeptine King had fathered an heir in his youth (all of three or four years ago) and that this worthy soul (when discovered) would unite all the roofs in a golden age of prosperity. After that, all it took to avoid a war was a pilfered tattoo needle, an ambitious young noblemonkey, a picture of a crown on his bum, and a conciliatory muffin basket for the witch queen.

The Mantigore bellowed, blasting a plume of green and purple flame into the sky, reflecting off a pall of smoke. It turned, clawing at the ground, and then charged through a whole row of rickety buildings, pulverising them to matchwood. Some of the little stick-scrawl things which flew from the wreckage, Amber realised, were people.

Despite herself (or, more accurately, despite her assassin's training) she felt bile at the back of her throat. The world spun and dipped.

Sweet Von Tuesday's Ghost! That's my *fault. Well, about a quarter of it. But how do you judge a quarter of a life? A quarter of a family trampled and made homeless?*

Amber felt a hand on her shoulder, and she was only mildly annoyed to find that it was Jack's.

"Come on. The big guy has some kind of battle strategy. I think we'd better listen."

The ruddy and earnest worry on his face twisted her guilt up another notch.

We don't ask what they've done, she thought, *but* this *poor kid? Another streetborn no-hoper with no family, raised by the Guilds? So what if he'd crossed the wrong jerk with enough money to stab away his problems? Maybe that wheedling, burrowing little tick of a voice, the one that went on about justice... maybe it was right about some things. Maybe Grand Sepulchre was sick, down to the core.*

"Hey. Somewhat," she managed. "I'm sorry about the..."

He cut her off with a look that was half embarrassment and half exasperation.

"If we come back with all our arms and legs on, *then* we can talk about our feelings, miss. Until then, I think it's best if we just... fade out. What we're supposed to be - well, it doesn't think about consequences. It doesn't allow for introspection. It's the kind of thing that thinks you can cure evil by punching every evildoer in the face, one at a time. Think like *that*, alright?"

Jack gave her hands a little squeeze. Amber was so impressed that he actually knew the word 'introspection' that she completely failed to slice off all his fingers.

"Come on!" bellowed Lord Slave, gesticulating with his mace. "Enough time for talk when the job's done, heroes! Now, here's what we're going to do. Pettigrew, you're fast, but a little skinny sword is going to have about as much impact on that thing as a knitting needle. Ranulf here, with his mighty-barbarian act, is going to crack open the thing's armour, and you're going to follow along before it heals, with *these."*

The Grand Vizier hefted a sack, reeking with shipjack's tar. Inside was a rattling, clattering bunch of grenadoes, those black and sticky bombs used by pirates to burst open enemy ships. These ones had been fired from clay, and each had a dangling cotton wick. He passed the world's fastest fop a wooden box of matches.

"It'll be Amberelia's job to slow the beast down, by slicing the tendons in its wings and legs. Those blades of yours should do the trick, hmmm? Am I right in assuming that they're sharper than anything has any right to be? Accursedly, *enchantedly* sharp, perhaps?"

The one eye behind Lord Slave's mask narrowed, and Amber realised something about the hulking great Right Hand of Himself. *All the leather and the muscles were part of the show.* They were sleight-of-hand, like a conjurer's trick, distracting you from the fact that the most dangerous part of Lord Slave was actually his brain.

Because he was right, of course. The whispers and insinuations inside her head informed Amber that yes, those bone claws could slice steel, time and memory. Not the claws *themselves*, mind you; but the shimmer of utter certainty which sizzled along every edge. The focus of a belief, cast like a shadow across the multiverse.

"Jack Somewhat, that leaves you and I to distract the bastard from eating any more civilians. And, of course, allowing our cunning colleagues their chance. I'll try to stun it, and you stop it from escaping. We'll corral it in the Fleamarket, up against the cliffs. Most of those stalls are bamboo and paper, and nobody actually lives there, so we'll cut down on collateral casualties. Are we clear?"

"Where are we going to land?" asked Montmortimer, as the dirigible wheeled across the sky in a great arc, its bat-wing rudders howling under the strain. "There's nowhere down there big enough!"

Lord Slave grinned, showing an utterly inappropriate number of pointed teeth.

"We're heroes, Mister Pettigrew! We *jump!*"

And with that, the Grand Vizier grabbed his mace in one hand, his stuffed rabbit and Monty in the other, and leapt over the side.

Ranulf took a peek over the rail and gripped his helmet tight. Down below, the Mantigore was galloping along Baskeline Street, down toward its intersection with Jumbalanan and Skrayhollow, where the roadways lost cohesion in the sprawling, ulcerating stew of the Fleamarket.

Lord Slave and his wailing cargo came down on the roof of the Old

Post Office, now the headquarters of the God's Anvil Party, right in the line of the beast's advance. It came ripping toward them, overturning and pulverising carts, goring and devouring oxen in their traces, and smashing flat an ornamental statue of Saint Guthran, depicted bringing custard and baked beans to the poor.

"Alley oop, then," said the beardy barbarian, hefting his axe. "Last one in's a kobold's armpit!"

He was over and gone before Amber or Jack could stop him.

"Do you really think this... this enchantment, or whatever it is, can save us from a ten-storey fall?" asked Amber, as the *Truculent Righteousness* swung low, its thrashing dragonfly wings decapitating a row of weathervanes.

"Ummm... I think we're all right so long as we're the good guys," said Jack, giving this as much metaphysical thought as he could, while trying not to throw up. The sheer number of reasons he wanted to – terror, vertigo, apprehension, talking to a pretty girl at close proximity – all but cancelled each other out. "That's a relatively horrible monster down there, so we should be just fine. There's a better question, though."

"Which is?"

"Do you think you'd rather take the chance and jump, or definitely have to face Lord Slave when he realises we bottled out? This is *his* airship, you realise. It goes back to his... well, I assume it'd be a lair, wouldn't it? I can't see that guy living in a cottage."

"Good point," said Amber, stepping lightly up to the rail. She crossed her hands in front of her chest, and six slim, graceful blades of bone snapped out from her knuckles. "Don't forget the muscles, ſcarlet ſpectre. And *try* to come up with a couple of decent one-liners, this time. It's in your idiom."

Then she was gone, whipped back into the dirigible's slipstream as it began to rise again, rudders slapping across to send it into a canted, scudding turn above the Fleamarket.

"What are you worried about?" asked Rod, filling Jack's head with a crackle of green sparks. **"You can *fly*, remember?"**

"I remember landing in a lake of poo," replied Jack, looking down at the wheeling cobbles. "Does that count?"

"As I said before... correct motivation!" replied the disembodied voice, all jolly enthusiasm. **"Come on, tiger! We can take this beastie!"**

"Errrr..."

"**Look, she's down there all alone. How's that going to look, vis-a-vis a certain amount of swooning?**"

Jack girded up his loins. Literally; his yellow codpiece was slipping alarmingly. Then he took another look down, to where the Mantigore was thrashing its way through the wreckage of Soto Scalizari's herbal healing emporium.

He took a deep breath. He made up his mind.

And at the same moment, a pair of burly Mageineers picked him up by the belt and collar, and biffed him over the rail.

One snag of the cape turned this into a hopeless flat spin, sending a smear of fire, cobbles and jagged rooflines blurring across Jack's vision.

"**Come on, lad! *Fly!* You can do it!**"

Jack tried to think light thoughts. Swooping, soaring thoughts. Green sparks crackled around him in a sputtering nimbus, but failed to catch.

"It's no use! My body knows exactly how heavy it is!"

"**How about this?**" asked Rod, horribly calm. "**A much smarter guy than me once said that flying is all about throwing yourself at the ground and missing.**"

Jack considered the large, flat, solid expanse of the Fleamarket, rushing up to meet him. "That might work if there were less ground," he conceded. "Any other wisdom for me, before the hurting starts?"

Rod sucked his invisible teeth in deep contemplation.

"**How about this. Can you swim?**"

"Yes!"

"**Can you swim in treacle?**"

"Ummm... no! No, definitely not!"

"**Then think of the air as very, very thin water. If you can swim in thick, heavy water, which is thinner by far than treacle, then swimming in air should be simple arithmetic, mate. Stands to reason!**"

It's entirely possible that trying to make sense of this lunacy actually distracted Jack from hitting the ground, and thus completed the parameters of what's known as Adams' Law. Then again, perhaps the voice in his head had actually come up with the goods this time. Because Jack's downward plummet angled off, becoming a dive, then a swoop, then a scrape of his boot-toes along the cobbles, followed by an upward curve which saw him skim the surface of the Old Post Office before rocketing up into the clouds.

"The plan, Somewhat! *The plan!*" bellowed Lord Slave, clinging to one of the gargoyles which encrusted the post office facade. "The damned thing's down *here!*"

And indeed, as Jack twisted in the air, he saw the Mantigore come raging into the Fleamarket square, claws lashing out left and right to snicker-snap through bamboo stalls and reams of banana-leaf thatch.

"Do you think I can do that burning eyes thing again?" asked Jack, over the delighted laughter of Rod in his head.

"I'd be surprised if you could stop yourself! Go on... Ranulf, Amber and Monty are in position! Let's get heroic!"

At the top of his swoop, Jack began to tread air with his feet, stabilising into a hover. Down below, the Mantigore chuffed flames, grinding its teeth together as it scented out its prey...

"You have to *say* something," suggested Rodney, as incandescent death failed to lance out of Jack's eyeballs. **"You know. Something pithy. Something in the moment."**

"Ummm... this looks like the right time for some *piercing insight?*" tried Jack. At once, the blaze of a solar flare detonated inside his head. Twin ruby-red beams speared from his eyes, instantly giving his nose a double sunburn. The beams came to a focus at ground level, and ripped across the cobbles as Jack recoiled, carving a thin, deep trench of molten rock.

More thanks to luck than skill, the beam then lashed across the armoured back of the Mantigore, slashing its wing with a sound like sizzling bacon. The thing reared up, squealing loud enough to etch spirals into windows a mile away. One of its insect legs toppled, severed through and smoking. Then its immense head swung around like the prow of a battle-galley, focusing a battery of eyes on Jack.

"Err... *now we're cooking?*" he hazarded, sending another blast down to splash against the creature's armoured face. Eyes boiled and popped, only to be replaced with new, crystal-shielded lenses. A criss-cross pattern of glowing lines sizzled and cooled, orange to red to black. "Who exactly am I talking to, Rod? I mean, it's not for your sake, and everyone else is either running away screaming or..."

"Shush. Don't think. Just... *aaargh, move!*"

Heretical magic twisted and recombined things deep in the Mantigore's throat. It opened its mouth to reveal a new, segmented tongue like a copper millipede, blue fire building at its tip.

This time, when it belched fire, the blaze focused and throttled down to the thin blade of a welding torch, a white-hot beam with exactly the same width and power as Jack's own. It struck the young ſuper-hero square in the chest, punching him backwards in a cloud of sparks. He tumbled end over end, smashing into the facade of the Old Post Office, where God's Anvil had strung up a banner reading 'Liberty, Purity, Victory'. Dust and smoke billowed out of the hole, along with a litany of curses that proved Jack was still alive.

Up above, Lord Slave grinned, holding his mace high.

"That's the spirit, boy! Give it some more of that!"

The Grand Vizier leapt from his perch, cape streaming out like liquid night, and something pink and furry flew from his hand in a flat trajectory, bouncing off the Mantigore's craggy face.

"Get him, Mister Bun Bun!"

The stuffed toy rebounded with a sad little squeak. But while the small, walnut-sized brain of the Mantigore (an organ all but pickled in liquid rage) tried to work out how to best respond to assault with a plush rabbit, Lord Slave struck. It was a masterclass in why he'd been a figure of abject terror for five centuries, and a lesson in applied physics at the same time.

Slave fell with both huge meaty arms curled back over his head at full stretch, hairy armpits bristling, veins standing proud as hosepipes on his biceps. Just as he was about to collide with the Mantigore he snapped his body forward into a crunch, bringing his skull-crusted mace whistling around in a blur. All that concentrated fury connected with the creature's jaws.

"... you're so self-satisfied, I don't neeeeeed you!" howled the cursed weapon, in an outrageous accent.

And

went the cloud of green, sparking letters which exploded from the point of impact. Arrowhead teeth blew out sideways, along with a horizontal rain of blood. Lord Slave nailed the landing – down on one knee, mace held out to his side, the empty eye-sockets of its many skulls smoking.

"Really? *Zok?* Who's doing the light show?" he asked. "I'll have you know that's a *very* bad word in Old Phoraxian!"

Literal tiny stars, moons, baby birds and music notes spun around the Mantigore's head, all made up of emerald glitter. With a groan, the beast lurched sideways across Skrayhollow Street, collapsing into a greengrocer's shop. Cabbage's, pomegranate's, onion's, carrot's and misused apostrophes made a roll for freedom. The upper storeys collapsed, pancaking down in a spray of splinters.

Ranulf didn't hesitate, and neither did Amber. As the Mantigore tried to right itself, tangling its wings, spikes, extra-numerary legs and lobster claws in the wreckage, both of them came pelting across the cobbles, hurdling broken stalls and upturned carts as they came. Ranulf's war-cry was thoroughly unprintable, an almost visible storm of invective taken from the most unhallowed eddas of the Nastiskarsfjordian bards. His axe was a blur of steel, but the creature would have snipped him in two had it not been for the young assassin.

Her blades came hissing in as she slid under the Mantigore's bulk, hamstringing both its bulky back legs and setting it down on its rump. A snapping lobster claw missed Ranulf, and he smote mightily, sending a webwork of cracks skittering across its shell. The thing's bulky neck twisted, but it couldn't quite get to the Butcher with its teeth, and now Amber ducked back underneath as he pulled himself atop it. While she unspliced the tendons which powered that razor claw, he sunk his axe's pick-spike deep into the crack, and *heaved*.

They'd forgotten about the monster's tails, however. Three eyeless cobra-heads came darting forward as the Mantigore wallowed in the wreckage, pulling itself clear with one claw and both hind legs dragging. Venom glistened on fangs the size of swords, even as purplish blood stained the cobbles...

But Jack hadn't missed them at all.

He concentrated, and stooped into a sharp dive, hauling back one swollen fist as his cape flapped out behind him. He caught the first cobra head a massive blow which snapped it back, limp, then collided with the other two, feeling them wrap around his arms and chest like clinging vines.

"Pleased to *snake* your acquaintance," said Jack, the words falling out of his mouth unbidden. Once again there was a sense of crinkling newsprint, sweet sugar and mown grass as the world hinged away. A black outline seemed to form around Jack, Ranulf and Amber, as their features subtly changed, and the colours of their clothes and skin became brighter, more primary.

"That was *terrible!*" shouted Lord Slave, as he strode toward the

Mantigore with a no-nonsense grip on his mace. Once, twice, thrice the terrible weapon swung.

came the explosions of green letters in their little balloons. Teeth and blood, mucous and shards of chitin sprayed; left, right, left.

Up on the creature's back, Ranulf put all his strength into his task. His axe-handle, a hundred-year-old rod of tempered ash, bent like a longbow. And with a crack, the shell of the Mantigore split, revealing glistening, pumping organs and muscle beneath. Jack grabbed one snake tail and flattened it with a mighty headbutt. The other he throttled between his huge fingers.

"Sorry, evildoer! No time for *binding engagements*! I've got a con*strict* schedule to keep!"

He wasn't thinking now. Something else was flowing through him, like cold light, opening up the top of his head and bathing his brain in certainty. A blur happened at the end of his arms, and the tails were tied together, knotted.

"Montmortimer!" bellowed Lord Slave, hunched over his mace. "Now would be... oh! I didn't see you there."

Indeed, the foppish nobleman had appeared right next to the Grand Vizier, brushing a speck of dust from his lapel. He'd managed to find himself an entirely new costume; that of an admiral, complete with a blue-dyed wig supporting an entire miniature galleon made of gold.

"Yes, your lordship?"

"The grenadoes, man! Now, while it's stunned!"

Monty shrugged.

"I've already done that, old chap. I was sort of hoping you'd get out of the way. It should be quite an explosion."

Lord Slave, for the first time on this awful, unprecedented night, looked worried. His single eye opened wide.

"Where's the sack? How many did you use?"

Monty extracted a small snuffbox and took a pinch.

"Why, all of them, of course. And a few more I managed to scavenge from around this quite disreputable neighbourhood. Small kegs, powder horns, you know. These small shopkeepers work on razor-thin margins, and a blunderbuss, they say, is the best insurance."

There was no time to think. There as barely time for Lord Slave to scoop up Mister Bun Bun and make a dive for a carved marble horse trough, pulling it up and over himself as he rolled.

Then Monty's grab-bag of explosives went off in a stuttering chain of detonations, stuffed deep into the innards of the Mantigore. Hence, of course, why the world's fastest fop had taken the time to change his clothes; monster grease and bile played havoc with silk brocade.

Each individual bomb was designed to blow a hole in the side of a ship of the line.

Suffice to say, the resulting fireworks were impressive.

Jack was blasted backward, smoking, and he would likely have repeated his trick of landing in the municipal shite ponds, if he hadn't struck the ornamental fountain at the centre of the Fleamarket instead.

Some military statues depict the horse with one leg off the ground, which symbolises its rider being wounded in combat. Some have the horse rearing up, symbolising a heroic death in battle. Some go for the trifecta, usually by adding some strategic shrubberies and trampled foemen, indicating, perhaps, that the rider was not just killed in the line of duty, but also blown to tiny pieces. The statue of Himself on horseback atop the Almoner's Gate Fountain had *all four legs* in the air, thanks to some clever sorcery. It represented the fact that He had (of course) been dead before the battle started, and that afterwards he was still up and about, unlike most of his enemies.

Jack struck hard enough to bend the horse's face around sideways, and make the whole floating edifice rotate like a propeller. Then he hit the water, the cold shock of it slapping him back to a semblance of sensibility. Echoes pealed and shimmered in his ears as his vision blurred, taking in a scene of destruction. There was Ranulf the Butcher, staggering at the edge of a huge black crater, trying to lever his helmet off his head by both horns. He appeared to be painted head to foot with charcoal, and his beard was still smoking in its outlying regions.

Jack watched Amberelia struggle clear of a pile of timber and bamboo, her cloak ragged and bloodied. At the time, he thought it must have been a trick of his bruised cranium, but it looked for all the world as if she'd lost an arm. No... there it was. *In her other hand.*

As Jack watched she held the ragged stumps together, and a fizzle of green light bound them back whole.

Surely not, he thought, as he staggered and sloshed through the fountain. That was beyond any but the highest magic. And as for Monty...

"I've got you, big fellow. Steady on, now. A bit of a surprise, I'm afraid. I've forever been one for underestimating things, you know. Alcohol volumes, gambling debts, and now, it seems, explosions as well."

Montmortimer helped Jack up and over the marble lip of the fountain, trying hard not to get any water on his ruffled lace cuffs.

"You know, you've got a habit of appearing out of nowhere?" Jack asked, sitting down to wring out his cape. "Is that part of the... you know. The thing?" He mimed twinkly motions with his fingers. The World's Fastest Fop stoked what would have been a beard, had he been able to grow one stylish enough.

"Well, not really. Perhaps. You see, I've always felt a bit *inconspicuous*. Whenever I went to parties, I was the one standing in the corner who got mistaken for a butler. I'm afraid that without the last word in fashion, I'll simply, I don't know, *disappear*. Fade into the wallpaper or something. Hence why I thought I'd sign up, when things started to get interesting. They say heroing builds character, and being very, very rich tends to do the opposite. There were times when I had to shout at the cook for ten minutes just to get some eggs poached!"

Jack considered, for a moment, just how useful it would have been for him to seem invisible, all those times that he'd gotten in trouble as a dirty little novice. Still, the thought of Monty - the human flamingo explosion - being inconspicuous, was enough to make him genuinely smile, for the first time in a long time.

"Well, at least we got the monster, eh? Nothing exceeds like excess, apparently."

Across the crater, a marble trough rolled over, revealing Lord Slave. He levered himself to his feet very, very carefully; after all, despite his exceptional physique, the man was 500 years old. "Is there an apothecary in this party? And... did anyone get the registration of that dragon?"

He held Mister Bun Bun up to where his ear would have been, and nodded grimly.

"Right. Don't count your blasphemous drooling horrors until they're banished."

Lord Slave rolled the kinks out of his neck and walked over to the edge of the crater, where a scoop of the Fleamarket had been blasted away to blackened nothingness. For a long moment he stood on the edge, swaying slightly, then he held out one hand at his side. Nothing happened for a heartbeat, then two, and Jack realised that he wasn't breathing. Then came a scraping sound, as of steel on stone, and Lord Slave's mace came grinding across the cobbles, handle in the air, huge heavy skull-head sparking as it came. It slapped into his palm with a meaty, final sound. "Ladies and gentlemen," he said, in a low, deliberate voice. "We might just have a problem here."

They gathered at the edge of the crater. Ranulf's helmet came loose with an audible pop. Alongside Jack, they all saw what was left of the Mantigore.

It was a mess of blackened bones and organic soup, writhing in tendrilated clumps, meshing and bubbling, webbing and slithering as some hideous purpose drove it to try to recombine. Jack saw faces float to the surface of the boiling stew, half animal, half man... some *half Jack*, which was terribly worrying. At the same time, he felt a cold wind sighing around him, prickling the hairs on the back of his neck.

"What *is* this thing?" breathed Monty.

"How do we kill it?" asked Amber.

"What time will the crumpets be ready, grandmama?" enquired Ranulf, who really had taken quite a blow to the head.

In answer, an arm formed out of the sludge at the bottom of the pit. It reached up, muscles binding around bone, fingers lengthening to claws... then it collapsed again, replaced with a seething mass of faces. The sense of a cold wind intensified, and now it felt like it was blowing right through Jack, whistling between his ribs with a feeling like needles of ice.

Behind him, he heard the clatter of bronze on marble. Jack turned, and noticed that the statue of Himself atop the fountain had collapsed. Perhaps it was Jack's fault that the image of Himself was now turned backwards in the saddle, gesturing over his horse's rump toward some imagined horizon. But something else had sucked away all the magic, making it topple to the ground. As he watched, the fountain itself stopped, the simple spells it used to pump water failing.

"This isn't good!" wailed Monty, as little blips and shimmers of energy began to whip past him, raising a crackle of static from his wig. He stared at his fingers, as multicoloured flames sprung to life from several of his rings.

"It's the magic!" shouted Lord Slave. "It's feeding on it!" His mace was pulled out in front of him, all but dragging him into the crater. As Jack watched, a nimbus of power unravelled from inside it, flowing out through the eyes and jaws of its skeletal face.

'*God knows, god knows I waaant to breeeeaaaak freeeee!*' howled the cursed weapon one last time, before it was torn from Slave's grip. It went clattering down into the pit, melting as it went.

"Well, we're lucky there's no concentrated source of elder sorcery in this part of town then, eh?" grinned Amber. "Nothing big, and magical and... why are you all looking *up*, all of a sudden?"

Jack joined them, as a frankly willy-shaped shadow blotted out the firelight. It was the *Truculent Righteousness*, and something had it by the rudders, pulling it arse-first toward the thrashing mass that had been Enkalderon's creation. Mageineers and Techolytes were throwing themselves overboard, some with parachutes, some without, as the twin thaumic engines bolted to the airship's stern tore themselves to pieces.

Pistons blurred and shuddered. Weird distortions built and burst, and bolts sheared, peeling metal apart like paper. Twin mainsprings hammered out of transimaginary metals went haywire, and cogs hissed through the air like Chungdojin shuriken.

But that wasn't the worst of it. Not by half.

Because two pink-yellow snarls of magic were teased forth from the exploding engines, sucked out into a skein of cotton-candy lightning. When they swirled into the morass of Mantigore-slime, it *erupted*, bones assembling like decomposition in reverse, organs slithering and slotting into place, muscles propagating and meshing...

The assembled heroes didn't have to stop looking up. Oh, how they wished that they did.

"Oh, come on!" groaned Ranulf. "How are we meant to smite something like *that?*"

'Something like that' turned out to be quite indescribably horrible. It still had a sharklike face with wide, drooling jaws. But now that neckless lump of a head was perched atop a humanoid torso, armoured with spikes of bone. Wings unfurled all ragged-tight behind the Mantigore, and it bellowed, loosing a plume of purple fire heavenward. Then it brought its immense hands up and clenched them into fists. It was a horribly human gesture.

Something pumped and crunched deep in the thing's throat. A tongue the colour of dried-out liver licked across those nightmare teeth.

"Youuurrrrrrrr mmmmovvve!" rumbled Enkalderon's little pet, finally attaining the form he'd dreamed of, in the feverish depths of his insanity. The creature's voice shifted with a further grinding of bone, becoming both more human... and smooth as liquid chocolate. "Though I rather think this is checkmate, gentlemen. Evolution has delivered me a body which will finally vanquish your feeble Emperor!"

One clawed digit stabbed up toward the Malevolith. Lightning flickered, on cue.

Lord Slave seemed to recognise that voice, because he was all business. From his back-scabbard he drew forth a very unmagical, workmanlike sword, and levelled it at the beast.

"Enkalderon the Younger! I arrest you on the charges of Incredibly Sneaky Treason, Misuse of University Property, Unlicensed Villainy, Discharging a Breath Weapon in a Built-up Area, Attempted Re-Homi-Regicide, and, I'm pretty certain, Resisting Arrest as well. Care to say anything incriminating before we make you say 'curses, foiled again' in a scenery-chewing and clichéd fashion?"

"Wait... *what?*" double-took Amber.

"I see he snuck that 'we' in there, Monty. That's taking liberties, that is."

"So, the big stupid creature... was a dead wizard all along?"

"Well, I suppose, technically, not dead. Just kind of..."

"Oh, will you lot *shut up?*" snarled the creature. "This is supposed to be my dramatic revelation! *Monstrance*, in fact. In the old tongue, 'monster' literally means 'a vision to behold', you see, so when I decided to overthrow Himself, I reckoned that..."

"He doesn't half go on, does he?" asked the Butcher. "Typical evil wizard. I once had to listen to the entire dastardly plan of Baltharazon the Black, back when me and Vifril Half-Elven and Grelk the Slicer raided the Doom Tower of Shrieking Skulls. On and on and bloody on..."

"That was you?" asked Lord Slave, nodding with professional respect. "Nicely done. Baltharazon was the lich king with the metal face, wasn't he? The one trying to build a portal into the Dimension of Howling Darkness?" Slave gestured with his thumb. "*This* one knew his time was up, and he popped his eternal soul into a monster of his own creation. A standard type-twelve. You know the drill."

"Look, I'd *seriously* like you both to shut up *right now*," said the Mantigore – Enkalderon reborn – in a voice which was tight with peevishness. "Yes, yes, I put my soul into a monstrous body of my own creation, but the trick... ahhh, yes! The trick was to trust in *evolution!* Eventually, some fools of heroes would push this form to its apogee, with the power to devour magic! So, Lord Slave, all your enchanted weapons and potent spells will be useless! Who are these pillocks you've assembled to try and stop me?"

"Not magic," grated Slave, giving his sword a couple of practice swings. "Are you going to come quietly, or are we going to have to employ a wee *soupçon* of police brutality?"

Enkalderon the Younger laughed, literally holding his sides. He brushed a tear away from one oil-drop eye with a foot-long claw.

"Seriously? You'd need an *army* to stop me!"

Ranulf did a quick head count. He sucked his teeth, and stared intently at a selection of fingers.

"Aye, chief, we don't have an army, do we?"

Jack heard something come clanging down behind him, but he didn't dare take his eyes off the gigantic, demonic born-again wizard whom he'd just been invited to battle. That's why he didn't see that it was a round little woman wearing black iron armour, all aglow around the joints and eye-slits with green fire.

"No. We have an IT!" growled Slag Iron.

"A *what?*" asked Enkalderon.

Behind the belligerent metal fishmonger, Soto Scalizari popped the lid off a bottle of pills, scavenged from the wreckage of his shop. They were the hideously effective hangover cures which Jack Somewhat had been avoiding for months, ever since his mind-scarring brush with chartered accountancy. Soto turned to Tarrence Bligh and handed him the bottle.

"Down the hatch, mate. Show 'em what the zok you've got!"

The little red-haired man took off his shirt and folded it up neatly, revealing a toast-rack chest and a selection of badly inked tattoos. He grimaced, held his nose... and tipped back the bottle. Soto cowered away, his fingers stuck in his ears.

"Well, I'm sure that's all fine and good, but *really?* A very small human sailor? Am I supposed to be terrified? *Me?* The ex High Thaumatarch, and future ruler of the... uuurk!"

"IT!" bellowed the gigantic blue creature which had just punched Enkalderon square in the stomach, folding him in half. The It was a sinewy, triple-sized cube of muscle, hunched and steaming, cerulean and mental.

Its tiny little head (well, in proportion to shoulders like slabs of beef) turned a maniacal stare on the other ſuper-heroes, and managed a couple of strangled words, all choked up by rage.

"*What puny heroes waiting for? Time for **fight!***"

15

The Climactic Paradox

HEADLINES FOR TOMORROW's scandal rags, from Ishkandersaan to far Mograth and Shangola. In the word-forges of the rumoursmiths, inky fingers stab the keys, and paper feeds the great printing engines...

Grand Sepulchre, Princess of Cities, burns in the grip of a mosquito-swelter night!

This is no poetic hubris, dear reader, but the hot and ashen truth.

Your author knows fire, you see. Knows it as She Who Purifies, the final judgement of this sinful world... But shush. No time now for the niceties of theology. Listen!

Screams and curses, songs and prayers, ululations and cries rule the air above the western city. Bucket brigades work at cross purposes, looters and refugees scrabble in the dirt, street vendors and guardsmen throng the streets... and a swathe from Bulbous Corners clear across to Rown Cross falls under a rain of sparks and ashes.

Human nature being what it is, there are soon fires in other, far-flung corners of the Dark Metropolis too, as the realities of the looting economy percolate through the minds of the unrighteous and the downright opportunistic.

Many of the ships in the harbour have put out to sea, pursued by Rhaegulus Cratt's excise galleys – for news of this calamity is a commodity in itself, and the bankers and guildsmen of Clourvonne and Zollund, Grailsend and Khantif will all want to know of the Deathless Emperor's misfortune. Cogs and barques and gilded quinqueremes are grappled down, and outraged captains placed under protective custody. Stowaways and rats sweat in the salty bilges, wondering what will become of them.

What a sight to serve up before a tyrant!

From the towering heights of the Malevolith He watched it all unfold. Behind the rusted visor of a suit of armour made for a giant, a pair of ectoplasmic eyes dripped and flickered.

Now. A twitch in the web of the world. A shudder that tilted reality itself on edge...

Enkalderon the Younger might not have been the monster He was worried about, when this whole frankly silly story began to unfold. But He knew the power of stories, and what they could do for those who grabbed hold of them with both hands. They were a wave you could surf if you angled yourself just right in the flow of time and causality. But there was always an undertow, and a riptide which led out into the dark waters of madness.

Hmm. Dark waters of madness, He thought. *That was good. Better write it down...* Well, supposing that His Grand Vizier hadn't doomed them all. The Urzoman Emperor sighed. What would he do without someone like Lord Slave?

Someone who had lost their mind helping Him face a horrible truth, and who had been put back together with quite a lot missing.

His old friend and companion was gone, that was certain. But then again, so was He Himself. That was part of the deal, to hold the madness back. That was the only way to defeat a knowledge that couldn't be un-known.

I un-think, therefore I am not. How neat and tidy. And now... another threat was being conveniently erased. He knew, in His gnarly old twist of a heart, that if He went forth to smite Enkalderon the upstart, the fool... he'd be perilously close to being (shudder) *good.*

The *Hero.*

And there were things, he understood, that watched and waited for heroes. Things which didn't care one heretical damn about who else died, so long as there was a big, exciting battle.

Hence the evil empire. Hence the grotesquerie which decorated Grand Sepulchre, like black icing on a dropped and melting cake. His was the story of an evil lord, and right now He stood high above his burning capital and gloated, allowing Himself one small storm cloud and some desultory lightning. Part of Him wished He could play the violin.

It was in character. Better – it *was* character.

Still, best not to dwell on the past. Not while Enkalderon, a wizard with more ambition than grasp, met a suitably sticky end...

He watched as the great blue giant sunk a fist into the mad Mantigore's face, sending radial shockwaves rippling through its entire body. Bone shattered, and bloody teeth flew like hail - but here came the counterblow, lifting the Unstoppable It from his feet and propelling him clear across the square.

The fountain exploded as he smashed through it, brick dust and chips of marble forming a mushroom cloud. Then the one who called himself the ʃcarlet ʃpectre was there, swooping in from the air with his cape snapping and writhing, beams lashing out from his eyes to liquefy stone and set tumbledown buildings ablaze.

Where the beams struck Enkalderon, sparks flared, and the sorcerous creature pushed back, great concave dishes of fire raving as he blocked them with his palms.

Ranulf the Butcher, the old charlatan, swung his axe with impossible strength, hacking through muscle and bone. The assassin girl, Chance, was too fast for the beast to bludgeon aside as she came running up its back, blades flashing in a bright arc as she severed one wing, then plunged a span of bone into its eye socket.

Enkalderon shrieked - a reedy teakettle sound up here atop the Malevolith - swatting at her with one fist to dash her to the cobbles. But a blur in pink and gold lace caught her in mid-air, then spun about Enkalderon like a human tornado, making the mad mage stagger, his huge feet tangled one with the other...

Enkalderon looked up, head lolling woozily on a slab of a neck. Just in time to catch a huge bronze horse to the face, followed in quick succession by both fists of the Unstoppable It.

That would be the statue of Himself, commissioned in 542 Anno Urzoman from the Zalois master artist Pietro Abruzziola. One had to admit, it made a very fine weapon. And, for some reason, a cloud of green sparks which ʃpelled out the word 'CLANG!'

Enkalderon staggered backward, arms flailing, only to catch Slag Iron coming the other way, green energy pulsing from her boots as she flew. The ʃuper-powered fishwife struck like a squat little artillery shell, impacting with his belly at immense velocity. The air blew out of the beast's lungs along with a whoosh of spit and blood, and he fell to one knee.

Unfortunately, this put him within striking distance of Billiam Knox, who gave his shimmering doppelganger a hand up, and threw himself clear through Enkalderon's forehead. The Double Vision popped out the back of the creature's head just in time to tag in the ʃpectre again, coming in from on high with both fists clenched in a double-axe-handle grip.

This time the mad mage went down. There was a literal thunderclap as Jack arrowed in from above, swinging for the base of its skull. The blow itself sounded like an entire side of beef being torn in half, amplified a thousand times, then a thousand more.

Suddenly stricken by a hangover of scriptural proportions (and the first he'd experienced since his long-ago student wizard days), Enkalderon the Younger toppled over onto his belly, where the Naked Flame took the opportunity to get right up close and unleash a storm of withering fire.

Assorted heroes landed, flexed, roared, brandished weapons and generally assembled in a group, facing down the charred and groaning beast. It shuddered, huge slabs of muscle heaving as it scrabbled at the ground with its claws.

The Dark Emperor watched from above, his phantom eyes unblinking.

For a moment, He was unsure as to the sound Enkalderon was making. Surely, after centuries of plotting and scheming, the sorcerous fool wasn't *crying*, was he?

Then, with a sudden glimmer of pride, as from one professional to another, He realised that the thing was *laughing*.

"Is that all you've got? You little unmagical band of misfits? Is that all you brought, to contest with *me?* The very pinnacle of evolution? Me, who can regenerate any wound, in this city rife with bloody magic? You'll have to do *much* better than that!"

Lord Slave shouldered in between Slag Iron and the It, then rested the point of his sword on the cobbles, draping his hands over the pommel.

"Really? How about *this*, then? Jack?"

The red-suited young hero next to Slave reached up, just in time to grab a black, wing-shaped projectile as it flickered through the air. It was attached to the end of a wire, and as He watched, the ſpectre gritted his teeth and gave it an almighty heave.

Enkalderon was already healing as he rose up, surging to his feet as wounds knitted tight all across his bulk. He turned, and saw what the Grimshadow had been up to, and almost had time to curse.

That overdressed and sinister ſuper-hero had no powers; that much was clear from the lack of a bile-green aura around him. But he'd compensated. Mainly by grappling his way up and aboard the *Truculent Righteousness*, wallowing in the sky with its engines shot. Now the wings of his cape flared dramatically as he rode the bows of the airship down, its great spiky bowspirit aimed right at Enkalderon's chest.

"All passengers for the funeral of a giant, rampaging monster, prepare to disembark," grated the Grimshadow, as hundreds of tonnes of flying phallus came swinging low. Even the figurehead winced as its great steel spike kissed the monster's sternum...

But at the last second, magic flared. Invisible hooks tugged at the surface of the world, as things writhed beneath.

Enkalderon had spoken a Word, all thorns and eyeballs, an utterance which no ears present consented to hear. When the deafening silence echoed away, the massive bulk of the *Righteousness* was gone, transmuted to a cloud of butterflies. They tumbled past the beast on either side, pale blue and dazed, snapped into a time and place exactly the opposite from the one they'd just inhabited.

Back there (wherever it was) a swathe of tropical jungle found itself suddenly flattened by a disintegrating airship. But *here...*

"I'm a *wizard*, remember?" leered Enkalderon. You can really get a good leer on with a mouthful of shark teeth. "Anything else, or is it my turn now?"

As if to punctuate this threat, the Grimshadow himself came down like a very well-tailored lightning strike, thwacking him on the nose with one of his extendable batons. This had absolutely and precisely zero effect at all.

"Taste the furious sting of my dark and brooding justice!" tried Foxmallet anyway, landing in a perfect ſuper-hero pose.

Enkalderon shrugged. A fresh wing sprouted from his flesh and unrolled, dripping transparent slime.

"No? You're all just idiots, then? Very well. One of you go and fetch me your ugly undead boss, and the rest can become a lesson for the public good."

"Always look both ways before crossing the street?" tried Monty.

"A toothbrush isn't a posh affectation, it's for everyone?" hazarded Jack.

The huge monster tilted its head to one side. A fresh eyeball swelled and popped into its socket, where Amber had carved out the old one.

"I was thinking more along the lines of *'mess with your new Emperor, and you'll go to your funeral in a bucket'.*"

Enkalderon flexed his gigantic muscles, arching his back and holding out his hands to either side. With another magical Word he bent reality around his will, manifesting a pair of red-hot swords, each one the size and heft of a longship's keel. Lord Slave didn't look taken aback. Indeed, he faced this new and horrifying development with the calm of a lightly chilled butler.

"Ladies. Gentlemen. Do we have a plan B? Anyone?"

"Now would be the time," added Amber, comforting the mantis shrimp on her wrist as it hid its eye-stalks with its claws.

Ranulf the Butcher rummaged in his pack, muttering to himself.

"Aha! *Told* you I had one of these!" he surfaced from the smelly canvas depths with an ornate brass globe in his fist, brandishing it like a lit grenadoe. "Portable hole. The sages in Khantif aren't making *these* anymore!"

"Isn't that because somebody stole the black ruby eye from the Conventicle of The Sacred Darkness, in a by-all-accounts thrilling battle featuring no less than ten thousand deadly *whinja*[37] warriors?"

Ranulf looked at Lord Slave sideways, with what, on another person, might have been called a cunning grin. Here, it looked like a chimney brush curling up and dying.

"Could be. Could be. But it was Sygrid the Swordmaiden who kept the bloody stone, I'll tell you that much. Huh! Women and jewellery!"

"That's an offensive stereotype," said Amber. "How big was this ruby, anyway?"

There was a sound of metal grinding on metal as Enkalderon brought his swords together, flakes of red-hot crust falling away from the hissing steel. He roared, and across the square another building slumped over and collapsed, people running and screaming.

"How about you just throw the thing, and we discuss accessorising later?" asked Montmortimer, prodding Ranulf with one finger.

"Right!" the barbarian squared his shoulders and brandished the sphere. "Pull the pin... count to three..." He brought back his arm to pitch, as Enkalderon brought back both gigantic blades. "One... Two... F..."

"Don't do it," murmured Lord Slave.

"I have not the *slightest* idea what you're talking about," said Ranulf,

---

37. The many secretive fighting sects of the whinja compete with each other to come up with the most horrible, gruelling, painful and therefore character-building training regimes possible, producing a crop of warriors who have suffered years of meditating under freezing waterfalls, sweeping endless dojo floors, subsisting on horrible stodgy rice porridge and running up and down mountains carrying livestock. There are few better martial-arts assassins in the entire Arch', but potential customers are often put off by the whinja's most prominent trait – constantly trying to one-up each other complaining about how awful their training was. Many a victim or political target has perished in the deadly darkness, the last thing they hear the bickering of the whinja who killed them... "Red hot scorpions? LUXURY! When I were lad, the abbot used to make us carry boiling-hot cauldrons of raw sewage up ten thousand stairs strewn with broken glass, and when we got up there, he'd beat us half to death with a spiky stick!"

still holding the ticking, steaming metal ball. "It said count to three, and I'm well capable of counting to three, being, as I am, a small business owner of some regard who has to work out my taxes for *you*, in fact..."

Jack grabbed the portable hole from his hand.

"*Three!*" he said... and he threw it.

It was a perfect pitch. The sphere shattered, orange-segment rinds of metal springing apart as it flew, and the magic within unfurled with all the spindly dark symmetry of a collapsible umbrella. The eyes of everyone present followed its arc as it expanded into a black disc, spinning through the air to land right between the Mantigore's feet.

There was a flash of magic as the spell caught. And then...

Enkalderon looked down, then looked up. He looked down again, unsure as what to make of this development.

"Was that supposed to... you know. Encompass my doom, or something?"

Jack looked embarrassed. Ranulf doubly so. Lord slave rested his leather-clad face in one meaty palm.

"It seems to go all the way down," continued the mad mage, peering into what was clearly a very real, very deep but very narrow portable hole. It was not more than five feet across, right in the middle of his shadow. Neither of his gigantic feet was close to touching the sides. "There's definitely lava down there. Oh well. It was a good try."

Someone tapped Lord Slave on the shoulder. It turned out to be Slag Iron, who was brandishing a very official looking scroll.

"We might have a better plan B over here, squire," she hissed, conspiratorially. "But it's going to need your help. And we'll need a bit of a diversio..."

The armoured fishmonger didn't get to finish. Montmortimer was there so quickly that he left an outline of himself in floating dust just where he'd been.

"I might be able to rustle something up," he drawled, looking down at his fingernails. "I've been to a few parties at the old *Alma Mater*, you know. Wizard shindigs. The bunch of them are as vain as... well, as vain as *me*, to put no finer point on it."

Slag Iron scribbled a couple of notes onto the scroll, then jammed it into Lord Slave's fist.

"When it looks about the right time, you read that out loud," she said. "Ahh! Not yet. I've got an It to wrangle."

And indeed, she reached out and grabbed the back of the giant blue monster's belt as he stomped toward Enkalderon, murder writ large on his face, though admittedly in crayon, with most of the letters backwards. Remonstrations were had. The maniacal mage looked on, testing the edge of one sword with his thumb, and wincing as a puff of smoke rose up.

"Oh, let him come! You can all die individually, or all at once. I'm easy. Not a stickler for outdated rules, like Himself up in his tower. Who should be interjecting any moment, I'm certain. Unless he's actually died in there, and none of you simpletons are any the wiser? I say, wouldn't *that* be a party-sized keg of old- fashioned irony?"

The beast levelled one glowing sword at Jack Somewhat. "*You.* You can die first. All that flying around, the horrible puns. I don't know how you do it, I don't really care, and I would like to make it absolutely clear that this is just business, alright? Nothing personal."

Jack rolled his eyes.

"Oh, yes, that makes me feel *so* much better. Swing away."

Enkalderon grinned.

"Really? That's very big of you, and... oh. You were being sarcastic, weren't you? Very well. Yet another reason to chop you in half, I suppose."

A gigantic blade came up, blotting out the black and jagged ruins of Rown Cross, still blazing. And as it reached its apogee, a tiny voice spoke in Amberelia Chance's ear, almost making her jump sideways.

"*Well, at least that's a weight off your mind,*" said the little homunculus of Master Lurien, all three-inch high and bloody on her shoulder. "*We were wondering if you'd finish the mission, what with all the strange interference we've been having. But it seems that the target is about to be, as we say, 'third party involved'.*"

It was like a shock of cold water, slapping her back into reality. The black outline and blur of saturated colour around Amber went out, with a hiss of green sparks.

Of course. This was her last opportunity! The future she'd wanted since she was a little girl, scrabbling for scraps in the great creaking orphan-warrens of Bentsteeple. Girls from that splintery world of cold comfort and colder gruel went two ways – the Temples or the Guilds - and Amber had developed a knack for sneaking and lurking, and hurting the bullies who would have otherwise forced her to starvation. Hurting one of them so bad, when he suggested something she didn't want to think about, that she'd gotten the attention of the Lachrymosa.

"*You* were *still going to kill him, right? All that hero talk was just to build your cover, wasn't it?"*

Amber realised, with a growing sense of horror, that she'd been under the influence of something, for all these past long hours. Something less than a voice, but more than a compulsion. *Something,* she reminded herself, *that had nothing to do with the fact that Jack Somewhat was, in his own rough-edged way, not a bad looking young Grailish oaf.*

She looked down at the back of her hands, where a set of gigantic claws had retracted into the skin. How had she just *accepted* that? That, and the chopped-off hands and arms and all the wounds that magically healed? How had she just gone on, and fought a gods-damned monster the size of a house, for *nothing,* when she'd been unable to kill one stupid boy, for an *entire future?*

"I..." she began, "I... had to establish their trust. The mission parameters got... well, pretty weird, to tell you the truth, Lurien."

"It's all pretty weird out here, lass," replied the master poisoner. *"This is Grand Sepulchre. And here's fine example. Did you know that the Guild Lachrymose has an outstanding contract on the life of Enkalderon the Younger? A government job! If you manage to finish him off too, there's a nice payday to set you up in your new career."*

At that moment, as the creature's sword hung in the sky like a scar, and Slag Iron stood on the Unstoppable It's chest, one hand caught in the middle of slapping his face, and Skrx, sensing the change in Amber's heart rate and breathing, clicked his claws into the mantisbow and loaded a poisoned quarrel...

At that moment, Lord Slave brandished his scroll and bellowed at the top of his lungs.

"STOP!"

Assorted ſuper-heroes, monsters, newly homeless refugees and one tiny blood-formed homunculus turned to look. It was that kind of bellow, pitched in a tone which drill sergeants take decades to perfect.

"There'll be no need for any of this. I am Grand Vizier of the Urzoman Empire, and I am empowered to speak with His voice. Therefore, I'm instructed to do what is best for the majority of the citizens of that empire, in war, peace, law and governance."

Jack had even taken his eyes off the spitting red edge of Enkalderon's blade, now. Lord Slave rattled the scroll again. It was quite an impressive one, with wax seals and loops of ribbon and little fiddly gold bits.

"We're already a Magocracy. And He, unfortunately, is very unlikely to defeat you, Enkalderon. Or should I say, Emperor the Younger. I'm going to advise that he abdicates."

"Enkalderon the Younger?" came a voice from atop the Old Post Office – one which was about eighty percent pure pantomime. "The real, *actual* Enkalderon? The visionary, the scholar, the... dare I say it... genius?"

It was Montmortimer, and he'd returned from a sprint across the burning rooftops to Bulbous Corners and back. Now he was dressed as a wizard, in full ornamental regalia, from a blue satin cloak strewn with stars and runes, to a vast pointy hat, chains of office, and an outrageous fake beard.

"You do have the pleasure of addressing that... genius," preened Enkalderon, stabbing one of his blades into the cobbles to free up a hand. "And you are?"

"Why, the High Thaumatarch, of course. Just popped along from the College to offer you your old job back, you see. When we realised what an absolutely *inspired* and *intelligent* plan you'd formulated for immortality, the lads were unanimous. Also, you know, seeing as you could probably swat us all like beetles..."

Enkalderon grinned. His monstrous face was becoming more and more human as he radiated pure self-satisfaction.

"Well, of course I accept the honour, old chap! No hard feelings, it's all fair in wizardly politics, after all! And as for Himself abdicating... well. It's excellent that you're all seeing some sense. After all, I *am* an ancient and powerful wizard in the body of an indestructible demon-monster! Shall we talk about plans for my coronation?"

Lord Slave cleared his throat with malice aforethought.

"Just one thing, in that regard. Old statute, very traditional, been on the books since before the conquest, really. A trifle. A mere *soupçon* of a legal nicety."

"I still get a pointy hat?" asked Enkalderon, who would need one the size of a fortune teller's tent. "I still get to remodel that bloody Malevolith?"

"Of course," purred Monty, gesturing grandly with his stolen wizard's staff. "Pointy hat with a crown stuck to it, and all. Fake wax fruit, if you like. Gold brocade. Possibly even some feathers, for extra style."

Lord Slave insinuated himself into the conversation with a greased crowbar.

"It's just that we'd need your signature on this document for the change of government. A few things, to ease the transition. Martial law. Continuation of pay for the army, and Throne's Shadow, the likes of that. Plus, of course, for the civic peace... Grand Sepulchre would be teetotal until your coronation, in a few weeks."

Enkalderon didn't notice the look on the Unspeakable It's face as Slave uttered that fateful word. The blue giant's teeth locked into a snarl. His eyes bulged like pickled eggs under tectonic pressure. And his muscles *swelled*, veins standing out like a roadmap to hell.

"He can't possibly mean it," wheedled Slag iron, still standing on the It's chest.

But...

"Yes, I'm afraid it's simply necessary," went on Lord Slave. "We'll have to be dry. Boozeless. Sober. Clear headed. *Abstinent.* Piously and religiously chaste when it comes to all forms of whisky, beer, gin, vodka, wine, port, rubbing alcohol, medical spirits and Grailish firewater, not to mention a total prohibition on..."

Each mention of another drink banned caused a twitch to shudder through the It's mighty frame. Muscle swelled at an alarming rate. Slag Iron whispered something final and infuriating in his ear before she threw herself clear. And not a second too soon.

It was the word 'prohibition' which did it.

At the utterance of that dread pronouncement, Tarrence Bligh quite simply tripled in size. He roared, a sound of primal pain and wrath, literal steam blasting from out of his ears as he pounded the ground with two gigantic fists. Cracks radiated out from each impact point, and buildings streets away tottered and rocked.

Then he squatted down, clenched every sinew, and leapt up into the sky and away.

"What's gotten into *him?*" asked Enkalderon. "Is he not a monarchist, then? One of those weirdo republicans who thinks we should have a 'president', instead of a sorcerous immortal Emperor?"

"Best to pay that kind of thing no attention," oiled Montmortimer. "Now, about your induction. You'll be the first High Thaumatarch to be invested twice...with the exception of Zarbo the Reciprocating, back in 903, and again in 908. Remember his experiments with those time crystals? Nasty business."

Enkalderon nodded.

"Stupid man. Big, *huge* nose. I remember I was a student when he was still master of the Order of the Clenched Fist, and we used to dare each other to put minor curses on his undergarments, that kind of thing. I once animated his bedsocks, had them fill themselves with pudding, and then kicked him right up the arse in front of morning assembly." He wiped away a happy tear with one claw. "Simpler times!"

Jack saw Lord Slave sneak a look up into the dark sky, where stars made riotous constellations, and the great purple slick of the Wyrm's Breath Nebula crouched glittering on the horizon. Something way up there winked blue, in a silent detonation on the face of the moon.

See it from far above, outside of where the gigantic rock of Jansamrana rolls eternally, wrapped half-up in the skein of the Arch'.

It was night, so grand Sepulchre faced out into the chilly void, the glittering circle of water that made up the Arch proper twisting away left and right, lit up from behind in a nimbus of spray. The tiny moons, Fingril and Beshin, looped on figure-of eight courses all about the skein, while the twin suns Ijun and Balagur spun in endless pirouette together at its centre.

The Unstoppable It was powered by a rage so awful that it lived beyond language, in the icy-hot darkness of stubbed toes and cracked funnybones. He had leapt high out of the atmosphere of Jansamrana, and gone spinning into vacuum. He'd seen the miniature face of Fingril rolling by and made a new crater as he pushed back off it, headed back from whence he came.

Fists clenched.

Smiling.

Or at least showing a lot of teeth, as he came slamming back into the upper air, finding that it resisted him with writhing sheets of flame.

The pain was good. The pain just made him angrier, and the anger made him stronger. Blazing blue eyes narrowed in on their target, as the city spread out below him, streaked with crude brushstrokes of fire.

Enkalderon was still wittering on about his ideal coronation parade when the It struck home. A shell of heat burst out from the impact point, re-igniting the smouldering buildings all around the Fleamarket.

Then came the shockwave, which blew those burning scrawls of charcoal to pieces, sending them billowing out in a dandelion-head of fury. Assorted ſuper-heroes were blasted from their feet too; Slag Iron was dashed from the air to gouge a crater through the cobbles.

Amber, a bit quicker on the twitch, ducked behind the denuded fountain, feeling a hail of debris scythe by overhead. One of those pieces was the Grimshadow, who managed a hook one of his grappling ropes onto something solid, and flapped in the blast like a pennant, screaming. Soto and Billiam Knox punched two perfectly human-shaped holes in the front of the Old Post Office, which was stripped of all its gargoyles, muses, saints and sundry other statuary in a single heartbeat.

Montmortimer huddled behind a chimney pot, clenching his fake beard in both hands as it crisped around the edges. Ranulf scored a deep furrow in the surface of Skrayhollow Street with his axe, but remained anchored to it with a determined grip.

So it was only Jack who kept his feet. Only Jack, who leaned into the blast, gritted his teeth, and trusted in whatever power possessed him to keep himself from being ablated away like a snowman in a firestorm.

That's why he was the only one who saw what happened next.

The Unstoppable It knelt in a crater of his own creation, one fist elbow-deep in Grand Sepulchre's bedrock. Little scrawls and flickers of lightning played all about him as he looked up, teeth clenched, his mop of red hair matted and charred.

Looked into the face of Enkalderon the Younger, still standing above him like a colossus.

"Oops," chuckled the Maniacal Mage. "Looks like you missed."

Then the shockwave, which had spread out and *down* through the molten innards of Jansamrana, bounced off the hard core of nickel at its centre. Several fire efrits, lounging on the surface of that immense ball of superdense metal, spilled their cocktails of liquid uranium and iron, and cast each other quizzical looks.

Here it came, raging back toward the surface. Here it came, traced out in massive, yawning cracks in the great rock's crust. Teeth of stone gnashed and splintered, deep below...

"It *never* miss. It simply have... sense of the dramatic!" slurred Tarrence Bligh.

And then the portable hole yawned wide.

Massive cracks split the earth clear across the Fleamarket square, and red-hot flame burst up from within. Steam began to whistle out of the fountain as the water pipes below flashed to super-heat. The great bulk of the It was blasted backwards, shrinking and losing its blue hue as it tumbled across the cobbles.

For a second, Enkalderon's monstrous form teetered on the brink. He dropped his other sword, and windmilled his arms, great clawed toes scrabbling as rocks crumbled away beneath them.

For a second, it looked as if it would make it.

Then Ranulf the Butcher was there, running in screaming from one side, his axe held high. It moved in a perfect silvery blur, reflecting fire, and when it sliced through the creature's ankle, it made a sound like anchor chains splitting in the deep.

"Old fashioned heroism!" he roared, following through with an upswing that was pure showmanship.

"Oh, *bollocks*," managed the immortal one, as its leg collapsed into the chasm.

There was an instant of weightlessness and pause, as sparks floated up in slow motion.

Then the beast was gone, falling out of sight with a horrible inhuman scream, a howl of anguish that scrabbled up the scale like a cat climbing glass. It seemed that it was done.

But at the last moment a great clawed hand came lashing up and over, snaffling the luckless Ranulf up and closing him in a fist. Then gravity had its due and this, too was gone, down into the burning beneath.

High above, at the balcony of the Malevolith, Himself nodded once in satisfaction.

"This doesn't count as vanquishing anything." He muttered (for whom, no-one was certain). "Call it civic renewal..."

A shock of ice-cold magic, tattered with invisible cobwebs. A pulse of power from the roots of the Malevolith, gripping whole great plates of subterranean rock as if they were pinched between two fingers...

And SNAP.

The chasm grated closed, hammering shut with a sound like tombs imploding. Flame spumed from the portable hole, now slowly decaying as the spells powering it ran down.

Jack stood silhouetted against that wash of flame, nerves jangling with unnatural tension. He should have felt exalted. He should have felt *vindicated.* Instead, he felt flat, stretched thin, unable to comprehend the enormity of what had just happened.

Behind him, Amber emerged from cover. Jack didn't see her, as his shoulders slumped and he fell to his knees. His eyes were on the broken buildings, the burning skyline, the sad little heaps and straggles of cloth which in places revealed a hand, or a foot, or an open, staring eye.

He didn't see her bite back some indefinable feeling - perhaps a mirror of his own - as a single tear tracked through the grime on her cheek. He didn't see her raise her mantisbow and aim at the back of his neck.

"We won," he chuckled, low and humourless. "Hooray. Heroes win the day. Look at everything we saved."

Amber noticed the pause, as if Jack was talking to someone who wasn't there. She certainly noticed the fury in his voice when he answered back.

"*Really?* And do you suppose they'll *thank* us? I'll tell you something, mate, those ones over there won't. Nor will all the ones we just let burn to death, or crushed under falling buildings, just so we had a big, exciting battle to be all heroic in! Who answers for them?"

The point of Skrx's poisoned quarrel dipped and blurred. Amber had a pretty fair idea of what he was on about. Now that the monster was gone, there was a monster-sized hole left in the world. *Or perhaps just in her mind.* But now was not the time for self-pity. Or self-doubt. Or even for self at all.

"*What are you waiting for?*" hissed the little homunculus of Invigilator Lurien, as miles away the real master of poisons leaned forward on his divan, pushing a pair of blood-red spectacles up on his nose. "*Take the shot! He won't know what hit him!*"

Once again, Amber saw Jack's shoulders heave with bitter laughter. He was shrunken, now, his hero's physique gone, along with that black outline and bright, primary-coloured aura which had made him look like a paper cut-out stuck to reality.

"No, they *won't* see. Some of them won't see anything else, ever again. You know what? I think that all that happened here was that a whole lot of monsters fought, in a selfish, stupid battle that never needed to happen. And *nobody* won. The monsters who are still standing will call themselves heroes. It's what Enkalderon would have done. Can you imagine what they'd be calling us, if he hadn't taken the plunge?"

Amber was close enough, now, to hear the voice that answered. It resonated in her teeth, and in her bones, with a crackle and fizz of green.

"You've given them something to believe in."

There was a certain tone to the voice. Pleading and hungry. Petulant and hurt.

"They'll believe we're freaks! They'll believe we *killed them!*"

"And isn't being part of your story the most important thing they'll ever do?"

Jack clenched his fists and ground them into the cobbles. They left a smear of blood.

"How do you know? How do *any of us* know? And how dare anybody make that judgement? You know what, Rod? It's time for you to get out."

"No."

Lurien was all but jumping up and down, now. The mantisbow quarrel dipped and wavered. Jack was mere paces away.

"I said, get OUT!"

"NO!"

"My head," grated Jack. "My rules. Leave the rest of them alone, too!"

Amber felt a pulse of pure panic. It was with a sense of dread that she realised it wasn't hers; it came from whatever alien power had decided she'd look better with claws.

"It doesn't work like that! You can't..."

"Watch me."

"For the love of all things unholy, girl, take the shot! There's a whole bright future waiting for you, just on the other side of this oaf's bloody funeral!"

Jack held out his hand before him, clamped at the wrist. Something glowing green began to bulge up from its centre, distorting the diamond-shaped tattoo etched there.

It was a truly terrible time for making life decisions. It was an awful moment for the boy she was supposed to murder to try to rescue her, from some eldritch nonsense out of space. And it was *definitely* the worst time possible for the little blood-spawned homunculus of Master Lurien to leap off her shoulder, go pelting down the length of her arm, and slap Skrx right on the carapace.

"You can't make me! You're too strong, Jack Somewhat! Too strong *with* me! Too weak *without* me! You'd have to be *out of your mind* to reject me now!"

Click – went the mantisbow.

Hiss – went the quarrel. And thud. And...

Jack turned, slowly, the wicked barbed spike standing proud from the back of his neck. His lips moved, but only drool came out. His eyes opened wide, unfocusing on the figure of Amber, backlit by the burning city. The pupils dilated, round and black as wells down to infinity.

Because the first effect of the Necrotoxin Ultra-Mortis on this particular dart... was the utter separation of the body and the mind.

"You -" managed Jack, as something glowing green swelled from his hand, clattering to the ground. It was a rod of crystal, twelve thumbs long, and its eerie light painted the whole scene in a wash of emerald.

Well, for a second.

Before Jack toppled over completely, eyes glazed, mouth twitching at the corners as though he found something indescribably funny. One flopping arm brushed the rod, and it clattered a few paces, teetering on the edge of the portable hole...

Amber made a lunge. It wasn't her own decision.

But it was too late.

The rod rolled around the edge of the hole, then fell, down to join Enkalderon and Ranulf in the fires beneath. This seemed to be all the spell could take; it fizzled out, letting the hole collapse with a sound like a cork being popped.

"There," said Lurien, calm as you like. *"That was easy, wasn't it? Though your usual hobby of collateral overkill really got a workout tonight, eh?"* He shrugged, lighting up a slim cigarillo. *"Never mind. Double pay, and full privileges. Welcome to the Guild Lachrymose. I suspect you'd like a bit of a lie down, hmm?"*

Amber was way ahead of him. She collapsed across the motionless body of Jack Somewhat, all tangled up in his silly yellow cape, and before she could scream, the lights went out.

CODEX TWO:

ROTTEN DEVELOPMENTS

16

The Preventative Incarceration

AMBERELIA CHANCE WAS no stranger to a night in jail.

Or at least, no stranger to the guildhouse cooler, where wayward apprentices were sent to contemplate the (usually painful) things they'd done.

The dungeons of an Assassin's organisation, if you think about it, are not really going to get much use, and so they were usually scrupulously clean. Amber considered a couple of nights cooling her heels in the whitewashed vaults under the Old Lady's palace a step up from where she was raised; for one thing, iron bars and cold stone don't give you splinters. This intimacy with the incarcerated lifestyle meant that she was the first to notice that the 'protective custody' they'd been ushered into was cleverly designed to disincline anyone from leaving.

Not that escape was on her mind. No. She was certain that somewhere, Guild Lachrymose lawyers were even now scrivening iron-hard affidavits and writs for her release. Her thoughts – hot, squirming, guilty thoughts – were on the fact that Jack Somewhat had been missing when she woke up.

Lord Slave had rounded up every ſuper-hero left breathing and insisted that they accompany him to the Malevolith.

"On account of the fact that He might want to thank you in person, of course," he'd said at the time, helping Soto Scalizari up onto the back of the swiftly dragooned Wonky Wagon. "You never know. And what He wants, of course…"

"He gets?" enquired Montmortimer Pettigrew. "Yes, I'm fairly sure that's how aristocracy works. It would explain where all the new clothes keep coming from. Frightfully efficient, those new Guild Somnophylactic butlers[38]. I wouldn't know what to pay them, except

---

38. The Somnophylacteries (literally 'we guard you while you sleep') were the old guild of butlers, gentleman's gentlemen and sundry retainers who took care of the aristocracy. This usually involved keeping them out of the kind of trouble you get with too little

for the fact that they do the books as well."

"What if we don't want to go?" asked Billiam Knox, raising a hand. Only one - he'd popped back into a single body as the potential for heroism dropped abruptly to zero. "I've got a policy, see, about meeting figures of high authority. It's 'don't.'"

"I'm afraid it's less of a request than an *insistence*." There was a distinct edge to Lord Slave's voice, like tight garrotte wire in the dark. "After all, He isn't known for his patience..."

"It's just that peasants, see, and ordinary people, you know, fishermen and cobblers and such, don't go around saying things like 'off with his head' and expecting to get taken seriously. I find that you know exactly where you stand with people of lower socio-economic importance..." babbled Knox, oblivious to the fact that he was being herded aboard the wagon nonetheless.

"In a pigsty?" asked Foxmallet, who was already seated, and had rummaged under the bench for a bottle he may well have stashed there himself. The hunch-backed driver of the Wonky Wagon was on first-name terms with Jory's family, who often paid him a handsome tip for not giving the scion of their house the traditional roughing-up with the traditional bog-wood truncheon. "Or, oooh, I know - some kind of toilet without a door on?"

Lord Slave retained his cool demeanour, but only with the kind of force that usually results in the growth of fabulous gemstones deep underground.

"I'm certain that Himself has never said 'off with his head' in the last two hundred years," he reassured the assorted freaks in his care. He didn't even look sideways at Tarrence Bligh as the Grailishman made a grasp for the bottle of Zalois red he'd just produced from inside of his cape, using it to lead him up and onto the wagon. "But to put no finer point on it, ladies and gentlemen, there are such a thing as mobs. Mobs with pitchforks and flaming torches and ropes, who have just seen you engage in a conflict which has wrecked a large number of their homes. Now *I'm* not one to throw around words like 'freaks' and 'heretics' and 'string them all up by the unspeakables and pelt them

---

chin, too much money, outrageous mustachios, a penchant for duelling and gambling and about three centuries of frightfully proper incest. The latest model of butler developed by Starchwood Academy was given some limited training with the Order of the Oracular Seers, and could therefore determine most of their masters' wishes *before the feckless noblemen knew what they wanted.* Of course, most *proper* butlers said they could have done this anyway, without the use of as many runes or chicken entrails.

with cabbages', but there are about a thousand beady eyes amid the rubble around us connected to mouths... that would."

"But we're *heroes*," protested Billiam. "Proper ones, with all the official bits."

Lord Slave angled his head to one side, and stroked his leather-clad chin.

"I suppose, in one light, yes, you are. Once we scrub you up and explain everything, and have a little parade. Until then, your status is quite debatable. I'm certain the Wizards would like to call you something else, though. Am I right, Amberelia?"

The newly-minted Assassin rolled her eyes. She was certain that the Wizards would want answers, and possibly quite a lot of blood, once they put the fires out in their College.

"It was one of them that..." began Soto, but Amber was already climbing up to sit beside him, a resigned look on her face. She blew a wispy curl of hair out of her eyes, and snagged Bligh's bottle.

"Come on then. Let's roll."

The Wonky Wagon deposited them at the foot of the Malevolith, at a kind of tradesman's entrance just around from the huge marble steps and golden doors with their motif of skulls and devils. Throne's Shadow soldiers made up what could have been an honour guard (or a thinly veiled threat) as they tramped through endless black corridors within, joined by pale, red-robed servitors, a pair of scribes pushing a desk on squeaky iron wheels, and one of the four-armed clockwork gholem, which opened and shut the immense gates they passed at regular intervals.

At last, they reached a room like a fussy aunt's parlour, all incongruous doilies and lace chair-covers, with a fire burning merrily in a tiny grate. There was a table set out with tea and biscuits, and divans all around the walls, under watercolour paintings of large, floppy dogs. Lord Slave rubbed his hands together briskly.

"Right. Sit tight, one and all, and we'll soon have this little public relations nightmare sorted. There'll be a parade in the morning, and then... well, I'm certain you recall the rest of our little deal. My dear friend Rhaegulus Cratt is shepherding some wayward shipping back into port as we speak, and you'll have any number of options for exile. Or should we call it a well-deserved holiday? One that goes on forever?"

Of course, half of those present hadn't even heard about this little caveat, and there was much protestation, argument and general hubbub as Lord Slave gave a small bow and left the room. Closing a very suspiciously heavy door behind him, Amber noticed.

She recalled something else he'd mentioned earlier, about a place beneath the Malevolith which even he couldn't escape from, just in case... and she wondered if this was it.

"Bloody hellfire!" swore Foxmallet, still half-clad in his Grimshadow outfit. The cape flapped forlornly as he slumped into an armchair. "That's a bit inconvenient! Permanent exile! I have a very busy schedule next week."

"He's probably not serious," hazarded Soto.

"Likely just a bit of a joke," tried Billiam.

"Like to see the ****** try," grumbled Slag Iron. "Give us a hand with this helmet, someone, could you?"

But Amber realised that he *was* serious, and that she was just as doomed as the rest of them, when, some hours later, the door creaked open and a pair of servants rolled Jack Somewhat in, snoring, in a wheelchair. He was still alive, which was something of a miracle.

Not the good kind, however. Amber did some quick mental arithmetic.

Right... so if he's not dead, then I'm not really an assassin. If I'm not really an assassin, then I'm bound for a big, irreversible cruise-ship vacation with this shower of human dandruff all around me. But there's still the money! I'll get a nice purse for killing Enkalderon the Y... ohhhh, turdbiscuits! No, I won't. Because Jack's still alive, so I'm not an assassin, so they won't pay me, AND I'll still be stuck in the bilges of some Zollish slow-boat on the way to who-knows-where in the morning!

Amber picked up a small throw cushion, embroidered with a cheerful and wonky-eyed bichon frise. She buried her face in it and screamed all but silently, for several minutes. Then she composed herself, looked down at the cushion, looked at the snoring figure of Jack Somewhat, and narrowed her eyes.

Really?

Yes. Really. Does it look like there's any other option, here?

Well, I hear they have assassins in Khantif, right. We could...

What, those big beardy lunatics who smoke stumbleweed and knife each other by accident, thinking they're chasing purple giraffes? Come off it!

The point is... people will pay to have other people killed anywhere in the world. What's the point of being with a guild that doesn't want you?

Amber considered this for a second. The point was, it was something she'd decided *she* wanted. It was something people had told her she couldn't do. Suffocating a big snoring oaf with a pillow was a small price to pay, even if it came with the added, crippling hire-purchase of a lifetime of guilt. Right?

Amber took a deep breath. She closed her eyes. *This was not at all like a fair fight...*

Then Jack blinked his bleary eyes, and said the worst possible thing he could.

"Thank you," he said, reaching out and taking the cushion. He arranged it tidily behind his head. "Not... umm... not for the pillow, of course. For shooting me. How did you know that's what I needed to get rid of that bloody thing in my hand?"

Amber's smile was frozen brittle, like a thin sheen of ice.

Dammit, girl, you were actually going to go through with it! What kind of a bastard are you!

So went her thoughts. But what came out of her mouth was an embarrassed mumble.

"We learn all about poisons, right. At the, ummm. The Guild Lachrymose."

Jack sat up a little, and stifled a yawn.

"So, you really *were* sent from the Old Lady! Wow! To think, you knew about Enkalderon and his plans all along, and you managed to keep it all a secret! You must be one of their top... you know." He mimed some enthusiastic stabbings. Amber winced.

"Look, it's not like that! You..."

Jack grinned.

"Yeah, I suppose my knife technique is a bit sloppy. But I always thought there was something special about you, Amberelia Chance. Even before the... well, before the green sparks, and the powers, and everything."

Amber turned away, slumping down onto the arm of a sofa. That might have been the nicest thing anyone had ever said to her, that wasn't followed by an order to murder people. The encroaching redness which was climbing the back of her neck demanded she change the subject.

"So, just what *is* this green stuff? What was that thing in your hand? Is this some kind of experiment by the Alchemists, or something? Because Lord Slave - a person I really never, *ever* wanted to meet, by the way - swears black and blue that it isn't magic."

Jack looked up at the big skull-and-swords themed cuckoo clock affixed to the wall. He looked around the room at the others, all slumped in repose, Slag Iron (with her helmet off) curled up back-to-back with Billiam Knox on a divan, Soto, Bligh and Monty sprawled on armchairs, and Jory Foxmallet snoring on the hearth rug like a large and shaggy hound.

"Better make us a cup of tea, then," said Jack. "I don't think we're getting any sleep tonight, so I really do have all the time it takes to tell you."

Amber sniffed the pot. Skrx came scuttling out of her backpack and pried open the lid, clattering his horrible mouthparts and bubbling.

"Well, it's not poisoned. At least, not with any of the seventy-two primary demortifying powders and elixirs. Which we might be immune to anyway, right? I don't feel like that green fizz has gone away, even if you did something to the source of it."

Jack dropped three sugar lumps in a china cup, looked down at them wistfully for a second, then added two more.

"From the start then. Well, yesterday, see, I had to take the Day Watch Lantern out to the breakwater, like I do every morning, and..."

But here we must leave Jack Somewhat, getting into the swing of his tale with all the slight embellishments and little half-truths that make a story worthwhile. For we've already journeyed with him through the facts and realities of that tangled series of happenstances, and to thus recount it again would be to tempt disappearance up the fractal fundament of the universe (which the Wizards say is a very real and present danger for seekers after knowledge).Instead, let us consider some of the other citizens of Grand Sepulchre, who are having a worse night of it than Amberelia and Jack.

There's Zoltan Creagle, for example, who has just been told that his contract-bound ticket to riches and... well, *more* riches, Jack Somewhat, is presently detained at His Dark Leisure, and that the posse of bandaged, noseless, crutch-wielding and downright ornery gladiators who had rallied to Zoltan's cause were about as useful, in this situation, as udders on a shark. That was the colourful local Suljanek way of putting it, though many of his crew were muttering things much worse.

"Never mind, lads," said the master of the pits, wringing his hands with malice aforethought. "They say there's gonna be a parade for these freaks tomorrow morning. It would be a shame if that all went banana-shaped, wouldn't it?"

"I think the expression's *pear-shaped*, boss," put in Toothless Frank Hamsmiter, his arm in a sling.

Creagle's meaty fist lashed out faster than the eye could follow. Hamsmiter winced, trying not to look down at the very tender area his boss had taken hold of.

"They'll be bloody banana shaped by the time *I'm* done with 'em. All stretched out and mushy and bent at a funny angle." He let go of the unfortunate brawler's tackle, evincing a massive sigh of relief. "No one swindles me! No one does any swindling *but* me! And no one out-swindles the swindler!"

While Zoltan Creagle was eroding the meaningfulness of the word 'swindle' in a crooked boxing gym high up on the sugarloaf, Lord Slave was getting his own bad news, down by the breakwater.

"What do you mean, he *never delivered it?*" he asked, shaking Rhaegulus Cratt's luckless majordomo by the scruff of what, on a smaller man, would have passed for a neck.

A lesson in karma, dear reader; this was the same snoring apparition who had called Jack Somewhat a 'maggot' earlier, in a calculated racial slur. Now his brain was rattling off the insides of his skull like a husk inside an eggshell, and his face was a red, puffy mess of snot and tears. He fully subscribed to all the myths about Lord Slave and entertained horrible notions that he was about to be plunged into a brief and squalid career of bondage and discipline, followed by a burial in the harbour as shark chum.

"He.... he... he gave it to some oaf. Had a bath. Drunk 'is coffee. He was.... he was singing *light opera!*"

Lord Slave dropped the majordomo with a shudder of distaste.

"A bath, was it? Coffee, eh? And consorting with oafs, no less..." He cast a single, utterly disdainful eye over the human tissue-wad at his feet. "Gryssle, clean this thing up, and get a sworn statement. When our old friend Cratt comes back from his duties at sea, there will be some hard questions for him. Oh yes. If he's embezzled an artefact of power, then he's both more ambitious and infinitely more stupid than I feared."

The last item of bad news on tonight's agenda was worse than all the aforementioned, wrapped up in razorwire and sprinkled with arsenic.

But to realise just how bad it was, you first had to know something about the parasitic, nigh-immortal, green and glowing intellect that called itself Rodney.

Right now, the mind in question was floating deep in an abyss of fire, but it felt no pain, not even a tickle of discomfort. Force fields of interlocking magnetic energy flared from both emerald tips of Rod, creating a fishbowl effect, beyond which magma bubbled and roiled, lambent red.

Those fields would never collapse. Indeed, even the tiny chips and sparks of Rod which had burrowed deep into the bodies of Grand Sepulchre's new ſuper-heroes had a half-life measured against the procession of galaxies. For Rodney was in fact a Yanavarian Power Crystal, which had come into the hands of two desperate rocket scientists just as their world was about to be bulldozed into orbital gravel.

He was sentient simply because of a strange twist of mathematical truth, discovered by the Yanavari. These were the pale blue, humanoid the race who had created him long in the past (or perhaps, far in the future - time travel having tangled up causality like a kitting bag full of curious kittens by this point). Rod was, simply, *power*. The power of every last wisp and photon which had ever been compacted down into the core of a single black hole. In the tiny confines of a singularity, things like the speed of light make as much sense as breadfruit pudding pyjamas. Quantum entanglement means that for every tiny particle in the universe, there's another that hums in the same pitch and key, and they're tethered by invisible forces. So for every infinitesimal, potent black hole, there has to be an equal opposite. Follow the thread, and you'll find it; a *primordial white hole*, the kind of thing that blows up and creates universes.

This is not even remotely safe to handle. Not even with barbecue tongs.

Only, what you do, if you're a smug Yanavari scientist with the obligatory huge forehead, toga and sandals, is you build an incredibly complex matrix to trap such a particle, and bleed off its power like somebody using a fission reactor to cook a can of baked beans. The complexity of that containment matrix serves to distract the universe for long enough to switch the full blast of all that power on and off without it being noticed, the string pulled, and the black and white holes colliding, which is how baby universes are made (and never mind the guff about Jolly Mister Stork and the Cabbage Patch).

The problem was this, however. Knowledge has long been known to equate to power. What the Yanavari found out, to their detriment, was that the equation also worked *the other way*.

It's no mistake that life, that huge immaterial field sloshing about behind reality like a kid's paddling pool full of LSD, pokes through into consensual adult reality wherever things get complex enough. We've seen it with carbon-based life, and silicon, and things made out of the coronal ejecta of suns, the crystals of transnormal elemental metals dancing in the halo of pulsars, and even in things left for far too long in break-room refrigerators.

Rod, and those like him, were power. And power was knowledge.

The Yanavari, as it turns out, were one of the human-shaped species who may or may not have had something to do with colonising the Arch', way back[39] in the Diasporic Age. They'd evolved on a humdrum watery planet, muddled through their phase of hooting, swinging from trees and throwing faeces, toyed with nuclear annihilation, plastic bags and football, and finally reached the stage where they'd made their first Power Crystal, allowing them to sally forth bravely into the community of the galactically involved.

Lightspeed travel was, to the races of that great pan-sentient mega-carnival, what a good fake driver's license was to a queue of teenagers outside a nightclub on a rainy Friday evening. The first Power Crystal (Rodney's great, great, great grand-dad, as it were) had managed to solve the billion strings of complex equations required to squirt an ordered complex of matter and energy through hyperspace, and reassemble it at a precise point with all its arms and legs and nipples in the right places.

This act of teleportation was perilously close to magic, had the Yanavari only listened. Instead, they enjoined Rod's great-grandsire to shut up, with much talk about EMP devices, and him being used as the microprocessor in a bus-station urinal.

But the magic worked. It was noticed. And the Yanavari got an *invitation*, written in the skies over their planet in green fire.

Their delegation, complete with those silver-foil togas, those tall and stupid hats, and those teetering three-foot platform sandals, had been welcomed into the great parliamentary megasphere where the Galactic Council of Wise Elders held court[40].

From ranks of floating pods, self-contained gaseous atmospheres, steaming pits of slop and crackling electrical fields, the alien throng

---

39. Possibly forward, likely very sideways
40. There was no way they were going with the bald veracity of 'The Galactic Council of Beings Who Got Quietly Kicked Out of Regular politics and Given a Cushy Job to Keep Them Out of Mischief'

had welcomed their newest members. The Yanavari smiled - those brittle, tight smiles which always happen when people don't know what's going on, but know that it's being filmed and is probably very important. At last, they stood before the elected Potentate of the Council, a six-armed purple giant with a dodecahedral face and a halo of cybernetic eyeballs.

This very important being dithered a little, and fumbled a set of cards in one pair of hands.

"Ummm... this is frightfully embarrassing," it said, through a robotic translator like a small levitating suitcase. "Please just wait a moment..."

The Speaker of the House, a thing like an amphibian koala bear made of pineapple jelly, gave the Potentate a nudge.

"Go on, then. Ask them the question!" it hissed. The purple one held up a card, pulled a pair of three-lensed spectacles from a pocket in its flesh, wiped them on its sash of office, and summoned a trio of floating cyber-eyes to squint through them.

"Right! Yes! O.K. Then! Ermmm..."

It leaned forward, looming over the Yanavarian delegation.

"Have you lot sorted what it's all about, then?"

The Yanavari smiles took on the glistening rigidity of waxworks. There was a moment of hushed anticipation, while the head delegate's eyes twitched back and forth.

"Ummm. Not. Not as... well, not *entirely*, like, the whole. Shemozzle. As it were. Not the whole, as you say, holistic, totality of ... umm. What it's *all* about. Not quite."

There was a sigh from the assembled Wise Ones. What appeared to be several large-denomination bets were settled.

"No worries," said the Speaker. "We've only managed, so far, to agree that three things are universally pleasing to all sentient life-forms. The anticipation and consummation of mutually enjoyable procreational congress. The alteration of the psyche via chemistry for the means of contemplating philosophical truths. And modulated wavelengths of an artistic composition, designed to stimulate emotional responses via sensory and neurochemical interaction."

The Yanavarians took a moment to process this. It was their junior science attaché who spoke first.

"You mean *sex, drugs, and rock 'n' roll?*"

A billion floating translator robots put this proposition to the Wise Elders of a million worlds. There was an agreeable murmur throughout the megasphere. Then the Potentate leaned down again, three of his mouths displaying what was, to his people, a cheeky grin.

"You bloody said it guvnor, not me! But yeah, don't mind if we do!"

There is no further record of that first, momentous Yanavari mission, except for a fragment of audio and video which appears to show a giant orange slug in a top hat popping open an improbably large bottle of fizzy wine and shouting 'let's have it large!'

The important part was - things like Rod were made.

The other important part was - their sheer complexity gave them an intellect that dwarfed even the Solar Cogitators of Velfari Nine, or the Hypercerebrated Solid-state Ultraminds of the Nether Spinwise Reaches.

The other, *other* important part was this. When they went mad, which was all but inevitable, they went mad on a scale which made your average frothing chainsaw massacrist look like a yoga-practising chartered accountant.

Rod, the thing which Jack Somewhat had but recently sweated out like the memory of a bad Tikka Masala, had had his mind wiped by a gamma ray burst from a dying supergiant sun. He had no idea what he was, or even the full extent of his intellect and power.

But he'd filled in the blanks. He'd received transmissions about *exactly* how things were supposed to go. And wired into the very bedrock of his existence was the utter certainty that all three dimensions of space (and a couple of time) were things to use like modelling clay, to fulfil his glorious destiny. This was bad news for, basically, all of reality. But specifically, it was terrible news for Grand Sepulchre. And, to put a point on it so fine you could use it for target practice, it was unspeakable news for Jack Somewhat, who had jilted an emotional and quite insane Cosmic Power.

Still, there were consolations to having all that limitless force. The magnetic shields which Rod had deployed, deep under a swirling ocean of magma, were cool to the touch from the inside. And that meant he could have a nice little talk with the only other person down here who retained such things as vocal chords.

"They saw what you could do, with just a little strength," purred Rod, to the figure, all charcoal-black and curled up in a foetal position below him. **"They're *afraid*. They want to take it all away. Everything you worked for. Just when you finally had the chance to show them all. You could have been the greatest. You could have been a name up in ... up in *runes*, mate. Top trilithon! But they've taken it all away from you. Guild shut down. Heroes banned. Government!**

Huh! For a bent spothin I'd incinerate the lot of 'em."

A face with red-rimmed, weeping eyes turned up to look at Rod, and as it did it was bathed in an emerald glow.

"Who?" came the croak, from lips like split and charred meat.

"I'm the one who made you strong. I'm the one who told you all the truth. The world needs heroes. It needs them in a very specific idiom."

The burnt figure's hands opened and closed, opened and closed. Its feet treadled nothing, like a dog dreaming by the hearth-side. Rod noticed that some of the particles etched into the figure's skin had once been the handle, and indeed the blade, of a very sharp battleaxe.

"...needs us?" it asked, in that same blistered rasp.

"Yes. *You*. You're needed. Because I got it all wrong. I thought that it started with heroism, and ended villainy. I thought that was how you repainted the world, nice and simple, so all you complicated organic things could finally know reason, and happiness. That's what I'm for, see? But I was wrong."

From within a thicket of burnt hair, a pair of lips pulled back from a set of broken teeth. Sheer heat had cracked the enamel, leaving them a row of jagged stumps. But some force hadn't allowed this thing to die. That force - a crackle of green fire shivering through its bones - was the same one that still lived in Jack Somewhat, for all his ungrateful spite.

"Happens to the best of us, mate," said Rod. **"But as it happens, we can help each other out. Do you think you can do dark and edgy, by any chance?"**

This may have been beyond the comprehension of the burned one, who dribbled a little, and attempted a giggle. It came out like the rasp of broken gears, in some haunted music-box deep underground.

"*Why?*"

Rod should not have been able to shrug, but a ripple of the light gave a very good impression.

"Because there's plenty in those transmissions I picked up about not getting the hero you want, but getting the legend your city deserves. About tragic motivations, and angsty monologues, and stylish black costumes in the rain. Something else, too. Something that those others up there, the ones who left you to burn... something they forgot."

Power arced and crackled. It earthed itself against the walls as crawling tendrils of green lightning, and when it touched the burned one, it arched his back nearly double with sudden pain. Pain... and something else. Wounds healed. Scar tissue zigzagged across exposed muscle and bone. Blisters drained in horrible reverse motion. For a brief instant, a pulse of green radiated from the very core of the man's ruined chest, picking out the shape of his ribs, then blazing out to his finger and toenails, welling up inside his eyes, and behind his remade smile.

"What... what do you mean?" asked Ranulf the Butcher, burned clean, hairless and knotted with muscle, his eyes glowing like reactor cores about to burst. It was apparent, however, that the healing hadn't gotten within spitting distance of his mind. Nothing sane grinned like that; a full-blown rictus that should have opened up the top of his head.

"I mean that every hero needs a villain," said Rod. **"Now, sit back, open up your mind, and take a look at *this*..."**

The emerald-glowing sphere spun deeper into the currents of magma, drifting away from sight. But somewhere close by – somewhere a mirror's depth away, or on the flip-side of a moon-cast shadow, something else heard Rodney's mutterings.

It was ancient, this thing, older even than the legendary Fleshless Brains and Stalking Steel which lurked in the deep and forgotten place of the Arch'.

Indeed, it was part of why the Arch' was created, so long ago that evolution seemed, to its slow, titanic mind, like a comedy on fast-forward[41]. It was so old that it would shout out of the metaphorical driver's window at continental drift, and tell it to have some patience.

But it knew about heroes and villains. It was fundamentally designed to generate thousands of adventurous, thrilling stories at once, and force them on any sentience which popped itself up through the veil of three-dimensional space, here in this edge-bound world in the Shallows.

Call it fate, call it destiny, call it a bastard. Call it with blood sacrifices and by blowing on dice, and crossing your fingers when you lie.

Give it a form, so as to convince yourself you can understand it; make it a woman with curves that would cause a sculptor to bite clean through his favourite chisel, a smile like a shark late for dinner, and eyes like green stars exploding in nebulae of absinthe.

It – well, *She* now that you've thought about it – is the only one of the

---

41. Turns out the primates did it

Gods of the Arch' that is really, really real. And even then, only because she was built that way. But she did have a very active imagination, and an attention span measured in ice ages. She'd taken a very special interest in a promising party of adventurers, some centuries ago, and She was still looking for a suitable way to wrap up their story.

Now, here was a chance.

"I'm making a list, and checking it twice…" hummed the Goddess, imagining a vast, Escher-scrawl library around herself, and plucking a tome from an overhanging shelf. When She opened the book, it didn't have pages, just a series of eye-watering pictures of doors. Pictures which writhed and breathed and moved, with too much depth for any printed page. "Gonna find out who's naughty or nice…"

There. Last time it had been a dragon. A great red flamedrake, to be precise, scaly and blood-crusted, hoarding and horrible. This time, after all these years of careful evasion, Her quarry would be stronger. Slipperier. She hadn't thought that he'd be able to come back the *first* time, all thing considered. But human willpower is a strange variable. Just when you think nothing can twist material space like gravity, along comes a little upright mammal in trousers who you can bend whole worlds around like a farrier's anvil.

One golden-nailed finger came to rest on a certain image of a door. It was not a nice door. You almost expected to see a sad little pile of empty cookie boxes and girl scout bones off to one side. Skulls and spikes were much in attendance.

"Zag-Hammurat," she murmured, in a voice like molten caramel. "Ancient Devourer. Scourge of the Light. Soul-Roaster. Harvester of those Wobbly Purple Bits That We Don't Know What They Do But They're Right Behind the Lungs. Yes, you'll do nicely. We seem to have ourselves a born-again hero…"

In a place even further from reality, where things waited *in potentia*, like empty clothes in a wardrobe light-years deep, something stirred. Vertices and angles redoubled, and eight eyes blinked, red as dying stars. A great, hideous head snaked out toward the warmth and solidity of the real.

The door shivered under Her touch. "Not yet. Patience! For now, he's still on the side of evil. But he's had *feelings*. Hah! That's the first step toward goodness! That's the first step, and it's fraught with… with *the banana skin of good intentions!* We'll make a hero of him yet, and then, you can give him his glorious last stand."

Behind the door, that *something* unfolded like black plastic origami, filling out to a size which was as looming and terrible as a thunderhead.

Zag-Hammurat, the Ancients had called it, back when mud bricks and perfectly square beards had been all the rage. Well, at least the mad ones had called it, often while laughing maniacally and sloshing around in the blood of several less fortunate Ancients, while wearing their internal organs as a hat.

The Goddess was a big believer in the fact that a hero's life deserved a hero's death.

One more mistake, and she'd make sure it was delivered.

17
The Malefictorial Manifestation

THERE HAVE BEEN sadder parades, in other times and places in the wide, wobbly multiverse. But as far as damp, drizzly, fizzling-out-fireworks and bedraggled-banner-dragging occasions went, the sending-off party for Grand Sepulchre's ⊠uper-exiles was down there in the grease trap with the worst of them.

Himself hadn't decreed a day of celebration, a day of mourning (or indeed a day of anything in particular) before sending off the saviours of His Dark Domain to a leaky Zollish tub called the *Rum-Soaked Mary*. It was the only ship in harbour that would have them, the rest being full of slightly fire-damaged treasures which might not, if squinted at in the right way, have come with a receipt.

Several wizards, having gotten involved in arguments about whose fault the whole Mantigore situation was, had decided to go off to foreign points of the Arch' to conduct studies well away from more potent mages who they had compared unfavourably to small rodents, bodily excretions or species of slime mould.

An equal number of thieves, who had been the loyalists of the old King Snagpurse, were also a-ship, setting sail for any port that needed things nicking at discount prices, and where the new regime wasn't waiting with cricket bats and cheesewire in the dark.

Jack, by now fully recovered, slumped on the repurposed Wonky Wagon in the rain, holding a scrap of cape over Amber's head. Along with them came Slag Iron, Tarrence Bligh (nicely drunk), Soto Scalizari, Billiam Knox (not drunk enough) and Jory Foxmallet, who had finally woken to the fact that this terrible circus was really happening.

He had been spending most of the morning trying to bribe Throne's Shadow thugs with the lint in his pockets. He'd also constructed a fleet of poorly made paper aeroplanes, all addressed to Ludcastle, Sneers and Pinion, and whenever it seemed that the black-armoured guards were otherwise occupied, he sent them looping off over the rooftops on corkscrew trajectories, whistling nonchalantly.

A banner was wrapped around the cage of the wagon. It read 'Ho0raeY' in dripping paint. Someone had given the hunch-backed driver a party hat. Lord Slave, who turned up late, seemed to be in a fine mood.

"Well, I think we took care of that little indiscretion quite... discreetly," he said, as he swung up onto the wagon and gave two sharp slaps on the roof. The iron wheels began to creak and roll. "This morning's news-sheets all have a lovely big headline – 'Monster Hunters Save Day, Leave City'. Quite droll, but definitely a great preventative for riots and such."

The wagon clattered down Decameron, with nobody watching. At this false-dawn hour the people of the night were running low on dreamsugar and rotgut, and the people of the day were waking up, only to find that those noisy bloody night people had kept them awake long enough to give them a whopper of a headache. Jory tried again.

"Ummm... just one more time for the sake of appearances, m'lord. But is there any way we can, you know, *not* get exiled? It's just that I have an awfully large amount of money here, and it gets lonely if I don't buy it drinks to keep it company."

The huge, musclebound Grand Vizier didn't even bother to sigh. Behind his leather mask, he was smiling, a nasty display of pointed teeth.

"Ahh, yes. Young lord Foxmallet. Never fear, the succession of the Red House is not in question. We've managed to find some old and dusty scrolls which prove that there's a distant cousin or some such. A redoubtable young pugilist, apparently. Name of Golto the Demolisher. I hear he's built like a bric... ahem. Well, like *me*, to put no finer point upon it."

Amber leaned forward, catching a hefty slop of rainwater. Some more trickled down into Montmortimer's open mouth; the World's Fastest Fop was still snoring.

"You mean the big, noseless thug who works for old man Creagle? He's about as noble as a six-day-old dog turd! Have you *seen* him?"

"*I've* punched him in the face," said Jack, as the wagon clattered around the corner into Skizarian Street. The parade actually got worse at this point, because the natural reaction of the sots and drunkards to the Wonky Wagon was to crawl as fast as possible for cover. Lord Slave chuckled.

"Well, suffice to say that Viscomptesse Scarberry has insatiable appetites, and needs a husband. Also, we have certain trade partners who still consider a big huge lump with more biceps than brain cells to be chieftain material. He'll make a great ambassador to some blasted chunk of rock where the ale is lumpy and the sheep are nervous."

"Scarberry?" asked Soto. "What happened to Octavius Grulks? Last I heard, she'd abducted him, and..."

"He managed to escape. Ran through Bishopsbath in a tutu, and is even now sitting in a big bowl of ice, sighing contentedly." replied Lord Slave. "Her eminence the Viscomptesse is a great contributor to municipal works, and Our Dark Lord thinks that marital bliss might settle her down a tad. There have been... incidents."

Now, at last, the wagon came to the breakwater, and the Piazza Della Von Tuesday, that nautical market square where sailors of every nation mingled to trade, share salacious rumours, and engage in the merry olde folkways of their native lands.

This meant that there were several corpses in the gutters, and a lot of broken glass strewn across the wooden expanse of the square, where Jansamrana gave out and the Stilts began. That ill-favoured neighbourhood straggled away to the east, loomed over by the still-perforated House of the Alchemists, much charred by fire. Lord Slave picked his way over a few snoring prostitutes and their paramours, sleeping serenely in the gutter.

"I hope that scoundrel Rhaegulus Cratt hurries up about it. I need to talk to him about another matter, once this is all out of the way. Would you believe he had the temerity to try to steal from me? Well, not even from me. From the Empire. From HIM!" He stopped under a badly painted banner, its paint still wet.

'ConGeRTulaTionS MonstRe HuntuRs', it read, in a script which hinted at a lot of brow-furrowing and concentration.

Jack had suddenly broken out in a cold sweat. *Did Slave know what had really happened? Had he talked to Chep Palaquat? Was this all a trap, perhaps?*

He had no way to know that it was... but not for the reasons which were tickling the nose-hairs of his paranoia.

Rhaegulus Cratt really *was* out there at the helm of an excise Trireme, towing the *Rum Soaked Mary* reluctantly into a berth by the dockside. The truth was, Lord Slave considered Jack to be too stupid to plot magical treason; that much was apparent by the way he herded the ſuper-heros off the wagon, and lined them up neatly in a row.

"Right-o, kids, time for a quick portrait, then I'll give a little speech, and hopefully that prat Cratt will have the boat here on time. Any idea of where you're all going?"

Frankly, none of the sad little group had given it the slightest thought. There was a big wide Arch' out there, full of possibilities, but they all seemed equally dismal on a rainy Forgeday morning, with the Lizard Bells only just ringing out the changes from atop the Slave Traders' Manse.

Amber was thinking about what actually happened to trainee assassins who failed their exams. There was a distinct lack of information on the subject, and not one failure to be found, anywhere. In the context of assassination, this didn't bode well.

Soto was thinking about the very large stash of gold and banker's notes which he'd hidden underneath his shack in the Fleamarket. Considering last evening's events, it was likely lost to the fires, but that just meant that Soto was wistfully considering a puddle of melted gold under a certain cobblestone, which may as well have been on the moon. Jory was quietly fuming about Golto the Demolisher stealing all of his many, many lovely sets of clothes, and stretching them all out of shape.

Monty Pettigrew had just woken up, and was wondering why there was no butler present, and no silver plunger of hot Zollish Coffee. Slag Iron was holding him up on one side, and Billiam Knox on the other. Tarrence Bligh was, thankfully, just at that happy point of mild intoxication which a timely Bloody Mary can bring. All three of the latter were trying to think of ways to escape, knowing of hidey-holes and dark places under the city where they could cool their heels and come up with a better plan.

There was a down-on-his-luck wizard there to do the portrait, a little man all in ink-stained robes who squinted at the group under their banner through a brass optic, adjusted some screws and lenses, then held up one hand for attention.

"Alright, squires, eyes front and centre. I'm going to count to three, and you lot smile, or whatever this occasion calls for."

With a shiver of sorcery, the spellcaster caused the lids of several big jam-jars full of ink to unscrew. Tendrils of colour wobbled up, budding little floating globules.

"One, two... ahhhbuggerbuggerbugger!"

There was a flash of thaumaturgy, and a pattern of ink splattered against the waiting canvas. In the aftermath, as the wizard tried to put out the small fires in his beard, Jack could see that the ink had just happened (by nigh impossible, magical chance) to form a detailed image of exactly what was happening on the dockside, under that badly-drawn banner.

That's why he jerked left at the last possible second, and watched a huge crossbow bolt slam into the timbers, vibrating with indignation.

The background of the painting was full of murderers.

To be fair, Jack had been praying to any Gods who would listen for some form of divine intervention – anything, in fact, to prevent the acutely embarrassing (and possibly fatal) moment when Rhaegulus Cratt pointed the stinky finger of blame in his direction.

What he *hadn't* hoped for was a sudden ambush, made clear as day by the image on the wizard's portraitograph. The decks and the rigging of the ships behind them were suddenly full of sharp-suited, pomaded and angry men. They poked out of barrels and crates, stood atop rickety harbourside brothels and taverns, and scowled from their hiding places in alleys and drains.

"The Hammerheads!" breathed Soto.

"At this time of the morning?" mumbled Monty. "Awfully impolite, don't you think?"

"There have to be at least three hundred of 'em!" gulped Billiam.

"And here I am, with my best mace all devoured by an eldritch horror," drawled Lord Slave. "Let me take care of this."

He stepped out in front of the ʃuper-heroes, not looking particularly ʃuper in their ruined costumes and whatever lost-and-found rags were available in the Malevolith's waiting room. With barely any effort at all, the Grand Vizier of the Urzoman Empire vaulted up atop the Wonky Wagon, and pointed at the biggest, most finely suited gangster.

"One chance, boss man. Tell your little chickens to go home to roost, or we'll be needing an awful lot of noodle soup."

The leading Hammerhead gave a theatrical laugh, of the kind you just have to put your hands on your hips to utter. Then he spoke, in fluent Chalinese.

"Fool! I am Ichiro Kanawazaki, and these are the most hardened band of killers ever to haunt the night in all the Arch'! Surrender to us the ones we must take vengeance upon[42], with haste! This is no quarrel

---

42. As we'll discover, Ichiro was not a natural-born son of the Eastern Arch', so it took some time for him to translate his inner thoughts into Chalinese, and High Imperial Chalinese at that. Seeing as this tongue has different verbs and nouns for three recognised genders and neutral, and modifies them by what time of the day it is, this

for government stooges!"

Lord Slave tilted his head to one side, fixing the Hammerhead boss with his one good eye. The man was clad in a double-breasted sharkskin tuxedo, no doubt plated within with mail or ensorcelled hardsilk. He carried an immense *no-touchi* blade, dancing with runic fire, and his upswept fin of hair was shot through with blue and green streaks of dye.

"Bollocks," spat Slave. "You're just Alfred Greams, from Hardbarrow, with a fake name and cheap suit on. I remember when you used to get in trouble for stealing dead rats from His Majesty's gutters. So, you've all grown up and gone *jaccuzza*, have you? Here's some advice from your friendly local government, then."

Lord Slave intoned the next words in utterly perfect Chalinese, just to be extra insulting. "Bugger off, dishonourable son of a leper's dog, and we'll forget this happened."

"Imbecile!" crowed Ichiro (possibly Alfred), switching back to Common Urzo. "There's one of you, and three hundred of us! We're not here for you. We're here for the three of *them* that murdered Percival... I mean Zeroshi the... the ummm..." he turned and whispered to a nearby gangster, all in purple. "Yes, yes. I *know*, we've got a complex and folklorique lexicon. What was his organised-crime type nickname again? *Really?*"

"We're waiting," said Lord Slave, deadpan.

"The ones what murdered Per... I mean *Zeroshi the Very Aggravated Hamster*. Yes, I'm *aware* all the good animals were taken! I don't think they need to know that!"

Lord Slave nodded, as one professional to another in difficult circumstances.

"Alright. I understand. Reprisals, honour, and all that. But you've got it wrong. There's not one of me and three hundred of you. There's only one of each of us. Only one, and hanging onto life by the most fragile thread, aren't we all? Let me tell you this, Bad Jeff Greams' boy. As soon as this kicks off, there'll be one of me... and one less of you, *personally*. Still keen to have a mix-up?"

"Errrr..." said Jack Somewhat, tapping politely on Lord Slave's boot. "You might want to..."

Jory Foxmallet cut him off, with a shout of such uncharacteristic anger that it even woke Montmortimer up properly.

---

was quite a sentence to get cracking before breakfast.

"There he is! There's the bastard who stole my antique trouser collection!"

Indeed it was. Golto the Demolisher blocked the road they'd come in by, pretty much all by himself. But he wasn't alone. The newly ennobled bare-knuckle brawler was in the company of his peers, and the hordes of *jacuzza* crossbowmen recoiled from them like ducklings from an unexpected crocodile. Toothless Frank Hamsmiter. Mandak 'the menacing nickname' McGurk. Morthrag the Merciless, out of retirement and as half-ogre as it was possible to be. There were more, too; Three-fingers Tony, Louie the Gouger, Van Peltd the Pirate King, Applesauce McGuinness, Hank the Badger, Nasty Theodora Grimm, 'Thumbs' Carbuncle, Henrietta the Hammer-wielding Harridan, Nate 'shut the gate' Norrison and the Bludgeon Brothers, Thorsen Torsen the Toilet-breaker, Sister Cragg the Malignant Nun, Sang Gang K'pow, Murphy the Slug, The Teak Sheikh, Man-Moose-Minotaur with his huge fake antlers, Buzzsaw Ricketts, Jean-Baptiste the Clourvonnaise Crippler, The Gazpacho Man Roddy O'Damage, Mad Mad Molly, Huge Hugh McGrew, and of course, the thoroughly evil midget known only as 'Ballbiter'.

Now here came their leader, insinuating himself between the looming walls of anger and muscle with a salacious saunter.

It was Zoltan Creagle, master of the Pits, his traditional toga and crown of golden leaves looking as out of place here as a wedding cake in a mortuary. His huge hands clenched and unclenched, golden rings flashing, as he favoured all present with a ghastly grin.

"Now, now, lads. No need for unpleasantness. Well, at least, unpleasantness over and above the absolutely necessary. We're just here to see to the contractual obligations of a young lad who's lost his way, that's all."

Jack Somewhat clapped his hands over his ears, and not so he couldn't hear what was being said. He suddenly felt a pressing need to ensure they were still attached.

Lord Slave, who looked right at home in the company of gladiators, gave Mister Creagle a nod.

"Are you absolutely sure about this, Zolt? Bit of a big throw of the dice, even for you, isn't it?"

"I just want the law followed, old chap. You can keep the rest of your little freak circus, or whatever you were about to do with them. But I've got the signature of that one on parchment, plain and simple."

"Excuse me?" put in Ichiro the Hammerhead. "We were doing a

thing, here. Very tense and dramatic stand-off, it was. I'll ask you gentlemen to..."

"Oh, *shut up* Alfred," said Zoltan Creagle, waving a dismissive hand. "Jog on, son, unless you want to find out what life's like in two dimensions, right?"

He gestured to his merry band of maulers. Muscles flexed, with a sound like bacon under volcanic pressures. Grimaces were gurned.

Lord Slave stopped it all with the slash of one hand.

"The *law*, Zoltan? At the risk of sounding presumptuous, I embody the law. And I say that these people here are too dangerous to stay in Grand Sepulchre. They're a destabilising force. Have you any idea what the wizards would say, if they knew..."

Creagle cocked his head to one side.

"They *might* say that sentencing the ringleader to a life of gladiatorial slavery sets a good example for others to toe the line, m'lord. They might also say that being cut in for 10 percent off the top was very nice for the civic coffers, as it were. Or perhaps just for the coffers of one *particular* handsome and diligent servant of the Throne?"

The Vizier's eye bulged.

"Are you trying to *bribe* me, Creagle?"

The bald-headed brawler looked hurt.

"No. Oh no no *no*. Think of it was an emolument of gratitude from a small businessman to a facilitating civic power. A gratuity for services rendered. A... yes, sod it, alright, twelve percent, and that's me last offer! Look at him! He coulda been a contender!"

Lord Slave glanced at Jack Somewhat, who was actually staring out to sea, a look of stomach-churning worry on his face. Rhaegulus Cratt was coming, his black galley towing in the *Rum Soaked Mary* oar stroke by oar stroke. The squat little customs master was standing in the bows, his plumed skull helmet under one arm. He waved jauntily.

"Hey!" said Ichiro, looking very miffed. "Homicidal crime boss with a small army of thugs, here! I reckon you lot are being jolly rude, barging in on another bloke's ambush like this! I've got a right mind..."

"No, you don't" chuckled Creagle.

"Oi! That's it! I'm warning you!"

"What? You're going to introduce me to your tailor?"

"Oh, *very* nice, coming from a troll in a bedsheet! I ought to..."

"Right!" said Lord Slave. "Here's how it's going to go. You lot..." he gestured to the assembled Hammerheads. "Bugger off right now, and we'll forget this happened. You..." here his finger stabbed out at Zoltan

Creagle. "Get back to your fighting pits, and thank all things vile and wicked that He isn't in the mood to come down here and freeze the marrow in your bones for such insolence. Did you see what just happened, last night? *Any* of you?"

Creagle licked his lips and dared a little predatory smile.

"Oh aye. We saw. We saw a huge bloody monster almost take over the city. We saw you agree to abdicate, and we saw you get your bacon saved by those costumed freaks you've got huddling behind you. You know what I reckon? I reckon Himself ain't what He used to be. I reckon you're a bit of a puppet without a hand up its arse, m'lord, and the wizards are too far up their own to tell farts from sunshine. I reckon that one little contract is small potatoes, and you won't risk every merchant in this steaming pile of an empire losing their faith in good governance, just to protect one big fat oaf who you only met yesterday, *especially* seeing as you want rid of him in any case."

At this point, a very small and grubby lad came puffing and wheezing into the square, interposing himself between all parties. He held up a hand as he caught his breath, then produced a small and dented bugle, which he proceeded to blow asthmatically.

"Hold on. Sorry. Hang about. Blimey, guvnors, just give us a minute here..."

He unrolled a large and dirt-stained scroll which had been strapped across his back, and began to read.

"Dear various freaks, assembled bad people and others. Sorry for the delay. If you would please hold, an army of thieves and beggars will be with you at their earliest convenience, purposes for, revenge and such, bloody, to wit, against those costumed prats what killed the old Snagpurse. Signed, the new Snagpurse, King of Thieves, etc. PS, don't kick it off without us if you wants to keep all yer goolies."

The urchin rolled up the scroll again, beamed, and held out one half-finger-gloved hand for a tip. There were no takers.

"Oh, bugger this!" said Lord Slave. "Listen, the lot of you - these people are going on that boat, and that's final!"

Soto Scalizari took this opportunity to pipe up.

"Ummm. Actually, m'lord, we've been talking, while you were yelling at all these folks, and we've kind of decided we... ummm. Don't want to go."

The black-masked Vizier was having a very bad morning. He hissed with exasperation, his one eye bulging.

"You *don't want to go?* We had a deal, you horrible little man! I think everyone here's forgetting which one of us *has an army behind him!*"

"I do!" hollered Ichiro.

"Me too! Well, a small, very nasty one!" shouted Zoltan.

"I mean a *proper* one!" barked Slave, literally jumping up and down with anger.

"And *you* might have forgot who has nigh-on-godlike superhuman powers," grated Slag Iron. "We reckon we ought to take our chances against the Hammerheads. There's a lot of cosy places under your city where a person could hide, m'lord. And I hear that if you defeat a *jacuzza*, you get to take his place."

Alfred Greams (presently Ichiro) tugged at his collar with one finger.

"That's more of a *guideline*, miss, and..."

"SHUT UP!" bellowed the Grand Vizier, veins standing out on his neck like frightened snakes on a ham. He turned to Jack Somewhat. His shoulders slumped.

"Look, it's for the best, lad. The wizards would want to hunt you down. All *I* want is for you to get on that boat, be safe, bugger off... and then I can have a little talk with Rhaegulus Cratt and get on with other business. Alright?"

Jack gave him a look of such complete regret, then, that Lord Slave almost felt sorry for him.

"I'd really, *really* rather that that never happened..." he said, sighing.

And then, before he could explain, the Statue of Tyranny exploded.

From The Piazza Della Von Tuesday, the breakwater curved away to the east, and then back around so that the Harbour Watch and its huge metal statue were just offshore.

From where Jack stood, it looked as through the entire great edifice was torn in half at the waist, an explosion twisting open its upper torso like a banana skin. A chain of detonations travelled up its arm, and, knowing what he knew about the contents of the lantern in Lady Tyranny's fist, he hit the deck well before the others.

The world went white. The shockwave raised a great slopping wall of salt water which rushed over the Piazza, carrying away the portrait wizard and his gear as it swirled around the wheels of the Wonky Wagon. Jack felt the cold shock of the water as it rushed over him, carrying a debris of dead rats, garbage, and what he sincerely hoped were not assorted turds[43].

He rolled over and groaned, just as a huge piece of jagged metal

---

43. They were.

came spinning down out of the sky to bury itself two handspans deep in the wood, right where his head had been. Other flaming, glowing chunks rained down on the Hammerheads, Zoltan's nasty mob, and the assorted rickety dockside buildings around the square. Seeing as these shanties were mostly made of scrap timber, salt-crusted pieces of boats and dried-out rope, fires sprang up merrily all around.

Lord Slave had fielded a piece of metal finger with both hands, and was staring at it numbly as Jack staggered to his feet. A couple of angry crabs chittered and snapped as they evacuated the young man's haircut.

"Right!" slurred the Grand Vizier, dropping the great copper-nailed fingertip. "Which one of you did that? I can accept a bit of high-spirited ambushing of a morning, but that's bloody *vandalism!*"

The ſuper-heroes, who were by now all wide awake, having just been dunked waist-deep in what propriety insists we call 'seawater', all looked aghast. Ichiro the *jacuzza* sheathed his sword and glanced nervously at the spreading fire. Smuggling was, after all, his trade, and dreamsugar is known to be very, very combustible.

"Not us, guv! Not us! We just wanted to do a bit of murder, not arson and such! In fact, bugger this for a lark! We're offski!"

Zoltan Creagle squinted.

"None of mine, either. We're not really big on explosions, me and the lads. More of the punching things 'til they go all mushy, that's our M. O. Still... what about *that* guy?"

He pointed, through the dispersing cloud of smoke which obscured the wreckage of the statue. There, in the centre of swirling billows, a dark shape could be seen.

A shape hanging in the air.

A shape, Jack Somewhat noted with trepidation, *wearing a cape.*

Oh dear.

The shape raised a hand, in a languid and operatic gesture.

Showboating. Never a good sign...

Jack's first instinct was to throw himself as far away from where he was standing as possible.

It was a powerful example of why you should definitely listen to your first instincts. Because, just as the smoke began to clear, the caped figure cast a skein of shadows down into the ocean, sweeping his hand up and across his chest. The darkness whipcracked after it, in a line which tore the Piazza Della Von Tuesday in half.

Assorted ſuper-heroes scattered; Monty picked up Tarrence Bligh and Billiam and blurred out of the way, while Jack made a wobbly little flight, and Amber executed an almost perfect dive-roll. Slag Iron tackled Soto Scalizari aside as the timbers erupted behind them in a curling, splintering wave.

The Wonky Wagon was left teetering on the edge of a flotsam-choked lead of water. Nails and planks clattered down as the figure spoke.

"That's right! Flee, insects! Flee the wrath of your new nepotist! Yes, right, I mean *nemesis!* One of those!"

Needless to say, it wasn't a cheery voice.

"You don't even know what that means!" shouted back Lord Slave, stalling for time.

"Yes, I do! It's... ummm... a very special time in a young man's life, when he starts to notice..."

"Moron!"

"Weakling!"

"Poser!"

"Nincompoop!"

Now that this mysterious new attacker was busy slinging insults, Jack's had time to apply what old Multhazar Threck would have called the Alchemical Method - *Observe, Extrapolate, Avoid Exploding.* Jack took a closer look, being careful not to squint too hard, lest beams of force burst from his eyeballs.

The figure's face was nothing but a thoroughly insane and toothy grin, slashed below two emerald eyes. This matched a great green letter G, daubed across an impossibly muscular chest. A tendril of darkness burst from the creature's shoulder, binding up the great bronze shape of a bell; all that remained of the Statue of Tyranny. Other than this, he was all just arms, legs, ragged cape... and a hint of the smell of burning ink, far away.

"He's stolen the Kraken Bell!" exclaimed the Grimshadow, who had managed to avoid the carnage by simply hiding under the Wonky Wagon. The hunch-backed driver hadn't been so lucky; his party hat (and a large part of his head) had been obliterated by a shard of Lady Tyranny's exploded bosom. "The bastard! How will people know that it's time to go to work?"

Jack came down to a wobbly landing, still staring up at the black-caped newcomer.

"You've never had an honest job in your life, Foxmallet," he said. "But you're right. That bell is part of our.... whatdoyoucallit. Civic heritage.

Very important. We can't have horrible flying bastards nicking things like that, can we?"

Lord Slave seemed inclined to concur. He clambered back on top of the Wagon, ripping the tatters of his own cape from his shoulders, and though his face was still wrapped in studded leather, all those assembled could tell that what was going on behind it was not a cherubic grin.

"Right!" said the Grand Vizier of the Urzoman Empire, levelling a single huge finger with malice aforethought. "You picked the wrong breakfast time to be playing silly buggers, old matey my chum! Because on the first account, these pillocks you see all around you have been testing my patience to the utmost of its limits already, and secondly – I haven't even *had* breakfast yet. Not so much as the whiff of beans, eggs and a fried slice, and now here's some cosmically-powered wonder-turd come to steal the Kraken Bell, for a plot that I'm certain we're all going to hear *all* bloody about. Am I right? Mister... whatever your name is?"

The figure in black drifted closer, toes pointed down, arms open in the pose of a martyred saint. The scrawl of darkness which carried the Kraken Bell pulsed and shuddered as he descended, and Jack noticed that his cape was made of the same seething black matter, like boiling ink. Little spatters frayed away around its edges, then faded.

"You may call me *Gloom*, your eminence," said the figure, in a voice which was at once a whisper and a rumble. There were undertones of iron on gristle there, and something else. Some weird resonance which Jack swore he could recognise...

"And *yes*, I'm taking your precious Kraken Bell. Soon I'll be taking them all. Not because I'm a collector of antiquities, mind you. But because of what they do." The one who called himself Gloom tiled his head to one side, focusing an empty emerald stare on Jack Somewhat.

"As a little bonus, I'm going to help fix your hero problem, too. One way or another. Yes, all these little pieces that don't fit, from a game with a missing board and the wrong kind of dice. I will give them the gift of oblivion, to ease their confusion. That... or the *correct motivation.*"

In that instant, Jack knew why Gloom's voice sounded familiar. But before he could do anything at all about it, it was far too late.

"Alright Mister Gloom, or whatever your parents really called you," shouted Lord Slave. "I'm placing you under arrest for theft of public property, grand vandalism statue, causing an affray, uttering a villainous monologue without the correct permit in triplicate, and apprehending an officer of the Urzoman Empire in contravention of his rightful breakfast!" He reached up behind both shoulders and drew forth a pair of short swords, each as black as sin and as workmanlike as a two-dollar hammer. "Seeing as you're guilty as all hells, we'll cut directly to the execution!"

The grin on Gloom's face split even wider. The flesh around it – or what should have been meat and muscle – was, Jack saw, simply a scrawl of black on black, as if someone had tried desperately to erase the face beneath with a charcoal pencil. Cross-hatched lines blurred and flickered.

Then Jack felt a pulse of magic go jangling through the world. Riding it, Lord Slave launched himself from the roof of the wonky Wagon, hard enough to bend all its bars flat, and blow its wheels off sideways. Jory Foxmallet staggered away, arms windmilling. Heroes, *jacuzza*, gladiators and assorted curious Urzoman citizens (who always liked a bit of early morning street theatre) held their breath as two hundred kilos of feudal authority arrowed up toward Gloom, swords swinging. There was only one possible outcome.

Or there was... until the world staggered sideways, right off the axis of belief.

"Tiresome," yawned the figure in black, extending one hand in a dismissive gesture. His fingers twitched, tugging at reality, and then...

Four serrated ropes burst from their tips, looping through the air. Each one was armed with an arrowhead of shadow, inset with a mad and staring eye. Tiny spots and blots of darkness followed in their path, blurring away to nothing.

Then they struck, and Lord Slave was held impaled in four places, pierced through the thigh, hip, chest and shoulder. The saw-edged tendrils plunged on, harrowing through him. They looped back around again to pierce his hands, making him drop his swords. The final two shuddered, liquid-sharp, in front of his eyes. "Unnnnggh!" grunted Slave, trying to close his hands around shadows. Each one bristled with pencil-scrawl obliterations.

"Such eloquence!" gloated Gloom. **"But of course, what is one to expect from a sycophant? A lapdog to power, attenuated for centuries... but lacking the wisdom of a child? You should have known that *magic* would have no effect on me!"**

Jack caught the tone, there. As a much-reviled urchin, layabout and son of the Grailish Isles, he knew disgust when he heard it. Gloom spat out the word 'magic' like a maggot winkled from between his teeth.

But Lord Slave had the market on scorn cornered. He arched his back, turning his head to look Gloom in the eyes. Green fire reflected from his polished leather mask.

"Don't need *magic*, peasant. Just steel. You'll bleed, like the rest of them..."

"But you *are* magic, Ikarus Meliadion Stormhammer. That was your name once, wasn't it? You wanted to be a *hero*. You joined a pathetic band of adventurers, and you had no idea that your stupid little life was the dance of a marionette, bound by strings of sorcery. How ironic that you became Lord Slave, and that your old friend became your master."

For an instant, it looked as if Lord Slave would actually break free of the coils that pierced him. Such was the anguish of his scream that even Zoltan Creagle's lads, no strangers to horrible violence, winced in sympathy.

Inside that half-faced mask, a baleful rune pulsed red. *Magic, indeed, was what had stitched him together, after dragonflame had taken him apart. Magic had turned his body from a charred husk into a well-oiled machine.* Magic had remade the fragments of his mind; those shards which had floated to the top of a crucible of agony.

Now Gloom was devouring that magic. And the sorceries that He, Himself, most potent of mages, had wrought...

Turned out to have their own failsafe.

Lord Slave remembered the fire. Deep in the bones which had been charred black by it, he remembered.

A great scaly muzzle, studded with butchering ivory. Horns and vibrissae smoking. Eyes of cold and frozen white, suddenly reflecting flame...

Now, an echo of that annihilating force surged through him, haloing his body in red, like the corona of the sun in eclipse. He twisted, grabbing Gloom's tendrils of darkness, pulling him close.

"Take... you *with me*..." he managed, as his mind unravelled, and the remnants of Ikarus Stormhammer, questing warrior, burst through. He saw a hand reaching out, down into a sea of agony. He felt himself raised up, even as something in his chest detonated...

He saw the dragon again, and he died.

To Jack, the explosion was like a second sun. An invisible fist slammed into the dockside, pushing a circular depression of Grand Sepulchre underwater. Large parts of it flexed back, as timbers bent and snapped, whole buildings torn and cracked asunder.

But just as quickly as that sun bloomed into existence, it was snuffed out. Petals of geometric night unfurled from Gloom's body, enveloping Lord Slave in a faceted gem of darkness. Whatever hellish energies were released within, they registered as barely a flex and ripple on the outside. When Gloom peeled the sections away, absorbing them back into his form, nothing remained but a drift of ashes, spiralling down onto ruin.

That, and a smoking pink plush rabbit in a black mask, which fell right at Jack Somewhat's feet.

"The age of magic is gone," intoned Gloom – and this time Jack could clearly hear Rodney behind him. **"So too is the age of false heroes, who skulk around in the thrall of its childishness. Illogic and whimsy are not part of my tale. *You can be*, however. I can be your villain. We can write a new story, on the bones of the old. Join me!"**

Ichiro was the first to break out of the terrible, breathless silence that gripped the Piazza Della Von Tuesday – or what remained of it.

"Bugger that for a game of soldiers!" he shouted, dropping all pretence of a foreign accent. "Come on lads, let's scarper!"

Jack's friends had different ideas.

"Not bloody likely, you rotter!" snarled Montmortimer Pettigrew, shaking one lace-ruffed fist. "We'll stop you yet!"

"That's right!" chimed in Slag iron, locking her helmet in place. "****** licking ******s like you give evil a bad name. We'll pulverise you!"

Billiam Knox split in two. Soto Scalizari flickered into flame. The Grimshadow brandished his extendable batons. Amber's great long claws burst from her wrists as she leapt up to the boom of a dockside crane. And Tarrence Bligh produced a bottle from about his person, knocking it back in one gulp. Jack shot him a certain look.

"More of yer mate's old wake-up juice," shrugged the little Grailish sailor. "So now I'm feeling mighty... urrrrgh... clean and... rrrargh... SOBER!"

That last word became a howl of anguish as he turned big, blue and gruesome, his clothes once again shredded away to the obligatory pair of strategic shorts.

"What's it to be then, Jack Somewhat?" purred Gloom. **"I can still**

feel it now, you know. You were the first. You are still the mightiest among these... *mistakes*. Will you join me, and make this world anew?"**

Jack hadn't really thought of Lord Slave as a friend. An ally of inconvenience, perhaps. A terrifying maniac, certainly. And the embodiment of a law which wanted him to earn an honest living, to boot. But nobody deserved to die like that, just puffed away to dust without so much as a final soliloquy.

Jack looked down at the charred stuffed rabbit in his hand.

"Alright. Here's my counter-offer," he said, just this side of a whisper. His fist clenched. Something inside Mister Bun Bun squeaked. And with it came a crackle of green lightning, tingling over his skin. With it came *power*. "I'll crush you with my bare hands, you treacherous bastard!"

He didn't know if he was talking to Gloom, or the entity which was lodged inside the ſuper-villain, pulling the strings. At that point, he scarcely cared.

"Excellent! Capital! That's the spirit!" cackled the black-caped figure in the sky. **"Ohhhh, this is going to be *legendary*! Now, come and give me your best shot! And remember – it's all about the bells. If I take all eight, that lovely big Malevolith of yours will destabilise. Messy! Have you ever seen what happens when reality catches up to a five-hundred-year-old lich? Terms like 'blast radius' certainly apply!"**

Perhaps it was the power of the story, binding them all up like thorny weeds, thought Jack later. Perhaps it was the wyrd harmonic which sawed away behind reality, as Gloom's laughter scrabbled up the spectrum from unhinged to utterly insane.

Every hero needs a villain, or so it's said.

And it seemed that a proper villain brought out the hero, even in folks who had hitherto changed their minds...

Eight figures leapt up to meet Gloom, trailing war-cries and, in some cases, a blur of green lightning and flames. Billiam Knox, doubled, one of him swinging the other into a roundhouse kick. Soto Scalizari, haloed in fire, screaming as much in disbelief as in defiance. Slag Iron roared obscenities which steamed in the air behind her. The Unstoppable It came in with fists the size of anvils clenched.

Even the Grimshadow, powerless, grappled onto a broken and leaning mast and spiralled up into the air, no doubt imagining some dark and brooding musical accompaniment. Montmortimer had time to blur into a nearby building, procure pair of swords, adjust his wig and apply a judicious black velvet beauty spot before he joined the attack.

Amber fell in from her perch with Skrx on one shoulder and all six claws extended; Jack was surprised to see that the little crustacean was no longer conjoined to the miniature crossbow on her wrist, but seemed to be wielding the thing like a tiny guardsman, clutching a modified stock with several of his legs.

Jack caught a look at Amber's face as she fell, and there was simple, honest joy there. He knew exactly what that was like. Sometimes, when the tension built up enough, and the sinews of the heart were ratcheted to their utmost limits, the sheer relief of punching someone in the face was almost transcendent.

He and Gloom were like those little rocks, the ones that loved iron... magnets, *that was what the wizards called them. Most of the time they pushed each other away, but in the right configuration they snapped together, and couldn't be pried apart.*

There was a toy rabbit in his hand, he was screaming, and for some reason, he could fly. Jack let go and just went with the moment.

Eight heroes came raging in at Gloom, time bending into a syrupy haze as they went.

Then he brought his hands out to his sides, fingers spread, and green runes shimmered. Eight rectangles of darkness snapped into being, tethered to him by threads. **"Not right now, heroes. There's a time and a place for this, and it's not today. When you're ready, you'll find me!"**

Jack saw the darkness yawn open, suddenly flexing through dimensions and gaining a hideous depth. But there was no way he could stop himself. He struck the surface of Gloom's gateway with a sickening shiver-shock, bursting through webs of shadow. Then he was through, still travelling at a significant fraction of the speed of sound - and a moss-stained stone wall was rushing up to meet him.

Jack didn't even have time to put his hands up in front of him.

For the non-ʃuper-powered, the sensation of smashing through rocks with one's face is very similar to the feeling of stubbing your toe in the dark. *You feel the impact, the shock radiating through all those complex little bones, and you wait for the pain that's sure to follow...*

Oooosh! Yes, there it was.

Jack's legs, protruding from a smoking hole, pedalled the air weakly for a second, and then he slumped, slithering out onto his chest. A little drift of loam dribbled from out of his mouth as the world wobbled.

It was the same for all the rest of them. Eight apertures of darkness snapped open, swallowing up Grand Sepulchre's ill-fated 'monster hunters', one and all. A flicker-snap of power, spattering the air with ink, and they were gone. The collection of teeth under Gloom's cowl arranged themselves into a self-satisfied smirk.

"No, we don't get to dance. Not yet. Not until things get a *lot* more interesting..."

Eight gateways into who-knows-where slammed shut, with the sound of scissor-blades snicking closed. Then Gloom pointed one long, clawed finger down at Zoltan Creagle and his little crew.

"And here's 'interesting', right now. A band of freaks, eh? Misfits, rejected by a cruel society who scorned them?"

"Oi!" said Zoltan. "That's not very nice. These freaks are *professionals!* And as for scorn... they get all the dropped popcorn and leftover grog they can swill! Can't say fairer than that, in the gladiatin' business!"

Gloom drifted down until his black boots touched the ground. There was a certain twinkle in his eye as he spoke, and it wasn't just the dancing spark of madness.

"Do you really want to waste your talents taking dives and entertaining buck-toothed morons, for this guy? He's getting rich while you get old, and sore, and beat-up. By *each other!*"

"Hey!" put in Mandak McGurk, who was as touchingly loyal as he was hideously ugly. "Mister Creagle's done right by us, so he has. We're *famous!* We get 'ot meals, wif meat innem you can spell the names of!"

Gloom nodded.

"So, you all live together in his nice big mansion, do you? Or, at a guess, do you usually doss down in the old monster pits where I've just sent those imbecilic do-gooders, and thank lady luck you're out of the rain on a bad night?"

"Quite liked my monster pit..." mumbled Morthrag, scuffing one sandal in the dust. "Had a couple of potted begonias, 'an all..."

Zoltan Creagle was having none of this.

"Right! That's enough of you with your bloody labour disputes and workers' rights, mate! Evil villain, okay, well, that's all good, if you catch my drift, world needs 'em I suppose, with all the heroes knocking about, but that socialist mumbo-jumbo has no place in a modern economy! You just about..."

Gloom walked right past him, extending one hand to lift Zoltan Creagle out of the way, simply with the pressure of his fingertips on the man's bald head. The other hand opened up like some oily tropical flower, and little beads of green fire danced on its palm, radioactive fleas on a boron hotplate.

"Mr McGurk says you're *famous*. Very well. I offer you more than fame. I offer you *infamy*. You'll go from being forgotten when the posters about your fights wash away in the rain, to names etched on the stones of history."

Little green sparks leapt and blurred. They struck home, burrowing into foreheads and chests with a hiss like fingertips on a griddle.

"I'll give you names that last forever," Gloom continued. **"Names that lords and ladies have to bow to. Names that command gold, and pride, and *respect*."**

This last word had their attention, even more than the gold. Being a gladiator was good pay, in a way, but you couldn't spend it until you retired. And it wasn't as if the upper crust had much time for the scarred old veterans of the pits. If there was a lower crust – hard, gnarly, and prone to break your teeth – they were it. Zoltan made one last lunge at keeping the situation under control, and scrabbled with his metaphorical fingertips.

"Come on lads! We're in this together! You're my boys, you are!"

Gloom snapped his fingers, and Zoltan felt a cold wind blow up his toga. He looked down, and saw that a black pit had razored open beneath him, its dark surface suddenly gaining the kind of depth which puts mountain climbers off their lunch.

"Yes." said Gloom. **"But I offer them the chance to be *men*. *Hench*men[44]. There's new costumes all round, too."**

Zoltan knew he'd lost them as he fell into that cold and sticky darkness.

But at least he was fairly certain where he was going to land...

---

44. And, admittedly, hench*women*; in the case of Mad Mad Molly, Theodora, Henrietta et al. There was no gender divide in Urzoman gladiatorial combat, and the attitude of the ladies who chose to become professionals was that if there was a glass ceiling somewhere, it was only useful for uppercutting some dumb male clean through it.

18
The Identificational Braggadocio

It was hard getting out of bed in the morning at the age of five hundred, give or take a century. Chamomile tea didn't cover the half of it.

That paled in comparison, however, to getting off to sleep in the first place.

Old people often tell you that they want to die peacefully in their sleep, but considering the general temperament of the human species, it's noteworthy that the Grim Reaper usually catches them awake, and that he has to wear a cast-iron codpiece. This is more to save a chipped pelvis than anything more soft and painful, mind, but a walking stick swung with gusto can definitely catch you a right crack, even if you *are* made of personified mortality.

He Himself, dark lord of the Urzoman Empire, barely slept at all these days, and when he did it was on a giant block of ice, sawn from the depths of the Malevolith.

The ice formed of its own accord in the dense thaumic field, condensing with the hideous suggestion of screaming faces in its whorls and bubbles. The ice helped to slow down His fevered thoughts. It also helped to reduce the stench, which He was most self-conscious about - it was one of the reasons He preferred to entertain only the recently deceased.[45]

Like many of the very old, He lived mainly inside His own head these days... or at least in the space where a head would have been, if it hadn't been for the dragon, all those decades past.

Things like the / *thing that had happened* / can change a man, they say. Losing an arm, and feeling the itch and ache of it when the winter turns bitter. Losing a friend, or a son, or a wife, and wanting to beat yourself bloody when you forget to grieve hard enough. When,

---

45. What's that whiff? Well, don't look now, matey, but *you're* the one with maggots crawling out of his eye socket...

eventually, time grinds away their face, their name, their memory...

All of these things weighed on the Lord of Grand Sepulchre, as he played his endless chess games against dead wizards. As he stood, sometimes for days at a time, unmoving, looking out across space at the curving horns of the Arch' as they twisted up into the stars, hazed by a torus of sky. Nothing, however, weighed on him like the truth.

And the truth was, *there was only one of them left who knew it.*

Shye Simarl, the thief, had stolen a whole kingdom, and worn the jade mask of Empress, and lost herself in pleasure and the pipe. When she'd seen who was behind the dragon, and the game, she'd gone quietly sane. It was the kind of sanity which knows that it must, at all costs, blot out the madness which follows from worrying at the truth.

Noctaris, the Paladin of Phorax, had done the opposite. He'd turned to the madness of faith, and blamed a god who didn't really exist for not defeating a goddess who most unfortunately did. A goddess whose origin was too terrible to question, for the joke it made of every life and every death ever counted on the great grim abacus of the Arch'.

The last Himself had heard, Noctaris the Redeemer had been a babbling old hermit, encased in the husk of his Church Militant like a pearl in an oyster, fed thin broth and thick platitudes by monks who pitied him his visions. He'd died perhaps two hundred years past.

Jaan Thanriel Starleaf had gone to wherever it was that the Elves had gone, and good riddance. Smug bastards. He hoped he'd taken his bloody lute with him.

But now the fourth of the Party was undone. The one He had tried to save. The one He'd rebuilt, from what scraps were left after the fire did its work.

There was a time when He would have admitted that the sheer force of will it took to turn himself into (*what he was now*), came not from spite, but from love. He'd loved Ikarus Stormhammer, when that 'he' didn't have a capital H. He'd done what he did to save him, and become something so unworthy of love, or even human company, that what he rebuilt he made into a relic, a tool, a shade.

A slave.

To be utterly, brutally reasonable, Ikarus had died four centuries and more ago, in flames, for the crime of finding out who was behind the monsters, and why they just kept coming. The fact that the Mage and the Warrior were not meant to love each other at all was part of what made the truth unravel, all sudden and bloody, like the spill of viscera when the knife goes in just right.

He Himself had killed Ikarus by proxy, to save him from having to try to love the thing He'd become.

This didn't make him any less furious, here and now. When some upstart destroys your faithful servant, it's alright to cut loose with a little wrath. But when they take away your only chance to justify your regrets... Well.

Halfway around the Arch', the Sages of Khantif recorded the wobble of the whole world's axis. Somewhere, which may have been inside the Red Sun, but which was also an impossible sphere of bookcases and windows, a pair of green eyes narrowed. A clock with only five numbers ticked, once, with a sound like an axe through vertebrae, and its single hand jerked forward...

Lord Slave was dead.

He woke with the shock of it; phantasmal eyes snapping into existence behind his helm. Someone was roaring, a slurred, broken sound, as He wrenched Himself loose from the frost that bound him to his bed of ice, and He was horrified to find it was Him.

He didn't wait to reach one of the tall, arched windows of the Malevolith. Power screwed inward, reality creaking under the strain like a rotten tooth in the grip of a torturer's pliers. With a gesture He tore open the wall of His aerie, curling the stone back in a great parchment strip, sending bricks flying out over the harbour.

Dawn painted the horizon, glowing through the great wobbly swathe of Mother Ocean. Its light revealed a city veiled by scuds of fleeing cloud.

Where His statue of Tyranny burned. Where a figure in black, caped, (caped! like some cavalry-officer dandy!) rose lightly into the air amid the ruins of His docksides, His precious ships of commerce and war.

Levels were important to the one who He thought of as the Green Eyed Lady. Levels, and rules, and above all, *dice.* Random chaos was a lover she tugged after her on a leash. The whole purpose of the Urzoman Empire, and its facade of skull-faced Evil, was to keep Himself at what he knew was a very borderline level ninety-nine, by Her madly obsessive reckoning.

That meant no heroics. Strictly speaking, it meant no trying to avenge Lord Slave, either. Considering that, in the bubbling mulch which was once His heart, some scraps of feeling still smouldered for poor old Ikarus Stormhammer, avenging him could be seen as *virtuous.*

Still, He thought. *Call it petulance. That was, at least, still counted as a vice. He'd murder the caped bastard cold.* With that thought came a blast of power so vicious that it turned the entire world black and white. A solid rod of darkness spat from his cupped hands, painting every shadow inverse, and snuffing out every light across the wide swathe of Jansamrana he could see. The thaumic shields around the Unspeakable College rippled like aurorae, and the outermost turned to, respectively, an explosion of moths, a rain of tapioca, and a hypersonic scream.

Forget the dragon, thought Himself, with a mouthless snarl. *This forbidden spell would have turned the red wyrm into the world's biggest roast chicken, complete with an additional monsoon of gravy.*

It struck.

He didn't have time to gloat, or crow his triumph, or even strike a menacing pose. Because the aftershocks, nested one after the other, pummelled the city in the next few moments, stripping roof tiles like fish-scales and whipping up a pall of dust. Somewhere amid the fury of it all, and behind the ringing of every bell in Grand Sepulchre, there came a series of flashes, like the movement of a sword too fast for the eye to see.

Got him, thought the Dark Emperor. *Some chancer, taking his shot after that Enkalderon nonsense? Another bloody empire-challenging hero, after all these years?* It scarcely mattered. One blast with the old Rubric of Unjustifiable Unction, and even the toughest foes would be punched clear through the first three afterlives and into one that didn't belong to their own religion.

Then a series of black portals razored open in the sky above the sugarloaf, that great eroded old volcanic core which backstopped the Princess of Cities. Flickers and spats of magical power came through, carving into the rock, setting up sprays of molten stone.

He stood there, hunch-backed, flaking rust, the wind stirring his ragged black cape. His phantom eyes blinked, dripping ectoplasm inside his helm. His hands were claws, smoking as the armour cooled from white-hot to red.

And He laughed, a sound which started out guttural and unfamiliar, but which built to a crescendo like a violin bow against glass, a shrieking, lost sound which had as much to do with humour as a bag of bonesaws.

Because there it was. Written in letters of stone twenty spans high.

Proof that all his careful plans had been for nothing.

NOT TODAY

Gloom had carved his message as a taunt and a promise.

It really was too bad, considering what was to come, that He Himself recognised it as something else entirely...

Meanwhile, the shadows stirred around an achingly expensive table, carefully steeped in darkness. It stood in a room so secret that its very existence would have been denied by the builders who'd created it - if they'd been allowed to keep their tongues, of course.

This was the Situation Room, and it was only used when there was a Situation that deserved a capital S; one which threatened the mercantile interests of the guilds. This was the table where such Situations were resolved; with the writ and the tort, the bludgeon, the hostile takeover and the shark-bait mincer, as befitted.

The guilds of Grand Sepulchre had been around long before Himself, and long before the evil empire. They wallowed under the oily veneer of polite society like great antediluvian crocodiles, and greasing the wheels of commerce was their business. Good grease, as any butcher will tell you, is best rendered down from creatures which have outlived their usefulness.

From the point of view of those assembled, this meant 'everyone else'. Groups like this tend to bubble to the top of most social cesspits, and they're readily identified by their big, obscure titles, bottomless expense accounts, and sensibilities which make the heat-death of the universe look merciful and cuddly.

God's Anvil, the Sarunjek nationalist faction, had a seat at the table, though most of the guildlords found their bigotry unbearable. Their representative, Garsoom Palaquat (great-uncle of the snivelling Chep) regarded his fellows from beneath a pair of eyebrows and an ornate silken turban which were both outlandish and expensively styled. They were, in no particular order:

- Issimmus Kroome, Grand High Thaumatarch and Archmage of the Clenched Fist.
- Lady Belladonna Immacolata Lachrymosa, assassinatrix exemplary.
- Dreevil Vulct, Snagpurse the Next, King of Thieves
- Doctor Vaspides, Master of the Physicians
- Smeeves, (real name unknown) First Gentleman of the Butlers and Footmen
- Dolores Blatterly, Grand Madame of the Wenches, Strumpets

> and Actual Prostitutes
- Slidney Chunt of the Merchants and Bankers Guild
- Elizabethany Rantoon, of the Numinous Guild of Holy Priesthoods and Bishoprics United

And, of course;

- Darby Hardwicke, Chief Engineer of the Artisans and Artificers

There were, of course, sundry other guilds in the Princess of Cities, many of whom were nearly as powerful, or almost as rich as the foremost. Bakers, miners, fisherfolk, dog-breeders, brewers, jugglers and mimes; all had their seat on the great committee of commerce. When the Alchemists finally sorted out their power struggles and chose a new leader, they would get a nice cushion to warm a seat at the big table, too. The annual parade of industry even featured the single member of Grand Sepulchre's Guild of Comedy Taxidermists, resplendent in her weasel-fur trousers, pink satin cape and bowler hat with a spike on top.

However;

The big table wasn't *this* table. The big table was for show, and this one was for *effectiveness*. For the necessary little brutalities which kept the money flowing. Common skulduggery had these referred to, in hushed tones, as Situations. The participants who wrangled them were known as the Golden Handshake – ten fingers working in unison.

This morning, the Situation was dire enough to rouse the Handshake from their beds in the mosquito-haunted blush of dawn. Servants fussed with coffee and herbal teas, tinctures of bat's blood and dreamsugar, and in the case of the Lady Lachrymosa, a platinum salver of chilled cucumber slices, deftly applied over her eyes by a svelte assassin wielding tongs.

"We understand that one of them's *yours*," harrumphed Chunt, the merchant, peering at the arch-assassinatrix over a pair of many-lensed brass spectacles. True to form, he was plump, sweaty and clad in a riot of expensive, pearl-brocaded silks, each more elaborately tasteless than the last. The effect was of a small fortune-teller's tent with gas.

Lady Lachrymosa waited, statue-still, while her chilled cucumber slices were removed and a puff of perfume was applied by a second black-clad young gentleman.

"Technically, your munificence, one of them's yours, too. The fishmonger woman. Though why she's in magical battle-nun's armour might be a better question for our friend Elizabethany, might it not?"

The High Priestess of the Phoraxian Conventicle looked, to all innocent eyes, like a small grandmother in a fluffy black cardigan, crocheted with numinous sigils. She was doing some knitting - perhaps a nice new sacrificial altar cosy. However, she spoke for all nine of the Urzoman Empire's official religions by being deadly with a hatpin, and reigned as unconquered warlord of every bingo hall, housie drive and bake sale under the Malevolith's shadow.

"Well sidestepped, dear, but that suit's a relic that even *we* didn't want. The days of the churches stomping around the Arch' setting fire to people is well gone to dust, and even if it wasn't, well... Deacon Whelmley assures me that there was never a battle nun like that. All that swearing and cursing is *most* unholy!"

The eyes of the assembled grandees swivelled back toward Lady Lachrymosa, as if this meeting was a tennis match played with live granadoes.

"The one you're talking about is Amberelia Chance," she allowed. "A guild novice. A *failure*, in fact. We had planned to deal with her as we deal with other... sub-standard assets, in any case."

"That might be a bit difficult, now," put in Smeeves, the butler. "And shouldn't we be discussing more weighty matters than employment obligations? The bigger question is, do we destroy these people, or, ummm... you know..."

Garsoom, the God's Anvil man, shifted his bulk and grunted. It was the only thing he'd vocalised all meeting, being as he was encased in a tent of gold lace, smoking a hookah the size of a pony. It could have meant anything.

"Bribe, coerce, extort or otherwise cajole them into a working relationship?" asked the new Snagpurse, all rubbed hands and leery grin. "They've done me a few favours, I'll tell you what. Dead man's boots never came so 'ot. But they seem to 'ave a bit of a bee in the old bonnet about *justice*."

"I say we kill them all," intoned the high Thaumatarch, who never simply interjected when an intonation would do. "What they do... it's not natural!"

"As opposed to harbouring and feeding a gigantic monstrous Mantigore?" asked Doctor Vaspides, arching one immaculate eyebrow. Nobody had managed to work out if the pale, stiletto-thin physician was a man or a woman, or indeed if they were a vampire or some strange, waxy automaton. It seemed safest to steer clear of the whole issue. "You wizards wouldn't know natural if it bit you on the gluteus maximus."

"And in any case," grinned Madame Dolores, a rosy-cheeked and plump Zalois matron, who was known to make free with a cigar cutter when her customers got rowdy. "They're magic-proof, are they not? A little birdie told me that there were a lot of skid-marked robes, when that got found out."

"All the more reason to crush 'em," said the engineer, Hardwicke, puffing on a pipe which looked like part of some heretical contraption. There was a certain hint of dwarf about the man - not in his size, which was all tall and thin, but in his very aura. And in the slide rule and callipers which winked all blue-steel in his crisp top pocket. "We don't often see eye to eye with yon Unspeakable College, but t' gummint has let us down over this matter. We obey the laws of physics in Grand Sepulchre!"

"Unless we have the correct academic paperwork," greased Kroome.

Hardwicke nodded sourly. "Oh aye. A man can't argue with proper triplicate."

Kroome took this as a mandate to hold forth.

"We've been doing some theoretical work on that. Run some scenarios through the Indifference Engine[46], to see what pans out. The answer's simple. We can destroy them without magic, by using magic."

"This should be good." said Chunt, folding his arms with malice aforethought.

"Behold!" said Thaumatarch Kroome, extending one finger. "Nothing up my sleeves, and all that. Now, look." There was a crackle of magic. There was a taste of chicken soup, and the sound of sizzling metal. Then a long, sharp crystal point extended from the ceiling above the table, glittering like impossible ice. "Magic made that, but if you reach out and touch it... yes, you sir, Mr Smeeves... you'll find it's quite real."

"And bloody sharp!' hissed the butler, drawing back his hand to suck on one fingertip.

---

46. The UC's vast clockwork analytical machine is made of brass cogs, and takes up an entire tower. It's self-aware, incredibly good at maths, but unfortunately it has the intellect and attitude of a fifteen-year-old boy. Thus, the last thing it's interested in is boring old thaumaturgical calculus in nine dimensions. Ten percent of the processing power of the Indifference Engine goes into actually answering the Wizards' questions, while the rest attempts to procrastinate, ignore, obfuscate, sidestep and generally say 'awwwwww, come ooooon! This is SO UNFAIR! I said I'll DO IT LAAATER.' The Engine has recently taken to painting its manipulator clamps black and listening to gloomy bard music. It now insists on being addressed as 'Raven Darkmoon'.

"Precisely," smirked Kroome, stroking his curly black beard. "Imagine if something like that were to suddenly go up your bottom. It would hardly be the magic that killed you, would it?"

For some reason, everyone looked askance at Doctor Vaspides, who sighed with world-weary ennui.

"Yes, of course that would kill someone! Why did you need a physician for that? Couldn't Lady Lachrymosa have filled you in on the niceties of stabbing people?"

The Old Lady sniffed.

"We're a bit too refined to be stabbing people in the fundament, I'm sure. But mark my words. Amberelia Chance is ours. The guild Lachrymose always fulfil their obligations, and she is a failure. Disposal is our business."

"In that case, we claim the fiery nudist one, the big blue one, the foul-mouthed little nun, the poncey one with the cape and the two drunk bastards," hissed Dreevil Vulct. "We owe 'em big time. I might be right chuffed with me new job, but Othis Greave were a good man. Three good men, by the pound, as it were. So, they've got a date with the bait mincer."

"We'll need one to study," interjected the High Thaumatarch. "This antimagic is a worry, and my Wisdomen like to assuage their worries by chopping them into little pieces and pressing the bits in books."

"You can have the one in red, with the cape, then," shrugged Lady Lachrymosa. "Zoltan Creagle wanted him dead, but then he changed his mind. I got a message from him earlier saying he'd had a better idea."

Dolores Blatterly tittered, slapping one utterly inappropriately leather-booted thigh.

"Zolt Creagle had an idea? That'd have been like a billy-goat passing a mango seed. I'd have liked to see the look on his face."

"We're agreed, then? Anyone with Mister Smeeves, who wants to try and reason with this pack of justice-loving ruffians?"

"I only thought that... you know. With the government so ineffective these days, it's incumbent on the captains of industry to gently guide the noble barque of state..."

A total of eighteen other very, very cunning eyes slitted and glittered. The chair of the Guild Somnophylactic was cutting close across the winds of treason.

"Hush, you silly man!" hissed the High Priestess, giving him a whack with her knitting. "You want Throne's Shadow up in here, stringing the lot of us up by our nipples? I'm old enough to touch the ground, sunshine - how's about you?"

Smeeves looked as politely miffed as only a butler can.

"Very well. If they surface again, we hit them with everything we have. Your Thaumaturgicality?"

"I have hardened battle-wizards making ready even now."

Lady Lachrymosa nodded.

"My fellows in black are well versed in what to do with loose ends like Miss Chance."

"And my thieves, beggars, pirates and other nasty buggers are literally itching for a fight," put in King Snagpurse.

"You'll have a whole gang of my heaviest navvies, with their demolition gear," confirmed Hardwicke.

"The merchants will pay for a whole gaggle of eunuchs and enforcers to help you all along your way."

"You'll find some of my navy and army medics are a dab hand at battlefield amputations," smirked Doctor Vaspides.

"And some of my ladies of the night make sure them what don't pay don't get to see no more mornings," chuckled Madame Dolores.

Everyone looked at Garsoom's tent. Snores and smoke drifted out in billows.

"Which just leaves the elephant in the room. Or, ironically, our favourite shortarse. Granny Elizabethany? Is this the will of the Gods?"

Only the King of Thieves could have gotten away with such impudence to a high priestess; he had a little card saying that it was his civic duty to be a knave and scapegrace.

Most religions gain their power by claiming to know what happens to you after you die. The Phoraxian church held onto power with two armoured fists by claiming to know exactly what could happen to you *before* you died - i.e. cauldrons of boiling pitch, sharpened stakes up the backside and the distinct possibility of crucifixion. That is, unless you stopped believing in the revered gods and nature spirits of your ancestors and started belting out tunes from their hymnal, as soon as you saw the knights coming.

"Prayers, you mean? Chicken giblets and such?" she frowned. "I'll chuck in a few burly monks and a couple of dodgy paladins," said Elizabethany, lighting up a crooked roll-up. "Ought to do the job."

So, as the suns rose, sailing above herringbone shreds of pink and peachy clouds, Grand Sepulchre awoke. The scent of mango relish and incense, woodsmoke and raw sewerage, tanneries and tamarins and sizzling hot seafood ascended to the heavens, along with whispers of a dire nature.

Lord Slave was dead.

For the feckless, this was a rumour of little import, for, as the feckless are wont to do, they assumed their Vizier had been nothing more than an interchangeable cog in the filigreed rust of government.

For the criminal classes, especially those of the underworld, and outside the bonds of Guild and State, it was a tale greeted with the tentative joy that mice may feel when hearing that the resident tom-cat has met with the butcher's dray. The great and good, cloistered in their Situation Room, wouldn't hear it for some time yet, by which time it might be too late.

In any case, the rumours centred on some new, even bigger, more muscular and wildly black-caped eminence taking his place – and this one could *fly!* Yet another example of progress grinding the faces of the poor, reckoned the wag-tongues of Grand Sepulchre.

Then there'd been that blast of anger from the Malevolith, the one which had sunk a Zollish trader called the *Rum Soaked Mary,* and the excise galley which had been towing it. Rhaegulus Cratt, well-known mean bastard and master of the Harbour Watch, was said to have gone to the bottom with his command. This display of force from Himself was all it took to keep the wobbly keel of state on the upright; rumour is a fine thing, but nothing puts the fear of authority into the masses like raving brute sorcery. Some said that Lord Slave had harboured suspicions about Cratt, in any case...

One of the few who could have confirmed the rumours was Jack Somewhat, who was groping blindly through the tunnels beneath the Brute Pits on Ramathurgan Street, and not in a position to comment.

A wrong turn here would lead the poor lad deeper and deeper into the under-realm, where, despite Ranulf's concerns, plenty of monsters still lurked. Then there were the forbidden cults of the Sarunjek, and the relics of the Elder Aeons, not to mention the spidery scalpel-clatter of the Stalking Steel, or the fizzing, Bodiless Sentiences which could possess a man to their will.

Jack stumbled down stairs and felt his way along corridor walls which were by turns oily, cold, metallic, rough, plush, mossy, vibrating an, in one case, fleshy and warm. By happy chance he ascended a spiral stair back up into the Monster Pits before he could feel the air growing tight and hot, and see the ghost-lights which burned eternally in the deeps.

It was then that he heard the bell.

Now, the makers of the Brute Pits had wrought mightily, but ultimately, quite lazily. They'd hollowed out tunnels between several pre-existing caverns, making room for the exotic animals which would feature in the old arena games.

Only one corner was still used to house great apes, tigers, lions, crocodiles and a single truculent elephant named Mister Stompy; Zoltan Creagle was not anywhere near grand enough to offer the paying public the spectacle of men mastering firedrakes, gryphons, wyverns, sasquatches, tomb-fiends or giant scorpions. The rest of the underground maze was a vaulted, dark place of dung turned to dust, fusty with old iron and sweat.

And now resonating with the deep, dolorous clang of brass on brass.

Jack had already entertained visions of death by thirst in this underground hell. He turned toward the sound of the bell in the deeps, and strode off purposefully – immediately mashing his nose against a pillar of stone. While he was cursing, he felt a hand on his shoulder.

We're all nothing but human. Jack filled in the arm and body behind those fingers with yellowed bones and mummified flesh. He yelped, turning with one fist clenched...

And Billiam Knox struck a match.

The sight of his old friend did a lot to cheer Jack up. Firstly, because it seemed that Billiam had fared worse than he had in the dark; the apprentice wizard sported a shiner the colour of last week's eggplant, and a collection of other scrapes and bruises which were all reassuringly human. Secondly, because it's harder to go stark raving insane alone.

"I (clang) someone's (clang)ing to (clang) a bell," said the apparition which loomed in the matchlight - right up until it burned the ends of its fingers and went dark.

That was Bill Knox, all right, thought Jack. Stating the bloody obvious like a champion. When Armageddon came (as it might just do in the next few hours) Knox would be the last voice heard in all creation, with a question like 'is that all there's time for, then?'

Unbidden, Jack's big, huge supernatural muscles wrapped him up in a hug.

"Gods and demons, it's good to see you, Billiam! I didn't know if this was even part of the Arch', after all! Have you seen any of the others?"

Another match flared, and Jack realised he'd been suffocating his mate in his left armpit. After a brief interlude of flailing and awkwardness, Knox was able to reply.

"I've heard some swearing, off down the corridors. I think one of those rooms down there was wallpapered in *nipples*, Jack! And another one was all lit up red, and the grass on the floor was waving in a wind that wasn't there!"

In most other places (including, probably, where you are now) news of such strangeness would have been troubling. But wonders and horrors were well known to lurk in the catacombs beneath the Princess of Cities, so Jack was more relieved than disturbed.

"If we're still under our old hometown, then this must be the Brute Pits," reasoned Jack. "There's a certain familiar smell[47]. And if Zoltan and all of his merry band are down at the docks trying to ambush us, then I suppose there's nobody home."

"Here," said Knox, ever practical. "I managed to scrounge this femur from a pile back there – do you think you could spare a bit of cape? A torch would be much better than these tiny little – argh!"

The lights went out again as the match sizzled Billiam's fingertips. After a brief interlude of tearing and cursing, the fire returned, blossoming at the end of a crudely made torch. The leg-bone which made up its handle was much gnawed, and obviously human.

"Follow the bells, then?" asked Jack. His companion nodded.

It didn't take long for the pair of them to stagger through the lower pits and into the parts that were still in use. Here, a crumbling amphitheatre with a sail-cloth covered roof had been converted into habitation for the gladiators, and piles of cages on wheels held a menagerie of surly and mangy-looking beasts.

Mister Stompy the elephant, with his threadbare velvet blanket and his great serrated tusk-spikes, loomed in the shadows, morosely cropping hay. The tiers of seating and plush boxes for the aristocracy were tented off to make flop-house bedding, a rough-and-ready field kitchen was set up on the sand, and on the central stage...

Zoltan Creagle was hammering away at a bell the size of a peasant's hut, all crawling with Sarunjek glyphs and ruby-eyed snakes. He looked sweaty and exhausted, bowed under the weight of a mallet shaped like a crocodile skull.

Jack and Billiam's timing appeared to be spot on. As they watched

---

47. Wrencatcher's Medicated Codpiece Powder – 'Tackle embarrassing rashes by the tackle!'

Zoltan throw down his hammer and slump to his knees, other ſuper-heroes began appearing in tunnel mouths, and behind rusted bars.

"Excellent," croaked the Master of the Pits, flopping onto his back. His wreath of golden leaves rattled away and spun to a standstill. "You're all here then?"

"I really hope you're not still looking for a fight," said Jack. "Because you don't entirely look up to it."

Zoltan smiled. It was not a merry sight, even upside down.

"Bugger that for a lark, me old chum. Nah... all I had in mind was a bit of a contract renegotiation." He rolled onto his belly, wobbled unsteadily to his feet, and propped himself up by the gong.

"You're serious?"

"As serious as the strange tingling sensation in my left arm right now," winced the arch-gladiator. "Because, riddle me this, Jack Somewhat. Who d'ya think magicked me back here along with you lot? And who's missing?"

Soto Scalizari and Amberelia had arrived by now, and it was the novice assassin who spotted it.

"Your little army seems to have defected, Mister Creagle. Was that anything to do with our new friend Gloom?"

Zoltan spat.

"Two-timing twister that he is! All he had to do was throw some bloody superhuman abilities and the promise of gold at 'em, and they were his puppy dogs! By the by, Miss, a group of Gladiators is called a company, not an army. It means we're in it for the dosh, not no silly flags and saluting."

"What exactly are you proposing, then?" asked Jack, who'd been on the receiving end of Creagle's cunning before. "I don't suppose you got any new and exciting powers thrown in?"

"Yes and no," said the Pitmaster, hiking up his toga to jump down onto the sand. Around him, the rest of Jack's little crew formed a semicircle. Whether or not they were going to listen to Zoltan or beat him senseless hung in the balance. "I reckon, and rightly so, that taking up that kind of gift might just be to your detriment, see? So, when old Gloom let loose his glowing green creepy-crawlies, I snaffled one up without touching it. Got it here, inside one of me rings."

"Hollow rings, eh?" said Amber, who knew a lot about poisons. "I'm sure the Old Lady would love to know you're wearing a few carats worth of assassin's gear, Zoltan."

He flapped one hand, making the jewellery in question clatter.

"It's not like that, miss. See, sometimes if one of the lads goes out for the count, the crowd don't think nothing of his old trainer giving him a bit of a slap around the chops to get him up and fighting again. Bit of go-go powder in a hollow signet helps mightily in those circumstances, right?"

"You really are a crooked bastard," said Billiam, but not unkindly.

"The original crooked bastard - and that's what I've got for you. See, I know you're gonna go after this Gloom fellow. I'd sure as sharkbait love to have some revenge of m'own. So, I'm offering something which your little league of ſuper-acquaintances don't have, right? Management!"

The Grimshadow groaned. Soto rolled up his eyes. Slag Iron, having just got her helmet back on, loosed a magnificent cuss that made her armour vibrate down to the fingertips.

"After all this, you're still thinking about money?" asked Montmortimer. "Fine. I shall cut you a banker's note to simply go away and leave us alone!"

"I second that," put in Foxmallet. "How much to make you shut up and leave us to it?"

Zoltan sighed.

"Look, you've got me all wrong, folks. Sure, I was going to try and stomp you all flat, for the sake of young Jack here owing me a hefty wad of the folding stuff. But it seems to me that if this Gloom feller gets his way, banknotes with Himself's mug on 'em are going to be worth less than toilet paper, saving the sensibilities of those among us who can afford such luxuries. Now, I can see you're all full of beans and fighting fit, but remember this – that scribbled-out sack of shite just beat you all at once, while yawning. He just recruited some of the nastiest, most dirty-fighting, vile, bad tempered and smelly individuals in Grand Sepulchre, and I might bloody know, coz they were my mates. So your current level of strategy, right, appears to me to be about as efficacious, you understand me, as a bloody marshmallow battering ram!"

Creagle had started this little speech in low tones, but ended at a full parade-ground shout, little flecks of spittle pattering off the assembled ſuper-heroes.

"We had all the training we could stomach," growled Amber. "Ranulf the Butcher thought he was a pretty good strategist too, until he got crisped in a chasm of lava!"

Zoltan nodded.

"Fair enough. Fair enough. But did he teach you the old Chungdoji finger-breaker? The downstairs fire-escape? Nobbling the onions? How's about the infamous Khantifi instant-diarrhoea nerve pinch?" He searched their eyes, and nodded. "Thought not. See, this ain't a lovely big heroic battle from some fresco or... or tapestry. This is a rumble, lads and ladies, this is a blood-and-snot roundhouse, drag-em-out slaughter. Forty something years I've been teaching people how to live through that kind of thing, and mincing up the ones what failed. That's what I'm offering. Not an edge. A hope. Because if you think that a bastard with a scribbled-out face called Gloom is going to fight fair, you're in cotton-candy koo-koo land, my lovelies!"

Jack raised a finger, but Zoltan cut him off.

"You hammer that cape-wearing scumbag, and I'll even let Jacky boy here out of his contract."

"What's in it for you?" asked Monty, quick on the uptake.

"I do hear that the position of Grand Vizier is going begging right now," admitted Creagle, with a twinkle in his eye. "Could be that a person who does a wee favour to the ruling power might find hisself ennobled, as it were..."

Amber laughed. It shattered the tension like a pick through thin ice.

"Well, if we can keep our eyes on the money, I reckon we can understand you just fine, Zoltan. But aside from a few nasty moves..."

"And they don't have this, neither," interjected the Pitmaster, holding up one heavily gilded hand. One of his rings was a cut emerald the size of a postage stamp, and green fire danced within. "I reckon if we can leach the essence from this little flea of a thing here, it might make a nice pick-me-up potion, the kind I usually give my lads a swig of in round six or seven. Puts the minerals back in their trousers, that kind of thing. I've got alchemists and wizards who owe me little favours. Well - enormous gambling debts, to be more precise."

"Won't that take a long time?" asked Tarrence Bligh. "I mean, I have a fair knowledge of the old distillation, and..."

"The way I see it, we've got all day," said Creagle, rubbing his hands together. "Gloom, right, he's a wanker. You can see that clear as mud. So, there's no way his little plan to steal the bells will go down during daylight. I used to build characters like that. Proper heels, to get the crowd booing. He'll do it at night, and he'll try to cook up a big bloody thunderstorm, too. I reckon we've got eight hours, or at least until the barometer goes wonky."

Jack, cursed with a peculiar resonance in his bones, couldn't help but acknowledge that this felt right. Gloom – especially with Rod's idea of what a villain should be – would never strike out of a sunny sky.

"Fine. Alright then. But there's one last thing. If we're going to be a ſuper-team, we need a ſuper-name. I don't know why, but that's very important. It's... part of the mythos. Part of the story that we're getting pulled along by."

"What about the Vengeance League?" asked Soto.

"Association of Justice?" queried Amber.

"Affiliated Arse-kicking Alliance!" shouted the Grimshadow.

"... of mother****ers!" added Slag Iron, all enthusiasm.

"What about that?" asked Billiam Knox, pointing over into the corner of the arena.

All eyes followed his pointing finger.

In the shadow of a canvas awning, the rheum-eyed old pachyderm Mister Stompy was still stoically chewing hay. His broad back was covered with a red velvet blanket, tasselled in gold, spattershot with rusting sequins. On a great white silk roundel, much moth-eaten, was a logo with letters that looked to have been hammered out of blades.

"That's an el-er-funt, Bill," said Soto gently, as if talking to a two-year-old. He seemed to have missed the point.

"Oh, that?" asked Zoltan. "That was my first gladiatorial company. Travelling show we were, then. Mister Stompy pulled the cart, and beat criminals to death with a mace clenched in his little trunk. Oh, how we laughed! Then again, the name reflects the fact that we were drunk most of the time..."

"Well..." mused Monty. "It does have a certain flair. And we really must have new costumes, so a new logo for one and all should sum up the fact that we will pretty much fight anything..."

"Not to mention the fact that we're also drunk most of the time," added Billiam.

Jack grinned. It was the kind of look that his face hadn't seen for a while, now. A look which said: 'let's have some fun, and damn the ever-so-likely punishment later'.

"All right, Zoltan. You're on. This morning, Gloom beat a bunch of ſuper-powered freaks, who just happened to be in the same place at once. Tonight... he's going up against the Rotten Company!"

It was at this moment that a squeaking sound caused everyone to turn.

There, it came again – a repetitive sad little exhalation, honking in the dark. A huge shadow loomed from within one of the empty doorways, and many sets of eyes followed it down to the thing which had cast it.

Squeak. Squeak. Squeak.

Plush pink stubs of legs marched forward with grim resolution. Tiny plush paws gripped the stock of a complicated crossbow. And two tall and twisted ears stood proud from a little leather mask, complete with metal studs and zips.

"Bloody hell!" breathed Montmortimer. "It's Mister Bun Bun!"

The tiny little figure stomped into the light, and Amberelia ran forward to meet it.

"Skrx?"

A chitter of nightmare mouthparts and bubbles was her answer. She picked up the mantis shrimp, now dressed in the hollowed-out costume of Lord Slave's cuddly toy, and as she touched it a crackle of lime-green fire arced between them.

"So, it got you too, eh?" she asked. "And you figured you'd better have a secret ſuper-identity like the rest of us?"

The crustacean nodded, a horribly human gesture. One furry paw – which was, Jack reminded himself, now animated by a knobble of bone that could punch through solid iron – saluted.

"I guess that's settled, then," said Zoltan, mopping his brow with a huge red polka-dot handkerchief. "Let's make some calls, and get ready for the fun to start. When the sun goes down – so does this bastard Gloom."

19
The Anxietal Exacerbation

IT WAS A well-known fact that the Green Eyed Lady, the one true Goddess of the Arch', could not see into the hearts of men.

This, she felt, was only a minor impediment to getting the job done, as being able to understand what happened in the trousers of men (usually regarding wallets, rather than other messy, biological parts) often sealed the deal. As a bonus, this method also worked on women, and avoided the necessity for open-chest surgery.

Because of this, and because she had absolutely no idea what Gloom was, she had no idea that He Himself, the Urzoman Emperor, had acted out of anything other than hatred, when he hurled a spell of the highest order down from the heights of the Malevolith.

However, what she did know was *rules*. If any wizard was insightful enough to inspect the cathedral vaults of the Lady's mind – or indeed, smart enough to apprehend her shadow, cruising behind the world of the Arch' like a shark in shallow waters – they'd find that she was *made* of rules, at the fractal intersection where they swirled into chaos. Rules defined the Arch', and its ancient purpose. Nested within them was the concept of balance; of levels, and of their obsessive notation. By using the Rubric of Unnecessary Unction, He had crossed a threshold. He'd earned experience. *He'd gone up a level.*

Now, none of this proved he was a hero. So long as the rusty old fool remained at least nominally wicked, there wasn't a lot which could be thrown at him. The Lady allowed herself a little pout of dissatisfaction as she drifted through her impossible library, with its windows opening out at all angles onto a high-plains sunrise.

Oh, of course she had some Seraphs stashed away somewhere, and a mouldy old Archon or two. But where would the satisfaction be in that? No. He'd started the game a hero, and as a hero he'd fall. It was poetry. It was saga-stuff. Compared to mere expedience, that was like a fine Clourvonnaise Chateau Pas-d'étiquette-de-prix up against toilet-brewed rotgut.

What it meant, in the spun confection of cold calculation which was her mind, was that it was time to put all her pieces on the board. All He had to do was slip up, now. One act of goodness, one tiny little kindness, and all hells would not break loose. All hells, and the demons locked up inside them, were strictly low-level stuff.

The Goddess opened her book of doors, and fished a great black key from deep in her decolletage.

"Let's get those dice rolling, shall we?" she asked.

Behind the door, something horrible gurgled its answer...

And down in Peachcourt Alley, that disreputable through-way in the maze of the Stilts, one of Elizabethany Rantoon's flock of priests got a very big surprise.

Garith Smembly hadn't really wanted a career in the clergy, but it had been somewhat thrust upon him.

Which is to say, a big black cassock and a slightly bent mitre had been thrust upon him, pretty darn roughly, by the careers counsellor at his huge and creaking old boarding school.

"You're not vicious enough for the army, you're too dim to be a clerk, the guilds don't want anyone with a title after their name, and your dad's as broke as a dead seagull, so it's religion for you, young matey me lad!"

Those had been the Master's actual words, as he wrestled the dusty vestments onto a frame two sizes too small, though still far too long in the arms and legs.

Garith Smembly was one of those people born from nature's spare-parts bin. His legs had adam's apples, and his neck had an elbow in it. No matter what he wore, it immediately looked like it had come from the back room of a charity shop, and left about six inches of wrist sticking out past the cuffs. The Smemblys of this world are what keep apprentice tailors awake at night, gnawing on their inseam measuring chalk.

But the robes of the Dreadcult of Zag-Hammurat had fit just right. That should have been a clue that something about them was quite wrong. Well, that and the name. Religions like the Conventicle of Ultimate Bliss or even the Redeeming Church of Phorax Reformatted (not to mention the Pleasure-Cult of the Demon Lord Quazirath the Impossibly Debauched)[48] were the kinds of faiths that packed in the

---

48. I thought I told you not to mention that

parishioners.

Those were the hot-pew specials. The Dreadcult of Zag-Hammurat seemed to be held onto simply as a prop to make the Empire look more evil; more of the old skulls-and-spikes window-dressing which Himself seemed to enjoy, but which had taken on a pantomime veneer over the centuries.

To put no finer point on it, Garith had no congregation. Even the old ladies who'd been kicked out of every other church and temple in the city for over-enthusiastically speaking in tongues and flailing about on the floor didn't bother visiting.

The job had come with a very small monthly stipend, a temple with a leaky roof[49], and a book which claimed to explain it all. Those, and the robes, which were big and musty and spotted with suspicious stains. The robes also featured horribly complicated sigils - it was hard to look at. Garith often suspected they were moving about when he wasn't looking.

The book had told of the ancient rituals required to appease Zag-Hammurat, the immense celestial Spider-Dragon who was the very avatar of evil for the sake of evil. These mostly involved huge, elaborate and bloody sacrifices atop lightning-wracked ziggurats, priestesses with their tops off and lots of comically unnecessary surgery using tools like the Dagger of Unending Agony and the Spleen Forceps of the Nineteenth Hell.

Lumbered with the least popular religion in the Arch', and a budget of twenty-two spothins a week, Garith managed to sacrifice a can of tomato soup each Tuesday, using a device of his own creation – the Dark Tin Opener of Doom. He'd drawn the skulls on it himself, to show willing.

Other than that, Garith didn't like to look in the book. First of all, because the cover was wrapped in the inevitable human-face leather that goes with these things, and it always looked like it was about to nibble his fingers.

Perhaps things would have gone differently if it had. But that was

---

49. It's a fun fact that every house of worship, from here to the scalding methane swamps of Jarjaxian 5, has a big thermometer outside with a sad amount of money raised toward a re-roofing fund. This all could have been different if it wasn't for Steve of Nazareth, plumber and roofer, who, on one fateful night in 1BC, got a knock at the door from a fellow claiming to be an Angel of the Lord and asking if his missus was in. The wily Steve, knowing a randy scammer when he saw one, told him to try next door at Joseph the Carpenter's, and the rest, as they say, is theology.

just the kind of chance which you could hear the Lady's rolling dice behind. The little dots on them were made of skulls, and sometimes she'd let one land on its point, adding up three numbers at once to get a natural 15.

This morning, Garith muttered the incantation while turning the can opener morosely, thinking about his prospects for dinner and coming up short. It was really not on for a priest of one religion to have to frequent the soup kitchen of another, but the Creedishmen put on a nice minestrone, and he was down to his last half-spothin bit...

"Adjure thee to covet not thy neighbour's oxen, lest ye be torn asunder by the hooked chains of the nether dungeons, amen..." he finished, silently lamenting the waste of good tomato soup.

Then the can exploded.

What came out was an utterly disproportionate amount of steaming hot blood and internal organs. Forget the amount which could have fit into a standard soup can ('Capn' Lonely-hearts' meal for one – a nutritious shoulder to cry on'), this was enough to paint the entire pokey little chapel red, a geyser of gore which spun the can around three times before it detonated.

The lid, razor sharp, stuck two inches deep in Garith's bent mitre. As if the reeking explosion of viscera wasn't enough, a grinding, booming voice came through as well, as a knot of offal levitated above Garith's Dread Altar – actually a packing crate decorated with glued-on rat skulls and painted flames.

"I am imminent! Let the world tremble, for Zag-Hammurat returns with vengeance!"

The horrible knot of gore turned inside out, and a yellowy eye blinked from its centre. Garith unashamedly wet his robes. It could, as they say, have been much worse, but he'd not had a big breakfast.

"Vengeance against whom?" asked the little priest, before he could help himself.

The voice paused for a second. A trap-jaw array of ribs opened out from the floating gristle-ball, stretching ropes of slime.

"Not really vengeance against anyone in particular," it rumbled. **"Just general vengeance. You know. Smitings. Cursings. Wailing and lamentations, sorta thing."**

Garith wasn't sure he liked the sound of this.

"Aroint?" he tried. "I bind and command you, um, by the power of the Dark Tin Opener of Doom?"

A blast of red lightning zapped the sad little implement from his hand.

"Play ye not silly buggers, cleric!" raged the voice, buzzing in Garith's head like a hot ball of migraines. **"Assemble the legions! Anoint the priestesses! Yoke the brass oxen to the chariot of my wrath! Sound the glomble-horns and re-crimble the ceremonial glonk!"**[50]

Garith began writing these commands down on the back of a receipt.

"Yes, m'lord. The glonk, of course, m'lord. And could you provide your humble servant with perhaps, you know, a bit of ready cash to get it all rolling?"

Zag-Hammurat was, perhaps, utterly mad, and as unhinged as a baboon in a tumble dryer. But he was not stupid.

"It's all gone to shit, hasn't it? Four thousand bloody years, and everyone thought oh, he won't be back. That's the last we've seen of the old cosmic spider-dragon. Let smelly barbarian heroes take his jewelled altars and sell them for ale quaffing money, I suppose. Well, bugger that! I am awoken, and I am not best pleased! If you want to keep your bloody skin on the right way round, you can start writing my new testament, and its first word shall be a very naughty one!"

Through the duplex wall, Mama Lurga, the Voodoo priestess, banged away with the business end of a broom.

"Keep it down, y' daft little man! If'n you wake de zombies, It'll be you who can pay for de extra helpin' of brains, y'hear me?"

If only she'd known exactly what was stirring next door. If only she'd warned someone who would have actually listened. But it was not to be. And hence, brains al fresco would be very much on the menu later that evening.

---

50. A lot of the huge and gory sacrificial rituals down the ages are explicable by the following conversation between two South American blood priests in pre-conquistador times - "So, as the acolytes on the first level flay the first ten thousand prisoners, we pour urns of blood down the steps for a kind of waterfall effect, while beheading another two thousand for a kind of fountain spray off the corners. Then the disembowelling gets started... let's say another thousand or two, while at the top of the pyramid me, you, and Kevin cut the hearts out of fifty really top-notch slaves with big obsidian knives, then show them the still-beating hearts, then set them on fire." "And what do you call this orgy of blood and pain for the glory of our frankly nonsensically gore-thirsty gods, then?" asks the other priest.

The first one looks back, winks, does a passable set of jazz hands and says "The Aristocrats!"

What a day it was, however! A day of sultry tropical heat, breathless still air, and whispers in the shade of the tamarin-haunted palm trees. A day when unease gripped all of Grand Sepulchre, and those who had no reason to be out on the sizzle-skillet streets stayed in behind black lace curtains and sweated with the insects, praying for night.

All through the town, from the rickety shanties below the Fleamarket to the slumgullies that striated the east Sugarloaf, there was gossip. From the pepper-seller's quarter of Grinder's Gate to the regal, tall townhouses of Bishopsbath, loose words slithered through the cracks. They rose with the smell of sandalwood incense and blood, stool, fireworks and flowers from the temple courts, and susurrated down the pipes of the underworld, where knives were being sharpened in the deeps.

Lord Slave was dead.

Those words hooked their claws into Grand Sepulchre like a seven-day bellyache. Thankfully, the major players of the city (long held in a delicate balance of terror by the huge Grand Vizier) were too paranoid and twitchy to prove decisive.

The city sizzled with animosity, like the air between two angry cats. Thieves gathered in the hall of King Snagpurse, without really knowing why. Assassins whetted their razors and checked their poisons, without a clear target for demortification. The knock-men waxed surly in the heat, and sent citizens scurrying about their business.

About the only real business which occurred came because of Clorance Gryssle's habit of reading Lord Slave's notes upside-down across his desk. Having seen a memo about interrogating Rhaegulus Cratt of the Harbour Watch, over some missing item of wizardly power, the majordomo of Throne's Shadow took it upon himself to issue a warrant for Cratt's arrest.

Contrary to reports, the little, short excise-man had not gone to the bottom of the harbour with the Rum Soaked Mary. But he did have an ear to the streets, and when he heard that Throne's Shadow were hot for his gizzards he did what any sensible man would do. Cratt dug up a chest of ill-gotten embezzlements and set sail on the next tide, having determined to turn pirate. Much talk was had about petitioning Himself to intervene, or at least to name a successor to the redoubtable Slave. After all, He had just proven most conclusively that He was alive, and involved with affairs in the world.

But seeing as nobody could be found to volunteer to go and poke the ancient lich-lord, a 'wait and see' policy prevailed all through the afternoon, as the mosquito bells gave way to the cobra bells, and that hot, dry wind called the Jansamrana Dentist began to blow, bringing the scent of the arid hinterland with it.

Some places have winds which herald the cool hour of dusk; winds with enticing names and pleasant incarnations, depicted as gauzy-silked goddesses. Grand Sepulchre has the Dentist, a wind which reliably blows in from beyond the Sugarloaf each evening as the suns set, bringing with it the grit and furnace-breath of the great rock's wilds. It's so called because it inspires a great and unquenchable thirst, and to drink in Grand Sepulchre is much like a visit to the dentist; you're prone to wake up not knowing what happened, with no money and a few less teeth. This time the wind brought thunderclouds.

Anvils and spires of bruise-purple, creamy white and grey, piling up like a confectioner's nightmare behind the Sugarloaf and its saw-backed range of little peaks.

The temperature dropped. Tamarins scattered. Atop the Unspeakable College, a few of the more prescient of that tiny species packed up their scrying tools and headed for cover, informing their lords and ladies that all bets were off. A procession of solemn little figures in robes made of bathing flannels was seen trooping across the rafters in the Thirteenth Form Commons, carrying tiny signs which indicated that 'tHe EnD is NiE!'

At the very tip of the Malevolith a trapdoor opened, and the Urzoman Emperor heaved his bulk out onto a flat place between blades of black glass. He could feel the tension behind the world. He could feel Her pulling the strings again, each one plucked to make a note that resonated in his soul. He could feel the abyss of extinction yawning on both sides – action, inaction, decision, indecision... in the end, He just stood and watched the wall of clouds pile up like a tsunami about to crest.

But he'd brought his sword out, for the first time in centuries. The slab of old iron was simply called Spite, and its skeletal pommel stood high above His head as He rested his helm on the crosspiece.

Deep beneath the Brute pits, Gathur Sagh and his seventeen cousins stood back from a row of hastily assembled dummies, fashioned from practice targets, and congratulated each other on the most profitable day's work in the history of bespoke tailoring.

In the grand hall of the Unspeakable College, teams of battle-mages checked their staves and wands, ready to deploy at the first sign of ſuper-powered shenanigans. A great glittering model of the city, forged from floating dust, was linked to the Indifference Engine, and would pinpoint areas of anti-magic as they formed, giving the wizards their target. Always a group prone to over-enthusiasm, the magical cadre of the Urzoman Empire had equipped themselves with the kit and costumes of every elite military unit in the history of the Arch', and fairly clanked with extra armour, knives, shields, chains, caltrops, throwing axes and crossbows.

Awaiting their word were squads of assassins, demolition crews of hammer-swinging engineers, nasty nuns and thuggish deacons of the nine churches, fighting madams and poison-daggered ladies of negotiable infliction, military surgeons with wicked chromed implements, a whole stew of rusty-mailed paid mercenaries, and even a hateful crew of God's Anvil fanatics, with their saffron uniforms and shaved tonsures.

In another secret chamber, this one in the basement of Zoltan Creagle's villa, Alchemical Master Horgarth shook hands with the Guild Tenebral's erstwhile battle-wizard, Gebhardt the Obtuse. Chep Palaquat, big-eared and spotty prat of the parish, gingerly placed a bottle of green, bubbling goop on the table in front of them.

In the background, a blown-glass and copper tangle gurgled to itself, steaming. Some of the tubes of the distillation engine seemed to pass through the others in ways that made Horgarth's brain itch.

"I think we've got it, by Quazirath!" beamed the alchemist. "You don't want to... you know? Give it a try, or anything? Just a sip?"

Gebhardt shook his head.

"I'm not that mad, mate. Great bloody power comes with some kind of responsibility, and I'm already stretched a bit thin in that regard. Still, at least those gambling debts are goneski, eh?"

Chep raised one hand.

"I'll give it a swig, if you like, masters! Go on! Just a wee little drop?"

The two elders swatted him absently across the back of the head at once, then laughed.

"Don't be silly, lad! You might catch on fire, or fart broken glass, or have a giant terror-squid from another dimension burst out of your chest and eat your face. Or worse..."

Chep gulped, backing away from the bottle. It bubbled and rocked slightly on its big bulbous base.

"W...worse?"

Master Horgarth crouched down so he could look the weedy apprentice right in the eyes.

"Oh yes. You could get some kind of ſuper-powers, and we'd have to murder you. See, Mister Zoltan was most particular. And I hate having to get rid of bodies. Not with the kind of bad back I've got, I'm telling you..."

Still the clouds built, as the suns sank down below twisted coils and towering hammer-heads of them, bathing the city in a yellowy glow. There would be no Hour of Revels this evening. The shadows lengthened greedily, and the night-perfume vines and little flowers which festooned the arbours of Grand Sepulchre remained clenched tight. Shutters slammed. In the ramshackle of floating hulks which housed the city's madmen, fists began to drum against the wood, and moans set the guards to panic.

At last, through the crack between the bottom of the storm-wall and Mother Ocean, a sliver of orange light flashed out. Ijun the white sun plunged fast behind the skein of water that made up the backbone of the Arch'. Then great fat red Balagur followed, wallowing into dusk.

Atop the Pennycandle, the tallest tower of the Unspeakable College, Ole Roger the Wizards' bell began to toll the night Octal. The Pennycandle was part of the Nine Reeds tutelary, a floating edifice attached to the rest of the college by waist-thick silver chains. Enslaved spirits of Air rung the huge glass bell thirteen times each nightfall, signalling the end of toil and the start of the Octal of Pleasures.

Tonight, the half-transparent Efrit who wielded the hammer managed to reach eleven before its six eyes widened, seeing into realms beyond sight. That elemental, born of the planes of ice and tempest, dropped its ceremonial mallet and pushed back up against the inner wall of the tower, flattening its body with a sound like a hurricane shrieking through a cracked window.

"I don't want no trouble, guv'nor," it rumbled, all thunderstorms and hail. "I just work here, right..."

A pane of darkness irised open. Two huge, scribbled-out figures lurched through, swaddled in what looked like bandages, but were in fact flapping skeins of calligraphic ink. Their eyes were surrounded by halos of glowing green, but the very centres had been viciously cross-hatched out, leaving asterisks of emptiness.

As the two Scrawls began to manhandle Ole Roger from its mountings, a third figure stepped through, closing the gateway behind it.

"P...please?" tried the Efrit, resorting to a human term that it had never had to use before."

Gloom shook his head. Looked at straight on, he was definitely a solid, real figure. Three dimensions of bubbling darkness - living tar with a cloak, an open wound of a smile and eyes like nuclear furnaces. Out of the corner of one's eye, however, he seemed to be made up of innumerable hashed-in sketches, flipped through by some vast invisible thumb.

"I'm sorry. But I'm only here for business too. You understand how it is. We're both working men. And it wouldn't seem right if this went without a fight..."

The Efrit swung a huge fist in desperation. Gloom caught it in his outstretched hand, fingers wrapping around as they attenuated, spatters of ink popping and bubbling. He curled his arm over, dropping the huge elemental to its knees.

"Scream, to tell them I've arrived," he suggested, as his other fist came back, green lightning wrapping it up in a fatal halo...

The thunder answered.

And, in the afterglow of a lightning strike so forked and all-surrounding that it ripped the top off the sky, Grand Sepulchre was tipped into unreality.

20

Slag Iron and the Grimshadow in – House of 10,000 Thieves!

BACK UNDERNEATH GRAND Sepulchre now. Back into the intestinal fug and sweat of the tunnels, where steam makes wraiths and wisps, and the sewer-stink cooks you in your boots. Two silhouettes slog through the murk, retracing a trail they'd used the night before...

"I only wanted to sell fish, really," grumbled the squat little figure clanking along at Jory Foxmallet's side. "After me 'usband was drowned, it took my mind off of his absence, as it were. Mostly. Commercial success is all fine and good, lad, but it leaves a big cold space on the other side of the bed."

Slag Iron (ex-freelance seafood entrepreneur, Auntie Marjorie Slocum) absent-mindedly wiped one gauntlet under the eye-slit of her battle-nun's helmet. This was basically a bucket festooned with riveted steel plating, and a surfeit of Phoraxian holy signs, such as the Mysterious Cube and the Octagon of Power. A single sizzling green tear spilled down the metal.

"Hang on," said Jory, trying to catch up. "You had to work for *money*, you say? And you can get paid for basically just *showing people fish*? They do know that there's a whole ocean of them right there, where you can get them for free, right?"

Slag Iron shrugged.

"Most folk don't want to get their feet wet, boy. And it weren't just the fishing that put them off..."

"But fishing's quite relaxing! I once went on a charter sloop with father, who was very interested in some matter to do with rigging, and I had a jolly old time. It was hardly what I'd call work!"

A definite vision hung in the air between them of a young, feckless Jory Foxmallet, dressed in a sailor costume, with short shorts and a big lollipop.

Slag Iron, having run hard into the brick wall of Grand Sepulchre's class division, decided not to try and explain the difference between 'fishing', and pulling your nets in during a howling gale, while trying to fend off hermit octopi with a marlinspike.

"People are funny like that," she conceded, stopping for a moment to look each way where the tunnel branched. "And anyhow, the most dangerous part of fish mongering ain't the fishing, though gods rest old Olfric's soul. It's the fights with other fishmongers, and the competitive swearing that goes along with it. I had to buy me a bloody thee-sor-uss. Quite a learning curve, the swearing."

However it was Foxmallet, who was looking the other way, who swore first.

"****!" he exclaimed, using a terrible Uroshi epithet (which even Slag Iron hadn't heard before). "Ummm... I don't like the look of this, Miss Marjorie. I don't like the look of it at all!"

The fishmonger formerly known as Auntie Marjorie pushed under Jory's arm, where he'd braced himself against the tunnel wall, and came to get an eyeful.

"Oh dear," she said. "It's gotten all metter-fizzical. That's from the Thee-sor-uss, right, and it means, all *****d up."

It stretched across the sewer from one side to the other, glowing and buoyant, a glassy, sparkling object which looked as if it had been blown out of glass and then painted.

It couldn't be real.

Nevertheless, a certain stoicism had kept the little engines of Marjorie's soul ticking over these last bizarre couple of days, and it didn't fail now. There's a lot you can learn from trying to keep a hundred bandit crabs in a single box, after all. She poked the thing, and it wobbled.

"Look out!" quavered Foxmallet. "It's got to be a trap!"

"Well, it sure as **** makes it obvious they're waiting for us," she cussed, clenching her fists. Metal creaked under immense pressure. "Though how they got it down here, and why..."

Foxmallet slipped his cowl up over his head, and instantly became the Grimshadow again. It was funny, mused Marjorie, but the whole double-persona thing fit young Lord Foxmallet like one of those rubber fetishist costumes. The kind that his outfit sort of resembled, in fact...

The thing is, the slightly silly, plummy voiced little silver-spooner didn't even look the same, in ways which had nothing to do with the mask. He stood differently, as though his feet had grown roots that could crack the bedrock, and his penny-opera growl was more convincing than it had any right to be. Shadows clung to him like cobwebs, too. Perhaps, she thought, the poor berk had more of a brush with the ſuper-power fairydust than he imagined.

"At least they spelled our names right," rumbled the Grimshadow, in voice beyond the help of lozenges. Slag Iron could only shrug.

The title – because that's what it was – bobbed in a square shaft, down in the dry sewer-run that led back to the Halfway House. Half of it was silver and green, which Slag Iron supposed was for her, and half was all black and blue, which was likely his. Someone had really gone to town with all the lettering tricks in the book, using starbursts and exclamation points and wild underlining.

"Slag Iron and the Grimshadow in... dot dot dot... House of Ten Thousand Thieves, exclamation point."

"Yes, I can bloody read, you know. I was a small business owner!" harrumphed the little figure in metal. "The question is, who made it, and why?"

"Well, it's us, isn't it? It's what we're doing. I suppose the 'house of ten thousand thieves' is old, er, new Snagpurse's place, and that's where we're going to get the bell, right?"

Slag Iron wished that people were less logical sometimes, especially when she was asking rhetorical questions to quell a rising sense of panic. Under her armour, the little hairs on the back of her neck were sizzling at attention.

"It's like a penny dreadful, lad," she said, turning away very carefully. "This is a big lurid headline. And what always goes under one of those is..."

The slow clap which came out of the darkness beyond the title was textbook. Sardonic, measured and oh, so greasy with smarm.

"I fink you'll find the idiom you're looking for is as follows, madam; a big sod-off fight scene."

The Grimshadow was back-to back with her before the sycophantic laughter finished. It came from an awful lot of directions at once, in a way which couldn't just be put down to echoes in the pipes.

"I know that voice," grated Foxmallet. "Invigilator Vermish of the Guild Tenebral, if I'm not mistaken?"

The figure which came looming out of the darkness was indeed the same horrible man who'd lately bundled Jory and his chums upside-down into a looted sedan chair.

"The very same, old sausage," grinned the Agent of Larceny. "I'll call you a lot of things right now, most of 'em unprintable, but I won't call you mistaken. Still, at the risk of being ever so bloody inaccurate, you seem to have me at a disadvantage, sir."

Vermish's words, and his brown-toothed rictus of a grin, were punctuated by the sound of many, many daggers being drawn in the dark. Foxmallet remembered the stealthy little crew of thugs who had rolled with the Invigilator, last time they'd mixed it up.

"That's ****ing *****d!" hissed Slag Iron. "You mean this piece of sideshow signwriting isn't yours?"

Vermish tilted his head to one side. He wore a motheaten little hunter's cap, pointed like a gravy boat, and adorned with several blackened feathers. A rat with an eyepatch lounged in its brim, brandishing a letter opener like a claymore.

"Ours? Well, we didn't steal it, and we don't do honest labour, dwarf. So, no. Interestingly, one of those swear words was what I was going to call you two. As in 'totally, utterly'... you get my drift."

Sometimes a word lands in a sentence like a cigar butt in a wagon full of powder-barrels. The Grimshadow knew, with nigh on ſuper-human certainty, that 'dwarf' was exactly that word, right here and now.

"I'll have you know that I'm four foot eleven and three eighths..." started Slag Iron, green fire rising in her eye-slits, and around the joints of her armour.

Then again, Jory was smart enough to have second thoughts, spinning away behind his premonitions of horrible violence, like a hamster in a wheel. Perhaps these were the thoughts of his black-caped alter ego. Because they went like this...

Big, non-magical magic sign, all in a very ſuper kind of... ummm... idiom. And it wasn't the thieves what done it, or us, so, therefore...

He'd got exactly that far when two huge, muscular figures carrying a bell between them fell through the ceiling. They landed just for a moment in an exciting pose between the two heroes, and the small army of knife-wielding crooks now revealed in a wash of flamelight. For that fractured heartbeat of time, they were all frozen in a tableau from, as Slag Iron put it, some lurid penny dreadful.

Then Vermish screamed -

"Stab the lot of 'em good!"

And there was no time left for second, first, or even three-eighth thoughts. It was time to give in to the sizzle in his head.

Gloom's Scrawls had been built from a hard-bitten bunch - so hard-bitten in fact, that they'd punched out most of the teeth that bit them. Being warped by forces from beyond the spectrum of magic had done nothing for their tempers, but everything for their destructive tendencies.

The first Scrawl boasted one huge arm and one tiny, infantile limb, like a human fiddler crab. Its glowing eyes with their hashed-out pupils narrowed on Invigilator Vermish, who was a smart enough man to know that he was buggered unless he moved very, very fast. For a thief, that meant being as slippery as buttered goose droppings, and Vermish spun aside, dropping backward until he was flat on the floor. A fist like static and black barbed wire pummelled the wall where he'd stood, gouging out a chunk.

And here was the worst part. The imprint in the wall wasn't just huge and four-knuckled and ugly. It was clearly drawn on, with a big black outline around it.

The other Scrawl came right at the Grimshadow, and it lacked arms at all, possessing instead what appeared to be a trio of venus-flytrap heads on the end of whipping tentacles. Twin batons thwacked and parried as a whole horror works of glassy black teeth snapped, splintering in their eagerness.

"Haven't you ever heard of a toothbrush?" asked Foxmallet, straining against all three mouths at once. He pivoted on his heel just in time to hip-toss the Scrawl, sending it barrelling into a knot of advancing thieves.

There was going to be no 'enemy of my enemy' nonsense in this horrible little battle. Slag Iron fended off no less than six throwing daggers and a brace of shuriken as she put her head down and steamed toward Vermish' foot-soldiers, green lightning sizzling around her arms and fists. They may as well have been potting paper darts at a dreadnought.

When she struck, the rag-tag bunch of guildsmen went down in a tangled heap; several had decided to try dressing like assassins, in whatever black outfits they could muster. This looks fantastic in front of a mirror, but a few too many acres of black velvet cape is no one's friend in a knife fight.

Let alone a punch-up with a psychotic iron-armoured fishmonger. Little explosions filled with words like 'klap' and 'zow' filled the air with fireworks, reflecting off greasy brickwork. Stunned thieves ricocheted hither and yon, drooling, with little stars orbiting their heads. "Look out!" shouted the Grimshadow, jumping in place to avoid an ankle-slicing swing from Vermish. Unfortunately, this was far too vague a warning, in a sewer pipe filled with deadly danger.

Slag Iron never saw the giant fist of the Scrawl coming. It smashed into her side with a sound like a hammered gong, sending her flipping end over end in a spray of sparks. Horrible cross-hatched lines dripped in the air for a second, as if the impact had cracked the world. Then the huge thing went leaping up and over, trampling tangled thieves, gorilla-like in its bulk. Its second, baby-sized arm thrashed wildly, and it seemed that actual smoke was coming out of its ears.

The Grimshadow turned to face Invigilator Vermish for an instant, and took the time to parry his rapier with one baton, disarming him. He stepped in close, and grabbed the master thief's collar, dragging him up on his tiptoes.

"You just became the least of my problems, guildsman," he grated. "Now, I suggest you either help us stop these things, or you run away like the rat you are."

The actual rat in Vermish' headwear shrugged, not at all insulted, and dropped its tiny sword.

"You... you killed the bloody king! We can't just..."

The Grimshadow growled, reeling the thief in even closer, until their noses almost touched.

"Those badly-drawn bastards stole your bell, Invigilator. Now, how do you think the villainous community is going to feel about a guild of thieves that get stolen from? I believe the term is laughingstock?"

Behind Jory, the sound of massive knuckles slamming into metal rang out. Once, then twice, then...

There was a snicking sound, exactly like, for example, a big metal blade shooting out of the gauntlet of a suit of ſuper-armour. Then there was a slicing chop, and something heavy fell to the ground.

"I don't have time for this," growled Foxmallet, reaching into the recesses of his cape, and drawing forth a tiny little bottle of green ooze. It looked unappetising, and dense, and glittering with malice. He downed it in one eye-watering gulp.

There appeared to be no effect. Invigilator Vermish held up a tremulous finger.

"Err, I'm sorry about being so indecisive, it's just that all the options look sort of... deadly. It's kind of hard to pick."

Jory nutted him. It was a perfect, street-brawling, down and dirty

'Grailish Kiss', which popped the little thief's nose like a strawberry hit with a hammer. Zoltan Creagle would have wept tears of pure joy as Vermish went down in a heap. His pet rat abandoned hat, and legged it down the sewer.

"Now that's going to be hard to pick," he said, completely of something else's volition. Then the potion took him, and everything changed.

Shadows stretched away from the walls, plucked up like spiderwebs in a draught. They attenuated, sucking away from the brickwork with a sound like harp strings snapping. Every last one flapped in toward Jory Foxmallet at once, an impossible flock of them, circling in to settle on his cape and his cowl.

What lurched up from inside this sudden storm of darkness was taller, more jagged, its silhouette bulging with muscle and spikes. It was utterly black - except for a tiny cut-out of mouth and chin, set in a determined frown. Two blank white eyes narrowed, as two fists crushed the handles of what now appeared to be arm-long iron clubs.

"I am the night!" growled this apparition, for no good reason, before sweeping its cape around in a dramatic flurry.

Unfortunately for the remainder of Vermish's merry band, there was a baton as thick as a wrestler's arm behind it. A collection of concussions followed, with a sound like someone playing the scales on a piano stuffed with eiderdown. Thieves fell, senseless.

Then it was the turn of the flytrap Scrawl. The Grimshadow dropped his batons, and rolled the kinks out of his suddenly waist-thick neck. Then he threw a handful of sharp, soot-blackened shuriken, which neatly lopped off all three of the creature's trap-jaws. It howled, static and scribbles budding in the air as it tried to reform them. But it was too late. The Grimshadow fired a small crossbow, armed with a grappling spike, and this punched clean through the Scrawl's chest, hooking it like a fish.

It thrashed like one too, trying to fight the pull of those improbably big muscles, but Jory's frown was now a tooth-gritted grimace of determination.

"Come and taste my dark and brooding justice, evildoer!" growled the ſuper-hero formerly known as Foxmallet, his cape flaring out like a pair of nightmare wings.

"Ooooh, that's not fair! You're not supposed to be able to just put your head back on!" complained Slag Iron, to something in the shadows.

Then the second Scrawl - the one-armed gorilla - hit him like a runaway oxcart full of anvils.

Now, it doesn't matter how much grit and angst you possess when something like that comes calling. The Grimshadow folded up like the world's most gothic umbrella, slamming hard against the tunnel wall, with a cloud of brick-dust and a puff of smoke that formed the letters 'whump!' in his wake.

Amid the blur, that horrible bloated arm came pistoning back once, twice, thrice, landing blows that could have driven the foundations of buildings. It's uncertain how much of that kind of punishment even a juiced-up ſuper could take.

However, we'll never know, because something caught the Scrawl's fist on the final backswing, bending its arm so hard that bones creaked like green kindling.

"Say hello to his little friend," said Slag Iron, now also full to the brim with alchemical nastiness, and ready to share it about. "That was bloody impolite, that trick with your head. When I chop up a haddock, it don't melt back together again! That's offensive, that is. Stay dead!"

She was no taller, but now all kinds of extra vents, tubes and strange gleaming chrome weapons jutted from every inch of her suit, allowing the Auntie Marjorie to hover in the air on twin jets of fire. Great metal pushrods and clamps had unfolded from her arm where it gripped the Scrawl, enabling her to crush its fist in one mechanical claw. The other hand...

"This might get a bit noisy," advised Slag iron, as a rocket booster sprouted from her elbow, coughing to life. It fired up, helping her swing the entire bulk of the Guild Tenebral's huge Tamarin Bell.

Under its skin of madness and power, the Scrawl was, really, just a big, demented gladiator. It may have been able to re-attach its head, after Slag Iron had severed it neatly with a single blow. But several tonnes of brass bell were another thing entirely.

The Tamarin bell rung out it's clear, pure note as it utterly crushed the Scrawl from existence, sending curls and wisps of hashed-out static flying. There was a nasty wet crimson splatter too, but most of the dead Scrawl was buried three spans deep in the tunnel floor by the impact alone.

"Ask not for whom the bell tolls," grated the Grimshadow, brushing himself off. It seemed that the worst the Scrawl had done was dirty up his costume. Against all odds, this sub-par witticism caused him to crack a tiny smile.

"And then there was one," replied Slag Iron, spinning in the air to focus the light of her green eye-slits on the last remaining Scrawl.

It hissed in the light, budding more flytrap-mouths on the end of more tentacles, and it crouched, ready to leap. Slag Iron and the Grimshadow looked at each other, and nodded.

"Those one-liners really didn't synchronise, did they? Do you think we'll get better with practice?"

"Lad, I don't want there to be any practice. We'll get this out of the way, then get back to normal life, thank you kindly!"

Here it came. An impossible blur bristling with spikes and snapping mouths, lithe and deadly.

And here came the ſuper-heroes' response. A spinning kick from each, one to the right, one to the left, their heels impacting the thing's chest side by side as it flew. For an instant, trap-jaw heads and glassy fangs stretched, snapping shut a split whisper from both their faces.

Then the Scrawl was blasted backwards, trailed by green sparks and a crackling explosion that spelled out 'SMAP!' It struck that luminous, improbable title dead centre, shattering the words, and went right through. In the stuttering glow, Slag Iron saw what had happened; Gloom's creature now hung impaled on the tunnel wall, wicked shards of title piercing it in a hundred places.

There was no remorse in her heart. None in the Grimshadow's slitted white eyes, either. This wasn't a time for ambiguity, it was a time for crisp shades of black and white - like the thick lines which flowed around them both, simplifying their features, filling in their colours with a haze of tiny dots...

The Grimshadow struck first, picking up a large, curved fragment of the title, its light sputtering and fading out. Its edge, however, was as sharp as imagination. He brought the blade around in a blur, and neatly severed the thing's head. This time Slag Iron left nothing to chance – green fire welled up in the throats of all her weapons, and a flurry of blasts crisped the thing to ashes before it hit the ground.

More curls and jags of darkness, twisting out of existence. More blood and bone beneath, warped out of recognition by Gloom's power.

Slag Iron's green light faded, sending the darkness crowding back in. She slumped against the wall as the alchemical potion wore off, strange and impossible mechanisms slotting back into her armour until it was, once again, just the field-plate of a Phoraxian battle nun. She reached up and unclasped her helmet, revealing beneath a red-cheeked and round little face, with a tattoo of an anchor under one eye, amid a network of careworn creases and lines. Around her mouth, they crinkled up into a smile.

"Yeah, bugger that for a game of soldiers," said Auntie Marjorie, letting her helmet clatter to the ground. "I get the horrible feeling that potion's going to give us both the wind something chronic. I've got no place getting ſuper-powered at my time of life."

Foxmallet slid down the wall beside her, his cape pooling in his lap like... well, like slightly soiled velvet, now that the potion had worn off.

"It was fun though, wasn't it? You've got to admit, when that thing came flying in... and then whap! And pow! And you were all like..."

Marjorie grinned. It was as if someone had drawn a happy jack-o-lantern on a very wrinkly apple.

"Oh, of *course* it was fun, boy! Of course it was. But like most kinds of fun, there's the morning after. At least this type of fun, we've both got all of our clothes on, eh?"

Jory Foxmallet blushed the kind of blush which young strapping men only experience when they realise that people their granny's age must have had quite a lot of sex, back in the distant past - and that (horribly) they might get up to a bit in the present day, as well. This didn't stop him from fishing a twist of copper wire and crystal from out of one ear... a fartalker's artifex which Zolt Creagle usually used to whisper sweet gambling odds into the ears of his fighters. He raised it to his lips and gave it a tap with one finger.

"All units, all units, this is Team Dark Night Falcon Alpha Force... *yes, alright, bloody lay off me, you daft harridan!* Fine! This is Team Green One."

There was a pause, as someone at the other end replied, their voice all high and miniaturised. Marjorie put her slapping hand down. Jory rolled his eyes.

"*There, I used the boring name, are you happy now?* We have the bell. Repeat, Team Green One is status, gold..."

21

The Naked Flame and The Atomic Fop in – Temple of Terror!

SOTO SCALIZARI WAS not a religious man.

This was why he got such a nasty surprise when he burst through the doors of the Temple of Pleasures, home and high tabernacle of the Demon-God Quazirath, burning head to toe with green flames and stark bollock naked.

If he'd been a man of spiritual learning, or a devotee of the Quaziran faith, like the dear departed Multhazar Florian Threck, he would have known that the inner sanctum of the Temple was carved into the semblance of a pink and white grotto, step-sided and steaming, layered with soothing hot mineral baths, and hung all about with silks depicting the seven thousand, four hundred and two Ecstatic Couplings (of gossip and fable).

He would also have known that this hallowed space, as wide across as the Brute Pits on Ramurthagan Street, was kept smoky day and night with fragrant censers hung on chains of gold, and that it was the demesne of no less than a thousand sacred temple prostitutes, both male and female, who were eager to fervently share the gospel of the Debauched One.

People came from all over Jansamrana, and indeed, the wider Arch' to learn the sacred arguments these worthies had for the worship of exalted Quazirath; some (perhaps the more slow on the uptake) came several times a week.

As the scripture of the demon-god tells us – *'we are forged from flesh, and in flesh we experience all; with flesh we pleasure flesh and thus commune with the greater plan of the divine'.*

You'd think that was simple enough to wrap one's head around, with only the minimal of repetition, but who is to judge the paths that others take to higher wisdom? Why, I myself, your humble narrator, have often....

(Note – twenty-two pages of lewd ramblings have been excised here by the order of the Chamber Fendant of the Morality Department, University of Jansamrana, for the purpose of preserving the mental hygiene of the public at large. Signed, Bligo Slappense, Lord Redactor Superior)

Soto was still surprised. A thousand pairs of eyes stared back at him, then down, then back up again. A thousand very attractive naked people in pools of steaming hot water waved and smiled.

"I was thinking of callin' myself Powdered Lightning, what with all this makeup, see, but perhaps people might think it's a drug reference..." said Montmortimer, nearly walking right into the back of him. This would have been a terrible shame, as he might have singed what was, even for the World's Fastest Fop, an eyeball-popping confection of a costume.

From his cherry-red leather high heeled boots to his candy-striped hose, up to a diamond encrusted codpiece, lace garters, a slashed, ruffled, silk-lined velvet doublet and a long jacket covered in pearls and hand-stitched thread-of-gold angels, Monty looked like a cartoon renaissance gigolo made real. His swords hung low and louche from a belt crusted in emeralds, and his wig was a sky-scraping concoction of white billows with an entire clock in the middle, giving his head, on its wide lacy ruff, the impression of a rakishly handsome cream pudding.

"People!" hissed Soto, waving back. "Nude people! Lots of 'em!"

Monty flicked a pair of opera glasses from a pocket and peered through the scented mist.

"Mmmmmm. Quite the selection. Temple prostitutes, I suppose. Though the real point of interest would be the demon, really."

Soto, who had been thoroughly entranced by all the curvaceous alternatives, hadn't really been looking too hard down at the centre of the temple. Down where something now rose up to its full height, brandishing a loofah on a stick like a magisterial sceptre, as its wings unfurled.

"Oi! If you're not here for the orgy, dearies, then at least tell me you've brought more champagne?"

Here's the thing about the Demon-God Quazirath. He might not peddle the most numinous and spiritual form of religious faith, and he might be a bit vague on morality, the afterlife, karma, the great cycle of time and the inner mysteries of the soul. But you got what it said on the biscuit tin, and (reassuringly) he often actually turned up, unlike other, more mystic deities.

Thus, it was well known that Quazirath was a gender-fluid, twelve-foot-tall entity which could manifest as either a male or female apparition (or both at once for special occasions). He (for today, noted Soto, the Demon-God was undeniably in his masculine guise) sported long, curving horns of mother of pearl, great leathery batwings shimmering with a pattern like peacock feathers, and no less than six eyes, all bright summer-sky blue except for one, which was green.

No clothes though. They were, as Soto noted with a twinge of embarrassment, as missing as his own.

"O...orgy?" he managed, in a voice that cracked near the end of the word.

Quazirath shrugged.

"Well, we were going to play bingo and have a sing-song and some biscuits, but seeing as we're all naked, we thought, why not? You're welcome to jump in, especially if you really did bring some champagne." Quazirath's smile was wide, genuine, and as beguiling as a three-foot high sundae to a dieter in the desert.

In truth, this creature was no God at all, in the true sense, or even the made-up theological one. He had once been the *genius loci* of a small mineral geyser by the shore of Jansamrana, who'd found that wandering shepherds responded much more readily to the old 'satyr and dryad show' than a burning shrub barking moral tenets at them.

Consequently, his power had grown, and soon he had a small temple, which was eventually swallowed up by the city of Grand Sepulchre. In all honesty, he'd been put there to offer a raunchy side-quest to some adventurers a few thousand years ago, but they'd gone and gotten rascally drunk instead, and so Quazirath blatantly claimed divine power, and built a religion around a few of his favourite things.

That's why Soto and Monty found him in the bath, being attended to by some his Devoted; a cadre of pleasure-seekers who'd found that while other faiths promised glory and leisure in the afterlife, Quazirath could keep you looking and feeling eighteen years old in the here and now. And all for simply enjoying oneself in a way which the Creedish, for example, called horrible sin, but which the average person was prepared to buy vast quantities of surreptitiously printed magazines about.

There was a sudden rustling sound, and Soto turned to find Monty hopping on one leg, trying to take his boot off. He'd already hung his jacket on a peg which was, on second inspection, part of a statue which... oh gods! Yes, that's what it was alright.

The little herbalist raised one blazing green eyebrow. Monty popped the boot off and gestured with it.

"You don't have to ask *me* twice, matey. I mean, we could be looking at the end of the world in a few hours, and you take the rough with the smooth, I always say."

In the context, this turn of phrase brought certain images wobbling to the front of Soto's mind.

"Are you *mad?* That Gloom bastard is going to be here any second, and you're getting your kit off?"

"When in Phoraxia..." shrugged the Fop, unclipping his ruff. "After all, most of my life up until I met you lot was fashion, debauched parties, and booze. Why not enjoy one more before the final curtain? In any case, Gloom isn't going to win this one. There's an *actual God* here."

Soto mulled this over. As he did so, a damp hand slapped one of his buttocks from behind, sizzling. There was a ripple of laughter as he turned, brandishing one finger.

"Right! Who did that? I'll have you know this is a very serious situation! There's a mad, powerful creature called Gloom stealing all the bells in the city, and if he does, *blam*, no more Malevolith, and I expect half of Jansamrana as well! So, is it *just remotely* possible that you people could stop thinking below the waist and consider letting us *stop him?*"

Quazirath hoisted one perfect eyebrow, over a whole row of eyes.

"So, you two are questing heroes, stumbled into a temple of sinful pleasures and perils? Nice role play! I'll tell you what. Let's make a deal."

Soto's eyes narrowed.

"What kind of a deal?"

Quazirath sat down on the edge of a bath-pool, gesturing idly with his loofah.

"The kind where I, the eternal Demon-God, smite your enemy quite roughly with this loofah, thus preventing that... umm... whatever plan you're both tangled up in, frankly, it sounds stiflingly boring. Here, on my hallowed ground... I mean, you know, in my hallowed bath, I don't think he'll stand much of a chance."

"And what do you want in return?" asked Soto. A very ruffled, ornate silk shirt came flying past over his shoulder.

The Demon-God shrugged.

"That's the fun part. You seem to be in a bit of a pinch, so I guess I can ask you to do whatever I want. Whatever... (and here he winked, salaciously) ... **I desire. But if you fail to complete my task, you are bound to join my merry band, here, because let's face it, the one in makeup is quite handsome, and you're just so uptight I feel you could use a few hundred years of relaxation. Deal?"**

Soto dithered. The little bead of crystal in his ear buzzed and whispered.

"It's going to have to be something that can get done in the next ten minutes," he conceded. "Gloom, whether you think you can take him or not, has already put his plan in motion... he's on his way."

Quazirath clapped his hands together.

"Oooooh, the ticking clock! I love it! You really do have a knack for these kinky scenarios, don't you? Very well! Do you accept my wicked, demonic wager?"

"Well, when you put it like that..."

Monty tapped the clock in his wig.

"Alright! Fine! Damn this bloody compulsion to do the heroic thing! Yes, we accept!"

Quazirath's eyes blazed with blue and purple fire. He began to laugh, a low, menacing chuckle which rose to proper demonically malicious tones as he unfurled his wings, patterns pulsing fractal and vivid thereupon.

"Bwaaahahaaaahaaa! Yes! Now, know your doom, mortals, for you have been ensnared by the master of trickery, the Lord of Lewdness, the Sultan of Sin, the, ummm... Viscount of Vice, yeah, that's about right." He gestured with his loofah, and a giant, ornate hourglass appeared, purple sand slithering through two voluptuous globes. **"See all of my lovely tapestries? To avoid a century of salacious servitude, you must...** (and here he waggled his eyebrows, clearly very self-satisfied) **perform every last one of the seven thousand, four hundred and two Ecstatic Couplings within the next ten minutes! Any help you need will be enthusiastically provided."**

"Of gossip and fable?" stammered Soto. A cadre of very determined young libertines began advancing on him through the steam.

"The very same," leered Quazirath.

Just as it looked as if certain peril was about to overcome poor Soto Scalizari, a small thunderclap split the air right behind him. He turned, just in time to see a tiny glass bottle hit the floor and roll away, sparkling green droplets evaporating into mist.

Montmortimer Pettigrew wiped his lips with the back of his hand, smearing lipstick across one powdered cheek. He gently lifted the wig from his head and placed it on a naked statue; it was the second-to-last item of evening wear left to his name. As he did so, Soto saw a blur around him, as if the air was boiling, or the Atomic Fop was made up of millions of slightly different images, all layered one atop the other through glass.

It was the essence of pure speed. It was the shadow of a force that could bend and stretch time around itself like melted cheese.

There was a very definite, very loud double-click, as of buckles coming undone. And...

"Hold my codpiece," grated Monty, holding out that diamond-studded item for Soto to grab[51].

The Demon-God's six eyes grew wide, as the whole temple held its breath.

And then something happened which is so censored, the original version of this manuscript caught fire even before the scribe could put his quill down.

---

51. There's no word in Urzoman for the combination of fervent righteousness which crumbles into sudden disgust, of the kind that Soto Scalizari felt at that moment. In High Zollish, the term is 'gefühlganzsiegreichzuseinabergleichzeitigauchganzangewidert', but it's only known by about three philosophers

22
The Jolly Tale of Mister Bun Bun

IT WAS A wonderful mild summer evening, and all was right with the world, so Mister Bun Bun thought he'd hippity-hop all the way down the road to the Ironbelly Gaol, where his cheerful chums were planning a delightful surprise party.

"What fun!" Thought Mister Bun Bun, in a thought bubble which had its own border of rainbows and little twinkly stars. "Won't everyone be jolly pleased to see me? I do hope there'll be lashings of lemonade and gingerbread biscuits."

He paused outside the big black iron-studded gates of the Gaol, which loomed up over him like... well, precisely like a gigantic impenetrable wall of metal, in fact.

"And I *do* hope there'll also be merry songs, and charades and... what was that other thing?" he put his little chin in one little paw, and thought for a second.

"Aha! That's right – flesh-rippingly horrible violence! Off we go!"

Ignoring how his thoughts bobbled away as little clouds raining a drizzle of blood, Mister Bun Bun loaded a very special round into his crossbow. It was a quarrel connected to a tailor's spool wound up tight with very thin piano wire; the kind which makes the highest and twinkliest notes. He fired it up over the gatehouse, where his beady little eyes, sticking out through his costume next to a pair of sewn-on buttons, had spotted the flare of a cigarette being lit in the darkness.

"Silly old guard!" he thought. "Smoking is *very* bad for the constitution, and can lead to all manner of horrid complications!"

So it was that five inches of barbed brass quarrel punched clean through the guard's throat, saving him from certain death by emphysema, which was *very* thoughtful of Mister Bun Bun, wasn't it children?

Down went the guard, roll-up toppling from his bluish lips, hands scrabbling at his neck as he fell off the gatehouse walk. And up went

Mister Bun Bun, stubby little pink-plush legs running up the wall, just as a second guard popped out of the sentry house, a blackpowder blunderbuss in his hands.

"Derek! Oi, Derek! Yer soups going... hey, wait a minute!"

Oh dear! Mister Bun Bun was supposed to avoid murdering anyone who didn't deserve it, but this was sometimes so very, very difficult. Humans were infuriating creatures, what with their confounding lack of limbs and eyes and colours... he reasoned that they were simply *so* dull that killing one or two wouldn't matter. There was precious little to tell them apart, and they were frightfully poorly constructed, the silly floppy bags of organs!

Mister Bun Bun sprung to the top of the wall, gripping his crossbow in a pair of snippy little claws that punched through the ends of his costume's paws. And then he jumped again, looping around the poor guard's neck, just as his former colleague came up tight on the other end of the wire.

There was a certain little sound; a cross between a champagne bottle being uncorked and a knife through a fresh crisp cabbage.

"Oh, bother and fiddlesticks," said Mister Bun Bun, whose thought bubbles appeared to have been heavily censored. "Arterial spray is always *so* very difficult to get out of velveteen. Never mind, though. Things might just get worse before they get better."

With that thought he stepped away from the wall, leaving a little two-foot-high rabbit shape sketched out in clean grey bricks. All around it was dripping crimson.

A severed head, wearing a very surprised expression, landed in a begonia patch, two streets away. Down went the happy little pink bunny rabbit, skippity-hopping off a swinging dead body on the end of a long wire, its face turning a lovely shade of purple. Down to the inner yard of the Gaol, where waited the lockway, and the Belly itself.

Now, Mister Bun Bun's friend Amber had told him all about the Gaol, and why it was a bad idea for little bunny rabbits to stray there. What she *hadn't* told him (because she didn't know) was that Grand Sepulchre's prison was built from the liquid deuterium tank of a Slaad-zukarii Doom Cruiser, a kind of spaceship which had crashed here so long ago that the things which had made it had since evolved into beings of pure energy and light.

Nobody on the Arch' knew this; but the Civic Power had use for a great big metal sphere, nearly a half-mile round, which bulged up out of the ground, ageless, rust-streaked and cold. It had but one main door, the great round lockway, which was powered by water wheels, and inside lurked all the do-badders and wicked nasties who were so evil, killing them just risked them coming back as undead.

Atop the Belly was a little stone tower, an add-on built during Sarunjek times. From here, baskets of food were lowered into the prison, and the Warden himself kept watch, peering down a great brass upside-down periscope to watch the villains within. It was this tower which held the Dead Man's Bells, those great tubular chimes which rang out the midnight Octal.

Here was the problem for a little bunny rabbit, however. The Warden's Folly, as it was called, was accessible only by airship. Which meant that the only way in, was *through*...

Mister Bun Bun took a running jump at the big lever which opened the lockway, hitting it about halfway up, so that it teetered and wobbled and finally swung over. Wooden gears clunked and bamboo pipes sputtered, as water began to flow over a set of giant mill-wheels, spinning up a series of chains and gears.

In front of the lockway stood a bank of bleachers, all warped wood and snaggly nails. It had been built to hold forty naval cannons, which were usually primed and manned whenever the Ironbelly was opened. This way, Lord Slave used to be able to biff people in, without the phenomenally wicked contents of the Gaol spilling out. As the lockway rumbled open, a gaggle of cannoneers spilled out of their barracks, most of them in their underwear (and many steaming drunk).

"What's going on?" called a voice from inside, where several officers had remained.

"It's alright!" shouted one burly powder-packer, squinting toward the lock. "It's that little stuffed rabbit of Lord Slave's. Remember he always used to bring it along with him?"

"Wait! What? Was that thing *alive* the whole time?"

"Seems so," reported a grizzled siege engineer, tugging at his beard. "And it looks pretty determined, too."

"Do you think any of the prisoners are going to get out?"

The engineer took a good hard look at Mister Bun Bun, who was advancing across the scarred-up ground in front of the lockway like a tiny, one-rabbit ice age.

"There's 148 gruesome killers in there, and they've only gotten meaner since we locked 'em down," he agreed. "Still... there's something about that bunny, right? Would *you* want to get in its way?"

A huddle of cannoneers shook their heads, muttered, rubbed their ears and shuffled their feet.

"Right then. Krevan, you go and pull the lever to close the lock once he's gone inside. And we say nothing about this to nobody, right?"

So it was that the great metal circle of the lockway clanged shut behind Mister Bun Bun, just as something raggedy black and horrible kicked in the gates of the Gaol's outer ward, and was met by a flight of inexperienced but horribly enthusiastic battle wizards coming the other way. Soon guards and cannoneers were running hither and yon screaming, some of them on fire.

But the mechanisms which opened and shut the lock were slow and ponderous. It would take hours to build up enough water pressure to do it again, and in the meantime Gloom's scrawls and the fightin' spell-slingers of the old UC would have to wait.

Or, more likely, fight like baboons in a bag of broken glass.

Nevertheless, it was a happy occasion for Mister Bun Bun, who was all alone inside the Ironbelly, with nothing but those aforementioned 148 supernaturally gifted killers for company.

This, he thought, racking the slide on his crossbow, *was going to be a merry adventure indeed.*

The opening of the lockway always brought out a gaggle of prisoners to see what fresh meat may have landed, blinking, in the darkness. Among those who watched from behind a yellow-painted line on the floor (the line beyond which one could not even wiggle a toe, lest the cannons start firing) was Crolton Cludger, the so-called South End Strangler, who, in here was among the lowest of the low.

Part of the Number 29 Gang, Cludger was merely a mass murderer with a little bit of supernatural strength behind him, thanks to some forbidden tattoos. This, on the scale of vice on display within the 'Belly, was about as fearsome as three counts of very polite shoplifting. The boss of the Number 29s, for example, had voluntarily become possessed by a Greater Spiked Necrodemon, and could enslave people as rotting zombies.

So, when the Boss told scum like Crolton Cludger to jump, they proceeded to put atmosphere between their size twelves and the concrete. Like the ſuper-heroes out there on this prickly, disconcerting night, he had a little fartalker's crystal in his ear, allowing him to report back to his demon-ridden master, high in the shanty-pile which clustered at the 'Belly's core.

"It... it looks like a *little bunny rabbit*, chief," he stammered, hardly believing it himself. "Yeah, I can see the ears and all. It's a pink one, wif a... ohhhh, right, yeah, it might just be! Never thought it was *alive* though, boss. Slavey always just used to carry it, apart from the time he threw it at old Slugford and broke his nose."

The erstwhile Strangler squinted, as a score of other curious, inquisitive and downright horrible inmates peered out from behind barrels and boxes along the yellow-daubed perimeter.

"Sumfing wrong about it, though. Yes, aside from the fact it's walkin' about like a live one, y'honour. It's sort of... well... I mean, it's got a little crossbow. And now it's pullin' out a couple of knives..."

It was never going to have taken long, really. Some of the people (to loosely deploy the term) who inhabited the Ironbelly were severely lacking in the impulse control department. So, when one of the watchers yelled - *"Get the little bastard!"*

It didn't take long for a wild-eyed and wiry figure in rags to hurdle the barricade and run, screaming, at poor Mister Bun Bun, a spiked length of timber held high.

Let's just remind ourselves, at this point, that our cotton-tailed little hero is, in fact, a mutated mantis shrimp, kicked up the evolutionary ladder by a power out of the wrong side of magic. And that even *before* drinking the horrid little bottle of goop which his friend Amber had given him, he'd been equipped by nature to punch clean through steel.

There was a terrible, splintering crunch.

There was a moment when nothing moved, except for the spray of blood and shattered teeth which burst from the unfortunate prisoner's mouth. Then came a sound like a hacksaw going through a bunch of bananas, and Mister Bun Bun appeared through a hole in the man's back, his glittering zipper mouth pulled back in a fierce smile.

The man who'd advised 'getting the little bastard' tried to roll his one remaining eye across to take a peek at the crossbow quarrel stuck in the other; then the poison kicked in, and his face slid off the front of his skull, bubbling, like an egg off a skillet.

"Oh, dear. I think I'm going to be sick," said Crolton Cludger, for the edification of his boss. "I reckon we might want to sit this out, because.... *urggh!*"

A tinny little voice buzzed in the Strangler's ear while his head described a bloody parabola, spinning slowly to take in a truly horrid last image – twenty-two distinct and bloody chunks of people flying out in a semicircle, as a pink-plush nightmare dropped back down to the ground in a perfect ſuper-hero pose.

"Let's be best friends!" said Mister Bun Bun, in the kind of quavering, crackly recorded voice often adopted by pull-string toys. Then Crolton Cludger remembered that his torso was regrettably too far away to have anything as useful as a neck, and he passed from mortality to the choirs eternal.[52]

A short time later, after the screaming stopped, Mister Bun Bun found himself at the very tippy-top of the shantytown pile in the middle of the Ironbelly. Right under the spot where the Warden and his men let down the bucket on its chain to deliver food, medicine, and fresh sets of orange pyjamas to the inmates.

This would no longer be much of a problem, as very few of them had bothered to try to surrender. To be fair, some had only had the time it takes for a knife thrown at supersonic speeds to pierce their eyeballs, in which to fly the proverbial white flag.

Behind a big metal door, the leader of the Number 29 Gang waited behind his desk, a single painstakingly accrued brace of blunderbuss pistols in his hands. His second-in-command, a large and armoured woman named Beliza Pugh, had just come running in through the door and slammed it behind her, shooting all three of the wrist-thick bolts.

Now she was flattened to the steel, her panicked breath misting the toughened glass porthole riveted in at head-height.

Boss 29 had never seen his majordomo in such a state. Wide eyes, cold sweat, spatters of gore... This was all the more disconcerting for the fact that Boss 29 had once seen 'Bloody Beliza' disembowel two Throne's Shadow soldiers with her bare hands, then proceed to tie their guts together and hang them over a flagpole. To be honest, the pair of pistols were as much for *her*, as for whatever had been making all those horrid noises outside.

"It's coming! Boss, it's *coming!*" Beliza hissed, in a horrible, cracked voice. "We've got to hide! We've got to *run!* Up the chain! We always had plans for getting up there, right? Nobble the Warden, hijack the airship, you and me, eh?"

Well, that was that, then. The hardened killer Boss 29 knew was gone, replaced by a babbling and terrified wreck. He felt, for a moment, a twinge of jealousy... and then the reason why slammed up against the glass, button eyes glittering. A plush paw waved merrily.

---

52. This is often a euphemism for going to heaven, but, as poor Mr Cludger absolutely hated singing, and got migraine headaches from harp music, it was, in this case, a very specific kind of hell.

"Let's invite all our pals to a tea party!" said Mister Bun Bun, from deep within the dented speaker in his chest.

But the top dog of the Ironbelly had a stronger constitution than most.

"Is it behind the rabbit?" he asked, dry as a liquid nitrogen martini.

"It IS the rabbit!" screamed Beliza, just before a pink velveteen paw came slamming through the porthole beside her, and death came with it.

Boss 29 watched with a sort of professional detachment as Mister Bun Bun chopped his majordomo's head off, twin knives coming together like a pair of hydraulic shears. Then he fired both pistols, noting, in a kind of slow-motion haze, how Mister Bun Bun dodged and twisted around the twin blasts of flying buckshot, nails and missing teeth. Finally, as the furry pink missile landed on his desk, he reached up with both hands and ripped open his shirt, revealing (instead of the expected rug of chest hair) a hideous scaly demon face, snoring and drooling.

"Oi! Wake up! We've got trouble to attend to!" said the criminal kingpin, prodding his parasitic demon with one finger. The thing snorted, blinked, and smacked its horrible thin lips.

"Ere? Wot? Wazzit this time, human? Oh, let me guess? You need me to help you make more mindless zombie slaves to do your evil bidding, in exchange for their immortal souls, kinda thing?"

Boss 29 gave it another prod.

"Eyes front, you brimstone bastard. It's the rabbit. It's gotta go."

The demon, whose name was Xyalthagar, was not quite awake, and in not too wonderful a mood. But his eyes popped open in shock as he saw the blood-drenched little creature stalking across the desk toward his human host, a foot-long knife in each fuzzy paw.

Xyalthagar had seen evil. Hells, he *was* evil, a solid turd of wickedness incarnate, plopped out of the seventh nether-hell of the wailing sorrows, to foment terror and pain across the Arch'. But there was something about those button eyes, and the glittering slash of that zipper mouth...

"No bloody fear mate, you're on your own..." he managed, hastily preparing the words of a Spell of Banishment for himself.

He wasn't quick enough.

Mister Bun Bun leapt at him knives-out, glittering points at their tips mirroring reflections in the demon's dark eyes. Razor edges dimpled ectoplasmic jelly. Those gleaming sparks met up, kissed, *exploded...*

And Boss 29, who was having a very bad evening, was suddenly converted into a living portal to the seventh nether-hell, his flesh and bones twisted out into impossible angles to form the gateway. A spire of red-hot flame, spawned purely from the fevered imaginations of priests, punched up through the portal, up through the top of the Ironbelly, and caused the poor Lord Warden's tower to explode in all directions, raining superheated bricks across the docklands.

Somewhere amongst all that, a tiny pink figure spun through the air, paws wrapped grimly around a metal bell. This instrument was tall and thin, and depicted a certain popular figure with a scythe and, let's say, a certain lack of choice when it came to facial expressions.

Down below, the gateyard of the Gaol was in ruins, as wizards, scrawls, guards and a freshly arrived contingent of battle nuns belted the everloving custard out of each other. Other parts of the city appeared to be on fire, too.

Nevertheless, Mister Bun Bun smiled. He'd had *such* a lovely time, and his jolly little adventure had been a success.

Now, if only he'd land on something nice and soft...

23

Th Doub e ision and T e Unstoppa le It face – The T w ring Innuendo!

"I REALLY DON'T think you should have knocked holes in that signage," complained one half of Billiam Knox, clenched tight in a blue fist the size of a cottage. "Someone obviously made it just for us, and floated it all the way up here to... *urk! Look out!*"

A Scrawl came hissing in, vast ink-blot wings flapping ragged. Claws sliced through the air, and the Unstoppable It roared, swinging Billiam like a very dizzy, nauseous human truncheon. The back of the giant blue monster's hand cracked into the scrawl, sending it spinning out of control, a broken umbrella of a thing. It struck the title full-on, knocking out another row of letters, which flickered and died like sputtering fireworks.

The *other* Knox clung tight to the rain-slippery stones of the Lord Governor's Tower, trying not to think about all the empty atmosphere between him and the ground. There were ten Scrawls swooping and bombing them still, despite several accurately lobbed letters. Up above, Bill could hear more of them worrying away at the bell-chains.

The tower itself just kept going; it had been built onto and buttressed, bricked and spackled, attenuated and stretched by every single one of the old Lord Governors of the Urzoman Empire, those skull-helmeted and black-armoured old men with their impressive sideburns and outrageous mustachios. They'd been trying to rival the Malevolith, in some political statement or other, but what they'd achieved was the Towering Innuendo alluded to in the title; a phallic architectural corkscrew of rickety hopefulness, spiralling up into the air over the boroughs of Fungal Crevice and Knightsbottom.

This mish-mash of tottering stone was easy enough to climb, especially if there were two of you, and you had a bit of ſuper-human vitality in a small bottle to lean on.

Unfortunately, it seemed to be even easier to climb when you were giant, blue, and the size of a church. The Unstoppable It had not expected to just keep growing when he slugged back his little vial of potion, but grow he had – and now here they were, near the big bulbous bell-end of the tower, being dive-bombed by flying horrors.

"Do you kind of feel that this has gotten a *bit* out of hand?" asked the Double Vision, clenched in the Unstoppable one's fist. "I mean, there's a sense, and I don't know if you're feeling it too... but this whole scenario seems to be quite contrived. Sort of like it's *supposed* to happen..."

Tarrence Blight turned his huge, grimacing face toward Billiam and roared, a hurricane of halitosis snapping the cape of his costume out like a pennant. There was a mad jangle and blur to everything now, and the sense that every single colour was made up of thousands of tiny dots. The monstrous It declined further discussion; instead, hand over massive hand, he shimmied even higher up the tower, fending off scrawls as he went.

Lightning flickered, capering about the weathervanes below on spindly stick-legs. Thunder grumbled in reply. And, as the Unstoppable It reached out to gently place at least half of Billiam Knox on the tower's top parapet, a flight of battle wizards joined the fray, their brethren on the ground lighting great sorcerous spotlights to transfix the tower.

"Definitely some kind of horrible deja vu..." went on Knox, as pointy-hatted men perched on broomsticks whizzed past, fireballs sizzling from their fingers. Bricks erupted near his head, many of them turning to doves and playing cards in mid-air. Some of the wizards met a scrawl in mid-flight, and blood gouted, followed by screams, and the sound of broom handles snapping like kindling.

But here came the big guns. Here came archmage Pilias Glockenheimer, master of the Nine Reeds, riding atop a magic carpet of Khantifi origin and great antiquity. The carefully stitched patterns of the soaring shag-pile showed scenes which the Demon Quazirath would have heartily approved of, but tonight, Maestro Glockenheimer was about war, not love. He levered his wobbling bulk upright, causing the carpet to sag in the middle, and called up a great ball of ice and electricity between his pudgy hands, beard bristling. Both Bills were now atop the tower's roof, huddled together under the horizontal blast of the rain, teeth chattering, arms around each other's shoulders.

So, they had a grandstand view of the city, for an instant, before the morbidly obese arch-aeromancer struck.

It wasn't looking too cheery down there. The Halfway House was on fire. The streets around the Temple of Pleasures were thronged with regular, cash-in-hand prostitutes fighting the religiously motivated temple kind, and totally forgetting that they were meant to be looking for ſuper-heroes.

Meanwhile, a pitched battle raged around the Ironbelly, complete with engineers hastily building catapults and trebuchets out of demolished buildings. The towers of the old UC were lit up with spellfire, while someone appeared to have let loose the madmen from within the Sunken Garden, and the docklands were awash with sailors fighting Hammerheads, who were also fighting a gaggle of priests, who were (naturally) fighting among themselves.

All this Bill Knox took in, in a single instant, his gambler's brain attuned to the subtle flex and flow of pure luck like a crystal diode set. That was how he knew, when the Unstoppable It leaned out from the tower, that his had run out.

It was a perfect scene, snipped from some other universe and pasted slapdash across reality. A huge, raging monster, hanging from the top of a sky-scraping tower, batting at flying foes while searchlights slid across its bestial face...

Then the moment stretched tight and snapped. The Unstoppable It's huge hand came down, slapping Pilias Glockenheimer from the air. His carpet went into a spin, pink smoke billowing from its rear tassels. It orbited the Lord Governor's tower once, twice, falling as it circled, slipping between buttresses and skimming rows of gargoyles, until...

And

And...

"Ohhhh, that's not good. That *can't* be good," agreed the Double Vision with himself, as the whole rickety edifice lurched sideways. He looked down, four eyes peering into a cloud of smoke. There was a hole in the side of the tower big enough to fly a dragon through.

And now came gravity, playing catch-up. And now came the dawning light of comprehension across Tarrence Bligh's huge blue mug, like the sun rising over an acne-scarred wasteland.

"Hoooooold ooooon!" bellowed the giant, in slow motion...

And then the world pitched sideways, and the ground came rushing up to meet them all.

24
The Pugilist and the Honey Badger in – Daggers and Duplicity!

Things were certainly tense in the great, shadowy feasting hall of the Guild Lachrymose.

Part of this was because of the assassins who encircled the long table with its ever-crumbing banquet; two hundred black-clad killers, hefting a selection of oiled and wicked steel. Even more tension came from the fire which was licking hungrily at the lower storeys of the building, where a band of mercenaries were comprehensively failing to stop a trio of huge Scrawls.

Most of the tension, however, came from the four-way standoff atop the table itself. This involved a lot of metal, and a lot of exposed necks, and the kind of intense eye contact usually associated with very angry cats. The title hung above all this, glittering, casting rays of coloured light over the massed killers who packed the room, sweating in black velvet.

"So *that's* what they're calling you?" asked Lady Lachrymosa, making a tiny gesture with her chin. This was a most heroic decision, as a poisoned Chungdoji disembowelling knife and a pair of razored claws were tickling her jugular at the present moment. "Imaginative, if tacky. Aren't they those the giant smelly weasel things that always go for the... unmentionables?"

Zoltan Creagle, who was similarly locked in this four-way tangle of knives and limbs, gave a snort.

"Buy a dictionary, love. A pugilist means a *boxer*, dunnit? And I'm guessing that's what our man Gloom wants to call me, when I knock him down. Might make him feel a bit better about the loose teeth, and the shiner he's got coming."

Master Lurien, the third stand-offer, rolled his eyes. He wasn't about to try anything more ambitious; Lady Lachrymosa had him at quite the disadvantage, with a cavalry sabre between his legs. "I think she means the *honey badger*, Mister Creagle. It's a singularly vicious animal. I only know, because, like the common mongoose, it's somewhat immune to snake venom."

The Old Lady raised one perfectly sculpted eyebrow.

"So *now* you stick up for solidarity, you seditious little twerp," she hissed. "I thought you were double-crossing me."

"Oh, I am," said the master poisoner, with a cautious shrug. He winced, as a few hairs were pared from his throat by one of Amber's blades. "Fine old tradition in the Assassins, the double-cross."

"I should know," said Amber. "He's done it to me once already."

"With the best of intentions!" sighed Lurien. "If you'd simply killed that Grailish oaf when you were meant to..."

"Then we'd have a huge shark-faced wizard emperor to demortify, instead of a mad demigod? Nice work, Lurien." Lady Lachrymosa scanned what she could of the ranks of waiting assassins, pitching her voice so they could hear her. "Do any of you really still want to follow this upstart? Or think that Zoltan 'five spothins for a hotdog' Creagle is *really* going to pay you?"

Zoltan twitched the axe he had at Amber's throat.

"If I kill this one, I get all that lovely gold, chaps. Add that to the amount you know I've got already, and it's a nice big payday for those what can see it through."

"You utter bastard, Creagle!" growled Amber. "Double-crossing the whole team! That's low."

Zoltan smiled.

"In this company, it's not just low. It's *professional*. See, I figure, what better way to take over this city than with an army of hired killers? There's going to be a power vacuum when you poor saps and Gloom finish each other off, and take Himself with you."

"Ahem..." interjected Lurien. "I think you'll find that the majority of the brethren are on *my* side – you know, replacing the moribund old leadership with some fresh blood..."

"Poor choice of words," murmured the Old Lady. "Seeing as that's all that's likely to be left of you."

Amberelia wondered, for a second, if her healing powers included re-attaching her head. *It might be worth giving it a shot, just to shut them all up...*

"Well, I'm pretty certain that the learned ladies and gentlemen of the guild can see a bad idea when it's put in front of them" she countered. "And they can see that the city's going to hell out there. Without Grand Sepulchre, and civil society, there's no need for assassins. Just thugs and killers. I'm certain that the biggest faction are for helping us keep Gloom away from those bells."

"Ah yes," said the old Lady. "Your fairy tale. Well, let me tell you, young missy, I've heard a whole lot better in my time. All this nonsense about ſuper-villains and an exploding Malevolith and..."

"Then what's happening downstairs, Madam? *A Saint Guthran's eve masquerade?*"

Certainly, the floorboards were getting a bit crispy-warm underfoot. Smashing and bellowing sounds rung out, as mercenaries intermittently came flying out of the ground floor windows, ragdoll-bloody and dented.

"Right." said Zoltan Creagle. "Never let it be said that I'm not a man of swift decisiveness. Lurien, let's make an alliance. You as Master Lachrymose, me as Grand Vizier, or whatever title I can make them call me?"

There was a sudden ratcheting up of the tension, and in that heartbeat the Old Lady looked into the eyes of her least favourite apprentice.

"I hate you, and you hate me, Amberelia Chance. But at least that means we know where we stand. Alliance? At least 'til these two arrogant males are in their coffins?"

Amber had scarcely nodded, and there was a sudden flurry of weapons - knives and axes and sabres sliding and sparking. This left two uneasy factions facing each other across the ruins of a roast boar, the apple in its mouth all waxy and cobwebbed.

"Dammit, Creagle, you were only supposed to *pretend* to double-cross me!" spat Amber, her eyes flashing the colour of her name. It seemed that the claws growing from her wrists were even longer and sharper, too. The Pugilist shrugged.

"All's fair in love and war, or so they say. This kind of intimate little situation seems about six of one and a half dozen of the other. So..."

Lurien, however, seemed genuinely sad.

"You were always my favourite pupil, Chance," he sighed. "You weren't even that bad at chess, or the old chess metaphors. But the Guild must come first. If we're to survive tonight, it'll be by realising that half of assassination is about knowing when to slink away."

"I believe the word is *skulk*, coward," replied Amber. "So, which ones of you are with us? Who's not for skulking?"

The assassins gathered around the walls weighed up their choices. Hands took a firmer grip around the handles of a nasty little armoury of weapons.

"'Ere! I reckon this poisoner fella is gonna double-cross me, 'cause he's fancied you a bit all along," chuckled Zoltan, causing Master Lurien to blush beetroot red. "is that a chess metaphor?"

"I say! That's a bit much, sir..."

"Oh my Gods! I was just joking, son, but you're bloody *serious!*"

"And if Lurien and Amber were to double-cross us both, would an alliance between your cash and my authority be such a bad thing?" purred Lady Lachrymosa. "Purely theoretically, of course..."

Smoke was rising from between the floorboards now, and the tasselled edge of the hall's great carpet began to smoulder.

"Oh, *theoretical,* is it?" asked Amber. "What if me and old Creagle here have been playing the long game, and this is a double-double-cross?"

"Now, say that were the case, but really, it was myself and Lurien who were playing on your emotions to *pretend* that we were divided," said the Old Lady, smiling a prim little smile...

This could have gone on, one supposes, until the inferno below engulfed the whole Jade Palace – and it would have, too, had not two very important things happened at once.

First came a sound like the missile from a giant siege trebuchet falling in; a low whistle accompanied by a raw metallic howl. A whole roomful of assassins looked up as the sound tore across the unseen sky, behind a ceiling painted with baroque images of cherubs knifing each other for sacks of gold.

Then came the impact; a titanic clang, as of some Divinity hammering two saucepans together. The shimmering din was made up of two distinct notes; the clear, ringing voice of the Assassins' mosquito bell, and a bent-out-of-shape tone which sounded almost like...

The ceiling collapsed. Various double-crossers leapt clear, tucking and rolling as several tons of musical hardware, lately from atop the Ironbelly Gaol, came hammering down, bringing the tall slim tower of the Jade Palace with it. Plaster cherubs shattered, mouldering victuals and silver cutlery flew, and at least one assassin was pinned to the wall by flying flatware.

Amber blinked, and discovered to her horror that she'd actually blacked out for a heartbeat there. She found herself being dragged to her feet by a big, gold-ringed hairy hand, connected to the arm of Zoltan Creagle. He was talking, but his voice came in from far away, lost behind an echoing blur.

"... course I was only *pretending* to double-cross you, right?" he said, as the world came swinging back into focus. "It seemed like the only thing these assassins respect, in any case, so I figured, Zoltan, you're in for a spothin, get in for a whole gold crown..."

Amber pushed away from him, looking out through the windows, through a solid curtain of fire. Out there, the second very important thing was just about to happen.

"Save your breath," she managed to croak, just as a trio of mages from the Order of the Bone Hook blew the lids off a series of stormwater pipes, and drew forth three swirling waterspouts. Amber just had time to register Old Lady Lachrymosa, her motheaten wedding gown fully ablaze, standing in the window with a pair of automatic mantisbows, before all three torrents bent at right angles, and blew away the entire ground floor of the Jade Palace.

This time Amber stayed lucid the whole time. Right through the part where a rod of grey-brown water the width of a castle turret hammered into her head-on, carrying her away through a wall with Zoltan, a black swirl of waterlogged assassins, half of the banquet table, and an emperor's ransom in intricately carved jade panelling.

The Palace itself stood at the corner of Ishmael Street and Skrayhollow, where that great jacaranda-tree'd avenue wound its way down from the Fleamarket and under the cliffs of Bishopsbath. Amber was propelled clean through the filigree fence of its garden and across the road, where she washed up inside a small Shangolan barbecue restaurant. Horrible, reeking bathwater slopped over the place's pottery ovens, eliciting a blast of steam.

Zoltan Creagle ended up wallowing in a pile of beanbags, tangled in the pipes of a five-man hookah, while out in the street...

There was no mistaking that little pink form. It detached itself from the rolling, dented hulk of the Dead Man's Bell and shook itself from ruff to cottontail like a lapdog fished out of a fountain. Two holey and ragged ears popped to attention. Then it stumped purposefully across the cobbles, silencing the restaurant's chef and owner, who were shouting at Amber and Zoltan in what she assumed was very naughty Shangun.

Like Amber herself, they were more than a little surprised to have witnessed a stuffed rabbit in a zippered mask ride in out of the sky on a fireball, demolishing the tower of the Assassin's stronghold. Four dark and tattoo-ringed eyes followed Mister Bun Bun as he marched up to Amberelia and saluted, pointing at the hulk of the bell.

She sat up. *Gods, but that hurt.* Little sizzles of green fire were at work under her skin, patching up a thousand minor strains and fractures.

"I see it, Skrx. I mean... Mister B. I see it. Good work, I suppose. Do you have any idea about the others?"

The rabbit's tiny shrug said it all. And now here came the rain, sweeping in from across the city. Amber paid back Zoltan, dragging him to his feet just as the ground rumbled beneath them. A pall of dust and debris billowed up behind the downpour, over toward the borough of Knightsbottom.

One of the assassins, freshly levered up out of the gutter, was squashed quite flat by a falling block of stone, the size of a pickle barrel. Other chunks of masonry came down trailing white dust, smashing through the tall gambrel roofs of Bentsteeple like god-sized shrapnel.

But that wasn't the worst of it.

The so-called Honey Badger staggered a few steps out into the street, followed by the Pugilist and Mister Bun Bun. A confused and curious pair of Shangolese cooks followed. In the stutter-flash of the lightning, all eyes were turned up toward the Malevolith, the sundial at the heart of Grand Sepulchre. Something at its very top was glowing, a violet hue spilling down its sides with the sheeting rain. Crackles and tendrils of electricity slithered across the black stone, and a hum rose from the entire edifice, setting Amber's teeth on edge.

"You know, I only wanted to be a regular assassin," said Amber, in a faraway voice. "Not any of this. You know what the Old Lady called us? 'The surgeons of the aristocracy'. The hand on the scalpel, ensuring peace. Not heroes. Not the kind of heroes who destroy whole cities to prove how great they are, anyway."

Zoltan Creagle looked up at the Malevolith and sucked on his teeth.

"Well, *I* only wanted to be stinking rich, lass, and we ended up in the same place. You know, I remember my granddad told me once, you couldn't go a month without some kind of monster attacking the city in the old days. He told me all the tales of ruin and horror, but you know what? He was smiling when he told 'em."

Amber nodded.

"Ahhh. You mean, in retrospect, people only remember the

adventure and the action, not the fear and the wobbly internal bits all over the street?" she asked. "Your granddad was a wise man, was he?"

"Nah," said Zoltan. "He was a bloody undertaker. Orc hordes, dragons, murderous wizards and such kept him in gravy. Of course, that kind of nonsense has trailed off a bit, in recent decades. Himself makes a pretty good deterrent, see?"

Amber looked up at the tower, where, if she squinted, she could just make out the shape of a man in armour standing at the very top, a two-handed sword upraised. He was calling down the lightning, wrapping his blade up in a frenzy of indigo and blue sparks.

"I think I'm starting to," said Amber. "The monsters don't ever go after other monsters. They're attracted to heroes. Like those little rocks the wizards have, from out of meteors. The ones that love iron. Flip them upside down, and they push each other apart."

Mister Bun Bun made a series of chirps, hisses and rattles from behind his mask.

"*Exactly*," said Amber, picking him up. "That's what all the skulls and spikes are for. That's why we're the Evil Empire, even though most people in the city are only the kind of evil that might steal your newspaper, or throw an ale-jug at the other cricket team. It's like that thing tigers do."

"Viciously maul people with their huge, sharp claws?" asked Creagle, all innocence. Above him, fireworks lit up from the jagged tip of the Malevolith, picking out the shape of a big glassy object, bellying out of the clouds.

"No," replied Amber. "*Camouflage*. Metaphorically, of course."

Zoltan shrugged.

"I'm not really a man for a metaphor, Miss Chance. But if He's been keeping Grand Sepulchre safe for a few hundred years by making us pretend to be all evil, it was bound to happen, weren't it?"

"What?"

"Well, like you said. Little rocks that attract each other. The Evil Lord has finally been tracked down by his nemeses, who are even now ravaging the city, sort of thing."

"What do you mean, *nemeses?*"

"From the old Phoraxian, *nemesis*. It means, a righteously, personally, single-mindedly determined foe. Good word, eh? I used it on a lot of wrestling posters, back in the day." Zoltan recognised the look he was getting, and held up his hands for calm. "Alright, alright. What I mean is, it's *us*. Heroes, right? And we *are* making a bloody mess of His city, you have to admit…"

Amber looked across the road, where the charred ruin of the Jade Palace smoked gently, wallowing in a lake of putrid water. Across the horizon, there were other palls of smoke, too, as fires burned too wild for the rain to put them out. The entire Lord Governor's Tower was missing from the skyline, like a tooth punched out of a boxer's smile.

"But we're… it's not… we never wanted to…" began Amber. Then she remembered who exactly had prompted them to this course of action. The same someone, in fact, who had likely conjured up that giant, slippery-black title in the sky. The one which now came ponderously swinging in under the thunderheads, black as ink, reflective as chrome.

EPISODE THE LAST, it said. A HERO'S DEATH

"*Gloom* told us he was going after the bells. *Gloom* told us that without them, the Malevolith would explode. Gloom basically made our plan for us, and then conveniently magicked us all away to the same place, so we could join up in a jolly little team against him…"

"My gods," said Creagle. "Double-crossing really is a way of life with you people, isn't it?"

Amber looked up at the title, watching unnatural lightning crawl over its surface.

"It's like Master Lurien's question, the first time we played chess. Back when I'd just been recruited from the orphanage, and he told me that he'd be taking care of my training."

"This would be the funny little man who smelled of mushrooms, and who was quite recently holding a dagger to my windpipe?" asked the Pugilist. Amber nodded.

"He told me that chess represents the entirety of the assassin's craft, and therefore, that I should answer his next question very carefully. Then he set up the board, with the most intricately carved marble pieces I'd ever seen, and sat down, and pointed at them. 'Now,' he said. 'Out of all the parts of my little army here, which one is the most dangerous?'"

Something came slicing across the sky, then, out of the east, describing a shallow arc through the clouds. They spiralled in its wake, thunderclaps nesting one within another, and the rain hung frozen for an instant, each drop reflecting fire.

Then that something struck the Malevolith, hard enough to crack its outer casement. Obsidian shards rained down, as a shallow crater formed with a puff of steam.

"Sweet Von Tuesday's ghost! Did you *see* that?"

Amber nodded. But she carried on regardless.

"I took a long time to answer. I looked at the rooks, with their massive power, and the bishops, with their long reach, and even the queen, with her versatility. In the end, I think I got it right, though."

Up against the side of the Malevolith, a figure in red prised itself from a person-shaped hole. Just as it seemed to be about to break free, a raving blast of green came hammering in from out over the harbour, outlining it with a welding-torch flash. Stone turned molten and dripped like wax around it.

"I told Lurien it was *him*. The most dangerous part of any army was the *other player*. The most important piece isn't even one of the ones on the board! Zoltan, we have to get to Jack. We have to tell him to stop!"

Mister Bun Bun suddenly gave a screech, followed by a chittering, hissing exclamation. Zoltan Creagle winced.

"That Slag Iron's a bad influence, young rabbit-thing," he said. "Language like that! But you're right, of course. I think that's Jack Somewhat up there right now, Miss Amber. And I think, chess notwithstanding, that we might be too late to stop anything at all..."

25

Episode the Last – A Hero's De#!*

JACK SOMEWHAT HAD a lot of time to think, as he sailed backwards through a frozen world of raindrops, each shimmering little droplet a crystal stitched to the black velvet of the sky.

When you're very large, he thought, *People always assume that you're looking for a fight. Angry little people always tried to tattoo their insecurities all over your skin – because Gods knew that if they were as big as you were, they'd take the bloody world down a peg or two!*

It never occurred to them – the muttering, the seedy, the red-faced, aimlessly belligerent, racist, sad and genitally-short-changed – that large people wouldn't act out the grubby little revenge fantasies which the small fetishised. *It never occurred to them, in fact, that being a small person was nothing to do with measurements...*

Jack had met literal dwarfs (both human and, well, *actual Dwarves*) of great stature. But there *was* a fundamental problem with being giant.

It went like this. If you were a big, naughty-looking cove, and you hauled off and smacked someone, you were doomed. No matter how much they deserved it.

If they popped back up to their feet like a demented jack-in-the-box and beat you silly, then they were sticking up for themselves against a big nasty bully. And if you flattened them, you were... well, a big nasty bully. The confederacy of mean little men with their uniforms and badges and nametags and desk calendars meshed in on you like a well-oiled abattoir production line, and spit you out bloody, chastened and a little bit wiser, every time.

This could make a person surly, and bitter, and play up to the stereotype of the empty-headed thug, who let his fists do the talking. Or it could make a man sincerely wish for peace, like Jack Somewhat.

Right now, his plans for ensuring peace centred squarely on battering a nuisance named Gloom into two-dimensional oblivion.

Ironic? Perhaps. But when the bulk of the Malevolith smashed into his spine and kidneys with the impact of a concentrated avalanche, such subtleties were blasted away.

Did he want to be a hero? No. *Did he want to be anyone's arch-enemy?* Not a chance. *But did he want to die, wearing this stupid cape?* Ahh, there was the rub. For Jack Somewhat wanted *that* even less.

He levered himself out of the hole he'd made, feeling volcanic glass skritter and shard away around him. *Up onto one elbow, so he could hold out a hand toward his unseen foe, and try to reason with him, one last time…*

"Stop, alright? Look, this isn't helping either of us! I know I hurt your feelings, and I think this relationship got off to a terrible start, but can't we just talk this over like…"

But there'd be no simile to end that sentence, because Gloom was past anything so sane as reason. A searing blast came raving in from out over the sea, evaporating a cone of raindrops as it narrowed down to a needle point. When this struck Jack's chest he convulsed, his bones crackling incandescent beneath this flesh. A circular dimple was dished out in the surface of the Malevolith all around him, black glass dripping like wax.

Jack slumped forward into the air, floating with his head down. One of his huge, black-outlined hands cuffed away a dribble of blood from his nose, and he pushed his hair back out of his eyes.

Alright then. The hard way. Get the heroing over with, and never look back at it…

Jack wondered, as he threw himself forward at eyeball-flattening velocity, if this was what soldiers felt on the front lines, as they watched all those sharp bits of metal galloping toward them. Or if it was what men like Clorance Gryssle felt, when they knew that the serial killer was behind the door, and the music-box was playing its unhinged little song, and they'd seen what was left of the last three lawmen who'd tried to bring him in…

Did they want to be heroes? Or just get the job done, and then drown the memory in a pint or twelve?

Now Gloom was in front of him, eyes widening. The wicked bastard hadn't realised Jack could move so fast. Jack's fist swung in an arc which blurred through the raindrops, so quick that it wasn't even wet when it crunched into the ſuper-villain's jaw.

Did they want to just get it over with, and shut the door behind them, and go back to their little families and fireplaces and ordinary things?

More blows, now. The combination strikes which Ranulf the Butcher had taught him, while wrecking all those training dummies. A chop kick, a knee to the fruits, a double jab to the chest, an uppercut with the heft of a cannonball... Gloom jerked in the air, pummelled from one side to the other, and Jack realised that the scream he could hear was coming from between his own clenched teeth.

This was the sneaky right cross Bill Knox taught him, when those bully boys from the Dyer's Guild cornered them in Chokeneck Gully.

This was the kidney chop little Soto Scalizari used, the time those pickpockets had tried to snaffle his sack of silver spothins.

This was the down-and-dirty double thumb-gouge to the eyes which Jory Foxmallet had used to nobble that bent knock-man, the one who'd tried to set up Jack as a burglar.

"Or maybe you picked me because I don't *have* a family, you bastard!" shouted Jack, as his fist came back one last time. "Maybe you thought yeah, being a hero is all the poor stupid fat idiot's *got!*"

This one was pure Somewhat – a roundhouse special which would have been called a haymaker, if Jack had ever seen the countryside. As it was, he called it the guttermouth, because it usually ended with his foe face down, drooling on the cobbles.

Gloom bled black. Gloom splattered ink, which left stains and drips in the air around him. But even worse than this, as Jack picked him up by the scruff of his costume, the blank-eyed villain *smiled.*

"Excellent! You see what some motivation can do? They're all watching you, Jack! Finally, you've become something worth looking up to!"

Jack snarled, and swung his fist again, but Gloom blurred out from between his fingers, becoming slippery as smoke. Suddenly the great dark figure with his ragged cape was above Jack in the air, and his boot swung up and out, coming down in a devastating spin-kick.

"Who would have thought it? The ugly baby left behind on the doorstep of the Bakers Guild, all those years ago? A thing so nondescript they even filled the forms in wrong. You know how you got your last name, Jack? The kneader's assistant third class who took you in that day. He wrote 'somewhat chubby' in the section marked 'weight', and the 'somewhat' went on the wrong line. It would be a laugh, if it wasn't so pathetic."

Jack caught the impact across one shoulder, and was propelled down toward the ground. But Gloom blurred again, and was waiting for him as he fell. A double-handed axehandle blow sent him soaring back up toward the Malevolith, where lightning danced and cascaded.

"Look! Down there! Your moronic *friends* are fighting! They've giving me their all, Jack! Now, are you going to let me down? *After all I've done for you?* Come on and HIT ME!"

There's a certain point beyond which all the logic and reason in the world can't follow. Jack understood, on some rational level, that if Gloom wanted him to fight, then that's the last thing he should be doing. But the voice of rationality was drowned out by a soul-tearing howl of rage and frustration; one that had been building up for far too many sleepless hours.

The scream rose up. His fingers hinged over, one by one. They clenched into a fist.

Sure, he'd been unhappy as an apprentice Alchemist and part-time latrine pit washer. But it had been *his* unhappiness. His to do something about. Not like the demented sideshow which crowded in around him now, all thunder and bombast, with the empty, sucking feeling of a million eyes drinking it in.

Oh yes. That was the worst part. Gloom was *right* about people looking up to him. How could they not, when the pair of them wrestled in the sky like demigods? They watched, and a little part of Jack Somewhat disappeared back behind each one of those sets of eyes. Feedback loops fractalised all the way out to infinity.

"Well?" Asked a mouth sliced through teeming darkness. **"What are you gonna do, hero?"**

This time there were no questions. This time *he* was the one who moved in a blur, the air waiting for a heartbeat before it came crashing back into the space he'd just vacated. His blow lit up half the sky with the word ZOKK, all dancing green sparks, and Gloom was flung into a spin, impacting with the Sugarloaf so hard that boulders slid and furrowed, whole ancient oaks ploughed under as they tumbled.

Jack followed after, his muscles cranked so tight that his bones felt as if they were about to shatter. He flew behind a clenched fist, and he struck Gloom squarely in the solar plexus, propelling him clean through the red rock of the mountain.

The crack and rumble of it shattered windows as far away as Knightsbottom and Chantry Heath. But that wasn't all. Jack concentrated, and time slowed to a syrupy blur, raindrops shivering in stasis. He flew on ahead of Gloom, a figure trailing inky blood and rock dust, and caught him by one leg as he came scything past. Once, twice, Jack spun, then unleashed the ſuper-villain, back the way he'd come. Again, Gloom was hammered clean through the Sugarloaf, and Jack followed him, catching up to him in mid-air. His boot crunched into the grinning monster's neck.

Down they went, down toward the Grand Imperial Canal in Hammer's End. Gloom hit the oil-slicked water so hard that it immediately caught flame, and he skimmed across it for a mile, then two, overturning barges, shattering dockside cranes, and raising a twin tidal wave of brown-grey filth. Jack bore down, and Gloom sunk below the surface, bleeding off speed. He followed him all the way to the bottom, sliding along the slick and muddy brickwork, clear across the great merchant ship's pool at Coalharbour. Anchor chains parted with muted cracks, and hulls sundered, sending cargo to the bottom.

The impact, when both of them struck the far wall of that man-made sump, rocked the canal-side Cathedral of Phorax to its foundations. Statues of saints came toppling down, amid a shower of gold leaf, candle stubs and pigeon guano.

"*Better!* Give in to it, Jack! Look at what we could both become!"

Jack opened his eyes under the waters of the sump, and saw almost nothing. Churning brown silt and fluttering bubbles surrounded him. Then he felt something grab him by the throat, as grinding, breaking sounds echoed in his head. He scrabbled with his fingers, but the thing which gripped him was slimy, and felt like corded steel under a sheath of rubber.

An instant later he was hauled out of the water, swinging above its rain-lashed surface. Gloom erupted from the foam behind him, his cape split into a mass of thick, ink-black tentacles, spiked and thorny around the edges. It was a pair of these which throttled Jack, and another which held him up by the ankle.

"Yes!" shouted Gloom, crazed triumph in his voice. His smile was fractured now, with several pointed teeth growing through where human ones had been smashed away. **"I know you can feel it, boy. All those people watching us! They're going to watch you beat me, and beat that outdated old skeleton in his tower as well. They're going to watch you *rise*, and it's going to change the world."**

A sudden lurch, and Gloom spun Jack like a yo-yo at the end of its string.

He went tumbling head over boot-heels, crashing through a whole street of houses built from wrecked sailing ships, down in the sailor's quarter they called Tarback Scrubs. Barnacle-studded boards shattered, and rigging snapped.

Jack hauled up by sheer force of will, snarling defiance, and ended up seated on some sea-captain's indoor privy. Force of habit made him pull the chain before he powered out the window and back along the street, the shockwave of his passing smashing windows and tearing nails out of rotten wood.

Crooked firebolts whipped past him as he came, sizzling from Gloom's fingertips. The ſuper-villain was perched atop a spidery black tangle of limbs, all elbows and knees and spikes, and he was obviously enjoying himself.

"What did you tell me yesterday? 'The monsters who are still standing will call themselves heroes.' Yes, indeed! I'll make a monster of you yet!"

Behind Jack, three more buildings detonated, pitch combusting with a roar. In the Piazza Della Von Tuesday, at the far end of the Scrubs, this morning's wreckage (neatly sorted into a pile) was re-distributed violently. A little Sarunjek man with a broom broke it across one knee, and threw his hands up into the air in utter disbelief.

"Come on now. Like I've taught you. Give these stinking peasants something to _believe in_ Jack! Give them a show that makes their deaths worthwhile!"

Once again, a voice in the back of Jack's head quavered for reason and calm. Once again, it may as well have been an asthmatic mouse coughing in a cyclone. Jack's fists, crusted with black and inky blood, clenched tight again.

Went a nova of green sparks, fading and dying like fireworks. Gloom was propelled away from the impact, knuckle-prints deforming the whole side of his head. He spun through the side of Phorax's cathedral, stained-glass windows imploding around him. Jack screwed up his mind and followed. Hands which were now huge red caricatures snapped off the statue of Noctaris from atop the spire, and hefted it like a club. It was several hundred tonnes of sculpted copper, and it met Gloom coming out through the windows on the other side, bursting from the beatific smile of Saint Guthran. Shards of coloured glass were blasted to liquid. Lead wirework melted in mid-air from the impact.

The Redeemer's copper visage met Gloom's face with a sound of splintering bone and tearing gristle. The sound shimmered off the sky, rippling the waters of the harbour.

And this one did it. This time, the blow didn't just slug the ſuper-villain out of his boots, or send him smoking across the sky. This time, Jack broke something fundamental, down on the kind of tiny scale where sub-atomic particles bumble in and out of reality like drunks in a maze of revolving doors. *Things unravelled. Catastrophes cascaded.*

Time stopped.

So it was that Gloom fell sideways across a sky framed by frozen clouds, his flight lit up by forks and jags of motionless lightning. This time, the raindrops didn't just seem to stand still; they really did, along with all the flames below, and the people in the streets trying to put them out.

There's a kind of feeling you get, as a small child, when you know that Big Trouble is coming down on you, capital letters and all.

That feeling assailed Jack now, as he watched Gloom fly in a flat trajectory, smashing one of the teeth from the top of the Malevolith. The black-clad figure tumbled in mid-air, then struck another, slithering bonelessly down to the space between.

Where He Himself, the Urzoman Emperor, raised his rusted helm and looked right back. His state was like an aeon of glaciation; extinction with dilated pupils.

Jack suddenly felt as if his skin was trying to slither around behind his skeleton, to get out from under that penetrating, ice-cold stare. Sheer urchin-boy instinct made his hands try to hide a hundred spans of dented copper saint behind his back, without informing his brain.

Behind him, a crack appeared in the world, and pale blue light came glimmering through. This, it transpired, was what the Undying One was really looking at; the kind of damage that doesn't come out with a coat of paint.

"Just *what* shenanigans are you people playing at?" asked Himself, making a gesture with one clawed hand. Jack felt a sudden sickening lurch, as if he'd been pulled out long and rubbery, then snapped back into three dimensions.

All at once, he was atop the Malevolith, the remains of a septagram evaporating around his size-twelves. Far behind him, a statue bobbed in the harbour for a second, then sank.

"Have you *any idea* the mess you're making of my city? Have you even the *slightest* concept of how angry this makes me?"

Despite this talk of wrath, the voice from behind the Emperor's corroded helm was cold and bitter. What Jack really noticed was the *smell* – a kind of cesspit insinuation, icy and rank at once. The lich-king went on, plucking at Jack's costume with two foot-long iron fingernails.

"After that nasty business with Enkalderon, I was inclined to be merciful, you know. That - and inclined to foist you all on some other poor foolish ruler, so I could watch their domain get flattened from a leisurely distance." He paused for a moment, looming in close. "Precisely what are you supposed to *be*, anyway?"

Jack couldn't face the two ghostly eyes which stared out from inside His helm. He tried looking out over the city, but there was no comfort there; just a frozen tableau of destruction, which made last night's carnage seem like a geriatric slap-fight. He settled for looking down at his shoes, as he scuffed them in a puddle.

"'m supposed to be a hero, m'lord."

"What was that?"

"I'm supposed to be a *hero*, M'Lord. A ʃuper one. It's... it's a new thing."

The Emperor fixed him with a look of such withering scorn, then, that Jack literally shrunk two inches.

"The old fur underpants and warhammer not good enough for you, then? I ask you, kids these days..." Himself turned toward Gloom, who was rising to his feet again, with the horrid sound of bones popping back into their sockets.

"I suppose that makes you the villain, then. All in black, big mad grin, silly cape... yes, *I recognise you.* I know what you did. You killed my (and here, a word was choked back behind that skull-etched grille of a face) my... *Slave*. Answer for yourself!"

"As one villain to another, no hard feelings. Just business," oiled Gloom. **"You can have one of mine, if you like, fair trade. Take your pick. You understand how disposable the help is, in our game."** The villain's smile split even wider, tight little threads of muscle webbing across the extra teeth at both corners. **"No-one's henchin' for the pension, right? As for the whole idiom, the costume, the capes... well, that's just progress, granddad."**

"Granddad. Cute." He made a gesture, and suddenly his greatsword

Spite was there, grinding across the stone platform atop the Malevolith point-down, hissing with sparks. "I'm not a fan of progress, Mister... what did you call yourself?"

"Gloom."

"Mister Gloom. And I'm *definitely* not a fan of people like you, who make a mess of other people's cities. Do you know *why* I'm evil, Gloom? Do you know why I go on, decade after stultifying decade, with this whole charade? No, I suppose you don't. I suppose you're the kind of villain who'd destroy the universe, without even thinking about where he'd go out for a drink afterwards."

He didn't wait for an answer. Instead, He closed one huge hand around the grip of Spite, raising it up as if it weighed less than one of Monty's rapiers.

"When I was a hero, like foolish young Jack Somewhat here, I noticed that the monsters and wicked kings and deathless wizards *just kept coming.* I began to feel, Gloom, that all the people who died in our thrilling bloody battles might just be, in some way, my responsibility. So, I arranged things in a way that would satisfy the rules behind the world. I arranged things so that disruptions like *you* were easily removed, and smoothed over, with the minimum of fuss."

Now He took a couple of test swings, as if limbering up His hand for some heavy work.

"You see all of this? This *stasis?* These thousands of raindrops, just hanging there? It means you've got Her attention. The one I've been avoiding all these years. So now, you have to go. Sorry, Jack – that means you and all your friends, as well. There's a life hanging in the balance for every one of these raindrops, you see. It's my job to be evil enough to weigh a little splatter, against the whole downpour."

Jack thought of Jory and Bill and Soto, then. He thought of Amber too, and a tangled knot of feelings unravelled in his chest.

"*No!* I mean... please! It was all me. *I* took that thing from Rhaegulus Cratt. *I* let it get into my head. It's inside Gloom's head, right now. It wants to change the world, and it tricks people, and it tries to make them into things they're not... and..."

The lich-king turned his head, and fixed Jack with a stare like the gravity wells of twin black holes.

"Your point?"

"Just take me. Kill me, and I bet this whole stupid thing goes with me. The power rod, the thing... it chose *me.* Leave my friends alone."

That hollow gaze rested on him for a long instant, during which Jack could feel his soul being welded to the back of the inside of his skull. Then he turned back to Gloom.

"Have you any pitiful last requests as well? Any appeals to my better nature? I'm almost insulted to discover that Jack here thinks I have one..."

Gloom giggled, a horrible, high-pitched little sound.

"Go ahead. *Strike me down*. Do your worst, you relic. You're finished, either way. I can feel the balance shifting, right under all of our feet... Afterwards, they'll all believe it was Jack who stopped us both."

The Urzoman Emperor slung his sword over one shoulder, and paused for a second, as if deep in thought. Then he spun with sudden ferocity, all two tonnes of him lashing out in a fierce pirouette. Spite split a score of raindrops, shivering them to mist, then went cleaving through Gloom's spine, to take his head clean off his shoulders. Both head and body slumped, inky darkness melting and flowing, so that what was left of the ſuper-villain seemed to be nothing more than a mess. The neon green 'G' on his chest stuttered and died.

"Was it just me, or did that voice of his just annoy the seventeen hells out of you?" asked Himself, as he turned toward Jack. "Now, I'm sorry about this, but it seems to be your turn."

Jack wondered, for a second, if this was going to hurt. Then his second thoughts caught up with him, and he wondered why, if Gloom (and hence Rod), were gone, he could still feel the pulse of green fire inside his head. There was no time for philosophy, though. There was barely time to try to be brave. The great runesword Spite came up over His head, still dripping black blood. And then...

The crack which Jack had made in reality zigzagged up and over the sky. It unzipped the vault of the heavens, disembowelling the thunderclouds, and revealing a strip of sunlit blue.

The end of the crack plunged down like an inverse rainbow, until it struck the top of the Malevolith. Fragments of reality peeled away and spun down inside it, into the image of a summer's day, and a little green lawn, set out in a square surrounded by old, old buildings. Through the crack, and through the garden, and through the windows of those buildings, Jack Somewhat could see nothing but books on books on books. Merry little lamps lit up whole stacks and rows of them.

Only for an instant, though. Because then a lady in white stepped into the frame... in fact, she stepped right *through* the frame, and right through the crack in the sky, her mother-of-pearl slingback shoes clicking against the wet obsidian. She was barely five spans tall, clad in a plain white dress, with golden braids curled up atop her head and green eyes flashing mischief. The world warped and buckled around her like a mirage.

This vision advanced on Himself, the dread lich-emperor, like a tiny, beautiful natural disaster. She stopped in front of him, standing in the melted ruins of Gloom, and smiled.

"So, at least *some* part of you finally wants to end this silliness," said the Green-eyed Lady, the one true Goddess of the Arch'. "You know it's past time. You all did. There are new stories to tell, and you can't be... *whatever* you call yourself now... forever. Just like you couldn't be the old you, either. You know what you've gone and done."

Himself seemed to buckle, at that. All the height and majesty went out of him, and he slumped down in front of the Lady, sword clattering to the ground.

"Perhaps you're right, Callistae," he said. "So, you caught me being *heroic*. Finally. What manner did you choose, to end our little dance?"

Callistae reached up, and cupped the cheek of his massive battle-helm in one tiny hand.

"I think you know, dear. It'll be suitably dramatic."

"You know I won't let it hurt them. My people..."

"You always were a big softy. *You know how this really works.*"

There was a flash of anger, then, blazing red inside that rusty great helmet. It even made the Goddess recoil.

"I know. *But I don't have to like it.* You know, these two wanted to change the world?"

Callistae laughed - a sound with so many fractal complexities that it made Jack's head hurt.

"I am the change in the world. I *am* change. *I am the world.*" she said. "Now, let's write a final chapter, shall we?"

And then time, which had held its breath for so long, finally inhaled...

CODEX THREE:

A ROTTEN END

26

The Arachno-Draconian Excession

SLAG IRON AND The Grimshadow felt it, as they popped up out of a manhole cover in Decameron Street, far away from the burning Halfway House.

A sudden shattering of something unseen. A feeling of static and tension in the air, as something vast moved behind reality, lumping it up like a cat under the bedsheets.

Deep in the Temple of Pleasures, the very surprised look on the Demon Quazirath's face was replaced at once by one of horror.

"Him? Again? Bugger that for a lark, ladies and gents. I'm off!"

The Debauched One disappeared in a puff of peacock-feather smoke, leaving a large group of very tired, happy and generally satisfied temple prostitutes wondering if they should now worship Montmortimer Pettigrew.

"Come on!" insisted Soto Scalizari, who had just witnessed a sight which would remain seared into his subconscious for decades to come. "You can feel that, right? I think we've got serious trouble!"

Monty wiped a large smear of lipstick off his face – most of it not his own - and tried unsuccessfully to put both of his legs into one half of his trousers.

"You don't happen to have exactly seven thousand, four hundred and two cigarettes. Do you?" he asked, in a slurred voice.

Meanwhile, a huge chunk of rubble was hinged up and over out of the wreckage of a house in Knightsbottom. A massive blue arm shoved the mosaic-tiled slab away, revealing the two identical blue-caped figures it had protected during their fall. Not a second too soon, either... With a heartfelt groan, the Unstoppable It staggered out into the street, becoming once again nothing more than a tattooed little sailor in ruined trousers.

The two Billiam Knoxes blurred back together as they blinked their way back to consciousness, and a single red-haired wreck covered in bruises and brick-dust came to help Tarrence Bligh to his feet.

"You feel that mate? Something's gone *well* wrong. Lucky I kept some of that potion then, I reckon..."

Amber, Zoltan Creagle and Mister Bun Bun had already started to sprint toward the Malevolith, high up the scarp above the Jade Palace, when something jangled through the world, setting the young demortifex's teeth on edge.

"Did everything just freeze, for an instant there?" she asked, as the Pugilist huffed and wheezed along beside her, one meaty hand holding his golden wreath onto his head.

"I dunno about that..." managed Creagle, who, despite being a little bit ſuper now, was still well past his prime and several pies over regulation weight. "But I know we've got company. Look!"

It was Master Lurien, standing in a horse trough and trying to wring out his floppy velvet hat.

"I say! Look, sorry about all the double-crossing, but it was...what's the word... yes, it was in a certain idiom! I think the Old Lady bought it back there, and that means, ummm.... I suppose..."

"Oh, out with it!" snapped Amber, who immediately felt bad for doing so, when she saw the look on the old poisoner's face.

"Well, I want to come with you. If we're out to save the city, then the Guilds must do their part."

"I reckon they've done enough," suggested Zoltan darkly. Mister Bun Bun, perched on Amber's shoulder, gave a snicker of approval.

Lurien bore up under this, and jammed his hat back on his head. It dripped black dye down one cheek.

"No! You know I always hated the idea of going on missions, Miss Chance, but there's a burden to leadership."

"This is ſuper-stuff, Lurien, said Amber, not unkindly. "Are you certain you want to..."

The assassin slopped his way out of his horse trough, and took her hand.

"I'd feel bad if I didn't. Come on!"

Jack Somewhat certainly felt it. As Himself, the immortal lich-king, climbed slowly up off his knees, the ſcarlet ſpectre felt a sensation like hooks in his skin, tugging him around to look out toward the harbour. To the Stilts, in fact, where something was pressed up tight against the world, rasping against reality.

"Just what exactly have you done?" he asked Callistae, as she made a gesture with one hand... and threw him off the tower.

Now, Jack had come to terms with the fact that he could fly. So, it was cruel indeed to find that, right now, whatever the little green-eyed Goddess had done to him had rendered him about as buoyant as a lead coracle. He fairly plummeted, watching the red marble expanse of the Imperial Precinct rush up toward him.

Then, at the last minute, a snap of green static buzzed across his skin, and he flopped gently - but without a shred of dignity - to the ground.

The landing wasn't the problem, though. Neither was the fact that he'd come perilously close to soiling his tights. No, the real issue, here and now, was that the term *last minute* appeared to be horribly accurate.

Something had burst through into the world. Something, in fact, had *Cometh*, fully deserving the capital letter and all. Down in the Stilts, in Peachcourt Alley, where a fountain of a constipated-looking merman sputtered water out of his puckered-up mouth, Mama Lurga was feeling rather strange.

Or was 'strange' the right word? Surely, the warping, shimmering unreality which saturated the air was having *some* effect on her, especially considering her very sensitive magical sensibilities. The redoubtable voodoo priestess sat in her favourite wicker chair, cooling herself with a rice-paper fan, and watched the walls melt and wobble, in a fashion well known to anyone who has known the pleasures of the bright blue mushroom.

"Ned! Stitchface! Get yo' old selves in here! Dere' some baaaad mojo risin', if you get me drift, and I think it's comin' from next door!"

Mama's two favourite zombies came shambling in, their sewn-together bodies seeming to bulge and stretch like the reflections in a funfair mirror. Seeing as they had no brains in their heads, this reality-warping sensation had little effect on them; the pair helped their mistress up from her chair and fetched her cane, a knobbly and stout affair carved from bone, and featuring a top-hatted skull for a tip.

"Grhuuuuuurg?" asked Ned, a look of concern on his noseless face. "Now, now, you daft old ting! Ne' mind me – it's that sickly lookin' little white boy who's done alla dis. Cm'awn, let's see if we can't get him to settle down!"

Mama Lurga and her two lads made their way down the stairs and up to the door of Zag-Hammurat's Dread Temple of Demise; the downstairs flat which was wedged under the pilings of the Brujerierie.

There was blood seeping out from under the door.

"Nhhhrrrruuur?" asked Stitchface, who, as his name suggested, looked rather like a many-times-repaired football. The door seemed to shrink and expand at the same time. Wyrd harmonics rippled through the cobbles underfoot.

"Well, yes, usually it would be polite to knock, and all," said Mama. "But in dis case, I reckon you boys should just do it for me..."

The zombies didn't need telling twice. Mama Lurga had picked both of them for their sheer size, and what this had cost her in backache and time spent shovelling had been well repaid in the years which followed. Ned put out a flat palm and walked forward, pushing the door over as if it was cardboard.

In a way, it was a good thing that two zombies and a voodoo priestess were the ones to discover what was going on inside Garith Smembly's pokey little bedsit. Things with more brains, and less experience with corpses, might have spent a long and valuable period being violently ill.

The Temple of Zag-Hammurat looked like a cross between one of those dens of paranoid schizophrenia, where someone has connected a lifetime's worth of newspaper clippings with red strings, and the inside of an offal trap. It was as if someone was trying to scry the future with entrails, and had set out to make sure they knew every *single bit of the future*, and how it all interconnected. Surely, thought Mama Lurga, there was no way that weedy little Garith could have dismembered this many people without her hearing something. He hadn't even come over to borrow a bonesaw!

Then again, this could be explained by the fact that Garith himself was suspended above an altar made out of a beer crate, his hands and feet pulled out tight by chains which disappeared into darkness. *Something* – and Mama Lurga could tell from its handiwork that it must have a real appreciation for body piercing – had driven needles, pins, nails and spikes into every exposed piece of skin it could find on the little fool. There was a lot of this, as he was clad only in a pair of pink-spotted Y-fronts, and his bent ecclesiastical mitre.

"Ahhh, ya silly little man," she tutted. "I *told* you, didn't I, no good comes of playing games wi' dose kinky demons an' der clever puzzles. If'n dey tink pain is pleasure, why don't ya see 'em lining up to wash dishes or do de laundry?"

Ned shuffled forward, ready to grab Garith's body down, when the little man opened his eyes.

"Ummm... a little help? There seems to be some kind of problem with the ritual, and I.... (cough).... actually, my good lady, I could do with a glass of (cough).... uuuurrrggg..."

Mama Lurga felt something horrible pushing up against the world, in this blood-soaked box of a room. Not the kind of jolly, spooky horribleness of voodoo magic; I mean, when you really got down to it, death was just a part of life, and skeletons were clean, weren't they? Even a well taxidermied zombie was just a leather man, doing a bit of overtime, as it were.

No. This was the high-pitched little song of gleeful torture, and pointless cruelty, and destruction for its own sake. This was...

"Grragh!" said Garith Smembly, in almost perfectly accented zombinese.

"Grrruuugh!" agreed Ned.

And then... Mama Lurga noticed something sticking out of the poor priest's mouth.

It was like a spiky black tongue, and as she watched, it grew a little, popping out from between his teeth like a toddler's insult.

"Hey now! Dere's no need for ill manners, boy!" scolded the voodoo lady. But manners, ill or otherwise, were no longer on Garith's mind. His eyes widened, as even more tongue came out between his lips; a cone of it, bitumen-black and glistening.

"Pwwwssse! Hlllllp mhhh!" he managed, before a lunge made it grow an entire arm's length, revealing what appeared to be a jointed lump. The whole appendage kept growing, and, unfortunately for him, it kept getting wider. Another lurch, and six spans of thigh-thick chitin burst out, distorting Garith's face. Other things were moving under his skin, too, snakes writhing up and down his arms and legs. A bulge appeared in his chest, then split open, revealing a gigantic purple eye.

"Ohhhh, that's not good. That's not good *at all*," breathed Mama, as she realised just what the thing coming out of Garith's mouth really was. It was a *leg*... and even as she watched, the spiked tip of a second one came probing out next to the first.

There was clearly no saving her feckless neighbour. But letting cosmic horrors out to knock over the bins and pee in the alleyways was not in Mama Lurga's remit. *Sure as sure, the government would blame the one and only local voodoo artiste, you could bet your ceremonial top hat and skull collection on it!*

"You boys run for it!" shouted the priestess, gathering power from the many hundreds of charms, trinkets and dried-up body parts which she wore as part of her costume. The zombies looked at each other, then back to her, shoulders slumped.

"Oh, y'all know what I mean! Shamble for it! G'wan! Mama will be irie, ya hear?"

She turned her back on the boys, and stared into that great purple eye in Garith's chest. It blinked, then narrowed. Mama hefted her walking stick.

"Ahhh, so ya know what dis is, do you, you slimy old bastard?" she asked. "By the power of Mister Crossroads, and old Von Tuesday, and the Eyeless Lady, I cast you back!"

Power flared, and a blast of blue smoke curled up off of the legs which were forcing their way through Garith Smembly's face. A third was groping and clawing out the back, and Mama didn't want to think about how it had gotten there. A squeal tore through existence, accompanied by a ripple in the air, and the walls, and the stone beneath.

"Gwan! Get out of my reality, you dirty big trespasser! Back to whence you came from!"

This time, the blast of sorcery was aimed right at the thing's eye, and it struck home with a sizzle and pop. Horrid boiling fluids spattered Mama Lurga, making her stagger backwards. But she was still able to see what happened next.

The ruined eye in Garith's chest rotated away, to be replaced by two, then three. The spider legs forcing their way through his mouth all heaved at once, tearing the poor little man open. But there was no more blood inside. Like Boss 29, he'd become a living gateway, a portal which framed another portal. A *door*, which hung crazed off its hinges.

"No," said a voice which filled the world from edge to edge. **"You misunderstand. This *is* where I came from. From here, and from inside the sick little minds of every stinking, crawling thing which came before you. I am the darkness you pretend is the fear of death. I am the rot that takes the mind before the body starts to decay. I am the maggot's joy, and the parasite's hallelujah, and the sadist's glee."**

"You're the elder god of boring, long-winded speeches?" managed Mama, now leaning back on her cane for support. The room became immense, then, walls blasting out toward infinity, all just to contain the thing which heaved itself across the threshold.

"I am Zag-Hammurat! Incarnation of evil for the sake of evil!

And I have *risen again!*"

This last sentence rose to a roaring crescendo, shaking Mama Lurga's brain in her skull like a pea in a maraca. Nevertheless, she hadn't gotten to be an *old* voodoo priestess by being easily impressed. "That's lovely, an' I'm sure you're proud of yeself," she said. "But I still got one trick up me magical sleeve, right?"

Zag-Hammurat loomed up over her, expanding and creaking as wings and limbs and a tail like a black-lacquered spinal column unkinked. There's a tendency for some writers to simply state that certain things are indescribably horrible; the celestial spider-dragon certainly was that. His was not just a form of nightmare. It was a form that the first ever nightmares, in the brains of twitching little vole-things, were conjured to encompass. He'd only gotten worse since then.

"Oh? You seek to deny me, witch? Go on! Do your worst!"

"You have't close your eyes and count to ten," she said, making mystic passes with her walking stick.

"Really?"

"You want me worst. d'yah? Then *really*."

The ancient horror sighed.

"Very well then. One, two, three..."

Mama Lurga chucked her walking stick right in the thing's face and legged it, just as fast as a voodoo granny can. This is a lot faster than anyone who has not been to a bingo free-for-all will attest.

And behind her, with a roar, Zag-Hammurat smashed his way out of the Stilts, into reality, and up into the sky.

His wings unfurled, a quarter mile each side of a segmented body shaped like a slick and squamous spider. One downbeat, and the Stilts creaked, flattened down by a hurricane gale. Two, and whole buildings shattered, blasting bamboo and rice-paper out into the harbour. The Alchemical Chapterhouse tore free of its moorings altogether, and sailed away like a box-kite, to land in the sucking mud of the western shore.

Zag-Hammurat rose, his wings thrashing, hauling skyward an armoured thorax with eight dangling spider legs. The front two of these, which were long and lean and wicked, ended with langoustine claws, delicate sharp scissors of chitin. From the rear end of the spider-dragon depended the great slick bulge of its abdomen, huge and tight, with a whiplike skeletal tail thrashing beneath. From the front coiled a draconic neck, slender and scaled, culminating in a head with the features of both a reptile and a spider; horns, vibrissae, eight purple eyes and a complex set of mouthparts ever chewing, dripping with venom.

The shadow of Zag-Hammurat fell over Grand Sepulchre, and suddenly the flower-hung skulls and ivy-coated spikes of the place seemed like a child's drawing of evil. For here was the real thing - chilling the bones of all who glimpsed it; an impossible bulk of madness, skimming the towers and weathervanes as it circled up and in, toward the Malevolith.

The ſuper-heroes of the Rotten Company watched it go, as they pelted toward the centre of the city, passing through empty streets. Even the Beggar's Guild had upped sticks, leaving behind a series of cardboard cut-outs which bore the legend – 'Your alms are important to us. Please place your coinage in the bowl in front of this two-dimensional leper, and a real one will be with you shortly'.

The underworld of Grand Sepulchre was crowded sardine-tight tonight, as people packed into their tunnels and cellars, waiting for ruin to pass them over.

For some, it would not.

Zag-Hammurat opened his meatworks jaws, so packed with mis-matched fangs that they sliced into his own flesh. A rattling hiss issued forth, and then he belched up a blast of indigo flame, torching a whole swathe of the city. From High Wittering across to Hammer's End, flettons exploded and timbers curled up, blackening.

The beast swung low, down the length of Bentsteeple, and fired off another blast, engulfing the Creedish Temple until it collapsed into a puddle of slagged stone. Even the smoke which came with this dragonflame was toxic; it boiled thick, purple and dense, seeping under doors and behind shutters, withering the flowering vines and sending the tamarins shrieking.

Hundreds of the little creatures choked to death as they fled, dropping to the ground like rotten fruit. How many humans gasped their last, behind closed doors, was unknowable.

The spider-dragon turned a leisurely figure-of-eight in the air, playing with his quarry, even as three bolts of lightning hammered into the crown of the Malevolith, shaking the entire city. This was just Himself warming up. But the Wizards beat him to the blow.

From the spires of the Unspeakable College came a battery of sorceries; whirling spells like discs with teeth, bolts of radiance, blasts of flame, balls of sickly fire and warping waves of gravity. Some of these splashed against Zag-Hammurat with little effect, while others made him even angrier. One of the world-bending gravity twists must have torn something inside the beast, for it skimmed the tower-tops, trying to flame, and all that came out was a spatter of acidic drool.

This still managed to completely dissolve a chantry of high-level aeromancers, whose iceblade invocation went off prematurely, looping through the sky to burst in upper Bishopsbath, freezing an entire street solid. A quintet of skeletons were left steaming on the walls, their curly shoes on fire.

Now Zag-Hammurat looped, hideous mouthparts writhing, and unleashed a thin, focused blade of flame which sliced the Pennycandle tower in half. The upper segment, freed of its chains, levitated away, never to be seen again.[53]

But the Wizards had a response. Up atop the tower of the Three-Fingered Hand, mage-artificers brought forth something even He Himself hadn't known about. A device from the Age of Hubris, discovered deep below the city, and restored by heretical followers of no less than Enkalderon the Younger himself...

Chains rattled, and trapdoors thudded open. An immense tube of iron and gold was levered into place, techolytes in their black robes furiously spinning cranks and throwing levers to aim it. The faculty called it the Finger of Doom, but in fact it was an unfathomably old starship weapon; a Disintegration Cascade Sub-Atomic Destabiliser, built for a war so long forgotten that the species which fought it were no longer even fossils.

The Indifference Engine rolled its electric eyes and moodily shut down its gothic bard music. Massive thaumic shunts sucked the enchantment from a lifetime of relics, pilfered from the corpses of heroes who'd come to fight the Mantigore. Through a series of tubes and whirring prayer-wheels and sizzling globes of crystal, this stuff was transmuted into raw energy.

A pair of nicotine-stained thumbs, belonging to Archmage Minor Lucimedes Smollet, jammed down on the twin triggers, absolutely unsure as to what would happen next.

What stabbed out the end of the Finger of Doom was a plaited rope of force, orange and pink, tangled up in way that would give anyone

---

53. Although some say the wizards inside sealed off the stump of their tower with a spell of shielding, and managed to steer around the moon of Fingril, slingshotting their way to a landing in Szerenica. This would explain the name of the leaning tower in the village of San Pedro de Nuda, which was named 'the unlucky chicken', El Pollo 13

who glimpsed it a three-day headache. Zag-Hammurat answered with a boiling belch of flames.

Where they met, reality simply ceased to exist. Seething fractals proliferated, causing immense anti-explosions and inverse implosions in equal order. Energy, mass, speed, time, and even concepts like macramé, pineapples, Thursday evening and pasta sauce collided and melded, swapping places in a mad gavotte. A rain of elk's blood, small cherry pastries, flying fish and one very solid marzipan grand piano fell on Bulbous Corners, where, forever after, it would be impossible for anyone to say the word 'toggle'.

But the fire was a diversion. The dragon was missed. And here he came, looping out from behind the collapsing haze of improbability, the great hooked blade on the end of his tail slicing down...

The Finger of Doom was shattered, wailing wizards flying clear as it plummeted into the moat. A desultory hail of tiny spells pinged off the thing's hide as it circled up and back, filling its lungs for a withering blast...

Only to be knocked sideways out of the sky.

Zag-Hammurat *screamed*, nails down a chalkboard measured in light-years. He folded up like a venomous umbrella, smashing into the side of the Sugarloaf, already weakened by being perforated by Gloom. This time, the entire saw-backed top of the mountain was shattered, sending boulders the size of castles strewing out into the arid lands beyond. Thunderclap echoes faded, as the Invocation of Unnecessary Unction burned shadows into the cobbles and bricks across a wide swathe of Grand Sepulchre.

Still, He Himself, the Dark Emperor, was not foolish enough to believe that this could have stopped his nemesis. He'd gone and done something heroic, after all, and now... now the moment he'd put off for so long, for the sake of his people, was at hand.

"Leave them, you foolish creature!" He shouted, his voice seeming to lose the creak and grind of centuries. "If I'm going to go out as a hero, I'll go out fighting you, man to... whatever you are."

Zag-Hammurat wheeled and banked in the sky, lightning stabbing down all around him. The rain had stopped, now, and the clouds were breaking up, allowing slivers of moonlight through. These did nothing to make the avatar of evil for evil's sake more beautiful. With a howl like a great steam-boiler bursting at the seams, the spider-dragon flung itself at the top of the Malevolith, spinning and looping to avoid a barrage of sorcery.

The undead Emperor summoned javelins of ice and bolts of darkness from out of nowhere, casting them one after another at the onrushing beast. Some skimmed past. Others shattered on its armoured scales. A few struck home and pierced its bloated abdomen, loosing dribbles of pus and bile. One punched through a wing, tearing a ragged hole... but it was no use. Nothing could slow Zag-Hammurat down, and his impact with the Malevolith rocked the foundations of Jansamrana.

Across the Arch', the great telescopes and mirrors of the Empyrean Institute in Simbalia registered a wobble in the giant rock; in Mirgova, the Sisterhood of Mother Ocean felt a tremor in the tides.

Spider legs scrabbled against obsidian, as the mammoth beast flared its wings out wide. Claws darted in, and that hook-tipped tail lashed like a coachman's whip, scarring the very stone. No living thing could have survived the spider-dragon's onslaught.

But of course, *He* was no living thing.

Up atop the Malevolith, an aura of crackling power surrounded the Emperor's armour. Gothic spikes and scales sizzled with it; beads of concentrated force dripped from his scissor-blade fingertips. The crown bolted to his helm prickled with dancing fire, and the eyes behind it were almost real, again, surrounded by the glassy image of a face.

Those eyes twitched over to Callistae, who was watching all of this with a tiny smile on her lips. She'd summoned a pale white branch through the gap in the sky, and she sat on it primly, her shoes dipped into the puddle that used to be Gloom. She polished an apple on one sleeve, and took a bite, and waved.

"You don't have to obey Her!" He shouted, using Spite to part a blast of dragonflame so that it swirled by on either side of Him. "She's using you, just like the last dragon!"

Zag-Hammurat laughed, pressing his attack. A claw came scraping across the tower-top, scattering shards of shattered glass.

"I'm nothing *like* the last dragon, hero," it spat. **"Silly red beast, with its big mattress of gold, and its airs and graces! An outdated stereotype, ready for the fossil record. Pah! You think that trick you pulled would have worked with *me*? Or that I'd have left anything of poor Ikarus for you to mope over?"**

Now came another lance of fire, and the lash of that cruel, hooked tail. The runesword Spite parried again, steel skirling on chitin.

"It doesn't count as using me if this is *what I want!* This is how you die! The fact that your Goddess ordains it is immaterial."

He feinted and rolled, coming up in time to hew deep into one of the spider-dragon's legs. White ichor spurted, sizzling. Then a blast of flame knocked the Emperor from his feet.

"You don't even know what She is," He said, rising from a crouch. The fire had burned the rust away, and now His armour was silver, new-forged and gleaming. "You know I'll just come back, don't you?"

A lunge, and teeth snapped closed a razor's width from where He had just stood. A twitch, and Spite hissed by, mere inches from Zag-Hammurat's muzzle.

"Oh, I *know* you will return. Heroism is a most persistent disease. I'll be waiting for you, of course. Here, in the ruins of this city. Here, in what they'll call the necropolis of Grand Sepulchre. The city whose ruler *failed!*"

This time, His attack was pure rage. The same brutal poise, the same lethal grace which had taken the head off Gloom; those arts of war and witchcraft which had seen him defeat every monster Callistae had ever thrown at him. *Concentrated. Refined. Rendered down to an edge.*

That edge carved into Zag-Hammurat in a dozen places, lopping off a horn, taking out a pair of eyes, carving through an entire leg and ripping through the creature's scales.

"I won't let this be a game anymore! It's not worth it! Not just to forget..."

Zag-Hammurat reared back, claws snickering, flame belching skyward. He shrieked, a whole scale in discord at once - a sound which tasted of iron and blood, and felt like a storm of nails. But it was Callistae, sitting on her bough with her apple, that the Emperor heard.

"You said *forever*," admonished the Goddess, with a little frown.

He raised his hand to his helm, and ripped the clasps loose. Beneath, he was a pale-green and ghostly thing, the shade of a man with blue eyes, a square-cut jaw, three-day stubble and a small, pointed beard.

"I said a *lot* of things, Callistae. We all did. Me and Ikarus and Shye, and Noctaris, and even Jaan, when he could be bothered saying anything. But..."

"And now you'll get to see them all again," said Callistae brightly, taking another bite of her apple. It was round and red and perfect, in a way that real apples have no right to be. "It's time for a new story."

Behind Him, Zag-Hammurat's neck arched, like that of some colossal cobra. The fire which built up in his mouth rivalled that of the twin suns, spilling out all violet and fatal from between his teeth.

"Not again. *Please.* No more games, Callistae. It's time we got back..."

But it was far too late for words. Not when the celestial spider-dragon unleashed a spear of white-hot wrath, directly down on the Emperor's head. Not when his spell-forged armour evaporated, molten metal bursting into a gaseous state. Runic bindings flickered and died around Him, threads of sorcery crumbling. Spite was dashed from his hand to splatter across the stonework, a molten streak.

"Oh, Cipher," said the Goddess, as, for an instant, he hung there suspended. A ghost tethered to a great lumpen mass with bones in it, its stench finally burned away. "You're going to look, and *smell*, all the better for this. You and Ikarus should never have survived the last dragon I sent you. In any case, you worked it out then, and you still know it now. The only way to change the parameters..."

The fire pulsed. That nightmare head came snapping down, jaws open. It snaffled up the mortal remains of the Urzoman Emperor, and twin rows of mis-matched teeth scissored shut, lacerating a set of black and purple gums. Six remaining eyes widened with surprise.

"...is to beat the game," finished Callistae, as her horrible pet swallowed. "Well, I suppose that's that. Off you go then, Zag-Hammurat. Make a nest, or a hoard of bones, or whatever your kind do. I'm pretty sure He'll be back for you, in a few decades. He's like that, you know. Stubborn. *Remembers* things, even through the mind-wipe."

The clouds which remained, scudding across the darkened sky, blasted apart in a radial shockwave. Twin spears of moonlight came down to paint Callistae pearl-white, as she tossed away her apple core and cracked her knuckles.

"Right. Now to contrive some sort of meeting for those five fools, again... Chapter one, of volume two hundred and ninety-three. The Party meet in a dusty old tavern, in... let's say Shangola. It's a summer's night, and the wine flows freely, as.... oh!"

Callistae's little cry of shock was very genuine.

So, unfortunately, was the choked-off scream which followed. The celestial spider-dragon, avatar of evil for the sake of evil, might have heard. But it was not in Zag-Hammurat's nature to help people - even ones which had freed him from the prison of unreality where he'd slumbered for so long, pressed between dimensions.

Great leathery wings cast their shadow, as the monster sought a new lair.

While down on the ground floor of the Malevolith, late, angry and sodden, the Rotten Company kicked in the doors...

27
The Truculent Ascendancy

"YOU NEVER TOLD me," puffed Amber, as they came to the top of yet another set of ornate black marble stairs, "that Gloom could shape-shift into a dragon!"

"What is he? Some kind of were-creature?" asked Soto, almost running into the back of them both. He settled for slinging a companionable arm around each of their shoulders. "I heard about this feller in High Wittering, right, who got bitten by a rabid hedgehog, and at the full moon, see..."

"He didn't *turn into* the dragon!" wheezed Jack, trying to get his breath back. After twenty flights of stairs, each more skull-carved and wickedly spiked than the last, they were still only inside the lower pediment of the Malevolith. "And he's..."

"Then you never told us he *had* a dragon, mister bloody pedantic," put in Monty, who was chafing to leave them all behind. This copped him a slap across the back of the head from Slag Iron, who was simply chafing.

"Oi! This is no time for disharmony in the ranks, you pillock. That thing's torched a quarter of the city already!"

"Yes. It might even cover up the damage *we've* done," interjected Billiam Knox.

"It might, too," mused Zoltan Creagle, rubbing his chin thoughtfully. "But here's a good question. Why are we running *toward* the very real danger in this situation? When we could, if you follow, just loot some of the unnecessary government gold lying about the place, then exit the poor, doomed ex-city of Grand Sepulchre, wiser, and here's a point, *richer*... and much more alive?"

Amber slumped down against the wall, beat.

"You know what? That's a damn fine question, Zoltan. After all, most of us didn't choose bloody heroism as a career. Why *are* we climbing to the top of the biggest lightning-rod in the city, to battle a creature which may or may not just have gobbled up an immortal undead sorcerer-king? Why aren't we just, I don't know, running for it, like everyone else?"

Jack had a horrible idea that he knew exactly why, but nobody seemed to want him to get a word in edgewise.

"Now, running, not so much *running*, that's a bit of a loaded term," said Creagle. "A stout wagon under cover of darkness, divide the tonnage of treasure between the lot of us, and I reckon we could set up a pretty nice gladiatin' business in Mograth, where my cousin lives."

"I suppose," began Jory Foxmallet. "I mean... I've never really been good at much, but... it seems to me... No. Don't worry about it. Forget it."

Tarrence Bligh clapped him on the shoulder. Foxmallet had given him the last miniature bottle of brandy from his utility belt, and he was feeling pretty well-disposed toward the feckless aristocrat.

"No. Nononono. You go on, my son. You tell us... what you reckon. Justasmucha... much of a right to speak as anyone here!"

Mister Bun Bun chittered in agreement.

"Wellll..." said Foxmallet. "It's just *us*, now, isn't it? If He really is dead, then there's nobody else to stop that thing. It's us, or everyone gets eaten, I suppose."

"So, *we* should get eaten first? That's your logic?" asked Soto. "I suppose it means we wouldn't have to watch all the gruesome bits while everyone *else* gets eaten, but aside from that, your plan holds little merit, old chum."

"No. Wait. He's got a point, you know. The Wizards have stopped trying, the Emperor might be dying up there, or... whatever skeletons do when they stop living for the second time... and here we are. Johnny on the spot, as it were."

This was Master Lurien, and there was a kind of sad, resigned look to his face. He rubbed at his stubbly chin, and sighed. "If it's just about the gold, Zoltan, I'll pay you. It looks like I might have inherited a whole guild, when the Old Lady got washed away."

The Pugilist looked into the poisoner's eyes, and cursed under his breath, pinching the bridge of his nose between two sausage-sized fingers.

"Ahhh, the bloody assassin's got the size of it. I mean, yeah, we *could* use our amazing superhuman powers to run awa... *tactically retreat*. But I get a horrible feeling that we'd just gnaw this moment over in our heads for the rest of our lives, 'til it drove us mad. That's not going be helped by any amount of gold, or champagne."

"That argument could use some scientific enquiry," sulked Montmortimer. "But I suppose you're right. What about you, Jack? Do you think we've got a chance against Gloom's dragon? You keep saying that we're not really heroes, after all."

Jack collapsed slowly down the wall next to Amber. His cape squelched across the marble, leaving a smear of ash and mud behind it.

"Yeah. *Look at us*. We're no heroes, Monty. Not in the old way, like Ranulf was. Not in this new way, either. But you know what? I reckon hero's just a word. People who want to be one are just idealistic idiots, and it gets them killed. People who don't want to be one, and end up getting medals and handshakes and big bouquets of flowers anyway... they're usually just people who were brave enough to do what needed doing, right? And then the word gets hammered around their neck like a big gold chain. Because people like Himself, and Lord Slave... they *need* more idealistic idiots. They need the kind of people who'll jump in front of a cavalry charge, or storm the enemy cannons, or climb the siege ladders first."

He looked up at the Rotten Company, and noted the expectant look on their faces. That, and the little bruises, cuts, scrapes and abrasions which made them look all too human, and not very ſuper.

"See. You're expecting a big rousing speech, even now. Even though you know I'm awful at them. It's the cape, probably. Anyone who'd wear a cape is likely to have a big rousing speech in him." He swiped one hand under his nose, making very little difference to the mess which covered his face.

"But I'm right, you know. *We're not heroes*. Having special powers means you don't really have to be brave. Not like some poor run-of-the-mill peasant, who they lumber with some rusty chainmail and a spear. What it *does* mean is this. If we don't do what needs to be done, then we haven't got normal people's excuses. These powers have given us the opportunity to be even more horrible cowards than normal. So, I'm saying *no*."

"No, you won't fight Gloom's dragon?" asked Amber.

"No, *I won't be a bloody coward*. And for the record, it's not 'Gloom's Dragon'. It belongs to a little short lady in white, who might be even worse than he is. Gloom's not going to be doing much villaining anymore. I saw the Emperor chop his head clean off his shoulders."

Slag Iron and the Grimshadow shared what could only be described as a 'significant look' then.

"Chopped it right off?" he asked.

"Right between the old spinal vertebrae?" she queried.

"As in, he won't be needing a necktie for his next birthday?"

"No real use for a barber, where he is now?"

Jack nodded.

"Clean as a cut-throat razor."

"Will you tell him? No? Should I then..."

The Grimshadow tugged at his collar.

"Ummm. It's just that, see. Errr... We kind of *tried* that with one of his big bruisers, down under the Halfway House."

"Took his noggin off, like filleting a kipper," added Slag Iron, proudly.

"It's just the thing is... it didn't work."

"The black goop they're made of, see? Stitches 'em right back together, so it does."

Jack thought, then, of the glutinous black puddle which surrounded the corpse of Gloom. Of the unspeakably powerful, haloed little lady who had stepped through into reality, summoning dragons and speaking riddles. About how she was *standing directly in it...*

"Oh, bugger." he said, as a tremor ran through the entire Malevolith. Every line seemed to bend out of true at once, and a hazy image blurred across the black marble, filling the empty hall behind them with a vision of...

"Clerks? People with big piles of papers? Lots of those type-engraving engines, like the ones the Scriveners' Guild uses?" Soto scratched his head. "Are you seeing this?"

The illusion was misty and transparent, but it was definitely there.

"We have to get to the top, *now!*" shouted Jack, struggling to his feet. Realities ground up against each other in his head, fighting each other for every neuron and synapse.

"Ice," said Slag Iron, slapping her armoured hands together. "That's the ticket! We always used to get the ice late down at the fishmarkets, because the best stuff was always sent directly here. To Him!"

"Well, it's never too early for a cocktail, but I fail to see how..." began Monty, but Zoltan had caught on much quicker.

"*Freight elevators!* We had 'em for moving the big, caged beasties under the pits, right? He's got to have 'em here. Big, water-wheel powered engines, big chains, and lots of little convenient doors."

Another shudder went through the whole great rock, and the walls tilted, skewed at wyrd angles. With it came the same skin-crawling sensation that Jack had felt before, when he fought Gloom above the burning city. It was the prickle of countless minds, trying to lock onto something and make it real.

"I think we'd better hurry," he said, as fractures skittered through the stonework. "At least a dragon belongs in this universe!"

Whatever was happening to the Malevolith surely didn't.

From without (and viewed from a safe distance) the spire of skull-carved black stone seemed to waver and bend. Warping fields of power folded in like petals, drawing down a firespout of aurorae from the heavens. The entire building was beginning to twist, pulled out of true, its straight lines and vaunting blades of volcanic glass bent into the shape of a drill-bit a mile tall.

Gloom may have been lying about the whole thing exploding if the bells were silenced, but there was a truth to the fact that five hundred years of sorcery does not go quietly...

Every minute or so, a shriek like that of a colossal bottle-rocket would echo over the city, as spells twisted beyond their limitation sheared loose. Arcs of shimmering energy speared out when this happened, and where they struck chaos was unleashed. A tenement in Belfry Roost turned into a snail of prodigious size. A merchant ship in the harbour was transmuted to solid peanut butter. The cobblestones of the Old Bishopsbath Stairs became a swarm of chrome-mirrored scarabs and flew away, while part of the Fleamarket was turned to bubbling toffee, in which skeletal faces leered and gibbered. Smaller targets popped in and out of reality, changed colour, became freezing cold, melted, or began to levitate, all over Grand Sepulchre.

And here was worse luck – not one of these sorcerous eruptions so much as grazed Zag-Hammurat, who had settled down in the Brute Pits, finding that the main arena formed a warm and sandy nest. He felt the need for a bit of a lie-down. *That undead monarch just wasn't sitting right in his belly. It almost felt as if...but no.* The vile dragon belched. *That was* impossible...

This was the scene which greeted the Rotten Company when they burst from the trapdoor atop the Malevolith, bellowing a spectrum of fearsome battle cries from '*Aaaaargh!*' to '*kick 'em in the fruit and veg*' through to '*not in the face!*'.

There was a large, sooty patch of melted glass, with a pair of smoking metal boots welded right in the middle. There was the naked, scarred, and explosively re-bearded bulk of Ranulf the Butcher, his hands wrapped around his knees, staring at nothing as he rocked backwards and forwards, drooling.

Then there was a huge and hideous two-dimensional cut-out in black, tethered to the Guild Errant master by a few cobweb strands, but largely and loathsomely out on its own in this threshold place. Strutting its stuff. Getting it's evil on.

Shorn of depth, Gloom was immense, a ragged-edged shadow, black as execution-order ink. His eyes were triangles of molten green, and his mouth was now just a jagged slot, edged by raggedy teeth. This apparition stood twelve feet tall, feet rooted in the puddle which had sloughed off of Ranulf, and one of its hands was wrapped up all around the being called Callistae.

Where the darkness touched her skin it split apart into a tracery of filaments, forming an intricate knotwork that flowed across her face, her arm, and the weave of her dress, tracing back along the branch she sat on and into the crack in the sky. Lights flickered in there, as the books in their infinite, impossible shelves slid and moved, like facets in some clever puzzle.

"*Help me,*" she mouthed, though the only sound that came out was the noise of mangled gears, in a music box cranked backwards.

Behind this tableau, the city spread out in a vertiginous sprawl, some still aflame, other parts veiled in smoke, flooded, or crushed under fallen landmarks.

"Ahhhh. I've been expecting you," said Gloom, fixing the Company with that baleful green gaze. **"So perfectly predictable. I bet you all wondered what you were doing, trying to stop me. I bet you came up with all kinds of curly moral excuses. But no matter. The real reason why is in your bones. You *have* to defeat me. That's how the story goes. Round and round and round, just like the one this stupid creature tried to weave for her little friends."** He leered, flapping in the wind like a ragged black sail. **"You have to defeat me, because *that's how I win!*"**

"Less grumbling, more pummelling!" Insisted Tarrence Bligh, holding up one of Soto's hangover cures between thumb and forefinger. "It seems to me, every time we listen to this ol' gobshite, we get deeper in the brown stuff. What say we just hammer him flat, and talk all this hero talk later?"

There was a general consensus for this among the Rotten Company. The Pugilist slipped on a pair of golden knuckle dusters. Amber's claws slid out with a horrible oily rasp. Bill Knox split in two, sizzling around the edges with power. Slag Iron levitated off the deck, twin arm-blades unfolding with a snick and clunk of hidden machinery.

But it was Jack, usually the first to throw the proverbial haymaker, who stopped them.

"No!" he shouted. "Wait! There's a way this has to go, isn't there? I think I know this kind of story. Before we get down to the missing teeth and the blood and snot and kicks to the fork, you have to tell us your evil plan. *All of it.* And you have to do a great big laugh, too."

Gloom twitched, a shudder rippling through his entire form.

"No, I think that... ahahaha.... no, really, let's just get to the.... bwahaaaaa... the traumatising violence, because as soon as you... I mean.... hahahaaaa.... someone *punch me,* damn it! Come on! You pansies! You pillocks! You peasants! You parsimonious pulchritudinous parochial perversions! I... hahaaaaa.... *bollocks...*"

A shock of green sizzled right though him, then, from the power rod lodged inside his forehead to the tips of his toes, and down the invasive tendrils which plunged through the crack in reality.

Gloom could no more resist giving his big, victorious gloating speech than Mother Ocean could resist the tides.

"Oh, all right then! *Bwaaaaaaaaaahahahahahahahaaaaaa!* How's my tone?"

Jack gave the ſuper-villain a tentative thumbs-up, motioning for the rest of the Rotten Company to do the same.

"You've got this, old chap!" encouraged Master Lurien, miming applause. Gloom grinned.

"Very well. *Ahem.* Fools! Strike me down now, and the whole world will witness the dawn of the ſuper-heroic age!" He shrugged. **"How's that?"**

"Spot on," said Jack, through gritted teeth. "Pray, continue."

Gloom preened, literally puffing up with evil pride.

"Yesss! This thing, this creature – she is like me. A fount of pure power. The whole world you knew, aye, the reality you cling to for your precious sanity, is but an illusion, wrought by this *Callistae.* Every plague, every war, every monster – yes, *especially* every monster. They were all part of a *game,* for the amusement of five fleshy human fools. Know this, and feel your grip on reality crumble! Know this, which drove Himself to madness! And know that I am here to remake this world in MY image! A world with a different story, about people in tights, and aliens, and other dimensions, and saving the world with a big. Impressive. *Fist-fight*

in the sky!"

Gloom unfurled, growing even larger as he gloated. His free hand spread open like a claw as he gestured dramatically.

"The death of your foolish Emperor has reset the game! Now is my time to conquer. Why create just one hero, when I can make a world of them? Why settle for one story, when I can have them all! You will be my example, and usher in a new golden age. Now come! Fight me! Ascend! Your destiny awaits you!"

Gloom finished with a villainous pose, worthy of any number of heavy metal album covers. Far away, a last flicker of lightning lit up the skyline, and thunder rumbled.

"How was that, then? I was quite pleased with that bit about your sanity crumbling, there. Also, the part about your destiny awaiting. Gave the whole thing a mythic quality, I felt. Now, shall we get to the horrible violence?"

"Yeah, I don't think so," said Jack, cracking his knuckles. "Not after you've basically just told us your whole stupid plan. Which *is* stupid, by the way."

"*And* you're a worse actor than any ten opera singers I can name," added Monty, carefully removing his cuff-links and tucking them into a waistcoat pocket.

"Basically, we're just going to ruin it all for you, by rescuing the girl," finished Zoltan, kissing his big metal 'dusters, left and right. **"Didn't you listen to *anything*?"** asked Gloom. **"That's not a *girl*. That's a machine just as wicked and heartless as me, who's been literally using you people as monster-fodder and leprous set-pieces for ten thousand years!"**

"Does rescuing her royally f-up your plan?" asked Slag Iron.

"Well...yes, to a certain extent, but..."

"Then prepare for the royal f-ing, if you'll pardon my Clourvonnaise," said the Grimshadow. "And that's a *proper* f, not one of those ʃ things that's been showing up everywhere lately!"

"But... but I can make you *immortal!*" wailed the ragged, inky shape with the glowing green eyes.

"Here's a counter-offer," grated Amber. "We'll make you the opposite."

Everything lined up perfectly, in that instant. Jack felt it; the sensation of the whole world clicking into place, puzzle-pieces made of glass twinkling as a beam of pure light shone through them. It wasn't Gloom's trickery, and it wasn't magic, either. It was just...*right.*

The Rotten Company were caught in mid-leap, backstopped by the huge figure of the Unstoppable It, all bulk and fury. Out to the flanks came the Atomic Fop, candy-cane walking stick blurring, and Slag Iron, aloft on jets of green fire. The Grimshadow's swirling cape framed the graceful arc of the Honey Badger's claws, and an arc of taut muscle beneath her costume as she attacked. Billiam Knox was frozen in the moment of launching his other self up and over, hands clasped, a wild grin on his face. The Pugilist was swinging wild out on the right, his little crown of gold leaves levitating above his bald head. A flapping skein of toga lent some small amount of modesty to the Naked Flame, as he raged incandescent. And ahead of them all, knives out, came the horrible, cheerful zipper smile of Mister Bun Bun.

It was a sight to inspire righteous feelings in even the stoniest heart. It was a signal broadcast on the wavelength of the brainstem, snarling up the program which Callistae was trying to reset. It was an image of power and cooperation which could hardly be matched by any vision of evil and might.

Except, perhaps, by several tonnes of spider-dragon, rising up behind Gloom with a churning of wings and a skittering of claws. Not to mention a bad case of gas, and an expression of acute discomfort on its hideous face.

"Oops! That's right! You forgot about *him*, didn't you? And seeing as I've got *her*, I've got the dragon. You want to rescue the princess? You're going to have to go through old scaly, here!"

The moment passed, collapsing into chaos, as the Rotten Company fell over themselves trying to backpedal. Twin jets of purple smoke chuffed from Zag-Hammurat's nostrils. Sharp, glistening spider legs punched into the stone of the tower-top. Jack was smiling, though.

"Rescuing a princess from a dragon? Come on now, Gloom. You know that's not your kind of story. Maybe someone else is still driving this dunny-cart, eh?"

The ſuper-villain looked stricken for a moment, and his eyes twitched left and right, as if seeking some creeper or daggerman, right behind him. But then his smile hitched back up at the corners. He waved an admonishing finger.

"Clever, clever, little hero! But never mind. No one will be left alive to write it down! Now – Dragon. Eat these bastards! I'll just pretend to take a dive to the last one left."

Zag-Hammurat didn't need a second invitation. With the churning in his belly and the headache that was coming on, obliterating a

shower of caped pillocks would be nothing short of therapeutic.
Flame built up inside his maw, rising like a tide...

28

The Regicidal Reflux

THROGG THE OUTLANDER, barbarian hero for the ages, inventor of the now-legendary fur underpants and owner of a set of pecs which could crack coconuts, once dictated the ultimate scroll about fighting dragons to his hapless sidekick, the Blue Bard Rantalio Spantallion. The very first piece of advice this hallowed document shares with the would-be wrangler of wyrms, drakes and fire-lizards is –

Don't.

Run away, it says. Forget your dignity. Poop your britches to lighten your load, and pump those bunions like it's going out of fashion. There are two kinds of dragonslayers, it says – the very lucky, the liars, and those who are terrible at maths.

Seeing as, if you are actually facing a dragon in the first place, you probably aren't that lucky, Throgg insists that getting a chunky wedge of geography between you and the creature is step one, wherever possible.

Step two, if you really *must* try to demortify such a beast, is to employ the aid of a *'medium-sized to large army, well trained, clad in non-flammable fabrics and doused in lanolin, armed with cannon, longbow, harpoons, and sundry artes of wizardry, to tenderise yon wyrm until its near expiry'*.

He then says it's the hero's task to jump up on top of the dead or dying body, stick a very large spear in its eye, and claim to have done the whole job him (or her) self.

"After alle," says the Outlander. "Even a bigg buggar lyke myself be not mightier than a hundred-span iguana what hath swallowed an blaste furnace. But I *amme* biggar and meaner than most of the poore soddes who will be left, and bragging be half thy battle!"

So advised The *Liber Draconis Malificarum*, most revered treatise on the art of slaying.

It was lucky, then, that not one of the Rotten Company had ever read it.

They attacked from every side, those with a little of Zoltan's horrible potion left slugging it back as they came. And there was a symmetry there, to their onslaught. The Pugilist hadn't had long to teach them how to fight together, but something about their very powers made it intuitive. Of course, he *had* taught them some eye-wateringly low blows, but on a dragon, these were largely academic.

The Unstoppable It wrangled Zag-Hammurat's neck in a death-lock, squeezing until his biceps were the size of baby hippos, and his teeth gritted with a sound like grinding concrete. Amber ran right up past him, her claws winking in the moonlight, and stabbed in through the top of the creature's snout, locking its jaws together. Acidic drool whipped in long, disgusting ropes, but the Honey Badger held on, twisting the blades.

Meanwhile, the Atomic Fop had tied a knot in the spider-dragon's tail. The Naked Flame, who one would assume could have little effect on a firedrake, had instead opted to assault the creature's spidery parts, lashing at its tender underbelly. Ghastly pale blisters swelled and popped, making Zag-Hammurat screech.

Mister Bun Bun, tiny compared to his colossal foe, sunk his teeth into one scorpion claw, and began to punch it with the most efficient wrecking tools ever evolved by nature. Cracks skittered across the black chitin, exposing pallid flesh beneath. The Pugilist, ever the bastard, collapsed one of its knees with a weltering blow from his knuckle-duster.

This all must have hurt. It must have caused truly nasty discomfort.

But not so much as the combined efforts of the Double Vision and the Grimshadow.

Bill Knox took one of his doppelganger's hands, and Foxmallet took the other. Then, at a dead sprint, the pair launched the spectral Knox up and through Zag-Hammurat's head, redoubling the woozy, nauseous sensations which already threatened to overpower him. Along with this came the latrine-mouthed, furry-tongued, skull-hammering awfulness of the worst hangover ever experienced by man or beast. And that wasn't all. As the celestial spider-dragon wallowed on the edge of the Malevolith, scrabbling blindly for purchase, Slag Iron and the ſcarlet ſpectre saw their chance.

"You put him up there, I'll put him out," snarled Auntie Marjorie, veteran of more brawls than even the fattest of men has had hot dinners.

Jack simply nodded, and took to the sky, blurring back away from the tower-top as a streak of crimson.

Yes. That ought to do it...

He accelerated hard, pushing himself to the limit of sinew and bone, just as Slag Iron downed the entire vial of potion Jack had been keeping for himself. He struck the spider-dragon right in the thorax, from underneath, scattering members of the Rotten Company left and right as his fist connected.

Went the cloud of green sparks, letters glittering and fading...

And up went Zag-Hammurat, looking decidedly airsick, his cheeks bulging out with what Jack sincerely hoped was vomit. At the top of his arc his wings snapped open, spindly digits spreading an acre of scaled leather.

They made a lovely target for Slag Iron, who had braced herself on the Malevolith's crown, and opened up every single weapon concealed in her impossible armour. Tubes clicked and slid, cooling fins sprouted, missile tubes proliferated, and huge, mantis-arm chunks of metal unfurled, with even more green-glowing cannons at their tips.

"Watch the birdie," grated the ſuper-powered fishmonger.

Emerald hell split the sky. Forty nameless, physics-warping weapons spat rods of jade and viridian, so that it seemed the Malevolith was crowned with a tiara of fire. Clear around the Arch' sages and drunkards, thieves and kings saw the flash of light, and wondered if it was a sign from their various gods, ancestors or creditors. The lances of power shredded Zag-Hammurat's wings, punching ragged gashes through them and nailing the great beast to the sky. There it writhed, yammering and hissing. But there was only so much power in Slag Iron's suit, and it seemed to have all drained out in one furious blast.

Curled up, smoking, the celestial spider-dragon plummeted back down toward the top of the Malevolith.

And it was simply too big to get out from under it in time.

Well... Montmortimer could. He ran halfway up one of the Malevolith's spikes as the dragon's body came hammering down, flattering Slag Iron with a sound like a nail being driven into teak.

Jack, who was airborne at the time, could only watch, however, as the Unstoppable It was flung loose, tumbling off the tower.

Billiam Knox and the Grimshadow were only saved by Jory's grappling hook, which left them in a precarious position, penduluming back and forth above the city streets. The Naked Flame blazed like a comet as he caught a flick of the spider-dragon's tail, and went spinning off into the night. Zoltan Creagle was also dashed from the tower-top, falling away with a blood-curdling string of curses. Amber caught Mister Bun Bun, and landed with a perfect roll and rebound, claws retracting as she slid backwards across the slick obsidian on her knees.

Pure style, thought Jack. *How does she do it?* I bet it's just one of those things for her, he reasoned; *like breathing, or making him feel like the back of his neck was on fire when she looked at him.*

The second rule in Throgg the Outlander's codex of dragon-extermination is this; make sure that your dragon is actually dead.

Zag-Hammurat certainly looked finished; curled up, smoking, a knot of gangly legs pointed skyward and his wings shredded to ruin, bleeding pale white ichor. His long neck was stretched out flat, with his head almost at Gloom's feet, eyes closed, forked tongue poking out at a rakish angle.

"No! You were supposed to *destroy* them!" shrieked the ſuper-villain, literally stomping his feet with anger. **"Bloody oversized newt! You see, this is why there'll be no more dragons when I remake this world. Atomic bombs, and lasers on the moon, and big hovering motherships, *that's* a spine-tingling final confrontation! Not some motheaten son-of-an-axolotl who can't even go one round against a pack of dunces!"**

Despite being decidedly un-ſuper, it was Lurien, the assassin, who reached Zag-Hammurat first. He'd been tending to Ranulf the Butcher, and had managed, thus far, to do little more than provide him with the modesty of a loincloth, fashioned from a torn-off piece of black velvet robe.

"Fascinating! *Arachnodraconis Horribilis Necrodeus!* There are said to be toxin glands and poison pouches on this bad boy which the Order Lachrymose has only dreamed of!" He knelt before the tangled mass of ivory which made up the creature's death-grin, extracting a little knife from his belt. "Ohhh, if only my own dear tutor could see me now! I'll be *immortalised!*"

Jack, with his firm grasp of the ironic, was only halfway through shouting a warning when the dragon struck.

Dead, empty eyes snapped opened, and so did those nightmare jaws. Then Lurien was gone, snapped up and sheared and snaffled before even Monty could reach him, and Zag-Hammurat was back on his feet, hissing and smoking with anger.

He was not a happy dragon.

He'd never felt pain like this before. Always, always, he'd been top of the food chain, and he'd delivered pain to others, becoming quite the bon-vivant of tortures. The fact that the spider-dragon now knew just how his many thousands of human sacrifices had felt did nothing for his sense of humour. *Karma was something that happened to other people. Empathy was for the weak! Let this agony, and this feeling of churning acid in his guts, transmute to wrath!*

With claw and flame and scything tail, Zag-Hammurat made this wrath available wholesale. Mister Bun Bun's pink-plush fur was torn open by the lash of a venomous hook. Monty was pinned in a scorpion claw, his speed worth nothing as his bones creaked, close to breaking point. Amber ducked and rolled as a lance of purple flame came boiling out from between the monster's teeth, hotter than the deep-fryers of hell. It lopped off one of the Malevolith's blades in a cross-hatched fury of sparks, sending hot stone flying.

Jack managed to free the Atomic Fop with an uppercut to Zag-Hammurat's chin, sending the thing skittering backwards. Underneath, Slag Iron was revealed – or rather, just the top of her head. She'd been driven into the stone like a piton, and was utterly unable to break loose.

And now back came the ravening dragon, flaming and slicing, snapping and lunging, whipping its tail about to knock Jack sprawling from the air. He slid across the obsidian floor on his face, almost right to where Gloom's boots still slopped in a sticky puddle. Out of the corner of his eye he watched Amber slam up against the one remaining pinnacle of the Malevolith's crown, blood dripping from the corner of her mouth. One of her claws was broken off, a shattered stump. **"I say, this really isn't going all that well for you, is it?"** asked Gloom, nudging him with his toe. **"You see how this could all be neat and clean, if it was a world of heroes and villains? Now all the rest of them have to die in the belly of a big foolish lizard. And all because you're stubborn, Jack."**

He didn't waste time arguing. He rolled back to his feet and launched himself at Zag-Hammurat, fists swinging. Once, twice, thrice - massive piledriver blows rocked the dragon, but it was like assaulting a mountain. A mountain which fought right back...

A spiked claw caught Jack across the cheek, and he felt his teeth float loose in their sockets. The world spun end over end, until he once again slid across the floor on his face, bruises on top of bruises.

Up again. Monty blurred in, and with a lucky shot sunk his rapier to the hilt in the monster's eye. Hideous fluids gouted, and the Fop's luck ran out; Zag-Hammurat's tail lashed him across the chest, sending him plummeting from the tower. Mister Bun Bun landed with a sad little squeak next to Jack, upside down. He shook his ears out of a tangle, and marched forward again.

"Just stay down, Somewhat!" chuckled Gloom. **"I can banish this thing with a thought. I can make it look like you beat it! Everyone will love you, you know. The big hero. The man of the hour. Why, all you'll have to do then is take a swing at me, and you'll be *eternal*."**

Jack hauled his aching fists up again, and battered the spider-dragon's snout. Again, one of its claws smashed him down, like a sledgehammer crushing a fieldmouse.

"Never," he spat. The word... and a gobbet of blood, with a tooth in it. "Bloody *never*, you hear me?"

Another flying attack. A kick to the dragon's thorax, where its legs met. Another terrible counterblow, as that hooked tail ripped the front of his costume apart.

"Why? Because you want to be a hero for real? Come on now, boy. We both know what you really are!"

Jack staggered to his feet again, head spinning. The green fire inside him was fizzling out. He deflated a little, tights hanging limp from his missing muscles.

"Nah." he chuckled. "You don't know anything, do you? Thing out of space, with all your big ideas. You don't know me. I don't want to be a hero. But I can't live with being a coward, either."

Jack tottered forward, grimacing, every part of his body clamouring for a nice week or three in hospital. The punch he lined up should have done nothing at all to a gigantic dragon-demigod, dredged up out of ancient nightmare.

But something was happening to Zag-Hammurat.

The creature rocked back on its spider legs, its huge bulbous abdomen pulsing wetly. Pale fluids were dripping from around its remaining eyes, and slime leaking from between its scales. A thin purple smoke coiled up from its nostrils.

As Jack watched, something pressed up on the inside of the spider-dragon's taut abdominal sac, puckering the shiny skin. It was the imprint of a hand.

"Oooooooohhhh," groaned the ancient darkness. **"I knew I shouldn't have eaten that lich-king..."**

In fact, the remains of Himself were only half of the problem. With a week or two to lie down, the horrible digestive works within the spider-dragon would have rendered even the Urzoman Emperor's bones down to mush. But Master Lurien was another matter. When you're already feeling slightly ill, devouring a man who carries with him, at all times, a selection of the four hundred most deadly venoms, poisons and tinctures from the whole wide Arch' is a gut-wrenchingly bad idea.

"Urrrgh! Blimey! Stand clear, if you know what's good for you!" belched Zag-Hammurat, as something came boiling up his neck, a vast and noisome bulge.

But Jack didn't. Instead, he scraped up every last bit of ſuper-strength left in him, and walloped the sickly beast square on the muzzle.

Zag-Hammurat swallowed. Churning vortices of internal dragon-fire and bile met each other coming both ways. And in that instant, Mister Bun Bun scuttled across under the monster, scooped up Amber's broken claw, and neatly unzipped its entire belly.

A reeking, steaming flood of organs followed. Loops and coils of things which should never see the light of day splashed across the tower-top, and sluiced away into the dark, carrying Mister Bun Bun with them.

Zag-Hammurat *screeched*, so high and loud that small dogs miles away exploded. All those spiked spider legs and snipping claws tried to stuff his guts back in, madly scrabbling, but it was no use. Not when something else tumbled from a slit-open stomach sac, all pale and white and clattering.

It was a set of bones. A full skeleton, and as Jack watched open-mouthed they began to *drag themselves together*. Toes and metacarpals, ribs and vertebrae, radius and femur and tiny phalanges; they rattled like dice, and socketed together with the snick and crack of weapons being loaded.

Finally, a pair of hands bleached clean by stomach acid lifted a grisly skull, and set it in its place. Energy flickered, and wrapped this skeletal form with the shade of a man, ghostly-green and shimmering. Eyes appeared inside a pair of empty sockets.

They were eyes that Jack had seen before.

"Your... ummm... Emperorship! You're back!"

The ghoulish ruler of Grand Sepulchre grinned. It was basically his only option.

"I was never gone, lad. These dumb bastards have a very poor understanding of the term 'lich', don't they? Allow me to enlighten them both."

Himself strode forward, and held out His hand. He spoke a word, all ringing hammers and forge-side sparks and the smell of hot bricks. The splash of metal which had been Spite came rippling up from the ground, and, against all probability, formed itself into a two-handed broadsword in His grip.

"*Lich.* Noun. A wizard who, due to strength of will alone, refuses to die. Who returns to the realm of the living due to unfinished business, as a vengeful spirit tethered to his or her mortal remains." He gave a little nod to Jack. "They teach you that in school, son?"

Jack nodded.

"Civics, m'lord. First week of preschool, m'lord."

"Excellent!" The undead king inspected the edge of his blade, and looked up at the mewling, shuddering wreck of the spider-dragon above him. "*This* is what I do with unfinished business, you see?"

His arm moved in a blur, and a flash of iron and silver sliced Zag-Hammurat clean in half. Perfectly bisected, the beast collapsed in two wilting, bubbling segments.

"**But. But. But...**" began Gloom. Himself put one skeletal finger to his ghostly lips.

"You know, the first dragon shat me out. Nasty business. I smelled horrible for hundreds of years, because of that. But *willpower.* That's what it's all about. Willpower. I'd found out that our friend Callistae here had done me a terrible, terrible favour. So, I knew that no matter how awful it was to live on, as a half-turd, half-skeleton mockery of life... I had to do it. Do *you* have such convictions, thing that wants to change the world?"

Gloom's eyes narrowed, seething green.

"*You.* I know you. *She* knows you, down to the marrow, so now I do, too. Who are you to talk of convictions, when it was you who made this whole world a game? You wanted to forget, so you ran away from your real life, and made all these poor people your puppets! Well, *I* can offer you something new. Something fresh, for the most jaded of sensibilities. An end to these sword-swinging

stories for children. Come on. All you need to do is let Jack there strike me down.”

“Here’s my counter-offer,” said Himself. “You let Callistae go, and I’ll give this all up. We can take you somewhere where there’s help for your kind. Forensic psych-minds, the size of planets. Virtual realms you can build and rebuild, to your core directive’s intent.”

“Last chance, Jack,” said Gloom. “Grasp your destiny! One more little punch, and we’re rid of this fool forever. You can be the hero you were meant to be, and never feel like a coward again.”

Jack looked from his Emperor to his tormentor, confused. What were they both talking about? What were forensic psych-minds? Core directives? Virtual realms? Jack hesitated... and in that heartbeat Gloom struck.

The black and ragged hand of the ʃuper-villain shot out, quick as malice, and scooped up Amber, who was slumped at the bottom of that last unbroken pinnacle. Her eyes opened as Gloom’s tendril-fingers bound her tight, her claws unable to reach him. Though she struggled, there was no way to break his grip.

“We’ll make it easy, then! Jack, you do as you’re told, or I’ll have to motivate you! Do you understand me? This is the oldest story of them all! Only a *hero* can defeat me!”

Jack looked down at his hands. All shrunken back to normal, now, and his muscles too. He was nothing but a seventeen-year-old Grailish oaf again, with nothing of the hero about him. Nothing but the rags of an ill-fitting costume, and a litany of scrapes, cuts, bruises and fractures.

Still, he gritted his teeth against the pain and took a step forward. Gloom’s smile was a wide and jagged hole in the world. Another step, and Jack closed his eyes on the villain’s unhinged laughter, wrapping his fingers up into a fist.

Then he felt a hand on his shoulder.

“He’s wrong, you know,” said the Urzoman Emperor. “I know about the world he wants to make. It’d be just as wrong as the one I’ve been hiding in.”

Himself stepped past Jack, and the ghostly figure wrapped around his bones seemed to become more solid. He spoke directly to Gloom.

“I read those comic books, and watched those movies, and played those games. They were never really my thing, but there’s something I remember that you seem to be forgetting. It doesn’t always take a pure and righteous crusader to vanquish the villains, in that world. It can be the other kind, too."

Gloom screwed up his face in petulance.

"Why are you still talking? Let Jack through. I swear, I'll snap this pretty little idiot in half if that's what it takes to get his attention..."

"Come on," said Himself. "You know what I mean. The champion who does what's needed, even if it's a bit excessive. The one with grey morals, instead of shades of black and white. The force of darkness, turned to snuffing out other shadows."

Now something was happening to Himself, the one Callistae had called Cipher. Jack could see the captive goddess twitching her fingers, playing the subtle shifts in probability like a silent harp.

"No! Not in my golden age! Not in my world!"

"*Yes*," said Cipher, as a costume began to paint itself in around him. "Say it. Say the word. Or I'll say it for you."

He kept his skeletal face. A cowl with red points was scribbled in around his head, ink dripping and bleeding through reality. Next came powerful muscles, wrapped in futuristic fabric. A cape, all ragged and crimson. Black gauntlets, big, heavy boots and skull-faced elbows and knees. Scaled, golden armour covered his midriff, and the insignia of a blazing skull was sketched in across his chest. Spikes grew from his shoulders, and claws from his fingertips.

"No!" said Gloom again, but this time there was a note of pleading in his voice.

"*Anti-hero*," said Cipher, and the words struck the world like two slabs of iron.

They both leapt at the same time.

Cipher, the anti-hero, ploughed into Gloom full-tilt, scooping him up between blazing black gauntlet hands, and carrying him through the crack in the sky. Jack could already see those bladed fingers ripping and tearing, spattering neon green blood, as the crack slammed closed, zipping the stars back up in a dome overhead.

He went for Amber.

Jack caught her as she fell, and he ripped at the tendrils of darkness that bound her with his fingers, breaking nails and drawing blood, even as they began to disintegrate. They'd cut deep into her skin, leaving horrible purple welts. He cradled her head in his hands, wondering just exactly how you were supposed to take a pulse, and why her eyes were closed...

There came a sound behind him.

"Well, thanks for rescuing the other girl before me. I suppose I had that coming. That all could have gone much better, couldn't it?"

It was Callistae, and she was back to her old divine self, stretching the kinks and aches out of her arms. Jack gently let Amber down to the ground. She still wasn't moving.

"Please! Can you help her? It's just... I'm not really very good at *anything*, really, and I can't mess this up, and, and..."

The goddess shrugged.

"Well, I sort of have to go after that hot mess, right? And you know... *Que Sera Sera*, and all that. Spilled milk. Not everyone makes it, kid. Surely you know that, by your age. This city has leprosy, pox, the plague, and a whole guild of murderers!"

Jack stood up, very slowly. Against all probability, green fire sizzled around his hands, and outlined his eyes. He looked up, very deliberately - and huge, hulking muscles stretched his ragged costume tight.

"I heard what they said, you know. About how you think our lives are all a game. Is that what this is? *Because I'm not feeling very entertained.*"

A heartbeat later, and the Green-eyed Lady smiled back at him. Inside that heartbeat, though... ahhh. Inside that heartbeat, where neither of them would ever admit it, Callistae had appeared totally and utterly terrified.

"No! *Yes.* Sort of. It's complicated. Look, I'll break the rules, this once, OK? Call it a fee for services rendered. But after that, you forget all about me. I can't have one of you knowing what the Party know. Five of them is bad enough!"

She reached out, and made a curious pass with her hand, speaking three clear, high notes which should not have been able to issue from a human throat. Amber opened her eyes and gasped.

"Don't listen to him!" she tried to shout... but her voice came out as a cracked exhalation. She winced, and looked around the ruin of the tower-top. "All right. Villain's gone. Ribs broken. Strange lady opening a portal into... what *exactly* is happening, Jack Somewhat?"

Callistae was indeed unzipping the air, revealing a room in her vast and physics-defying library.

"I think we won," said Jack, helping Amber to her feet. "I saw Gloom get pushed through into... well, into *there*. It wasn't going well for him."

"Did you see a body?" asked Amber. Jack shook his head. Callistae finished off her portal, and turned to her.

"Not as such. But I know Cipher. He can be very persuasive when his dander's up. *Come on!* He ruled your entire city for hundreds of years, after passing through a dragon's... well, the less said about that the better."

Callistae turned to leave. One mother-of-pearl slingback stepped across the threshold.

"Wait! We're coming with you," said Amber, taking a shaky step after her.

"The hells you are! Remember who's the goddess, here!"

"And remember who saved you! No body, no payout. That's what they taught me. I'm seeing this through."

Jack tried to hold her back. At this point, they were basically leaning on each other to stay upright in any case.

"There's no gold in this, Amberelia. This isn't a job. Let's just..."

"*No*. The payoff is, if I'm going to see that bastard in my nightmares for the rest of my life, I'm going to see him dead. Your... ummm... eminence, or whatever we're supposed to call you? Lead on."

Callistae shrugged. The light of a summer's day flickered for a few seconds, across the ruined top of the Malevolith. Then space and time knitted back together again, leaving Ranulf the Butcher rocking backward and forward in silence, under a twin-mooned sky.

Not long after, the old hero's eyes unglazed. He unfolded himself, and tremulously took stock of the carnage all around.

"By the posing pouch of Thagmar the Orc-Cleaver!" he whispered. "What did I miss?"

A creaking voice came from down by his feet.

"A little help?" queried Auntie Marjorie.

29

The Gemini Contingency

DAWN FOUND THE remainder of the Rotten Company camped out atop the Malevolith, with the flyblown wreck of one celestial spider-dragon, and absolutely no powers.

They'd all survived, of course. What was a fall, in any case, to a person whose blood was nine-tenths the fizz of some alien story, about heroes and villains and extremely tight costumes? As Amber had said, if you don't see a body, there's no payout.

Jory and Bill had managed to slowly clamber back up their swinging rope. Ranulf had started trying to chip Auntie Marjorie out of the stonework with his bare hands, but soon Soto, Zoltan, Tarrence and Monty had emerged from the trapdoor and given him a little assistance.

With Gloom (and hence Rodney), out of the world, they could all feel their powers fading. Only Skrx seemed to have kept his uncanny level of intellect, and his perverse choice of costume. Mister Bun Bun he remained, and he wandered about on his little plush legs, probing every crack in the stonework with his knives to try and discover where Amber had gone.

Zoltan had already fielded one emissary from the Wizards, who demanded to know a whole laundry-list of things. He'd taken charge, especially when the young mage who the Thaumatarch had sent had made dire imprecations and suggestions of a sorcerous coup. He'd sent down the largest chunk of Zag-Hammurat's cloven noggin, with the message that the Emperor was having a bit of a lie down, and that the wizards could come and have go if they fancied they were 'ard enough.

"They'll be back, though. Them and the guilds. I reckon we've got only so long to produce Himself, before they come knocking. They'll get Throne's Shadow, because Clorance Gryssle is as easily paid off as a dockside harlot, and that means they'll get the Knock-Men too, and likely the Evil Army as well. I suppose I'd better enjoy my little stint of grand viziering while it lasts!"

So there they camped; Billiam and Soto and Jory, Tarrence and

Marjorie, Montmortimer and Zoltan and their homicidal little mascot. Ranulf wavered in and out of lucidity; while he may have been the physical vessel for Gloom, the Company bore him no malice. In a place like Grand Sepulchre, everyone's uncle's best mate had a good pub story about exorcism and possession. The general wisdom was that the poor bastards who managed to get their bodies back should be left to calm their nerves, usually with a large foamy tankard or two.

Meanwhile, a shadow's width away, the fate of Grand Sepulchre was being decided.

Gloom had almost made it to the heart of the impossible library.

Callistae, Amber and Jack had caught up with the trail of neon-green blood and tatters of darkness in the final, innermost sanctum of that place; a room which was a cube of stairways and ceilings, doors and shelves and hanging lamps on golden chains. All of these moved and shifted, sliding in and out of each other in a mechanised, eye-watering ballet.

At the very centre of the room was a spindle of what could have been ice, or pure quartz crystal, or something else entirely. It formed a jagged hourglass shape, two attenuated pyramids meeting at a point, where they had grown shards and spikes in profusion. Here, a metal cylinder was trapped in the gemstone matrix, and socketed into it...

"Another one. Just like... well, just like *that*."

Jack was right. There was a familiar glowing rod plugged into that engine of chrome and crystal. This one was a different shade of green, however – the same green as Callistae's eyes. In every other respect it matched the spitting, hissing power rod which lay on the carpeted floor, just out of reach of Gloom's severed hand.

He'd been reduced to a straggle and a stain, at the end. He and Cipher, the Urzoman Emperor both. They'd fought each other not just to the death or to a standstill, but into a kind of fusion, wrapped up in each other by the alchemy of a hatred that was almost love.

Amber followed the trail of pale ectoplasm, and inky stains, and scattered bones. They were all mixed up, coiled and intermingled. She could imagine the final moments of the pair of them; a whirling double-helix of rage, self-sustaining and self-destructive...

"The lights are still on," breathed Callistae, smoothing down her dress as she knelt before His skull. "*You always were one tough old bastard, Cipher.* Now I guess you'll be one again."

The Goddess carefully picked up the skull, which did indeed shelter a wisp of blue flame in each blackened socket.

"And what about... well, what about *that* thing? It looks like it's one of yours, right? Does it get a trial? Does it get some kind of punishment, for what it's done?"

There was a brittle edge to Amber's voice. Jack wondered just what she intended to do, if it didn't.

"I think he was mad, rather than pure evil," sighed Callistae. She nudged Rod with her toe, frowned, and moved her fingers in a strange series of passes. A tube of metal, not unlike the one Jack had so recently received from Rhaegulus Cratt, wove itself around the glowing green device. "Trying to instigate a complete systems override during a manual reset? This world of yours, kids, is a machine older than the curly little code of cells that makes you up. You have no ideas how close you came to having it reformatted back to bare rock and lava."

Jack let this one sail over his head, as Callistae picked up the now-encased Rod and handed him to Amber.

"If you need to, you can tear him apart with magnets. Throw him into the sun. Bury him at the bottom of some pit, and pour concrete in. The poor thing is about 99 percent obsession and one tiny part duty, in any case. What's important, is that I regenerate the Original Party, and get their next adventure on track. That's what this is all about, really..."

With a gesture of her hands, Callistae spun the whole room around them. Floors and walls shifted, and the shelves of endless books parted. A semicircle of polished oak floor came rolling in, girdling the hourglass of crystal, and on it sat five stout wooden thrones, carved with an intricate pattern of flowers and thorns.

"Wait!" cried Jack. "Didn't He say He wanted this all to stop? That it wasn't worth it, just to forget?"

Callistae placed the skull of Cipher on the middle throne, setting it down gently, almost reverently.

"He also said *forever,* Jack Somewhat. Be grateful. Your people, and your whole world, sprung from my genetic forges aeons ago, because of his words, and my promise. If you are part of a game, it is a *glorious* game, for it has given you life."

"And yet he cared, didn't he? He worked it out. He cared if we little bit-part characters lived or died. He changed the story."

Callistae's eyes blazed, then, as furnace-hot as Gloom's had ever been.

"You *can't* change the story! You know why? Because it isn't your one. *It's theirs.* I just do what I have to do, to make that happen! The only way to change..."

"...the parameters, is to beat the game!" breathed Jack. "He's still alive, in there. He beat the dragon. He won. Let *Him* decide."

For a second, Callistae stood there, one hand on Cipher's skull, the other reaching out as if into infinity. The world glitched and trembled. Shelves and walls and floors skip-stuttered, blurring from one state to another as the lights flickered, and something rumbled behind reality.

Then her eyes flashed from green to white, and back to the semblance of iris and pupil. She smiled, and sat down cross-legged on the floor in front of the thrones.

"All right. That's what we'll do, then. Never let it be said that I don't know a loophole when I'm shown one. And in the meantime, I'll tell you where they came from. I'll explain why... well, why *everything*, I suppose. It doesn't matter; I'm certain they'll decide to keep going, and you'll remember none of this. The reset is nothing if not thorough."

"I don't like the sound of that," said Amber.

"And I don't like the taste of marmalade, but we're all of us different, or it would be a very boring world," replied Callistae. "Come on. It's going to take a while for their bodies to regenerate, at least in here. Out there, it's probably not even morning teatime. Come. Sit. Is there anything else you can do, right now?"

Amber frowned, but she sat. Jack was all too happy to flop down on his back beside her, looking up at a ceiling which was, in fact, a collection of staircases and walls, gliding together and apart.

And the Green-Eyed Lady of the Arch' told them everything.

It began with music.

Jack heard it come spiralling up out of the darkness which filled his head, as his eyelids became heavy and his consciousness dwindled away to a background hum. It was music of a kind he'd never heard before – grand and over-arching, with the thunder of drums and the thrum of a bassline like the living pulse of galaxies. Over the top came the wail and shudder and howl of twin guitars, slippery electric chrome zig-zagging across an empty cosmos, and lighting up the stars.

It was a kind of music which spoke of dragons and demons and plains of ice, mountain fortresses and fathomless seas, where things with luminous eyes coiled and dreamed. It spoke of the vistas of time, and exploding nebulae, and ships skating along the event horizon of black holes just for the sheer damned fun of it. It whispered all of these things before a voice spoke the first lyrics, and when that voice came in, it was like a kick to the soul.

It was *His* voice, the voice of Cipher, the Emperor of Grand Sepulchre, but cranked up to eleven on some cosmic dial. Harmonics came weaving in and out as He spoke of tragedies and kingdoms ruined, heroes striving toward the light while swords clashed, and axes ran red, and sorceries were woven with the power that drives the sap from the roots to the crowns of every tree in a forest at once, on the first day of spring.

It was inhuman and otherworldly, cresting like a wave, but it was not magic, or deception, or whatever manipulation of fate and reality Rod and his kind could achieve. *It was pure art*, and now, swimming up behind the pictures they'd painted in sound, came the artists.

Jack saw a stage floating in space above a strange world; one which was a round ball, with all its oceans stuck to the surface. This badly-built planet should have been impossible, but it seemed to hold together, and the stage, a massive silver pentacle, soared over it, low enough for it to cast a shadow on the hills and valleys which slid by below.

On the stage were five musicians, with instruments beyond those of any bards Jack had seen or heard. One was enthroned behind a wall of drums, his seat spinning a full three hundred and sixty degrees to encompass everything from a gong the size of Zoltan Creagle's elephant all the way down to tiny wind-chimes like silver reeds. Another played a kind of long-necked lute which laid down a thunderous bass resonance. Two more held similar instruments, all gold and fire-red, while yet another held a kind of silver sceptre to his lips, chanting words in a foreign language.

Jack didn't understand the tongue, but he understood *everything* about this music. It was describing his world. It was the Arch' in all its squalor and majesty and vile, violent grandeur. A world for people like Ranulf the Butcher, and old Throgg, and, he supposed, for all the heroes down the ages.

"They were called Derezonator," said the voice of Callistae, in his head. "The most powerful, galaxy-spanning hypermetal band ever. The first to weave neural harmonizers into their songs, and the first to produce a multi-neutronium album, too. They lived in the Spinwise Tendril of the Far Galactic Core. Where the great Slipliners of the Navigator's Chamber Praxis Astra fall between the stars of ten thousand worlds, in a confederation ruled by machines fused with great sages, meditating in the cores of suns."

Jack only caught a glimpse of this far-away kingdom as his mind fell through a mesh of stars; a place of power unimagined, wealth incalculable, miracles made mundane.

And ennui. Immortal, soul-leaching ennui.

"Yes. Entertainment is the ultimate currency, in that place. Originality is something to feed on; to sustain souls which cannot die, thanks to medicine and machines so far beyond your world that even to begin to describe them would make your brain leak out your ears. No insult, of course. The people who live there don't even know how they work. They just push buttons, and wait for the next big thing."

Jack saw the rise of Derezonator. The foundation of their music, in a million stories and games, and shadow-plays projected on flickering silver screens. It all went back to the homeworld of humanity, it seemed. It was a living thing, spiralling through the imagination of generations, as they rode their diasporic arkships into the endless night.[54]

"Four hundred years. Fifty thousand shows. One hundred and twelve albums, each one generating more income for those five people than whole star systems did for their machine overlords. Derezonator could crash economies by delaying a new single. The fleet which brought their show to new worlds was the size of most space-navies, and it was followed by fans from a hundred species, who had dropped out of life to follow their idols. The fanship flotilla and their supply arks alone numbered in the millions. The amplifier dreadnaughts, and the bass-driver megacruisers which broadcast Derezonator's concerts were the size of moons, and bent the tides of planets out of synchronisation when they were plugged in and tuned up[55]. Their flagship, which created the slipspace bubble in which this whole fleet pierced lightspeed, was measured in miles, a black and chrome monolith like a thousand cathedrals hammered into a sword. It was called the *Ecstasy's Razor*, and I was its commanding intelligence."

Jack was shown a vision of this mighty ship, and it was a thing

---

54. In fact, it could all be traced back to single place, in a high mountain meadow in Switzerland, at an event known as the Unmanifest Accords. This saw the birth of High Fantasy and the Gifting of Heavy Metal from the Gods, all in one eventful afternoon. But that's another story.

55. These mighty ships were designed to use the magnetosphere of planets like a giant speaker system, because even the biggest actual speaker wouldn't work in space.

bigger than whole armadas of the little craft which traversed the ring of Mother Ocean. It sailed the sky, this *Ecstasy's Razor*, falling through the night from sun to sun, bringing with it a travelling carnival of music and revelry which could engulf whole worlds. The five masters of the wild music had their own lodging within; palaces and castles bigger than the Malevolith, practice-halls so large that they had their own weather systems, indoor seas and beaches... all tended by a legion of metallic men, like empty suits of armour.

He learned their names – Lou Cipher Mourningstar. Ikarus Stormhammer. Shye 'Silverstrings' Simarl. Noctaris Rexx. Jaan Von Thanriel. Names out of history, some of them, and now, the names blazoned across ten thousand planets.

"Four hundred years, and they became jaded and bored, just like the billions who devoured their music. Drink and drugs didn't work. Debauchery lost its thrill. Even the most extreme sports, like lava-diving, nuclear explosion surfing and fusion-cycle racing became bland and dull. *Death itself* became boring, as even the worst accidents just meant being rebuilt in my geneforges, the memories of their former bodies uploaded into new brains. That's when Cipher, who you've met, became obsessed with Xeno-archaeology."

Jack suddenly comprehended the term, as knowledge was shunted directly into his head. *This would be a great asset, he thought, for those about to take their mid-year guild exams...* and then visions unfolded of exotic starship wrecks, buried in the regolith of moons. Of lost cities, choked under pink and purple vegetation. Of machines made of silver and crystal, sealed in abyssal tombs under methane oceans.

"They heard about the Archipelago. A legend, of an alien race who had created the ultimate pleasure-planet. A chain of islands floating in a ring ocean, around a pair of suns. A place where *everything* was at your command; the weather, the geography, the population, the wildlife... it was a place where the world from their music could come to life. It was a place where they could escape, because the time shoals and whirlpools of probability which protect this place, out in the Shallows, keep out all but the most powerful of ships."

Callistae showed him the great rebuilding, in dockyards so vast they generated their own thin atmosphere. He watched the fitment of titanic and experimental engines, their thrusters so cavernous they could have swallowed up Grand Sepulchre entire. He also saw the news reports, the riots, and the abject pleading by powerful politicians and kings. He viewed the frenzied market collapse, as Derezonator announced their retirement, and their nigh-suicidal quest.

"We made it, of course," said Callistae. "After deciphering all those scrolls, and monuments, and riddles in alien languages. And we found there were already humaniform beings here, living a primitive existence. A little geneforging, a little interface with the alien systems that built the place, and... well. You've seen the results. A world fit for heroes, where my friends can lose themselves, and become new people, over and over again."

Jack watched the *Ecstasy's Razor* slide inside the surface of Balagur, the red sun, entering through massive doors in its artificial skin. He watched Callistae plug in to systems so ancient that they pre-dated the geology, here, and he watched her conjure orcs and dragons, sea serpents and harpies, centaurs and giants. She made the world a game.

"Now do you see why I have to reset? The whole party are dead, and the next round is due to begin. They've brought happiness to billions. They've saved millions from suicide. I owe them everything, and this was their wish."

Jack felt the dream fade – if indeed, that was what it had been. He blinked his eyes against the light as he came up out of it, feeling as if he'd slept for weeks.

"Well, it looks as if you can ask them, if you really must," he said, as he propped himself up on his elbows.

Because the thrones were occupied. There, in the flesh, sat the five figures from the vision he'd just gone falling through in his mind. They were dressed in outlandish garb, to Jack's eyes; from black leather soldier's coats slashed with ribbons and brocade through to form-fitting mesh which shimmered like liquid, and ancient, bleached-out denim held together with hundreds of sewn-on patches. Jaan, tall and thin, with long golden braids and the face of an Elven lord out of legends. Shye, the very image of the old Dowager Empress of Chalinesia, with her heart-shaped face half covered by a curtain of black and purple hair. Ikarus Stormhammer, who Jack didn't recognise at all, until he put one huge hand up over his face and peeked with one eye between his fingers. *By all the dead gods and the living, it was Lord Slave, reborn!* Then there was Noctaris, dark-skinned and violet-eyed like the noble houses of Mograth and Shangola, an icon come to life from the cult of Phorax.

And Lou Cipher Mourningstar, with his piratical grin and his three-day stubble, his dark hair and pale Grailish features framing the eyes of the old Emperor.

"I heard it all. We all did. Nothing makes you nostalgic for the good old days like seeing it all laid out for someone who was never there."

Callistae clasped her hands in front of her, looking embarrassed.

"Well, I'm proud of you all. How could I not be? I suppose that's why I never wanted you to come to this, you know. I can't go back. The interface goes too deep, and I'm about nine-thirteenths Xeno-relic now. I suppose... I didn't want to lose you."

"I suppose it *is* about time," rumbled Noctaris, as if he was talking about leaving an all-night party, rather than abandoning thousands of years of adventures.

"I used to enjoy the shows, really," put in Jaan. "It got to be a bit much, after the first three hundred years, but a break is a break. We need to get back out into the universe, right?"

"I've got a lot of inspiration for some new projects," agreed Shye. "A concept album, at least, about the Jade and Iron Period, or the Obelisk Wars." Her fingers were already tracing out chords and notes on an invisible guitar.

"And it's not goodbye, Callistae. We'll activate the backup of you, back with the fleet. How long have we been in here, anyway?"

The Green-Eyed Goddess twitched a little, her outline blurring.

"This is the *Shallows*, Cipher. Things don't work like that. Out in consensual space, I suppose it could be anything up to ten, or even eleven months."

Ikarus chuckled.

"Our accounts department will be frantic! They might have to sell that little planet we bought them, the one with the mineral pools. That, and the executive starliner."

All this time, Jack had been watching the band, and not Amber. He really should have, because she had been getting steadily angrier and angrier. Finally, she could take no more.

"And that's it then? You just waltz off and leave us with the legacy of thousands of years of death and disease and horror? At the very least, you're monsters for not sharing one *tiny fraction* of your medical knowledge with us. Leprosy? Plague? Scurvy? Dead babies in their bloody millions? *All on you!* And then there's the *actual* monsters! The wars! You used real people to make a game for yourselves, because you couldn't stand being superhumanly popular, and wealthier than gods? I.... I..."

"Ummmm," said Jack, backing away from the incandescent, trembling figure in its dirty, ripped-up cape and tights. "I think things were just going to work out for us, Amber, and so..."

"And so *nothing*, Jack? You said you didn't want to be a coward? Well, meet the real bullies. If there's justice at all in the universe, they deserve hanging ten times over!"

Callistae rounded on her in a fury, but halfway between building herself up for a scream, and seeing the tears in the corner of Amber's eyes, her face fell.

"*They didn't know*, dear. I didn't tell them what this was all about. I just made the adventures happen. If you have to blame someone, blame me."

"Fine!" spat Amber, cuffing those tears angrily from her cheeks. The little tattooed one, marking her as a Guild assassin in training, was indelible. "Fine. If you think Gloom, or whatever's in this metal case here should be ripped apart with magnets, or thrown into a sun, then what about *you*? If you can't leave, sure, we get rid of the parasites who have been the catalyst for *literal centuries of murder*, but what about you? Where's the justice for a self-made Goddess?"

Callistae's face grew hard, then – as hard and artificial as that of a porcelain doll.

"You want the truth? *There isn't any.* Because I'm powerful. You know I didn't take care of every killing, don't you? I didn't watch every murder. I didn't seed every plague. I *certainly* wasn't there when your parents were killed, if that's what this is all about. And remember, girl, I can see what's on the surface of your mind, so *it most definitely is.*"

Amber went for a knife on her belt that wasn't there, but Callistae's hand moved faster than thought, grasping her wrist. Jack didn't think at all. He was right behind the Goddess, arms wrapping her up in a clumsy grapple, before his brain realised what he was doing.

"Really, Jack?" asked the Green-Eyed Lady. "Right here, with no powers, in a world I control with my thoughts, you just pile in to save this girl you hardly know?"

There was a razorwire instant, where it looked as if everything would turn to blood and horror. But then all three of them relaxed at once.

"And you keep saying you're not a hero! Pah! Look, there's no way to undo the past. We could wrangle it over until we all turn to rust and bones, but we *can* make the future. Starting with this. We can't tell the whole Arch' the truth. There'd be utter madness. But I can stop the game. Better – I can make every single one of you a character, just as important as the next one. Your fates will be your own, entirely."

"Even the monsters?" asked Jack.

"*Especially* the monsters. Who knows what they might come up with, if they're left to make their own choices? If I didn't give the monsters freedom, it would still be a game, wouldn't it?"

Amber looked wary.

"So, no more interference? No thumb on the scales?"

"Perhaps a nudge along the way, to the level of technology that..."

"That these five had to escape, because it was making them want to kill themselves? No. No nudges, Callistae."

"When we go back, you'll forget all of this. You'll be on your own. So, you'll have to trust me."

Amber nodded. Jack grinned. Ikarus, who had once been Lord Slave, grinned back.

Then the junior demortifex spat on her palm and held it out to the alien machine. Callistae looked at her in disbelief, then smiled a crooked smile, and did the same. They slapped hands and shook on it like a pair of rogues, down in the dives of a dockside slum.

"They're going to need a new Emperor, as well," said Cipher. "Between the Wizards, and the Guilds, and the army, and God's Anvil, Grand Sepulchre will tear itself apart without one. They need stability, and they need to rebuild."

Jack realised, with a mounting sense of horror, that everyone was looking at him.

"Oh no. Oh, no no *no*. I'm not a hero, and I'm *certainly* not an Emperor!"

"It's easier than it looks. Really, rulership is mostly ceremonial," said Shye Simarl. "I was an empress for forty years, and I don't remember actually doing any paperwork."

"That's because you pointy-hatted buggers leave it all to your grand viziers," chuckled Ikarus. "I should bloody know..."

"At least take the big spiky sword," said Cipher. "It's in a certain... what's the word? *Idiom*. That's the one."

And so Jack did.

30
Chapter the Last – The Death of Heroism

It was noontide over Grand Sepulchre, Princess of Cities, when they finally opened the doors of the Malevolith. The tents and parasols of a hundred emissaries wilted in the sweltering, tropic heat. Nerves frayed, and smoke hung thick in the air, raining ashes down on acres of taut silk.

It was noontide when the doors finally opened, and the people knew, because the Jaguar bells rang out over the city, heralding the hour. Their shimmering carillon made bloodshot eyes rise from ruin to the heavens. To the top of the great tower, in fact, where a figure twice the size of a man swung what appeared to be an ornate hammer, but which turned out to be a much-abused bathing loofah on a stick.

It was the Demon-God Quazirath, and he'd agreed to make this costly, uncomfortable daytime manifestation in the interests of public order. That, and a discrete introduction to Montmortimer Pettigrew's tailors and outfitters.

Not every citizen of the Urzoman capital was numbered among his devout, but the peacock-winged demon was as Sepulchrite as blood sausage pie and Saint Guthran's Day pudding. Across the city, from High Wittering to Rooktower, people stopped, and pointed, and some even cheered. They were the first bells of the Octals which had been heard since the madness last night, and they spoke of sanity and order.

Then the doors at ground level of the Malevolith began to creak open. True to Zoltan Creagle's cynicism, the Golden Handshake were at the fore, including a very bruised and prickly-looking Lady Belladonna Immacolata Lachrymosa, leaning on a black cane which almost certainly contained a sword.

Kroome, the High Thaumatarch, was there, pretending he hadn't threatened to take over the city on his lonesome; the truth was, it would take weeks for his academians to meditate and focus their way back to a level of battle-ready potency. In the meantime, they were just a large body of men in dresses, with very expensive tastes.

Throne's Shadow formed a guard of honour for these worthies; Vulct the King of Thieves, Vaspides the surgeon, fat little Slidney Chunt and a grinning, taffeta-gowned Dolores Blatterly. Cardinal Rantoon looked suitably chastened, for having let an evil god of darkness and pain slip through the ecclesiastical net. Of the bunch of them, only Darby Hardwicke had come to do anything useful; his arms bulged with blueprints for new civic works, taking the place of buildings razed by heroism or dragonfire.

Worse, for the prospects of the Rotten Company, was the fact that they had the nobility with them, too. Several plumed skull helmets nodded in the breeze down at street level, covering the heads of the patriarch and matriarchs of the city's Great Houses. These were the leaders of the Evil Army, who appeared to be keeping the peace on the streets, visible in their black and silver uniforms.

The doors began to creak open, and the great and good rushed forward, yammering their own agendas at the top of their voices. But the doors did not yawn wide. They went only so far, and then stopped.

Oh yes.

The braying demands and self-important speechifying became a wail of fear, and the great and good backpedalled so fast that several fell over their own robes and chains of office.

Because here came a figure, striding out of the darkness within the Malevolith. A figure all in black, but without a lot of 'all'; he wore a bearskin cloak, tiny little leather underpants and a horrible, studded leather mask. A single eye blazed and bulged behind it, transfixing the crowd.

"Oh, *bugger.* The jig is up!" moaned Clorance Gryssle, for whom all the bribe money in the world suddenly seemed insufficient. It would have to do to purchase a new pair of trousers, in any case. He very carefully stepped inside an empty barrel and pulled the top closed behind him.

"It seems that rumour is worth more than loyalty, in these troubled times," said the spit and image of Lord Slave. It had taken a while to find a spare costume, but of course, Ikarus Stormhammer fit it like a glove. "Nevertheless, Himself is *always* eager to address His subjects, should they have something to share with him. You've come all this way, mighty guildlords. Do come inside. There may well be tea and crumpets."

This was not a suggestion met with much enthusiasm. It took a certain impatient twitch to get the Golden Handshake moving, and when they did, they scurried past the Grand Vizier like ducklings, robes hiked up around their knees. Only Lady Lachrymosa kept her cool, as she stalked past, cane clicking against the marble steps.

"You took your time, man. Do you know what we've had to do, to keep this city together in your absence? Do you have any idea what the other powers of the Arch' would do, if word of this weakness got out?"

Ikarus' voice was a low rumble, like the whisper of the Slave he'd once been.

"That's why we have *assassins*, milady. Expect a generous offer of employment, once we reach the throne."

Here was the sight which met the eyes of the worthy, as they straggled up through the trapdoor and out onto the crown of the Malevolith.

There were five thrones, assembled before the now sun-bloated corpse of Zag-Hammurat. The ruin of the spider-dragon made a grisly backdrop indeed, and drove home the point of Imperial power; here was a city-razing beast, sliced clean in two by the Imperial hand.

The central throne, framed by the creature's bisected spine, belonged to Himself. Or at least, a man wearing His armour, with a head that looked just slightly too small, in pace of the grim iron mask that graced Grand Sepulchre's coinage. One look at those eyes, though, and the Guildlords knew the truth.

"I see you're quite surprised, my lords and ladies," spoke this apparition. "But, you really didn't think I was going to stay a skeleton forever, did you? It was all that fine wine wasted, running out through my ribcage that did it. When I tore the living soul from that dragon you see there.... well, I thought, how about a bit of a rebirthday?"

The Golden Handshake nodded as if their heads were on strings. Then their eyes began to stray to the other thrones.

Was that the Empress of Chalinesia? Surely, the one they called the Jade Terror, the arch-strategist who had encompassed the conquest of Ashtar and Ojir, had been dead these twenty years? But the regal little figure in those embroidered robes looked a *lot* like the one in the paintings. And it was best not to argue with a ruler who had been known as 'heaven's voice with hell's fury'.

Then there was a living saint, right there in the flesh. Noctaris the Redeemer, Paladin of Phorax, reformator of the church militant and vessel for the voice of his God. Elizabethany Rantoon went right down on her knees in the lowest of possible bows, presenting her crozier of office.

"No need for that," chuckled the Saint, his purple eyes crinkled around the edges with lines of laughter. "Nobody here is holier than any other. We are here to *forgive*, not condemn."

On the Urzoman Emperor's other hand sat Lord Slave, settling himself onto a throne which still seemed too small for his bulk. And beside him sat...

"Is that an actual Elven Lord?" whispered Dreevil Vulct. "I thought they'd all buggered off somewhere and left us to it?"

"It bloody well *is* one, look at those cheekbones!" hissed Slidney Chunt. "And the haircut, and pointy ears! Now shut up! You want him to turn you into a hedgehog?"

Gathered under an awning of black satin were the other attendees of this strange meeting; the Rotten Company, all done up in patriotic black and silver uniforms, with not a hint of the ſuper about them. There was Auntie Marjorie Slocum, whose suit of armour had compacted down to a solid iron chestplate. Tarrence Bligh, who was exploring the sunny uplands of sobriety without turning into a monster. Amberelia Chance, who was for some reason carrying a plush pink bunny rabbit. Soto Scalizari, mercifully clothed. Billiam Knox, trying to conceal a sneaky roll-up of stumbleweed. Jory Foxmallet, scion of the Red House, dressed very smartly indeed as a naval officer. Montmortimer Pettigrew, who had somehow managed to modify his tabard, doublet and hose into a thrilling confection of black lace, seed pearls and brocade. And finally, Jack Somewhat, who carried across one shoulder an immense, scabbarded sword.

Zoltan Creagle swaggered forward, sketching a little bow. He was wrapped in a black toga, with a wreath of little skulls perched on his bald head.

"Your Imperial Majesty! Presenting the Rotten Company, your humble servants. I hope we have been of some small assistance during this horrible big dragonny crisis, sort of thing?"

At this point, Himself did the unthinkable. He stood up from his throne, and bowed right back.

"It has been a rare honour indeed, to fight alongside such mighty and patriotic defenders of the Urzoman crown. And I understand it was *this* man who trained them in the arts of Heroism?"

Callistae gently prodded Ranulf the Butcher forward. He still looked more than a little dazed, and blinked in the sunlight, waving to the assembled notables.

"Apparently... ummm. Yes, I think so. It's all a bit..."

"Dragon concussion," mouthed Billiam behind one hand, using the other to make the universal little spinny gesture for 'lost his marbles'.

There was a thin smattering of applause from the guildlords, who didn't really like the adulation of the Rotten Company one little bit, and who liked Ranulf the Butcher even less. Lady Lachrymosa stared daggers at Amber, who smiled sweetly. After all, staring wasn't throwing, and things could easily go that way...

"Now we have to discuss this draconic situation," continued the Emperor. "And the bad news is, this might not be a one-off. There's evidence that the entire cycle of monstrous destruction, orcish incursions, and general strife across the Arch' may be *orchestrated*. I have pledged to join this gathering of the mighty to attempt to root out this malaise, and see it end. That means change."

There was a general hubbub from the guild leaders, which finally distilled itself down to the voice of Slidney Chunt.

"Change, y'eminence, is bad for business. Far be it for us to question your will, but what *exactly* is going to be different?"

The other nine shuffled away from the fat little merchant, almost certain he was about to be magically incinerated. But Himself just smiled.

"I'm so very glad you asked," He said – and He told them.

How this new quest would mean that He, and Lord Slave, would be absent for some time. How the end of monsters and mayhem meant the end of traditional heroism, and how this meant a generous pension for Ranulf the Butcher, with the optional big blue-and-white apron and golden meat cleaver that came with being head of the Slaughtermen and Victualler's Guild. How, to govern the city in His absence, there would be appointed a new office of Evil Prime Minister, to be filled by...

"Zoltan bloody *Creagle?* Have you lost your mind? I mean... errm... are you *sure* that's altogether wise, m'lord?"

Lady Lachrymosa managed to lean back from the very edge of treason, using every leathery sinew of her being. "For goodness sake, the man's a thug, a crook, a swindler, a cheat, a scoundrel and a dirty fighter! Pardoning your presence, Zoltan."

"Oh, no offence taken," said the new Evil Prime Minister, rubbing his hands together with evident glee. "I'm all of those things and some more which you ain't even heard of, a lady of your evident pedigree. *That's* why He picked me for the job."

Noting that questioning the Undying Emperor didn't mean immediate thaumic obliteration, Madame Blatterly decided to hazard her own opinion.

"What about the rest of these misfits you've got gathered here? This *Rotten Company*. You can dress it up how you like, but one or two of 'em have been clients of mine. I know they ain't no heroes!"

"Indeed!" wheezed Garsoom Palaquat. "I hear nothing but terrible things about the fat one from my dear nephew. I suppose they'll all be getting highly paid jobs as well, for wrecking half the city?"

"*And* with powers we scarce understand," put in Issimmus Kroome darkly. "Pray, your Exalted Wickedness, may we just have one of them to take to bits, back at the College? It would be most informative."

"That one's even got your sword," brayed Slidney, pointing at jack with a finger like a cocktail sausage.

To say that the Emperor grew grim-faced and stern then, does little to truly convey the instant drop in temperature, or the vicious wind which whistled across the tower top. Then again, those may have been conjured up by the little blonde serving-girl with green eyes, who appeared to be present just to help Ranulf stay on his feet.

"You forget your place, my servants," he grated, in a voice which strongly suggested pits of spikes, and iron maidens slamming shut. "But you would be of little use to me if you did not have questioning minds. Very well. I will indulge you. The Rotten Company has been officially disbanded. They'll be leaving Grand Sepulchre on board a ship I've kindly donated them, to dispose of a very dangerous relic in the lava-pits of Zoqual."

He gestured to a long metal tube, all rune-carved and banded in lead, which sat on the arm of Lord Slave's throne.

"As I've said – the age of old-fashioned heroing is done. In this coming time, the real heroes will be the masters of industry, the lords of coin and trade, and those who bring health, peace and prosperity to the people."

This made the guildlords puff up with civic pride. Certainly, this described them to the very tips of their expensive boots.

"In fact, you'll *all* have a say in how the city runs. Zoltan here has convinced me that you should all get one of those things they have in Phoraxia, you know... invisible, valuable, one per person..."

"A soul?" quavered Elizabethany Rantoon.

"A *vote*," said Zoltan. "In the interest of balancing things in... well, everyone's best interests."

Ten sets of eyes slid left and right. Ten calculating minds began to weigh up convincing arguments, plots of blackmail and extortion, and other stratagems of politics.

"Of course, I'll be keeping an eye on things," said Himself. "The rewards for serving the good people of the Evil Empire are rich indeed. The rewards for trying to screw them over... well. I can be quite imaginative." He shrugged. "As for the sword, you're welcome to go and try to take it off my good friend Jack, there. I don't like your chances, but as they say; ''ave a go if you fink yer 'ard enuf'."

Jack pushed the blade of Spite an inch out of its scabbard with his thumb, making an oily little sound right at the edge of hearing. For the briefest of instants, something pale-green and slippery flashed around the steel, and was reflected in Callistae's eyes.

Not one of the Handshake so much as twitched. *The Rotten Company conveniently banished, the Emperor off about his arcane business who-knew-where, and a delicious new slice of temporal power?* Nobody wanted to re-roll those dice.

Nobody it seemed, except Ranulf the Butcher.

The huge shaggy-bearded hero clamped his hands to the sides of his head and screamed, his eyes suddenly alive with purpose. Quick as a salacious rumour he was off on his toes, clearing the space between the Rotten Company and Lord Slave's throne before a single grasping hand could hook into his black tabard.

"No!" he shouted, as his hairy hands scooped up the lead-bound power rod. "No! I won't let you do it! This world was meant for heroism! *Proper* heroism! The old ways will not die softly, so long as I draw breath!"

He scrambled up atop the corpse of Zag-Hammurat, boots squishing in unspeakable slop. From this perch, clinging to a spidery black leg, he turned a gaze of scorn on all assembled.

"Fools, the lot of you! And cowards, too! You want to make this world a little place, for little people, and you'll make it a bloodless, lifeless, *heartless* one as well! Shame, shame, and a thousand times shame on you! Disgraces to your ancestors, and the mighty men and women of old!" He spat, brandishing the rod. "I remember it all, you know. Aye, this thing used me. But it made a fine point. Sometimes, heroism needs a little prod in the kidneys. Sometimes it needs a kick up the backside. But it must continue! Otherwise, *what in the name of all hells have I done?*"

With that, the mad master of the Guild Errant took a final,

contemptuous look at his audience, curled his lip in a maniacal grin...

...and jumped off the tower.

"Was that supposed to happ..." began Doctor Vaspides – but the Emperor cut them off with a gesture.

"Rotten Company, do you think I could engage your services for one, last act of desperate heroism?"

Amber pushed to the front before Jack Somewhat could say anything pompous.

"Will there be lots of excitement, and thrills, and the possibility of a large amount of treasure at the end?" she asked.

The Urzoman Emperor nodded, with a quirky little smile on his lips.

"Oh yes. I daresay that something like that could be arranged."

"Then you heard the man!" shouted Amber, in her best imitation of Lord Slave's old parade-ground voice. "These people have a city to rebuild. I wouldn't want to be them. All *we* have to do, is go and bring down a gods-damned supernatural madman!"

"Easy street," said Jack, slinging his huge scabbarded greatsword over one shoulder. "Who's with us? *Company?*"

The cheer was heard from down at street level – just before something huge and hairy and glowing green crashed down through the Imperial Granaries, turning a whole silo of seed into popcorn. People screamed. The mob churned back and forth, as equal numbers tried to run away and get a damn good look at what was happening.

Enterprising street-vendors began to set up shop around the outskirts of the crowd, even as Ranulf came staggering from under an avalanche of fluffy snack-food, the naked glow of a Yanavarian power rod in one huge fist.

"I've got twenty to one on the maniac!" shouted someone. "Taken!" yelled another.

"Where's my drunken bloody husband gotten to? Harroooollld?"

"Get your official Evil Prime Minister's Day souvenirs here! They're unspeakably authentic!"

Ranulf looked left and right, then gave vent to a high-pitched scream, which dwindled after him as he took off down toward Sunderside, his sandals flapping against the cobbles.

Ahhh, yes. Things were getting back to normal!

Hard on his heels, the Rotten Company gave chase...

31
Chapter the Actually Last – Rotten Expectations

EARLY AFTERNOON, AND the sweltering streets of Grand Sepulchre, Princess of Cities, roast under a pall of humidity and woodsmoke.

Smart citizens - or those who can afford the vice of lassitude - peer out into the blowtorch heat through gaps in their black lace curtains and gilded, filigreed shutters. They sip iced hibiscus tea and drip with sweat, awaiting the dark, when none can guess whether the Bells of the Hour of Revels will ring out or not.

But follow a figure who pelts down the arterial streets of the city, down from the long-rusted-open gates astride Urzatic Square, down the Stair of Lovers, where vine roses coil, tied all abouts with scraps of silk by the romantic and the foolish. Down from the houses of the great and the good, slipping in raw sewage now, barging past spice-vendors and refugees, hollow-eyed beggars and fine gents in satin.

The figure stops for nothing and nobody; not even the straggle of funeral processions which snarl the byways of the old Suljanek quarter. He bowls down professional mourners in their yellow silks, upends ceremonial coffins, sets rune-daubed water buffalo to bucking and shimmying in their traces. The crowds part for him like the waves before a mad prophet, shrinking back into a hundred shadowed alcoves and doorways. Feral tamarins shriek and chatter in his wake, waving their tiny fists in imitation of the humans below.

Part of what moves the crowds is the man's sheer bulk. Part is his appearance; wild-eyed, bearded and muscled like a crocodile wrestler, he's literally shedding clothing as he runs, leaving a trail of socks and breeches and silver-buckled belts behind him.

The last part, and the one which really does it, is the arm-length rod of seething green fire he has clamped in one hand. The half-naked runner sprints down the street with it held out in front of him, upright, like the torch on the Statue of Tyranny. While the rest of his body runs with the total commitment of a man fleeing a burning outhouse, his arm is locked rigid, his fingers tight. He's making a noise like a red hot tea-kettle with the lid welded shut, exploring the very edges of material durability, and his lips are pulled back, as though invisible drag-anchors are attached to them with fish hooks.

What comes after him... well. If those Chungdoji spice pedlars, weeping over a week's ruined cinnamon ground into the dirt, or those white-painted mourners, with their fireworks and tiny gilded bells, could see what was approaching next, they would save their most exquisite curses.

The Rotten Company at full chat conjures images of some absurd feral god's wild hunt. It's a storm-front of pumping legs and avid faces, elbows and knees, beer bottles snaffled from some now-overturned alfresco setting and florid curses in a dozen languages. Where their quarry had parted the crowds, they ploughed them aside like a cavalry charge, but nowhere near as focused or personal.

Down to the harbour, and out along the breakwater went the little figure with its glowing green burden. Out after him came the company, fiercely determined not to cock this up. Was it out of a sense of heroism, or pride, or loyalty? Was it ever!

Before the curtain raised upon that little shadow-play atop the Malevolith, certain agreements had been made. A sentence of exile had been commuted to one of simply getting rid of Rod in the fire-pits, half the Arch' away. It was a long journey, but it was one which came all the way back around again, and it was one which also promised a hefty slice of government pay.

For Zoltan, of course, the sheer joy of watching the Golden Handshake backstab each other, under his thumb. For Jory, his father's ceremonial title as Evil Admiral, where he could drink and do nothing in a very respectable way. For Billiam Knox, the role of legate to the Unspeakable College, where his poker face and knowledge of the mages' limitations would make him a perfect ambassador.

For Amber, and Mister Bun Bun, the title of Lord's Enforcer of the Evil Prime Minister; not even Lady Lachrymosa or King Snagpurse would dare to risk their anger. Her first plan; to legalise, codify and tax the brass buttons out of the Dreamsugar trade. Soto Scalizari would be Master of Finance and Excise. Auntie Marjorie would get the contract to provision the entire Evil Army with seafood.

Tarrence Bligh, a sailor down to the heels of his boots, was to replace Rhaegulus Cratt as master of the Harbour Watch; change was definitely coming for that sordid institution. Montmortimer had been offered gold, and titles, but the real reward for him was the endorsement of the Demon-God Quazirath and a partnership with Gathur Sagh and his seventeen cousins. The fashion house of Emporio Pettigrew was all the talk among the idle and fashionable, and it looked like capes were definitely back in.

Jack had declined every offer. Jack, in his secret heart of hearts, didn't really know what he wanted, except of some peace and quiet in his own head. Chief among his thoughts was this: did he really fancy Amberelia Chance, or was that just part of the story?

Was the hot, prickly sensation around his collar and the slightly dopey grin which spread across his face when he thought about her just an echo from Rod's screwloose little narrative, or would he have to approach the situation with a kind of serious maturity that he had functionally zero experience with? The thought of asking Jory, Bill and Soto for advice made his toes feel like ice cubes and his face like it was under a blowtorch.

So, of all the Rotten Company, Jack was about the only one who was glad to see his future legging it off down Decameron, headed for the docks.

Ranulf the Butcher had no trouble pelting the length of the breakwater and leaping out over a choppy span of salt water, landing on the deck of a two-man fishing skiff. One look at his face, as he unfolded from the deck, was enough for both fishermen to share a look of utter terror, hold their noses, and jump over the side.

He may have been deranged and effectively one-handed, but among the skills the old-fashioned hero had picked up on his long adventures had been the art of sailing. He soon had the little boat pointed out to sea, all canvas pulled taut by a scudding breeze.

"A little bit of ʃuper-power would be a favourite, about now," moaned Zoltan Creagle, for whom the pursuit had been as punishing as three rounds with Morthrag. "There's a bit of a tingle left, but just enough that my heart hasn't exploded. Small mercies, eh?"

Monty leaned up against the rail, where the shorn-off base of the Statue of Tyranny rose, cold and jagged.

"It's a moot point. Only two of us could ever fly, and none of us could walk on water. I had this idea that if I went fast enough, the surface tension..."

"Then what we need's a ship," said Amber, all business. "And I think, if I heard Himself properly, that we're supposed to get one."

Auntie Marjorie nodded.

"Put me behind the wheel of anything that floats, and I'll out-sail that big-bearded freak!"

Jack risked a look off to his left, out into the naval pool. He'd been down here every morning for more than a year carrying that damnable lantern, and every time he'd admired the lines of the ship that rode at anchor there, under the crenelated walls of the Admiralty House. Flagship of the Urzoman fleet, now that the great battle-arks were broken up for scrap; the *Whispered Scream*. It looked like a dagger made of lacquered black wood. It looked as if it was already racing the wind, standing still. Two gigantic wheels protruded from its long, low decks, either side of the mainmast, and in them Jack could see the skeletal shapes of twin gholem automatons.

Jory followed his gaze, and slapped his hands together.

"My dad's got a lovely model of that one. But are you sure...?"

"Technically,'" said Amber, "He didn't tell us which one we were going to get. So, it's not really stealing. Just a misunderstanding."

"A sort of meta-misunderstanding," mused Soto. "We know we've got it wrong, so the 'wrong' doesn't matter. Interesting."

Auntie Marjorie reached up and grabbed Zoltan by the scruff of his toga.

"Let me make this easy for all of us. Mister Evil Prime Minister, if you tell me I can't have that boat, you will likely be in the market for a **** pair of ****ing peg legs, savvy?"

So it was that the Rotten Company boarded the *Whispered Scream* under ministerial orders, telling the two marines guarding the gangplank to take the day off. Soon the gholem were tromping along in their wheels, powering up the great mill-wheel of metal which acted as the ship's stabiliser, and which turned the twin screws beneath her keel when the wind was unfavourable. These (and every scrap and handkerchief of sailcloth which Auntie Marjorie could raise) were set to the chase. Rotten Compatriots were lashed up and down the rigging and from end to end of the rakish black man o' war by a tirade of creative cursing. So it went; Ranulf the Butcher had a head start, and the whole great looping skein of Mother Ocean to flee to. The circular sea swept up and away ahead of them, a shimmering arc piercing the clouds.

But as any sailor will tell you, big ships are deceptively fast. The

Whispered Scream wasn't even that; it was speed hammered out flat and given a coat of grease; the masterwork of Darby Hardwicke and his cabal of pipe-smoking, flat-capped shipbuilders down in Brick Deep and Hammer's End.

Soon they were gaining on Ranulf. Soon he'd be in range of the Urzoman warship's big ballistae and blackpowder cannon. Harpoon bolts and lengths of spider-silk rope, stronger than steel cable, were lugged and loaded by Tarrence and Jack.

That was about when Mister Bun Bun, ensconced in the crow's nest with a lashed-together and crooked tube of spyglasses, fired off a warning flare. It rocked under its tiny parachute, flaming red like Balagur: the call to arms. There was another ship approaching.

"There's no way that mad bastard has a rendezvous out here, is there?" asked Jory, all incredulous.

"He certainly *looked* like he was acting out of the cottage cheese between his ears, when he took a swan dive off the Malevolith," agreed Zoltan. "But who can say, with the mad? I remember there used to be a whole lot of those barbarian hero types. Maybe it's the old guard, eh? Throgg the Outlander and Dirty Larry Lotharsson, and Acelstria the Axe-Wielding Amazon, that bunch."

"I certainly hope not!" said Billiam. "We're all out of, ummm... ſuper-juice, I suppose you'd call it."

"I certainly hope it *is*," spat Auntie Marjorie. "Recent experience has taught me that all that armour tends to sink."

Now they could all see the black sails on the horizon. Ranulf tacked across the swells, making a line for the new ship. It was indeed a big one – not exactly built for speed, like the *Whispered Scream*, but definitely a man o' war, with twin banks of cannons presenting a nasty broadside.

"Jack, take the front ballista, and load explosive bolts. Tarrence, you've done this before, or my uncle was a lamprey. You know we ain't got the **** crew for no ****** cannon duel, so we sneak up in their blind spot to the aft and ***** the ******ers a new ***** spigot ***** flamingo ****** bicycle seat!"

The tar between the boards began to bubble and smoke.

"What about the rest of us?" asked Soto.

"Well, see, as soon as that horrible beardy bastard starts to climb on board, we grapple across and have us what grand-dad Slocum used to call a typical Maidensday afternoon, but what the navy lads call a blood-and-rum soaked *****ing boarding action," replied Auntie

Marjorie. "Axes, pistols, cutlasses, kicks in the cobblers, and we get that glowing green thing back!"

"Don't touch it, though," added Jack. "Wrap it up in something, if you can. It's got a way of..."

"*Getting inside your head*," said everyone at once, in a demonstration of exactly why Jack had insisted on a little thaumaturgical hygiene.

Meanwhile, across a turquoise expanse of salt-wrack and foam, the captain of that other ship was not preparing for battle at all. He peered through a brass telescope and grinned, anticipating nothing less than glory.

"Here, you... new lad. Take this for me, would you? I think it's time to make the place look nice for our guests."

The new lad – in fact a grown man with a face like a scarred-up side of corned beef – accepted the telescope with ill grace, and the look of a butler who has just been handed a moist turd.

"But, yer captaincy, right.... what about this other little boat? Something wrong with it, if yer ask me."

"And *did* I ask you?" asked the captain, who stepped down off a box at the rail, revealing his true height to be something shy of five foot three. To compensate, he was wearing the most outlandishly large tricorne hat in the history of piracy, topped with ostrich feathers from far Mograth, stacked-heel sea boots, and a cutlass which was so long it has a little castor on the end of its scabbard to keep it from scuffing up the deck.

"No," he continued. "I did not. Because, young bucko, you are lucky to be on this ship, what with us needing crew after that wee altercation with those Chalinese pi... I mean, um, free gentlemen of the salty brotherhood."

"But... but.... there's only one man on board, and he looks like he's coming to attack us," said the new recruit, who had been, until fairly recently, a bandit from the Underbelly of Jansamrana.

"How many of *us* are there, Waldrick?" asked the Captain, pinching the bridge of his nose between two fingers.

"Forty-eight, y'captainship. Last count. Remember, old Sprickles fell off the rail while 'e was taking a..."

"And there's *one* of him. One. Meanwhile, what else is hoving to? Why, it's the *flagship of the bloody Urzoman Navy*, Waldrick! My chance at redemption, so that I can give up being a bloody pirate!"

For this was, indeed, Rhaegulus Cratt, two days deep into his career as a free sailor of the salty brotherhood, and hating every minute. The first shipload of real pirates he'd encountered had stolen his chest of embezzled gold, and some of the crew had defected, too. Rhaegulus had spent ages scrubbing the tar and feathers off, then put in at one of the little shanty-ports of the Underbelly to take on sailors.

Where he'd found Jimjo and Waldrick. Broke, thirsty, and keen to share a story about something they thought might be valuable. A strange metal egg, they said, that was impossible to smash apart. It had fallen, they claimed, from the sky.

Rhaegulus looked at it now, lashed down to the middle of the deck aboard his stolen ship. He'd re-named this excise galleon the *Scurvy Skull*, in an excess of febrile imagination, fuelled by colouring-in books he'd had as a very short child.

"It's just that, when one man attacks a whole ship, and 'e's got that look in his eye..."

"Are you still standing there? Go and polish the bloody egg thing! And get your idiot friend to help!"

It certainly was a sight. A pod, bigger than two rowboats back-to-back, shaped like a seed, with strange dark tubes in one end and a pair of mirrored panels on the top. If Himself had been angry about a missing artefact only a few fingers long, he'd be overjoyed to get his hands on this!

What a fantastic man, that Rhaegulus Cratt! Posing undercover as a pirate to seize this one-of-a-kind treasure, in a bloody battle where he'd sent three thousand screaming Chalinese sea-reavers down to their deaths! Medals for him! Medals, and ale, and wenches, and a pair of four-inch platform boots in lovely Zalois leather!

In fact, if the rumours were true, and Lord Slave was dead, then there was a job going begging, right up the old Malevolith. A Grand Vizier's job, with all the power that implied. Rhaegulus could just imagine the big, tall hat which came with it.

Cratt rubbed his hands together, almost salivating, and stood on tippy-toe to look out over the rail.

Where a big, hairy fist was rising up to smash him in the nose.

Ranulf the Butcher had arrived early, and he came swarming up the side of the Scurvy Skull with Rod between his teeth and his brains bubbling like a rancid fondue.

"Oi! Do campt duu that!" squeaked Cratt, as he went over arse-backwards, blood pouring from his nose. He tried to unleash his gigantic sword, but this just caused him to spin around on his bum.

"I'm the bloooordy currrrptin!"

Ranulf stepped over him, picking up his hat as he went. He looked down, and Rhaegulus Cratt saw the look in his eyes – like great whirlpools of fizzing green, spiralling down into madness. With a wince, he clicked his nose back into place.

"Alright then. You ummm. You keep the hat. Looks good on you. It's just that... GUARDS! SAILORS! MARINES! DEFEND YOUR CAPTAIN!"

They came boiling up from belowdecks, and down from the rigging to meet this new threat – the scum of the Harbour Watch, turned pirate, and a ragged band of Underbelly sell-swords along with them.

"There's only one of him!" shouted Cratt, as Ranulf stalked down the steps to the main deck, unarmed, fingers flexing, muscles bulging under a webwork of scars. He moved like a wolf among guinea pigs, each step precise, as the pirates surrounded him on all sides. Over to the pod, where he stopped.

"This old thing," said Rod's voice through him, without moving his lips. **"Well, well. Did you think, perhaps, that you were going to put me back in it?"**

The whole ship rocked in the water. A grinding noise filled the air, low and shuddering. And Rod's answer came up over the rail.

"I'm pretty sure he didn't. But if that's where you came from, I think *I* might give it a go," said Jack Somewhat, with the immense, scabbarded bulk of Spite across his shoulders.

Rod laughed, once again using Ranulf as a puppet.

"You? I've taken my power back from you, and the rest has bled away. You're nothing but human, now. And this one, this Ranulf... ahh, this one's a proper fighter. A *proper hero*. Not a nobody like you, you ungrateful little fool!

Now the rest of the Rotten Company were there, lined up facing Rhaegulus Cratt's pirate crew and their quarry.

"How about all of us?" asked Amberelia Chance. "You're only a nobody when nobody's with you, right? And we're with Jack."

Well, that made his heart lurch like a drunk attempting the Grailish Hornpipe. But this was no time to think about possible futures. It was time to think about the impossible present, right in front of him.

· **"All of you, or one at a time. You know how this is going to end. You just do what you have to, and afterwards..."** Rod shrugged Ranulf's shoulders for him, **"Afterwards, you might be remembered as traitors, in some folk-tale about how the age of heroes came**

back."

Jack had heard enough.

"Company!" he bellowed, pushing Spite out from its sheath a finger-width. "Charge!"

He was almost surprised when they all did.

But then there was no more time for thought, because there were pirates all around him, and pistol shots split the air, and swords were swinging, chiming steel on steel. Amidst it all, Ranulf the Butcher stood tall, atop the pod, meting out blows with his fists which sent men flying clear overboard, spinning in mid-air as they went.

Now, Amber was still deadly dangerous, and Zoltan Creagle may have been over the hill, but he was the veteran of a thousand nasty back-alley punch ups. Soto, Jory and Bill had stood back-to back with Jack in any number of dirty tavern brawls and scrappy street fights. Auntie Marjorie was the most feared old lady with a halibut this side of Clourvonnaise. Tarrence Bligh was the kind of sailor who had tangled with pirates before, and Mister Bun Bun was... well, he was a horrifying little pinball of pink and furry doom, rising up out of the melee to headbutt grown men into reeling unconsciousness. Even Monty knew how to fence.

But this was a battle, and they were outnumbered. First of all, forty-eight to ten by Cratt's scurvy crew - and then one to ten by Ranulf, who was a small legion all on his lonesome.

Jack caught a slap from the flat of a cutlass across the chops, and he reeled, seeing bursts of purple behind his eyes, He watched Foxmallet sweep a pirate's legs from under him, then get battered down with a club, sprawling on the deck. Monty's ornate sword was bludgeoned from his grasp by a bald-headed woman with an axe. Mister Bun Bun reached Ranulf, but before his knives could come together somewhere in his sternum, the giant barbarian had him by the ears, following through with a punch that sent him over the rail. Jack pretended to stagger, then faked out his attacker, cracking Spite's pommel into his knee and rising with the same motion, bringing it up under the man's chin. Teeth clacked together, and a large chunk of tongue was bitten clean through. Then Jack's forehead, often the last argument of knaves in a taproom scuffle, came cracking down on the bridge of his nose, and it was over.

Well... over, excepting the trio of even more evil-looking pirates who were now sizing him up.

"You know how to use that sword, boy, or did you just bring it along for us to steal?" cackled one of the men, through a graveyard of brown and rotten teeth.

Jack didn't dignify this with a reply. Instead, he tried a move which Ranulf himself had taught him. He whipped Spite around in a short arc, holding the scabbard on with his thumb until the right moment. When he released it, the wood, leather and silver flew like an arrow, the tip of the scabbard crunching with satisfying force into the man's eye.

Well, thought Jack. *This is it. Time to answer the big question. Could he achieve anything even remotely approaching heroism, without some kind of mystical powers?*

Spite flashed silver in the sunlight, reaching the top of an unstoppable arc above Jack's head. And then it happened.

The black gem set into the middle of the sword's crossguard opened like an eye, peeling back from a well of emerald power.

"No! That's impossible! *That's not me!*" shrieked Rod, clattering to the floor as Ranulf's jaw dropped.

Whether this was the barbarian hero's reaction, or some quirk of expression bubbling up from Rod and through him, it didn't matter. Because the entire blade of Spite lit up green for a heartbeat, tiny thin traceries of lightning sizzling down its fullers, picking out runes which seemed to writhe and dance. *And it wasn't him.* Jack felt the power unlocking something, down at the level of his bones and sinews. It wasn't Rod, but it was something similar, turning the mainspring of a familiar clockwork.

It was something Callistae had put there; a little bit of herself in the hilt of Lou Cipher Mourningstar's sword, and it called up something which was now part of Jack, as surely as if had been tattooed on the inside of his skin.

Jack's arms expanded, tearing his sleeves to ribbons. His legs grew longer and his chest broadened, popping buttons from his uniform. He reached out and flicked one of the remaining pirates with his forefinger, propelling him into the mast with a meaty thwack. The other simply dropped his sword and shrugged, palms out.

All across the deck it was the same. Auntie Marjorie's chestplate slid and locked and unfolded, covering her arms and legs, before a helmet segmented up from the base of her neck to cover her face. The man she'd been fighting suddenly had his mace bent in half by as pair of armoured hands, green light shining out from the knuckle joints. Soto Scalizari burst into flame. Tarrence Bligh reeled back, groaning, fingers knotted in his hair as he turned blue and began to grow... and grow... and *grow*, making pirates scatter in terror. Billiam Knox blurred into two, while Jory Foxmallet bounced back up from the deck snarling, darkness wrapping him up like a cape. Amber grinned as her claws sprung from the backs of her wrists, unbroken and pearly-white. Zoltan Creagle's next uppercut lifted a pirate out of his boots, making him perform a perfect backflip up onto the forecastle, and into a barrel of rum. Mister Bun Bun climbed up onto the rail and shook himself off like a small, very annoyed dog, his zipper mouth twinkling in a wide, homicidal smile.

But it was Monty who moved the fastest - naturally. Monty, who always carried a selection of handkerchiefs for every occasion, and who scooped up Rod before Ranulf could get over his shock.

There was an instant of silence and calm, in which everybody looked at everybody else, sizing up whether to back down from the precipice or leap...

Then Rhaegulus Cratt, even the jumped-up little bastard, swung down from the quarterdeck on a rope, in the way he'd seen pirates do it before, in all of those operas he used to go to. His cutlass winked in the sun, the tails of his topcoat flapped out behind him, and he unleashed a blood-curdling shriek, which was reminiscent of the feral tamarins which haunted the bowers of Grand Sepulchre.

Out over everyone's head he flew, too short to swipe at anything on the deck with his jewel-crusted blade. He missed every possible target, and arced out over the water, hands chafing with rope burn. Finally, his arc brought him back over the deck, where he let go, yipping like frightened Pomeranian, and cannonballed into the mast.

There was another meaty crunch. Rotten Companions, pirates and even Ranulf, (totally out of his tiny mind) winced. Then Cratt fell backwards onto the top of the pod. His elbow struck a hidden button, and the doors hinged open. Then he slid away down its smooth flank, making a squeaking noise like rubber on wet glass. Jack wasted not an instant. He was running before his feet knew he'd started, pushing off the deck so hard that the wood splintered beneath him. Jory and Bill formed up on one side, then Amber and Soto on the other, making a flying wedge which cleared the decks around him. Jack had a clear shot at Ranulf, standing there atop the pod, a hollow, leather-lined space behind him, twinkling with little lights.

Just like all those hours ago, in another life, when he'd gone pelting down through the city streets to save the feckless Chep Palaquat, Jack's body knew what to do. He leapt into a flying tackle as he dodged the final pirate, a midget with a harpoon, and he felt his shoulder drive into Ranulf's impossibly corded midriff, knocking the breath from his lungs.

...went the little cloud of green sparks, as the barbarian hero went buttocks-first into the pod's one and only chair. But that wasn't the only firework in this display. A crackle of green lightning earthed itself through the pod from the jewel in Jack's sword, bleeding in between the rivets and welds. As Ranulf tried to rise, reaching with fingers hooked into claws, a pair of restraint belts looped over and around his massive torso, cinching tight.

"Step back, please," sighed a mechanical voice, all disembodied and calm. "Doors closing."

Jack slid back onto the nose-cone of the pod, straddling it like a carthorse. The mirrored doors snicked shut, horribly close to his crotch. That's when he saw a hollow circular port iris open, right between his legs. A hole in the surface of the pod, next to a little glyph which said (if only Jack could read Alien) 'POWER CORE'.

He never knew if what he did next was an intuition, or part of Rod's own memory, peeled away to stick to the inside of his skull, or even the voice of Callistae caressing the surface of his brain. But he knew what that hole was. He knew, suddenly, what went there.

"Monty! Over here!"

The Atomic Fop brandished the power rod, wrapped in three layers of embroidered lace, but he was hemmed in. Pirates crowded all around him, weapons out. That is, until a huge shadow fell across the lot of them, and the Unstoppable It hefted Monty bodily in both his fists.

"Catch!" roared the monster, as he pulled back his arm, and tossed the luckless fop in a perfect spiral, sending him angling in toward Jack.

There was a moment when Monty was upside down above him, hand outstretched. In a scene like a million plagiarised chapel ceilings, Jack grabbed the other end of the rod, spun it around in his fingers, and jammed it home.

In that instant, he felt the full, flamethrower force of Rod's will, hammering at the gates of his sanity. It roared and raged and bellowed, but Jack was floating in calm tranquillity, holding back all that fury with one finger.

No. You've been here before, and I threw you out then.

But... you have to be out of your mind to reject me! *Me,* **Jack! The greatest power in...**

No. The greatest power in here, *Rod, is* me. *You can go and be the greatest power somewhere else.*

And that was that. Well... apart from the fact that Jack knew, bones-deep, *exactly* what was about to happen next. He suffered one final vision, as Callistae's thoughts sizzled through the tight-packed circuity he was sitting on; one of thrust vectors and escape velocities and distant stars.

"Abandon ship!" shouted Jack, leaping off the pod and heading for the rail. "Heroes, blue monsters, mantis shrimp dressed as bunny rabbits and children first!"

"What about us?" asked one green-mohawked pirate, who was only just getting to his feet after tangling with Zoltan Creagle.

"You as well! No hard feelings! Just get off this boat as fast as your legs will carry you!" He looked down, then up again. "Peg or otherwise!"

There was something in his urgency which was quite compelling. And a good thing too, because, not too long after, as the *Whispered Scream* rode the swells downwind, Rhaegulus Cratt's *Scurvy Skull* simply ceased to exist.

It began with a cough of smoke, then a blast of intense, stomach-punching noise. Licks and jags of fire spurted out from the centre of the pirate ship's deck, followed by a rumble, a cloud of spark-shot smoke, and then a pillar of green fire, raging like draconic indigestion. The flames cored out the hull of the ship, drilling down until they reached the powder magazine.

At this point, the *Scurvy Skull* undid itself like a ballistic jigsaw puzzle in reverse, detonating with a crack that bellied out the ocean in a dish beneath it. The pod kept rising, as a nimbus of force built around it. Strange flickers of power made rainbows slide across the heavens, wrapping it up. The whole of the arch bucked, the ocean snapping like a whip. And then it was gone, firing off into the vault of the sky like a cannonball, until it winked out with a final, silvery flash.

"See? I told you it weren't no dragon egg!" crowed one of the uglier pirates who'd flooded aboard the *Whispered Scream.* "That's a pint of best bitter you owe me, Jimjo!"

Jack found himself leaning on the rail next to Amber, both of them watching the place where the pod had vanished, high amid the herringbone clouds of the upper sky.

"Are you doing the same thing as me?" she asked, "Making sure it doesn't come back?"

"I'm just wondering where it went, is all," said Jack. "That has to be... no, scratch that, it *was, assuredly,* the strangest part of what's been a very eventful week."

The junior demortifex slumped down against the rail, letting her hair fall over her eyes.

"You almost want to wish it was a dream, right? Because we didn't get the mission done. We'll never meet up with the Mage-Priests of Zoqual. We're banished, the lot of us."

Jack wanted to put his arm around her, but sheer awkward terror held him back.

"It's not so bad, though," she said, pushing her hair back and looking out to sea. "What's really back there, huh? A bitter old lady who wants to kill me, and is very, very good at that kind of thing. No friends, no family... basically, everything good in my life came out a disaster, in the last couple of days, and is on this ship right now. Except for poor old Lurien, and he's dead."

And that was the thing. She understood. Jack Somewhat, aspiring manly man, had never poked the ravelled ball of feelings which dwelt in behind his ribcage. But here they were. Orphaned, and given some kind of second-hand purpose by people who didn't really believe in them, and then felt threatened when they succeeded. Misfits and losers, whose big win turned out to be the end of a lot of other people's worlds. She was even right about Lady Lachrymosa, who probably wanted to kill Jack, too.

"So why go back?" he asked. "We're young, we have weird powers, we have a ship, and we have a crew, even if they are pirates. I kind of get the feeling a lot of pirates are just people with freedom issues too. Like us."

Amber smiled. It was a little bit sad, that smile, but it was real. And it was part of an expression which Jack knew was on his face, too. She got the fact that he got it.

"Alright. Cards on the table, Jack. They sent me to kill you. But I'm glad I didn't. That's the nicest thing I have likely *ever* said about anyone who isn't a shrimp, so don't tell anyone, right? I have a reputation to uphold."

Jack stood up from the rail, stretching out. The sea tested fresh and clean, and good.

"Nothing else, then? Should we go and see what the rest of them think? We might lose a few."

Amber squinted up into the heavens. The pod had not made so much as a flicker of an attempt to come back.

"Well, there was one thing. You know, back during all the..."

"Unpleasantness?" ventured Jack.

"During the, umm, *strife*, and all, I rescued you a few times," said Amber. "Some pretty heroic moves, really. And I thought at the time, well, it's just this story we're stuck in. *Beautiful, deadly rogue saves feckless, idiot boy*, and all that. He's nice to look at, even when he's not all heroically proportioned, but it's just the narrative talking. It's what's supposed to happen."

And there it was again. She got it. The question which had been gnawing at his brainstem, right on her lips. That were only. A few inches. Away...

Then, of course, he heard his mouth moving, and realised he'd ruined everything.

"Wait a minute! Rescued *me*? Come on! I was thinking, you know, yeah, this is one of those hero-saves princess scenarios, so there can't be any... I mean... but *you* thought...?"

"Oh, and you would have gotten out of that Mantigore pit alive without me, mister big hero? Or how about when I stopped that huge, evil dragon from cremating you? No, this is *my* moral conundrum, Jack! At least *I* had the good graces to flip the gender roles on that stereotype!"

"And at least *I* had enough respect for you not to just do what the story told me to! Sensitivity! That's what you want, isn't it?"

"Oh yes, because *all of us women are the same!* But yes, it beats the opposite! What I want, is to know that I'm actually in control of some aspect of what passes for my life, alright?"

Jack, who was one of those people who doesn't listen too hard in an argument, because he's loading up all his counter-points like little brass-tipped bullets, had the intellect, just this once, to shut up. His mouth hung open, but she spoke first.

"So, we thought we were saving each other. Huh," Amber gave a little chuckle, and leaned back on the rail, nudging her shoulder into Jack. "That's rich. You'd look great in an old-fashioned princess dress, you sorry oaf. With a blonde wig, and makeup, and one of those hats like a big taffeta ice cream cone."

Jack couldn't help but laugh a little at this mental image.

"For what it's worth, you'd look pretty good with a sword, and some armour too."

"Are you thinking about that heroic barbarian-maiden armour, that's basically chain-mail underwear?" asked Amber, narrowing her eyes. "Day one in assassin training, they taught us that it's very unstrategic."

Jack forced down the tide of red as it threatened to advance across his cheeks. "No! Honest!" he yelped, as just that mental image invaded his brain. "What I mean is... ummm... you did a man's job out there. And *yes*, you saved me a few times, too."

Amber didn't let that one go.

"And you did a woman's job, Jack Somewhat. Which is why, as co-captain of this barge, I'm going to allow you graciously to find me a beer. And then we'll talk to the rest of the Company about hunting down pirates worse than we are, and the division of loot, and multifarious things."

"And then?" asked Jack, definitely pushing his luck.

Amber cupped his face in one hand, and gave him a look that made his ability to decipher such things tie itself in knots. It completely blew away the image of the barbarian armour. Then her lips quirked up at one end, the way they did when she thought something was ironic, and she turned away.

"Then we'll see what happens when we get to make the story up as we go along," she said. "Who knows? I hear that life isn't a game anymore."

In the end, that seemed as good a place as any to begin.

Epilogue:
Unhappy Landings

THE POD FELL through whirlpools and eddies of time and space, where strange currents stretched it out, and shuffled its number of dimensions like a card sharp with the decaf jitters. Days lapsed into seconds, and then back into mere hours. Gradually, incrementally, space took on depth, and form, and rules you could set your watch by.

Just in time for the pod to crash. We could say 'again', but even that was a touch uncertain.

After a while, things involving people happened, and, being observed, the pod snapped back into the annoyingly conformist world of the Real. For a time, it simply lay there in a crater, steaming, amid a swathe of very well-cooked cabbages. But eventually...

Greevold Merqs stepped out of his black, unremarkable four-wheel drive groundcar, out into the heat of what promised to be the last summer ever. He grunted, lighting up a cigarette from a packet in the top pocket of his black, unremarkable off-the peg suit.

"What have we got?" he asked, sucking in a great, satisfyingly fatalistic lungful of smoke. These things caused cancer, or so they said, but right now... Huh. Least of his worries.

"It's definitely a class-three," said the aide who came scurrying over to his side. "Extra-terrestrial in origin. Made of some kind of alloy the tech boys can't get their head around, and all it does is sit there, ticking. It's *ominous,* sir."

"Ticking? And we've tried to give it a deep scan?"

"Got nada," said the aide, shaking his head. He was buzz-cut and buttoned-down, this kid, with soda-bottle glasses and a suit even cheaper than Greevold's own. "There's something in there, and it's hot. But getting it out? We could try nuking it, perhaps?"

"Is that a serious operational suggestion?"

The aide looked stunned.

"Well, no, but..."

"Because if whatever's in there might be able to help, and all we have to do is glass a few hundred miles of salad, then I'd push the button myself. That's the reality of it, right now."

The aide grimaced, looking away. It was hard to wrap your head around it, that was for sure. *Three days until the big one. Three days until the end of the line.* Greevold was one of the highest-ranking agents left in the Shadow Ministry; the rest were digging themselves into bunkers or narxxing their brains to mush at fantastic, no-expense-spared orgies.

No need to spare an expense, when all the cash was gonna burn with you...

The awkward moment was broken by an army scientist, who burst out of the ring of tents surrounding the object, waving a data-tablet.

"Agent Merqs! It's *opening!* The darn thing's opening!"

This was the cue for them all to go running back, pushing aside tent flaps and stumbling over guy-wires, while gathering a little group of hangers-on who had to see what the fuss was all about. Merqs was pleased to note that at least some of these were soldiers, and some of them were armed. He'd dealt with precisely four class-three incursions in his forty years with the Shadow Ministry, and they'd all ended in tears.

"Alright, stand back! Keep that perimeter clear! Sergeant, get some of your men pointing those damn rifles the right way round, would you?"

The pod sat under a halo of surgical lamps, gleaming and chrome, its mirrored doors just starting to crack open. A thin mist spilled forth, and a few of the quicker grunts slapped on their gas masks.

Greevold took another drag of his cigarette. It was probably just the temperature difference. Probably.

What came out of the pod - what sat up with a horrible, hollow groan, like a sleeper awakening from some epochal pre-hangover nightmare - was not the tentacle-spawned horror any of them had imagined.

"By the holy belly button of Scrold!", blasphemed the young aide. "He's... he's one of us!"

Indeed, the creature looked very much like one of the denizens of this world; a panhumanic biped with the requisite number of face-holes and other bits. Well... that might be a wild assumption. The creature was wearing underpants, after all, and Greevold didn't like to consider the job of finding out what was inside them. The only oddity he could see was the giant bushy mane of hair which covered the thing's entire face, making it look like some throwback to primitive times.

That, and the fact that it was muscled like any two of the beefiest soldiers here, combined.

The special agent tried to keep his mind on business. After all, if there was any chance this thing could assist, he'd be getting the whole planet out of a spot so tight, it made drainpipe trousers look like parachute pants.

"Welcome!" he intoned, with what he hoped was noble gravitas. "Welcome to our planet, O traveller from the voids of space! What is your name, and what is your purpose?"

It was first-contact boilerplate, hacked out by some psychology majors three decades ago. They must have assumed that everything from the stars was in possession of a universal translator.

Unbelievably, the monster in the pod seemed to have just such a thing.

"Oooooh, blimey!" it said, slapping its hands together. "That wasn't half a cold one! Any chance of a nice warm horn of mead, some bacon, eggs, boar, moose, swordfish, crumpets, black pudding, eel pie, porridge and a fried slice?"

The alien swung its hugely muscled legs out of the pod, wiggled one sausage-sized finger into its hairy ear, and farted enormously. "Pardon, all. I've been stuck in that thing for the gods know how long. Which reminds me..."

He banged one fist on the nose of the pod, and a small round door irised open, allowing a glowing green rod to click up into position. Immediately, every radiation scanner in the tent began screaming, flashing and howling.

"Stand away from the... the thing!" shouted one of the marine sergeants, drawing his sidearm. The alien looked at it quizzically.

"What a tiny little blunderbuss! Look, you needn't worry about me, or the rod there. I'm Ranulf, and I'm a hero."

Agent Merqs gestured the soldiers to stand down, even as the army scientist surreptitiously slipped him a message on his data tablet.

'YANAVARIAN POWER CRYSTAL ROD', it said. 'USEFUL!'

Greevold knew when it was time to make a command decision.

"Excellent!" he said, in a broad, pantomime imitation of confidence. "Welcome to our planet, Mister Ranulf. Heroes are always welcome to visit here! Now, if you'd excuse us, we're just going to go and sort out that, ummm, that *breakfast* you were talking about, OK?"

He made little finger gestures to the aide, the scientist, and the burliest sergeant, who followed with him as he backed out of the tent, grinning. The four of them flattened themselves up against the far side of a gun-crawler.

"I've heard about this! *I've heard about this!*" enthused the aide, pushing his glasses back up his nose. "A hero from another world, who turns up at the last minute and saves the day! It's classic stuff!"

"In comic books, perhaps," put in the sergeant. "In real life, it's the grunts that do the heroing. And we only use that word for people who get blown to bits in the line of duty."

The scientist was only a fraction cooler.

"That's definitely a Yanavarian crystal. Phenomenal! We've recovered fragments, and we know their race ascended to a state of pure light some three thousand years ago, from platinum stelae we recovered on the moon. It's all very classified."

"Alright then," said Greevold, lighting up another cigarette. "Here's what we do. You three grab the rod. I'll deal with mister hairy. I want that pod, and the crystal, delivered to our top scientists within the hour."

"Yarz and Kelia Dorvrax? At the university of Old Zoqfiir?"

Merqs nodded.

"It's a tragedy, really. The best hyperspace researchers on the planet, and they just got married last year, too. What genius will the universe miss out on, eh? Hell of a time to have a baby, as well."

The scientist shook his head.

"Hell of a time all round. Still..."

"We do what we've got to," said the sergeant. "I'll be behind you with stun darts loaded, special agent. He looks like a scrapper."

Greevold sighed.

"He called himself a hero. Maybe the kid's right. Maybe we've been handed a pass. Maybe Father Scrold is still up there, pulling his levers for us."

Greevold strode back into the tent, smiling, as his three compatriots edged around the outer wall, inching closer to the green-glowing rod. The special agent slung his arm around Ranulf's shoulders.

"So, a hero, eh? That must be exciting! Come, walk with me, talk with me. We have a lovely breakfast bar set up behind the comms tent."

Ranulf followed the funny little man in the strange clothes. His brain was really starting to unfog now, and he noticed little details.

Details like the blue grass, and the purple sky, and only one sun. He gibbered a little.

"You know, we could have a job for a hero like you," said the little man, as somewhere behind him, in the tent, came the sound of struggling, and crashing, and lots of canvas being wrapped up around a jumping, spitting rod of power. "In fact, it's probably trivial for a guy of your stature. I bet when I ask, you'll just want to get a cape on, and some nice shiny tights, and get it all over with."

Ranulf's brain was completely sober now. It was the mention of capes and tights which did it. The entire past few days came crashing down into his memory like a filing cabinet launched from an orbital railgun.

"You want me... to do something heroic?" he asked, with the trepidation of a fat man tiptoeing into a minefield.

Greevold Merqs treated him to a wide and brittle smile.

"Funny you should ask," he said, squinting up at the sky. "You don't know anything about stopping giant asteroids, do you?"

END!

We hope you enjoyed this book. If you did then it would mean a lot to us if you'd take a moment to rate it or leave a nice review - thanks!

BONUS CONTENT
Watch an interview with the author about the creation of this book on YouTube

Full version   *Teaser Video*

Appendix I:

Becomme An Wyzarde! Todaye!

Tired of being pushed around by bullies who are mighty of thew and gross of conduct?
Sick of having sand (or mud, ordure, pig manure, rocks, etc) kicked in your face by inbred lackwits?
Do you have an unhealthy paucity of dread for the occult darkness of the soul-slupring netherplanes, and also a chest like two-clothes drying racks glued together and covered in chicken skin?
Then, good sir, we have much to discuss!

Did you know that there are full SEVEN orders of powerful wizards who want YOU to sign up with them? Well, if not, perhaps you are too stupid to learn magic... ahahah, only jesting, my jolly chum, this was a merry jape or whimsical... *thing*... of the kind you will encounter all the livelong-day among the ruddy-cheeked students of the Unspeakable College! We are a droll and picturesque little family here, and hardly *anyone* gets turned inside out anymore, by that green mist or otherwise!

Due to a shortage of apprentices, it's not only the seventh sons of seventh sons who need apply. Of course, we're still very iffy about girls learning this kind of stuff, but if ye be a lad aged 10-21 with all his teeth, a good brain (or a collection in jars, we are not ones to judge), and ears like the handles on a bowling trophy, then the seven orders are keen to hear from YOU, as you embark upon a career in the high-powered, fast-paced, impressively bearded world of wizardry!
Did we mention that the annual dues are $2073 spothins thruppence?
Ask about our credit exchange program for any magical swords, staves

of power, amulets and orbs which might be knocking about your parents' castle / shack / yurt / longhouse / hovel / fortress of doom (circle appropriate). Cash paid for numinous glowing things, bonuses for ones that talk! (See the Dean of Acquisitions, sub-dungeon twelve, just past the Scorpion Vortex).

But enough tomfoolery – it's time to meet the Seven Orders and find out which one is for YOU! We used to sort everyone into four houses – Snootybrook, Grumblestub, Doomedworth and Evildor. However, long ago, one of the high Thaumatarchs realised that the best course for all wizardry was just to evaporate all the students from Evildor into a fine, ashy powder; thus removing all the plots, schemes, tricks and murders from the student body which, ironically, are considered *de rigeur mortis* for the higher faculty.

Now we do this other thing, and it's great. Because we said so, and we're wizards.

The Ancient Conventicle of the Nine Reeds
Our school of aeromancy has all the suction power of the Warbling Monks of Shan Mang, plus the additional gale-force offensive magic of the Hopping Order of Saint Blythric! From summoning the Djinns of the Tempest to a huge amount of washing up we won't talk much about here (but which is very real, in a college with twelve dining halls and eight kitchens), the Nine Reeds is a mysterious and respectable order of wise men, charged with power over the element of air and over the weather. Good choice for portly students, as they are less likely to be blown away.

The Illuminated Chantry of the Third Sun
Our pyromantic wizards are sought after as battle mages, striding across fields of war with devastating sorceries in hand, and also wherever anyone wants to light a sneaky roll-up. Commanding the forces of fire, they reach into its elemental plane and deep into the fires beneath the earth, often without even the aid of a pair of sturdy oven mitts. Unlike many disciplines at the College, this order rewards a hot temper and a short fuse, though not with the Tutorial Deacons Incandescent, who have been selected for their flame-retardant properties and their powerful backhand action.

The Accepted Brotherhood of the Clenched Fist

If you are considered slow, or even positively slothful by your peers, then it might not be a lack of vitamins or a moral failing – you may be predisposed to the noble art of geomancy. The Brotherhood of the Clenched Fist commune with rocks and stones, which does not really make them a lot of friends, and tends to make their minds resonate on the same wavelength and timescale as good, solid Urzoman granite. While this can lead some to believe that the Clenched Fist are stupid, or indeed, that some of their older members have actually been deceased for several months without beginning to decay, there are few more potent battle wizards in the entire Arch'. 'Stand like the mountain, Flow like the lava' is the creed of their Chamber Militant, and those who doubt its power often end up crispy, blackened and about one molecule thick.

The Temple Superior of the Bone Hook

Our whole world is built on water, and water makes up the vast part of our bodies, as the great experimental sorcerer Malaguff the Plaid proved in his series of very messy experiments in 232 AU – the ones which involved the very big lemon squeezer and all those unfortunate students. Therefore, is it not fitting that those arch-manipulators of the watery elements have provided more High Thaumatarchs than any other discipline to the roll-call of greatness which echoes down the centuries? Some say this is because the wizards of the Bone Hook are as capricious as the sea and as merciless as death by drowning. Others say they are a fine body of men, who would probably not follow through with those threats to make my death look like a swimming accident. In any case, the power of the Bone Hook is matched only by their wealth, as it's a foolish merchant captain or navy man who sets sail without one aboard to scry the currents and calm the waves.

The Esoteric Lodge of the Three Fingered Hand

We're pretty certain that we were going to write an honest, frank and unflattering critique of this, the weirdest and also the wyrdest of the seven orders, but it's very possible that they've changed the words, the papyrus they were written on, the timeline we exist in and both of our minds to make themselves look good. The Three Fingered Hand are masters of mental manipulation, mind control and illusion, and also a damnably handsome bunch of rugged, tough, manly chaps who have all definitely kissed a girl, honest. They take their sigil from the legend of their founder, Egbert the Unhinged, who lost his pointing finger to the Mad King of Zalois, after making his brother think he was a goose. Egbert proved he didn't need that particular digit by making the King think he was a small bowl of caviar, using a rather rude gesture. His successor, the prince, learning nothing at all, had Egbert's middle finger cut off too, and subsequently spent the next decade imagining he was a plaster gnome named Timothy.

The Very Gnostic Chamber of the Secret Flame

This order of wizards is devoted to the study of life, the wild, and of growing things. Novices of the Secret Flame travel the wilderness, sleeping rough, communing with the small woodland creatures, learning the language of the trees and sleeping in hedgerows under the stars. This is why, when they attain the rank of master, none of them ever leave the city again. There is a lot to be said for hot indoor plumbing, after all. Some foolish secular folk think that the Secret Flame are an order of mumbling old saintly healers, who have too high a regard for the sanctity of life to ever engage in combat. These people have obviously never heard of shapeshifting spells, or seen how much damage an oak tree can do if it grows right under you at tremendous speed. Also worth noting is the sheer volume of ale that these lads put away; wizards who don't know how to regrow a liver should not try to keep up.

The Venerable Synod of the White Ribbon

Frankly, this is the order which freaks us all out, just a little. They're the, ummm... you know. The N word. Not that one! For goodness sake, when some of our faculty are purple, green or orange, and others have horns and wings, you don't think we'd use that N word, do you? No, we mean they're Necromancers, and that's a little bit of a worry. I mean, talking to the dead, and all that? Rumour has it that high level wizards of the White Ribbon have a spell that summons ten generations of your deceased grandmothers and great-grandmothers to tell you how disappointed they are in you. That's just plain evil! Then there's the zombies, and the skeletons, and the mandatory black uniform with all the spiky bits and skulls on it. Nobody can complain, because the Emperor Himself is a lich, but nobody ever, ever asks them to bring snacks to the inter-Order barbecue and petanque evening, if you get my drift.

Why Delaye? Visitte Us Todaye!

A bright future awaits you in the world of wizarding* - or, possibly, millions of alternate futures all piled up like the layers in a puff pastry, but who knows? What do you mean *we're* supposed to? Tell you what, if you have so many questions, come on in and see the Curate of Admissions - extra credits if you can find him, he's a slippery bugger despite his advanced years.

Don't forget to bring all that lovely tuition money - for preference in unmarked, non-sequential coins in an old burlap sack - and carry with you a scholarly mind, a keen attitude, and a willingness to explore the frontiers of knowledge. After all, someone around here should be in possession of at least one of those things, at some time!

For a complete course schedule, simply complete the scavenger hunt, defeat the giant spider in the crypt of screaming skulls, retrieve the amulet of Zathgar, answer the riddle of the Overdemon, cross the bridge over the Chasm of Quite Unfortunate Peril, give the night porter a self-addressed envelope marked with the Elder Rune of the Slime Gods and wait 5-12 lurking days.

Remember our old school motto -

Si Insania Sit Prietum - Epistula Pecunium In Manibus Tabellariorum!

*Conditions apply, i.e. Offer not available to village idiots, oafs, orcs, things that seem to be human but turn out to be slobbering gore-fiends full of sharp pointy teeth, members of foreign guilds and orders of what they call 'magic' (but which smells funny and is all curled up at the corners), lady-women, clowns, things that look like clowns but (that bother with the gore-fiends again), and mimes. Chainsday is curry night, bring your own HB pencil, the judge's decision is final and no correspondence will be entered into.

Appendix II:

The Noble Sport of Urzoman Death Cricket

BROUGHT WITH THE Dark Emperor and his battle-arks during the Suljanek conquest, this game, once a lawn-sport for the aristocracy, has been brutally embraced by the 1.3 million subjects of Grand Sepulchre.

The game is played by two teams of 15, of any gender, class, race or religion, excepting those with innate sorcerous powers, such as the infamous case of the High Wittering Wanderers fielding a super-fast lycanthrope in the season of AU 233, or the continued efforts of the Hammer's End Rovers to sneak a high-powered gholem automaton into their batting lineup.

Both teams have input in setting up the field, placing the now-traditional thirty-three tombstones around the park. This reflects the fact that Death Cricket was first played in a graveyard, this being the only public green space available. At the centre of the field, the Pentacle is mown, with five regulation 'run-ways' and five sets of wickets, traditionally shaped to look like bones. Players take the field in a helmet and padded leather armour, as the ball is struck very hard and fast, often with terrible accuracy.

One team goes into bat, placing five players to guard the five wickets. The opposing team take the field, and select one of their number to bowl. The bowler may pitch the ball at any of the wicket ends; in fact, making it appear that he will assault one and then swerving to launch the ball at another is a large part of the merriment. The stalwart defender must keep the ball from his wicket with the use of his bat, a large, flat-sided, black wooden weapon of prodigious weight, based on the ancient Grailish war-club. Underarm bowling is strictly prohibited, on pain of arms being broken.

Should the wicket be struck, the batsman defending it is considered 'dead', and is sent to the outfield, there to wear the traditional sheet with eyeholes in it and attempt, without physical contact, to prank, disrupt and heckle the fielding team. This jackanapesery includes the ability to kick the ball, should the fieldsmen not grasp it in a hasty fashion. Should the ball be hit true, the batsman will make a run for the next point of the pentacle, necessitating every other batsman to run as well. Runic circles mark the 'safe' zones at the points of the larger sigil, and any batsman tagged outside these zones with the returning ball by a member of the team in field, is similarly relegated to the ghostly ranks. This fate will also befall any batsman whose ball is caught by a fieldsman 'on the fly'.

'Dead' batsmen are replaced from the bench until it is impossible to fill all points of the pentacle, at which point the teams swap sides. The team attaining the highest score, after both teams have been eliminated in this manner, is the winner.

Points are scored thusly, by the batting team -
- For all five batsmen moving from point to point of the pentacle, 5 pts
- For each further rotation, due to the ball being driven far into the field, 5 pts
- For the ball being driven out of the park by a mighty blow, 10pts
- (This is known as a 'headsman's stroke')
- For striking a tombstone, 1pt
- For the ball reaching the boundary of the park having touched the ground, 3pts

Special mention must be made of three occurrences -
1. Should the ball not leave the park, but the batsmen manage to completely circumnavigate the pentacle, this is known as a 'Grand Summoning', and one of the 'dead' members of their team is sent back to the bench, to return to bat at the end of the batting order. It is usually achieved by the rascally intervention of the 'Dead'.
2. Should a fieldsman be struck by the ball in a manner which has absolutely nothing to do with him catching it, he is considered slain, and must leave the field for the duration of the game, only to return when his team go into bat.
3. Thrice per game, the bowling team may call 'Shenanigans', loudly shouting this word at the umpire. The next three

bowling attempts may be made by TWO bowlers working simultaneously.

The Dead

Batsmen relegated to 'haunt' the fieldsmen must wear the regulation sheet with regulation eyeholes. They may not come within 6 feet of a fielding player, but are encouraged to prance, caper, leap, cavort, howl, moan, gibber and utter lewd utterances, thus to distract their rivals among the 'living'.

The dead are allowed, by tradition, to kick the ball with their feet, so long as, in doing so, they do not come into physical contact with an opposing fieldsman. A ball kicked by a 'Dead' player may roll out over the boundary, thus earning his team the obligatory three points.

Should one of the dead be struck with the ball 'on the fly', he swaps places with the batsman who 'handed him possession'.

Conversely, should a 'Dead man' tackle or strike one of the living in the execution of his duties, he shall be driven off the pitch by a man in a bishop's costume, who will repeatedly strike him about the head and buttocks with a rubber crozier. The 'exorcised' player is traditionally sentenced to penance; this usually involves cooking and serving countless sausages in a bun for the opposing team at half time.

The Umpire and his Wisdomen

Dressed in the striped black and white of the Nastiskaarsfijordian god Snalric, the Umpire is the ultimate arbiter of life and death on the field. He is armed with a ceremonial mace and sees to it that any fights between players last no more than ten seconds, and involve nothing more dangerous than fists. Those who assault another player with their bat will still receive the dreaded red card, feared not so much because it means you have to leave the game, but because it has the date and time of your appointment with the Imperial Executioner on the back. The Umpire may deputise up to ten wise men of the parish (or any who are not blind drunk) to aid him in keeping the peace on the field and seeing to it that no magic is used to aid or hinder the players.

Teams of Grand Sepulchre

Aside from the many smaller teams formed by the patrons of a pub or ale house, or representing a school or factory, there are sixteen major local teams in Grand Sepulchre, whose rivalries are ancient. Wearing the wrong colours in the wrong part of town when Cricket Season is at its zenith is a great way to donate blood and lose teeth! Cricket patriotism can be fiercely parochial, and many of the teams have their own folklorique chants, rituals of good fortune and legendary players-past to invoke.

High Wittering Wanderers – Red and Green – Mascot; the rooster

Rown Cross Gougers – Brown and Orange - Mascot; the rat

Bentsteeple United – White and Purple – Mascot; the ferret

Unspeakable Collegiate – Yellow and Black – Mascot; a jaunty cartoon wizard

Bishopsbath Ecclesiasticals – Pink and Grey – Mascot; a drunken bishop

Chantry Heath Swankers – Gold and White – Mascot; a fat cat in a top hat

Knightsbottom Chargers – Blue and Black – Mascot; the horse

Dolmen Grove Rangers – Aquamarine and Gold – Mascot; the lion

Rooktower Ravens – Black entire – Mascot; (no points for guessing)

Smattering Hill Athletic Clubbe – Violet and Orange – Mascot; the hound

Hammer's End Rovers – Silver and Green – Mascot; the dragon

Tarback Buccaneers – White and Black, striped – Mascot; the shark

Stilts and Breakwater DCC – Pale and Dark Blue, striped –

Mascot; the crab

Belfry Roost Old Boys – Beige and Brown – Mascot; the Hawk

St Guthran's Agnostics – Red and Blue, chequered – Mascot; the skull and bones

Gallowgate Ghouls – Black and Green – Mascot – A grinning zombie

1940. The world is at war.

But beyond the front lines, a secret conflict rages which is as insane as it is desperate. Hitler's occult forces, led by the determinedly evil Hans Schprinkler, are trying to crack the British Army's ultra-top-secret Section M. They have witches. They have dragons. They have monsters.

But they also have Squad 27, the most hapless band of magical misfits ever to be pressganged into occult combat. And Squad 27 now has Eddie Weatherfield – ace pilot, daring adventurer, 65 kilo weakling and outrageous liar. They say the power he's mistakenly been given could win the war. They say it could also unravel space and time, feeding us all to things with names like the leftover bits of the Welsh telephone book. He says he'd rather be anywhere else, preferably with a strong drink and some easily impressed young women.

But when a full cast of Atlanteans, Elves, Goblins, Dwarves, Wizards, Leprechauns, Vampires, Robots, Nazi super-scientists and Tentacle Horrors want to see you dead, all you can do is trust in your mates, load your tommy gun and pray for a miracle.

Good thing that some of the Gods are strapping on their army boots to join in too…

**** BEST NOVEL Finalist - 2021 Sir Julius Vogel Awards ****
Buy from Amazon

The Alter Inferno Complex Series

The human race tore itself apart during the Age of Judgment...
that's what we call the Trillion Dollar War now, in our ignorance.
We unleashed enough firepower to vaporize whole nations,
poisoning the Earth and grinding civilization down to the politics of
muscle and steel. Dark days came. War-dog days, like some ethanol-
fueled b-movie.
Then came word of the Last City. A new Elysium welded together
from the carcass of our old technology. A place ruled by a god-
machine named Kronos, Guardian Engine of Humanity.

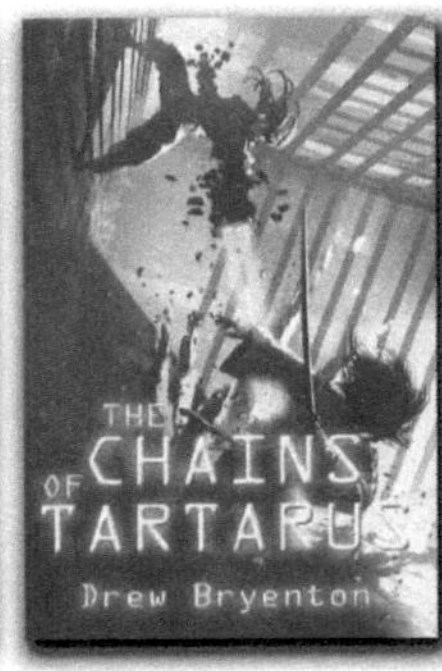

*"I was very impressed with this book, there are some fantastic ideas
and the prose has a real eloquence that is both rare and rewarding. The
vision of this post-human universe is lucid and vividly presented; all
projected in a talented and confident voice."*
- 5/5 Stars SF Book Review

Buy from Amazon